V🧬RAL
DREAMS

John Saenger

Relax. Read. Repeat.

To Debbie
Suspense & Wonder!
John Saenger

VIRAL DREAMS
By John Saenger
Published by TouchPoint Press
Brookland, AR 72417
www.touchpointpress.com

Copyright © 2019 Saenger
All rights reserved.

ISBN-10: 1-946920-82-7
ISBN-13: 978-1-946920-82-9

Editor: Melody Quinn
Cover Design: Colbie Myles, ColbieMyles.net
Cover image: Adobe Stock by Quickshooting

First Edition

Printed in the United States of America.

For Marie, my North Star
And for my parents: Helena M. and William R. Saenger

Nanologue

The genetically modified adenovirus particle, barely sixty nanometers in diameter, slid rapidly towards the target cell and began to initiate contact. It was attracted to multiple receptors on the surface of the cell, and as it approached it aligned its symmetrically icosahedral shape, enabling the trimeric fiber and penton base proteins on its surface to recognize and bind to the cellular receptors.

This interaction triggered an endocytotic cascade of signal transduction events that enveloped and transported the adenovirus into the cell, where it shed its capsid protein coat, migrated across the cytoplasm to the nucleus, and entered through the nuclear pores. Once inside the nucleus, the viral DNA took over the cell, commandeering its replication functions and transforming it into a virus producing factory…

Chapter 1

"Run your fastest, Megan. We've gotta hurry!"

The man had a tight grip on the hand of his nine-year-old daughter and was pulling her through the forest, weaving between the tall Douglas fir and Ponderosa pine trees that towered above them. It was late in the afternoon, and they were far from the hiking path that circled Crystal Lake, one of the popular camping areas five miles north of Mammoth Lakes, California. Sunlight filtered down through the trees, scattered into subdued beams by the dense pine branches that formed the high arboreal canopy. It would be dusk in less than an hour. But it wasn't the dark Max Tyler was afraid of.

"Daddy, you're bleeding," Megan said in a scared, breathless voice. She was sprinting at top speed and gasping for air.

Max glanced back at her and the blood streaming down his left arm. It was coming from a knife slash that had left a three-inch-long gash through his tee shirt and left shoulder. His shirtsleeve was soaked bright red, and the rivulets of blood had almost reached his wrist.

"It's nothing, Megs. Just a little cut. C'mon. We've gotta get out of here."

He pulled her along as he scrambled through the thick forest of trees, trying his best to lead them in the direction of their campsite. His mind was racing. Adrenaline rushed through his bloodstream and fueled the powerful, rapid thundering of his heart.

He mentally replayed the last ten minutes. What they had just witnessed seemed impossible, surreal...

Megan was gathering a posy of flowers while he leaned against a fallen tree watching her. They had decided to take a short hike before dinner. They'd found a trail that wrapped around the north end of the lake and strolled along the dirt path through the trees for fifteen minutes before coming across a glade blanketed with spring flowers.

It was early summer. The mountainous terrain boasted one of the best ski resorts in California during the winter. But this time of year, the days were mild. He and Megan were on a weekend camping trip, the first of several he'd planned for the summer and fall, and he was enjoying every minute of it.

It felt good to get away and bring her up here into the pristine sanctuary and quiet serenity of this towering primeval forest. The redolent sights and smells filled his senses, refreshing and renewing him as only the mountains could.

He looked away from her for a second to take in the tranquility of the glassy mountain lake a hundred yards to his left. He heard a small, muffled yelp. It was so soft it barely registered in his mind. Glancing back toward Megan, he caught a fleeting glimpse of her disappearing behind a copse of young pine trees, feet kicking in the air and arms flailing. Her mouth was covered by the hand of the burly man carrying her.

"Hey...Stop!" Max shouted in a booming voice. He sprang forward, covering the distance to where Megan disappeared in a matter of seconds, and raced behind the copse.

The man ran over a ridge and disappeared from sight.

"Stop!" Max roared, doubling his pace. He reached the ridge, ran down the slope, and leaped at the man, sweeping his feet out from under him and grabbing Megan before she could hit the ground.

The man sprung to his feet, pulled a hunting knife from a sheath on his belt, and rushed toward Max, who set Megan down and turned to face him. The man slashed with the knife, slicing Max's left shoulder as Max pivoted and launched a powerful, right thrusting kick at the man's knee. There was a sickening crunch, and the man, who easily outweighed Max by thirty pounds, cried out and crumpled to the ground. His knife clattered against an outcropping of rocks and skittered out of sight.

"Come on, Megs!" Max picked her up and ran at full speed through the trees, avoiding the path but heading in the direction of their campsite. The attacker's moans faded as Max put distance between them. He bolted at top speed through the trees until his arms began burning. Then he set Megan down, grabbed her hand, and ran towards their campsite, towards safety, less than a quarter of a mile away.

The man was sweating profusely when he reached the Jeep parked on a narrow dirt fire road used by the forest service. The knee of his left leg had swollen to more than twice its normal size, and he was exhausted from hopping half a mile on his good leg through rugged, uneven terrain.

He opened the door of his Jeep and pulled himself up onto the front seat. He couldn't touch his left knee without piercing jolts of pain shooting up his leg. He unlocked the glove compartment, pulled out a cell phone with push-to-talk, and switched it on.

"Nick, you there? Come in!" he barked.

"I'm here," a voice responded. "Didja get her?"

"No, damn it. I had her. Then her father came out of nowhere and attacked. I sliced up his shoulder, but he broke my knee and took the girl. Go to plan B."

"Got it. Plan B. Leave your unit on. I'll contact you. Out."

The man tossed the cell phone on the seat beside him and winced as he shifted his weight to pry his keys out of his pocket. He was outraged that Max had gotten the better of him. How was it that a guy half his size and nowhere near his muscular prowess had managed to take him down and snatch the girl? He didn't lose fights. Ever.

He fumbled with his keys for a moment before slipping the correct key into the Jeep's ignition and placing his hand on the black knob of the stick shift. Only then did reality slap him hard as he looked down and stared at the clutch pedal under his broken left leg.

This was not going to be easy.

Max and Megan reached their campsite. Everything looked peaceful and undisturbed—just the way they'd left it—but Max wasn't leaving anything up to chance. He had carefully scrutinized the perimeter of their campsite before they entered. He hurried over to the tent and glanced around inside of it. Then he went to check the inside of their white Chevrolet Suburban. Nothing.

He scanned the partial view he had of the nearby campsites on either side and across from him. No one seemed to be around. Max's stomach twisted. Something wasn't right.

"Daddy, I'm scared," Megan said, snapping Max out of his thoughts. "Why'd that man try to take me?"

"Megs, we aren't safe. We've gotta load up the Suburban and get out of here *now*!"

He took the keys out of his pocket, unlocked the Suburban, and opened the tailgate doors wide. Unlatching a side compartment, he took out a padded pistol case, unzipped it, and pulled out a Glock .40 caliber semi-automatic handgun. He grabbed one of the two fifteen-shot magazines from another case, slammed it into the handle of the Glock, and slid back the loading glide.

Ching-Chang. A 180-grain Winchester .40 caliber S&W hollow-point cartridge seated itself in the chamber. Lethal. Ready.

He slid the handgun into the waistband of his pants, ran over to the tent, and pried the stakes out of the ground. He'd once timed himself on how fast he could take down their 8' x 10' tent, roll it up, and pack it in its nylon carrying bag. His record time was three minutes and twenty-seven seconds. Today that record would fall.

Max stowed their camping gear in the rear of the Suburban, thankful that he had only brought the basic camping essentials.

Megan dropped her duffel bag next to the rear of the Suburban. She bent down and started fumbling with her sleeping bag, which she had bunched up and carried over in a heap. Max grabbed her duffel bag and stuffed it in the back with the rest of their camping gear. He was reaching for her sleeping bag when he heard a high-pitched sonic whine that ended abruptly like a mosquito hitting a window.

"Ow, it hurts!" Megan shrieked. "It stings, Daddy. It stings!" She arched her back and strained to reach between her shoulder blades.

Max stared in shocked disbelief at the cylindrical dart hanging from the upper middle of her back. He looked over his shoulder at the trees behind them, but he didn't see anyone. He yanked the dart out of Megan's back, opened the side door of the Suburban, and helped her climb in.

"Lie down! Don't even look up until I tell you!"

He dropped the dart on the floor, slammed the door shut, and pivoted, pulling the semi-automatic handgun out of his waistband as he raced around the rear of the vehicle. A second before he turned the corner, another whizzing, high-pitched whine zipped past him as a second dart slammed into the rear window of the Suburban.

Damn it! He thought and jumped back. *I'll teach you to mess with us.*

He peered out from behind the truck, both hands firmly gripped on the handle of the Glock. His finger was poised on its double trigger, ready to fire. He scanned the trees that bordered their campsite, looking for the slightest movement that would reveal the attacker. Their campsite was secluded in the rearmost location in the campground. Behind it lay nothing but deep forest and rugged terrain. Max had selected it precisely because of its seclusion, a fact he now regretted.

A soft mechanical latching sound caught his attention. He quickly homed in on its location near a large Ponderosa pine tree about sixty yards away. He knew that sound. He could picture it clearly: the well-oiled loading bolt of a hunting rifle seating another cartridge in its chamber and locking it into place.

Without taking his eyes off the tree, Max raised the Glock and wedged his shoulder against the rear of the Suburban. He tightened his finger tension on the trigger, aligned the front bead with the rear notch on his gun sight, and targeted a spot inches to the right of the massive tree and five feet off the ground.

Chest high.

He waited. Thirty seconds passed. Sixty. Nothing.

Then suddenly a gun barrel jutted out from behind the tree.

Max squeezed off four shots in rapid succession. The roar of the .40 caliber Glock was deafening. Bark flew off the edge of the trunk next to the rifle barrel as two of the shots hit the tree. The third grazed the shoulder of his assailant, who expelled a groan as the fourth slug embedded itself in his shoulder and drove him back into the foliage.

Got you, Max thought with grim satisfaction. He watched as the rifle lying on the ground was dragged back behind the tree. A few seconds later, the branches of saplings behind the tree flailed as the attacker disappeared into the forest.

Max rushed back to the Suburban and started the engine. He looked over his shoulder at Megan in the middle seat behind him, and fear gripped his chest. She was slumped over sideways, unconscious.

He put his hand up close to her nose and mouth. Her breathing was slow and shallow.

Some kind of tranquilizer dart. But what if it's too high a dose?

Slamming the gearshift into drive, he stomped on the accelerator and sped out of the campsite heading for town. The hospital emergency room in Mammoth Lakes was a fifteen-minute drive away. But today he would get there in five.

Chapter 2

❝She's going to be fine," the emergency room physician said, pulling the curtain closed behind Max as he entered Megan's partitioned examination area.

Max's left shoulder throbbed where eight stitches held his knife wound closed under a sterile gauze bandage. The Xylocaine they had injected prior to the stitches was wearing off. He ignored the twinges of pain and stepped forward.

Megan was lying immobile on a gurney with the side rails up, sleeping soundly. Max approached and gently touched her cheek. He felt her forehead and then took her hand. Emotions roiled inside him as he gazed at her still face.

He looked up at the doctor. "I heard you talking to the lab tech about Megan's blood tests and the tranquilizer residue on the dart I brought in. Is she really going to be okay?"

The doctor nodded. "Don't worry. Her vital signs and breathing are strong and stable. She'll wake up in a few hours after sleeping this off."

"What a relief," Max said, feeling his fear ratchet down a notch. He read the name badge pinned to the loose-fitting surgical green smock: Dr. Philip Linton. He gauged the doctor to be in his early forties. His tanned, rugged features made him seem trustworthy, and Max liked his calming manner and words.

"We're running a panel of toxicological tests on the residue left in the dart," Dr. Linton said. "We should have a lab analysis report back by morning. My guess is it's a mix of ketamine and xylaxine, the same animal tranquilizer combo the local forest rangers use to knockout and relocate aggressive bears that hang out around campsites."

"Animal tranquilizer…" Max shook his head. "How's she going to feel when she wakes up?"

"Groggy. And she'll probably have a pounding headache." Dr. Linton scribbled something in Megan's chart. "We'll start her on high strength ibuprofen the minute she's awake. A nurse will be by to move her to a holding room here in emergency where we can watch her for a couple of hours until she's fully awake. Then we'll move her to a room upstairs for the night. She should be able to go home in the late morning."

Max breathed a sigh of relief. "Is it okay with you if I stay with her tonight?"

"Sure, but expect her to be groggy for quite a while. I'll be by first thing in the morning to check on her."

"Thanks, doctor," Max said, extending his hand.

Dr. Linton shook it. "You're welcome."

Moments after the doctor left, a nurse pulled back the curtain. "Hi, Mr. Tyler. I'll be moving Megan into a room for observation now. There's a police officer out in the hall who wants to talk to you about what happened. When you're through, you're welcome to come in and sit with her. It's the first room on the left."

Max glanced at Megan. "Thanks."

The hospital emergency ward was unusually quiet for a Saturday evening. It lacked the usual parade of patients with cuts, broken arms, and heart attacks. The staff embraced these periods of calm, the lulls before the inevitable storms.

Max stepped out into the hallway and saw the police officer standing in the doorway of the nurses' station chatting with one of the nurses. As he walked towards him, Max sized up the officer—short dark hair, early thirties, six-two, linebacker build. The silver nametag above the badge on his uniform was easy to read.

"Officer Reynolds...I'm Max Tyler. I called in the incident out by Twin Lakes and asked to file a report."

The policeman nodded. "How's your little girl doing?"

"Doctor Linton said she's going to be okay."

"Glad to hear it. We can grab this room, and I'll take down a report." Officer Reynolds motioned to a medical dictation office across the hall. A small table and two chairs were partially visible through the open doorway.

"Let's go," Max said.

It took twenty minutes for Max to relay his story and answer the officer's questions. As Reynolds read the report back to him, Max closed his eyes and relived the details of the attack. He visualized the first attacker's face. His careful description in the report could allow a police artist to sketch a close resemblance.

"You're sure one of your shots hit the second guy?" Reynolds asked.

"Positive," Max said. "I fired four shots, and I hit him with the last two. Check the site for blood. Guarantee you'll find a trail."

Reynolds scribbled a few more notes then glanced up at Max. "The make of your handgun?"

"Glock 40-caliber semi-automatic," Max replied.

"Got a permit?"

Max nodded. "Fully licensed. I'm a former SWAT team leader."

"Really?" Reynolds looked up from his pad. "Who were you with?"

"Well, I started off in Chicago. I was part of their Special Weapons and Tactics team for about three years. My wife at the time wanted to be closer to her family in Southern California. I have a sister who lives in the Bay area, so we weighed the pros and cons and decided to move out west. I put out some feelers and got recruited by LAPD for their SWAT team. Stayed on the team there a little over ten years. I was team leader for the last five. I rotated off the team two years ago."

Reynolds took a closer look at Max's driver's license before handing it back to him. "What are you doing now?" he asked, closing the cover of his metal clipboard.

"I'm a part-time instructor at the LA Police Academy."

"No kidding. My younger brother graduated from there the year before last. Do you remember a Tony Reynolds?"

Max thought for a minute. "Sorry. Name doesn't ring a bell…"

"He graduated in the April class."

"That explains it," Max said. "I didn't start there until August. Besides, I'm only there to lead a special situations course a few times a year. The rest of the time, I conduct specialized training schools for SED—the Special Enforcement Detail of the LA County Sheriff's Department. I help lead the Advanced SWAT School and the Long Rifle School."

"Sounds interesting. You enjoy it?"

"Yeah. Great group of guys to work with." Max glanced at his watch. "Are we about through? I'd really like to get back to my daughter."

"We're done. I hope your daughter feels better real soon."

"Thanks. I hope so too."

Reynolds stood up and opened the door. "I'm headed out to the campsite from here. I've called our forensic tech to meet me out there to search the scene, collect blood samples, and see what else we can find. There might be a chance we end up with a DNA match from our database once the samples are back in the lab. From what you told me, it sounds like both your attackers will need to seek medical attention. Especially the second one for his gunshot wounds. I'll put out a high-level bulletin to every emergency room and hospital in the state to be on the watch for him. If we get lucky, I'll let you know."

"Thanks," Max said. "Do whatever it takes to get these guys, will you? I can't believe they shot my little girl with a tranquilizer dart."

"We'll find them," Reynolds said. He clapped Max on the back and headed down the hall.

Max returned to the holding room. A nurse was sitting by the far side of the bed filling out paperwork. He looked over the railing at Megan, who was starting to stir. Her eyes opened halfway and then shut again.

"She should be awake and ready to go upstairs in about an hour," the nurse said.

"Thanks," Max said. He pulled a chair close to the bedside and sat down. *You're going to be okay, princess,* he thought.

He took Megan's hand and began to wait. A gnawing ache grew in his chest and gripped his insides at the harrowing specter of how close he had come to losing her. It was going to be a long night.

Chapter 3

The gray Jeep Cherokee sat parked in a row of cars at the far end of the parking lot outside the Mammoth Hospital. With its dust-covered and weathered appearance, it blended inconspicuously with the other cars in the lot.

The driver sat slouched but alert in the front seat. He had been sitting there since dawn methodically scanning the parking lot. His primary target was Max's Suburban. It was parked near the front of the lot next to the emergency room entrance. From his position at the back of the lot, the man had a clear view of the Suburban and everyone who departed from the hospital.

It was a clear, crisp morning in Mammoth. Just another gorgeous day in this mountain ski town that had a surprising number of off-season visitors. It transformed into a bustling mini-metropolis during the winter when throngs of skiers took up residence, hitting the ski slopes by day and the bars and restaurants by night.

The driver in the parked Cherokee had been there since dawn. There hadn't been much for him to observe so far. He glanced at his watch and looked up to see a couple and their small child leave the emergency room and walk to their car. It was half past nine, and he was growing increasingly impatient.

Over the next hour, he scrutinized several arrivals and departures. A paramedic ambulance pulled in front of the emergency room exit with sirens blaring. The paramedics jumped out, slid the patient and gurney out of the back of the van, and disappeared through the sliding glass doors of the Emergency Room. The excitement lasted for thirty seconds, and then the ambulance left, and the parking lot was still once more.

The man stretched his arms over his head and checked his watch again. He reached into a white paper sack on the passenger seat, feeling his way to the last glazed doughnut. He wolfed down half of it with his first bite and wished he had some coffee left in his travel mug. As he started to take a second bite, his eyes swept the parking lot and came to rest on the double glass doors. They opened, and he almost choked. The girl and her father stepped into the parking lot and headed for the Suburban. The man stuffed the rest of the doughnut into his mouth and picked up his binoculars for a quick look.

Max and Megan came into full view. Megan was smiling. Max had a tight grip on her hand. He let her in the passenger side then walked around the back of the Suburban and climbed in on the driver's side.

The man watched the Suburban's backup lights turn on. He pressed the push-to-talk icon on his cell phone as the SUV backed out and started to drive out of the parking lot.

"Raoul to Nick, come in."

"I'm here. What's up?"

"They're rolling. Track 'em home to Orange County but don't intervene. I repeat. *Do not* intervene. We'll pick plasma samples up from the hospital lab. That's all we need for now."

"Understood. Track 'em only. I'm on it."

"Check in at 2100. Over."

Max drove out of the parking lot and headed toward Highway 395, the road that would take them all the way down into Southern California.

It took him a little over seven hours to make the drive. They stopped for lunch around noon, and Megan slept fitfully during the second half of the trip. They pulled into the driveway of their home in the foothills of Mission Viejo, tired from the long drive but glad to be home.

Max had wrestled the whole way with the mystery of why the men tried to abduct Megan. None of it made any sense. There were too many pieces of the puzzle he had yet to discover. Later that evening, he tucked Megan into bed and kissed her goodnight. As he left her room, he paused in the doorway and looked back at her. *I won't stop until they're caught. I'll get to the bottom of this.*

Chapter 4

The man glanced up and down the hospital corridor as he approached the patient's room on the third floor. It was at the far end of the wing, and no one was around. Just as he'd planned. He stopped before the partially opened door, listening to the still, tomb-like quiet of the hospital. It was half past three in the morning. The lone sound he could hear was the soft muttering of the two nurses in the distant nurses' station. They were the only staff on the floor, a bored skeleton crew working a slumbering graveyard shift.

Altogether there were thirteen patients on the floor. As recently as three days ago, the entire east wing of St. Andrew's Medical Center—all forty-five rooms—had been full, as well as half of the west wing. The place had seemed busier than a crowded mall at Christmas, bustling with patients' visitors, nurses scurrying to answer incessant call buttons, and orderlies wheeling patients to and from tests and surgery. Lab techs, like modern-day vampires, had descended on their wincing prey, drawing blood samples for laboratory tests.

He was one of those modern-day vampires. His name was Larry Drake, and he drew blood for a living. Or at least he used to. Anger welled up in him again with startling intensity, cresting into a familiar rage as he remembered the scene in Richard Berk's office over a month ago when he'd lost his job. He had been called to the hospital administrator's office by a curt note attached to his time card instructing him to report to administrator Berk's office on the first floor at three in the afternoon when his shift ended.

The meeting had not gone well. The hospital administrator everyone called "Iceberk" for his frigid curtness had become a seething fireball. He had accused Drake of stealing an assortment of drugs and syringes and showing up for work high on more than on occasion. He had ranted with scathing accusations and threats of legal action, but in the end, what he'd done was far more painful. He'd brought down the ax, severing Drake from gainful employment.

Drake willed the raging anger inside him to subside. He stood in front of the door, one hand gripping the doorknob, while he focused on his breathing. Gradually, his self-control won out, and he felt his anger subside to a steely calmness.

He took a deep breath and exhaled. Then he pushed the door open the rest of the way and stepped inside.

Light from the hallway spilled into the semi-private room, casting a dusky illumination over the two beds. The room was standard size. It would have seemed crowded if there were two patients in it, but the bed closest to the door was empty.

He pulled the door halfway closed to its original position and tiptoed over to the middle-aged woman sleeping in the far bed. She was lying on her back with her mouth open, snoring in a muffled, rhythmic cadence. The blinds on the window allowed thin slits of light from the parking lot below to fall across her bed.

When Drake looked down at her peacefully sleeping form, he felt no stirrings of compassion, no twinges of conscience. His own mother had died in her late twenties of a drug overdose—too much alcohol mixed with methamphetamine at one of the countless parties she frequented. The rough circles she had traveled in had finally slammed her into the grave, leaving him an orphan at age seven. He'd never known his father, and the drunken, violent uncle who raised him had favored harsh physical abuse as his preeminent parenting skill.

Drake reached into the plastic lab tech supply carrier he brought with him and pulled out a capped syringe filled with a pale yellow liquid. He put the plastic carrier down on the bed and removed the cap from the syringe. He pushed the plunger slightly and watched as the bubbles were forced upward and a small arc of fluid squirted from the tip of the needle. *Always ensure patient health and safety by following the proper technique for administering an injection.*

The irony struck him as he reached for the Y-port in the IV tubing that was going into the woman's arm. He made sure that bubbles wouldn't cause a pulmonary embolism so that he could kill her with a lethal injection of poison.

He stuck the needle in the Y-port and was about push the plunger when he felt the woman shift on the bed. He stopped and looked down. The woman's eyes were open, and she was looking at him.

"What are you doing?" she asked. A look of startled alarm grew on her face.

He smiled calmly at her. "It's just a medication your doctor ordered."

"What medication?" She shook off her drowsiness and reached for the nurse call button.

"It's an antibiotic. It'll help fight the infection you've got," Drake said. His gaze flicked to the call button and then back to the woman.

The woman's eyes narrowed. "My doctor didn't order any medication."

"Sure, he did." Drake fumbled with a piece of paper in his plastic supply carrier and pretended to read it. "Room 303. A ten-milliliter IV injection of Rocephin. Its generic name is ceftriaxone. That's the antibiotic I'm giving you."

The woman shook her head. "My doctor came by before I went to sleep. He said I didn't need any more medication. I asked him. He said the IV comes out first thing tomorrow morning when this bag of fluid is empty, and he's discharging me at noon. Somebody made a mistake on this order."

Drake fumbled with the paper. "Nope. This is the right room."

The woman looked over at the clock on her bedside table. There was something fishy about a technician giving a patient an antibiotic at this hour of the night.

Her suspicion hardened into resolve. "Take the needle out of there," she commanded. "I'm *not* taking any more medication."

Drake shrugged. "Doctor's orders, ma'am." He reached for the syringe dangling from the Y-port.

"*What's* my doctor's name?" she snapped.

He stared back at her blankly. Fear washed over her in an overpowering wave as she watched his face contort.

"Dr. Smith," he said, grabbing the syringe and pushing the plunger all the way down with his thumb.

"That isn't my doctor! Stop! Hel—" she began to shriek.

Drake's hand shot out. He covered her mouth, pressing her back into the bed. She bucked and fought him. She tried to grab the IV line going into her wrist, but as she lunged for it, he grabbed her hand and pinned it against the bed.

The drugs wouldn't take long to work. The combination of fentanyl, secobarbital, and vecuronium bromide was potent and effective. The sedative and hypnotic drugs thrust her down a spiraling black vortex as unconsciousness washed over her. Vecuronium, a neuromuscular blocking agent used by anesthesiologists, gripped all of her skeletal muscles in its paralyzing embrace and halted nerve transmission. Her chest diaphragm ceased to respond to the signals from the respiratory center of her brain. The simple autonomic breathing reflex halted, and as oxygen failed to enter her lungs, she suffocated. Death's approach was quick and silent.

Drake removed his hand from the woman's mouth and watched the perfect stillness of her form. Life fleeting before his eyes.

Then he slipped out of the hospital room, down the hall, and into the stairwell that would lead him out of the hospital, unseen and unheard.

Chapter 5

“It itches, Daddy. Itches a lot,” Megan said. She was feverishly scratching the swarm of mosquito bites that dotted her right calf and thigh. Her left leg and arms were similarly covered with the angry red welts. At first glance, she appeared to have the measles.

Max looked down at his nine-year-old daughter and smiled as he shook his head. “I swear, Megs...those nasty mosquitoes up there in Mammoth were trying to eat you alive. Now stop scratching. Here, let’s get something to stop the itching.”

He took her by the hand and led her up the wooden steps of the broad back porch that wrapped around the sprawling ranch-style house. The house was situated on two acres of land in the Mission Viejo foothills of southern California. The neighboring houses were spread out on larger lots that accommodated two to three horses.

The screen door slammed behind them as they entered the utility room off the kitchen. Max opened a cupboard above the washer and dryer and took out a slender can of Bactine antiseptic spray from the crowded middle shelf. Megan winced then relaxed as the spray worked its cooling, soothing magic.

Later that evening, Max was sitting in his favorite chair in the living room trying to read the newspaper. They’d finished dinner a half hour ago. His eyes moved over the words, but his mind kept wandering down dark, familiar paths. He lowered his newspaper and looked at Megan. She was working a jigsaw puzzle on the square coffee table. She was good at puzzles, and she loved ones with pictures of horses out in the countryside or kittens getting into mischief.

The scary events in Mammoth began playing out in his mind for the hundredth time, every movement reenacted in slow motion, every intricate detail dissected in sharp, analytical focus. He wrestled with the wild protectiveness that had gripped his insides and triggered his violent rage and defensive attack. *Why would anyone go to those lengths to kidnap a little girl?*

If he didn't hear from Detective Reynolds in a day or two, he'd call him at the police station to see if they had found a DNA match from the blood samples they'd collected from the campsite.

Megan pushed another piece of her puzzle into place and smiled at Max. He smiled and turned back to his newspaper, pushing the events in Mammoth from his mind. He managed to read most of a short article on hiking in the Sierra Nevada, but then a familiar painful memory of his wife, Carol, and that terrible night two years ago when he'd lost her washed over him.

An accident had taken her life in a single, horrific instant, snuffing out the most wonderful, loving woman he had ever known. She'd been driving, and another driver, either drunk or asleep at the wheel, had drifted into her lane. She'd swerved off the road to avoid him and crashed into a tree. At least that's what an eyewitness had told the 911 operator just moments after the accident.

The driver had swerved back into his lane and sped off. Carol's car collided head-on into the tree. The impact had ruptured the gas tank and caused the crushed car to ignite. Moments later, the car was engulfed in a wall of flames. It wasn't clear if she had died on impact, but if she hadn't, the fire had finished the job.

The one inexplicable miracle of that night was that Megan had survived. Somehow, she had been thrown free from the back seat. She'd escaped the accident with only a few scratches. She was still unconscious when the paramedics had arrived, and when she regained consciousness, she couldn't remember anything about the crash.

The driver who had called in the accident had tried to chase after the driver responsible for the accident. He pursued the car for twenty minutes at speeds close to 100 miles per hour he reported, but the other driver managed to elude him. He had called back with a more detailed description of the car and its driver along with a partial license plate number, but in spite of a thorough DMV search using all of Max's police department connections, they were never able to identify the car or its owner.

Max chased the darkness from his mind, but the clenched feeling in his stomach was slower to fade. He watched Megan work her magic on the puzzle for a while and then sat down next to her on the couch and tried his hand at a couple of puzzle pieces.

A half hour later, it was bath time. Then he read her a few pages from *Alice in Wonderland*—where Alice thought things were growing curiouser and curiouser—and Megan drifted off to Neverland.

Max lingered at the doorway after tucking his daughter into bed. She had fallen asleep as soon as her head hit the pillow. He gazed at her peaceful, sleeping form a while longer and found himself surprised as he often was at how much she resembled Carol.

A clutching dart of pain stabbed at his heart. He let his love for her wash over him. He vowed that he'd be the best father Megan could ever ask for.

It was well past midnight when the coughing awakened him. The loud harshness of it jolted him from a deep sleep. He lay on his back and listened to Megan, whose room was right down the hall. Her paroxysm of coughing was interrupted by brief periods of silence and then resumed with raw, painful sharpness.

Max got out of bed, switched on the hall light, and went straight to the medicine cabinet in the bathroom next to Megan's bedroom. Grabbing a bottle of Pedia-Care cough medicine and a plastic measuring spoon off the top shelf, he hurried into her room and flipped on the light.

Megan pulled herself into a sitting position as he came over and sat on the edge of her bed. As he started to unscrew the cap, another fit of coughing overwhelmed her. It seemed like it would never end. He felt her forehead and frowned. He didn't need a thermometer to know she was running a high fever.

He glanced down at the bottle in his hand and changed his mind. She needed something stronger. He took the Pedia-Care back to the medicine cabinet and exchanged it for a half-empty bottle of Delsym, a more powerful cough suppressant, and a bottle of children's Motrin.

Megan took both medicines without fuss and lay back on her pillow. Max tucked her in and brushed a stray strand of hair out of her face.

"Sweet dreams, princess," he whispered as he bent down and kissed her forehead. "You'll feel better in the morning."

The heat radiating off her skin unsettled him, but he was sure the Motrin would break the fever by morning. *It always has in the past,* he thought, as he turned out the light and went back to his room.

Early the next morning, Max awakened to the raucous squawking of two mockingbirds engaged in territorial battle outside his bedroom window. Sunrise was beginning to unfold, and the room was infused with the luminous glow of first morning light.

He lay still for a moment with his eyes open as the dreamy fuzziness cleared from his mind, and his thoughts coalesced into coherence. He listened, waiting for the strident paroxysm of coughing that had awakened him in the night, but the house was quiet. The Motrin must have done the trick.

He glanced at the clock radio on his bedside table that read a half past six. Time to get up. Twenty minutes later, he was shaved, showered, and dressed.

Megan didn't stir when Max walked into her room. He sat on her bed for a minute, watching her, then reached over and felt her forehead. She was burning up. He jumped to his feet, fear and panic pulsing through him. Her fever was much higher than it had been during the night.

He retrieved the digital forehead thermometer from the cabinet in the hallway. He swiped it across Megan's forehead and felt his chest tighten. 105.8 degrees Fahrenheit. He dropped the thermometer and shook Megan's shoulder. She hadn't stirred while he was taking her temperature.

"Megan?"

She didn't respond.

He shook her a little harder. "Megan, sweetie? Megan, wake up."

Her breath rattled in her chest as she rolled over on her side.

Max continued shaking her until she opened her eyes. It took a few moments for her eyes to focus on his face. Her sluggishness alarmed him.

"Megan, are you awake?"

"I'm…awake," she half-whispered drowsily. She tried to close her eyes and roll over on her side, but Max grabbed her shoulders and helped her sit up. "Come on, Megs. You've got to stay awake and take some more medicine." This time he gave her a double dose of Motrin. He was tempted to give her even more, but he wasn't sure if that would be safe.

"I'm so thirsty…" she said.

He gave her a large glass of water, and she drank half of it before lying back down. She closed her eyes and nestled in her pillow. She was fast asleep in less than a minute.

Max looked at his watch. *Two hours*, he thought to himself. *If her fever hasn't broken by then, I'm calling the doctor.*

Max finished his second cup of coffee and folded up the *L.A. Times* he had been reading. He glanced at the clock on the wall. It was almost nine o'clock. Two hours was up.

Megan was still asleep. Her forehead was sizzling to the touch. Max dragged the knob of the thermometer across her forehead. He held his breath as he released the button and the small screen displayed its measurement. A dizzying sense of alarm hijacked his mind. He turned off the thermometer, waited a minute, and took her temperature again. 106.7 degrees.

"Damn," he whispered under his breath.

He was gripped by the alarming thought that the multiple mosquito bites that covered Megan's arms, face, and legs were the likely cause of her fever. When he was growing up, he'd had an eight-year-old cousin die from a meningitis infection that he had picked up at summer camp.

He hurried out of the room and dialed the number of Megan's pediatrician.

"Dr. Green's exchange."

"This is Max Tyler. My daughter Megan is one of Dr. Green's patients. I need to speak to the doctor immediately."

"I'm sorry. Dr. Green is on vacation until next Monday. I can have his nurse call you."

"Thanks, but I really need to speak to a physician."

"Dr. Phelps is covering for Dr. Green, but he's in surgery for the next two hours. I can have the nurse call you. Is this an emergency?"

"Yes, it is." Max gritted his teeth and tried to keep his frustration in check. "My daughter Megan is running an extremely high temperature—almost 107 degrees. I'm getting her dressed and taking her to the emergency room at St. Andrew's Medical Center in Yorba Linda. Please have Dr. Phelps call me there in an hour." He ended the call.

Megan was limp as a ragdoll as Max got her out of bed and helped her put on her bathrobe. He grabbed some of her clothes and stuffed them in a duffel bag.

Mosquito bites. Meningitis. Encephalitis.

He put her in the car and sped to the hospital. Racing his thoughts.

Racing for Megan's life.

Chapter 6

Max insisted on staying with Megan as the emergency room team treated her.

He was sitting in the corner of a triage room behind a partitioned curtain. Megan, dressed in a hospital gown, was lying on a gurney, covered by a temperature modulating gel-filled cooling blanket. Max held her hand as the nurse checked the blanket's temperature.

The receptionist had taken one look at Megan in Max's arms and ushered them into the triage room, alerting the physician on call. Dr. Baker had listened to Max's explanation while he checked Megan's vital signs, lymph nodes, pupillary response, and general neurological function. The thermometer had given back-to-back readings of 106.1 degrees Fahrenheit. He gave her an injection of an anti-pyretic drug and two prescription-strength acetaminophen and ordered the nurses to immediately cover her with a cooling blanket.

It had taken over thirty minutes for Megan's face to feel noticeably cooler. Max kept placing his hand on her forehead to check her temperature. He felt a surge of relief when he realized her temperature was finally beginning to drop. He held her hand and waited another fifteen minutes. Megan's lower lip quivered, and her teeth began to chatter.

An emergency room nurse walked behind the partition and took Megan's temperature. She smiled when she read the thermometer.

"99.7. Almost there," she said. "Textbook normal is 98.6." She recorded the temperature in Megan's chart. "We'll keep her under the cooling blanket a few more minutes; then you can get her out and put her in this hospital gown. The medication Dr. Baker gave her should keep her temperature down for a while. He'll be over to talk to you in a minute and let you know if there are any tests he wants to run. He'll probably want to admit her. At least for the night."

Max nodded. "Thanks." He turned to Megan and took her hand. "Just a little longer, sweetheart."

Megan peered up at Max and squeezed his hand. She was pale, and her hand was freezing. "I'm c-cold daddy."

"I know, baby. Only another minute or two. Then we'll take the cooling blanket off you."

Dr. Beth Collins' cell phone vibrated with a text. She was finishing her examination of a teenager with an infected leg wound. He was dangerously close to developing septicemia. Gangrene was even possible.

She checked the phone number in the text and dialed it.

"Dr. Collins here," she said. "What's up?"

She listened to the nurse's request message and glanced at her watch. "Uh, sure. Tell Dr. Baker I'm with a patient and I have one more I need to check on, but I'll be up to see her when I finish. Should be in about thirty to forty minutes. What was her name again? Megan Tyler? Room 238, west wing of pediatrics. Got it. Thanks."

Beth finished rebandaging the teenager's infected wound that was now cleaned up and re-sutured. When she'd first seen it over an hour ago, it had been horribly swollen with pus oozing from the forty stitches that held it together.

Three weeks earlier, the teenager had been thrown from his motorcycle after being clipped by a reckless motorist accelerating through an unsafe lane change. Airborne at forty-five miles an hour, he'd hit the pavement and rolled, barely missing the car roaring by in the outside lane. He'd collided with a pile of branches on the side of the road. The sharp edge of one of the branches had shredded his left thigh, ripping a gaping furrow that was half an inch deep and reached from above his knee all the way to his groin.

Dr. Baker, the emergency room physician, had stitched it up and bandaged it, but the teenager had ignored his instructions to take it easy on that leg and change the bandage regularly. The wound had split open multiple times over the last two weeks.

His mother had rushed him to the emergency room again after the swollen wound began bleeding and oozing profusely. Dr. Baker was once more on duty. He called in Beth, the hospital's infectious disease specialist, for a consult before cleaning up and restitching the infected wound. She had the teenager admitted to the hospital straight from the ER and wrote orders for an immediate intravenous administration of Keflex, a broad-spectrum antibiotic.

Beth flipped through the teenager's chart, scribbled notes in different sections, and slapped the cover shut. He was her patient now.

"You're being discharged tomorrow morning, Scott, and I want you to listen *very carefully* to me." Beth looked at the teenager and his mother, who was sitting at his bedside. Beth gauged the mother to be in her early thirties, but she couldn't help but notice the multiple tattoos on her arms and the signs of premature aging on her lined, leathery face. A visage of hardcore living if she'd ever seen one.

Beth fixed Scott with a penetrating stare. "You didn't follow the emergency room physician's instructions after your accident. Your stitches broke open. The wound got horribly infected. I've never seen a dirtier mess of a stitched-up wound. You want to tell me how that happened?"

He shrugged and turned away from her with a look of impatient resignation.

Several moments passed, and she continued to wait for his answer, determined to make him verbalize responsibility for his infected leg. She glanced at his mother, who was growing more nervous as the seconds ticked off.

"I, uh, went riding with some buddies of mine out in the desert," he said finally, breaking the silence. "Did some hill jumpin' and racing. Guess I dropped my bike a couple of times. Had one major spill."

Beth waited through another gap of silence. She saw the look of defiance on his face begin to fade. "Guess it was…pretty dumb, huh?" he asked.

She waited a moment, letting his own words sink in.

"See this?" She held her index finger and thumb a quarter of an inch apart. "This is how close you are to losing your leg, and we're still not out of the woods yet."

She moved her hands down to just above his bandaged leg.

"Let's see…a wound this long, and as massively infected as you allowed it to get…I figure we would have to cut off your leg right about here." She pressed the edge of her hand on an area above mid-thigh. "Yep, we'd need to hack off at least *three-quarters* of your leg."

His eyes grew big, and his jaw dropped.

It was just the response Beth was looking for. "It's no fun living the rest of your life with one leg, Scott," she said. "Nothing hip, cool, or trendy about it."

Her look and the tone of her voice turned harsh and serious.

"You *will* stay off this leg for the next week. You *will* use crutches when you have to get up and about. No baths or showers, washcloth only. You *will* take antibiotic pills twice a day, every day, for ten days. And you *will* change the bandage and apply fresh antibiotic ointment every two days. *Do you understand me?*"

This time she didn't have to wait for his answer.

"I understand," he muttered.

"Good." Beth scribbled on a prescription pad, tore off a sheet, and handed it to his mother. "The ointment I want you to get is called Neosporin. You can buy it over the counter at any drug store. The prescription is for an antibiotic you need to pick up on your way home today. Take one tablet now then another before you go to bed. After that, twice a day for the next nine days until they're gone."

"What about school?" his mother asked.

"No school for a week. I'm sure you can contact his teachers and get his assignments. I want him *completely* immobile for a week. Then he can go back to school on crutches. In a week, you can wrap the bandaged part of his leg in Saran or Glad wrap, and he can start taking brief showers. Got it?"

She nodded.

"I want to see you in two weeks," Beth said. She pulled a business card out of her pocket and handed it to her. "Call my office and set up an appointment. Do you have any questions?"

"No. We'll make the appointment today."

"Good," Beth said. She turned to Scott and focused on him. "Now listen up because I'm dead serious. You've got to take care of your leg. Follow my instructions exactly, and I mean *exactly*. No excuses. Got it?"

"I hear ya," Scott agreed.

"Okay, see you in my office in two weeks." Beth began heading for the door.

"Thank you, Doctor," Scott's mother said.

"Uh, yeah. Thanks," Scott mumbled.

Beth looked back at them as she pushed the door open. She flashed them a guarded smile. "You're welcome."

Chapter 7

Megan was in a semi-private room on the pediatrics wing of the second floor. She had been isolated because her disease was potentially infectious. While the room could be partitioned, the second bed would remain empty as a precautionary measure.

Her room was three-quarters of the way down the west wing hall from the nurses' station. A muffled clamor of noise wafted into her room from the other rooms on the wing. Visiting children and the hushing admonitions of their parents generated a soft, constant background din.

Max was seated at the foot of Megan's bed reading *USA Today*. He looked up as a nurse came in to collect the lunch trays. Megan was playing with a square of red Jell-O. She gave it a whack with her spoon and watched it wiggle back and forth. She had eaten most of her applesauce and a few bites of a sandwich, but red Jell-O was her favorite.

"All through?" the nurse asked, picking up Max's tray that was lying on the foot of the bed.

"Yes. Thank you," Max said. "Megan, are you done?"

She was sluggish and slow to answer. Max thought he could see her fever rising in front of his eyes.

"Yes," she said. "But I'm still thirsty. Can...Can I have some more juice?"

"Sure, sweetheart," the nurse said. "Do you want apple juice again? We also have grape, pineapple, and cranberry."

"Grape sounds good."

"Coming right up," the nurse said. She reached for Megan's tray. Megan gave the square of Jell-O a final whack before placing her spoon on the tray and leaning back.

Max watched her lay her head back on the pillow. He felt her forehead, and just as he suspected, her fever was rising. *First, she gets shot with a tranquilizer dart,* he thought, *and now this.* All he could do was comfort her and pray she'd be all right.

He heard a knock on the door and turned to see a woman in a white lab coat step into the room. She held a hospital chart in her hand and had a stethoscope protruding from her pocket. He took in her attractive features in an instant.

She was in her mid-thirties, about five-foot-seven, with shoulder-length brown hair and high cheekbones that accented her creamy smooth complexion. He could see her skin had a healthy tone to it, and in spite of the unflattering lab coat, she looked fit and trim. Max guessed that she was no stranger to exercise.

She smiled. The penetrating blue-green of her eyes and brightness of her teeth was a striking combination. The contours of her face were slender and attractive, and Max felt a whirling thrill accelerate inside him, a brief free-fall that caught him entirely off guard. It was a feeling he hadn't experienced in years.

"Hi, Mr....Tyler? I'm Dr. Beth Collins." She extended her hand.

Max snapped out of his daze and stood up. "Nice to meet you," he said and shook her hand. Up close, her features were stunning, and the brief handshake quickened his pulse and the dizzying sensation inside him.

"This is Megan," he said, turning to look at his daughter.

"Hi, Megan," Beth said. She stepped forward and placed her hand on Megan's shoulder. Megan slowly turned her head and looked up at her. "I'm Dr. Collins, and I'm going to take care of you."

"Hi," Megan said. Her voice was weak and raspy. Her eyes blinked with leaden heaviness.

Beth dragged a digital thermometer across Megan's forehead and checked both of her ears. The temperature readout was startlingly high, so she checked it again. No mistake.

Turning to Max, she said, "I read the notes in her chart about the attempted kidnapping up in Mammoth and the tranquilizer dart. Pretty bizarre."

"Unbelievable," he agreed. "I have no idea why they were trying to take her."

Beth shook her head. "And what's with all these mosquito bites?"

"From camping, I guess. Neither of us noticed she was bitten until we got home. Then a couple dozen of them appeared. She was itching like crazy."

"I can imagine."

Beth listened to Megan's heart and breathing with a stethoscope and examined her throat. Then she checked the girl's eardrums with an otoscope. She felt the swollen lymph nodes on Megan's throat and noted that her skin was hot to the touch.

"Do you hurt anywhere, Megan? Does any part of your body ache or throb?"

Megan nodded. "My head hurts, and my neck's really stiff."

Beth palpated Megan's neck, feeling the tightness on the sides and back. "Do you feel tired? Maybe a little fuzzy too?"

"Uh huh."

Beth used a penlight on Megan's eyes to test her pupillary reflex. "How about your tummy. Does it feel upset?"

"Kinda…"

"Well, we're just going to have to make you better," Beth said. She patted her hand and gave her a comforting look. "The first thing we need to do is get your temperature down. I'm going to have your nurse come in, and after she gives you some medicine, she'll put cooling washcloths all over your arms, legs, and chest. Then we'll run a few tests and see if we can find out what's wrong with you."

She turned to Max. "Could you come with me to the nurses' station for a minute? There's a procedure form I need you to sign."

"Sure," Max said. "I'll be right back, sweetie."

Beth led him towards the nurses' station. Before they got there, she pulled him aside next to a storage closet. Visitors were entering a room two doors down, but otherwise, they were alone.

"Mr. Tyler…"

"Please call me Max."

"Okay…Max." She stopped and took a deep breath. When she looked up at Max, her eyes displayed confident authority and compassion. "Megan's temperature is elevated again, but that isn't my major concern. The extra strength non-steroidal anti-inflammatory medication and cool cloths I've ordered should bring that down. My major concern is the sum of her

30

symptoms…the complete picture. That gives me a strong indicator of what's wrong with her, especially in light of recent occurrences."

"Occurrences?" Max asked.

"Yes. In the past week, we've had six people admitted to this hospital with raging fevers very similar to Megan's. One was a young boy, and the other five were adults. All of them lived in southern Orange County. At first, we thought it was just a bad flu infection that was going around. When you catch the flu, the influenza virus can cause a fever, and occasionally it can get pretty high. But the fevers we saw were too high and tenacious. And the stiff necks and swollen lymph nodes indicate a different viral or a bacterial infection."

Max was staring at her with a growing look of fear. "And?"

"We performed spinal taps on the patients."

"Spinal taps? Don't you do that to check for meningitis?"

"That's right," she said, nodding. "The test also allows us to scan for any bacterially-induced encephalitis. Two of the adult patients had viral meningitis. We confirmed bacterial meningitis in the other four, and two of those we weren't able to save. The first was an elderly gentleman. He was in bad health to begin with, and the infection moved quickly."

"How quickly?"

"He died three days after he was admitted to the hospital. As I said, he was in exceptionally frail health."

Max forced himself to ask the next question. "The boy was the second one to die, wasn't he?"

Beth hesitated before looking Max directly in the eye. "Yes. He was two years old. His parents were illegal immigrants. They were afraid to bring him in for medical care. They let the fever go for two to three days, intermittently treating him with baby aspirin, but not keeping close tabs on him. The fever raged out of control, and the boy went into seizures. He was almost comatose when they brought him to the hospital."

Max reeled as his worst fear broke the surface. "So, you think Megan has meningitis?"

"She has all the symptoms of it. I think there's a strong likelihood this will turn out to be *viral* meningitis."

Max looked away, chasing his racing thoughts. It seemed that whenever meningitis was in the news, one or two people had already died from it.

"I can't believe Megan might have meningitis," Max said. He collapsed onto a nearby chair and leaned his head in his hands. After a few minutes of silence, he looked up at Beth and said, "I think I remember reading something about there being two main types of meningitis. Is viral the worst kind?"

"No, actually it isn't," Beth said. "*Bacterial meningitis* is far more serious. It needs to be treated aggressively with antibiotics to prevent permanent neurological damage and possibly death. *Viral meningitis* is milder. If that's what she has, the symptoms should disappear in a week or two without any lasting complications."

"Well, that sounds better," Max said, visibly relieved. "If she's got it at all, I hope that's the type she has."

"I agree," Beth said. "But to confirm a diagnosis of meningitis, we'll have to do a lumbar puncture. A spinal tap," she said when Max gave her a confused look. "We need to collect a sample of Megan's cerebrospinal fluid. Then we'll run tests on it, and that should tell us what we need to know. If she does have it, the tests will tell us which type."

Beth handed Max a piece of paper from her clipboard. "I'll need you to sign this authorization form to allow us to do the procedure."

"Okay," Max said tentatively. The thought of doctors performing a spinal tap was unnerving, but he read the form and signed it. "Oh, man, is this going to be really painful for her? She's afraid of needles."

Beth saw the worry on Max's face. "I'm not going to say it won't hurt, but the pain should be tolerable. Megan will get through it just fine."

Max felt comforted by Beth's warm, confident tone.

"Can I be in there with her when they do the procedure?" he asked. "I know it would make it easier for her."

Beth took them form from him and gave him a sly glance. "Easier for her…or easier for you?"

"Both…" Max laughed.

Beth made a notation on the consent form. "Of course," she said. "I think that's reasonable, but let me tell you what to expect so you're clear on what happens during this procedure."

"Sure," he said.

"Megan will need to lie on her side, curl up into a tight ball to flex her back, and then hold perfectly still through the whole procedure. The team will sterilize the lower spine area of her back with a Betadine sponge and then inject a local anesthetic called Xylocaine—a few injections—to numb the area. Remember when they gave you those stitches for your shoulder wound?"

"Yes," Max said, touching his shoulder.

"They injected you with the same stuff before sewing you up.'

"Good. I didn't feel anything but pressure when they put in the stitches."

"Exactly. So next, after her lower back area is completely numb, our anesthesiologist will insert the spinal needle between the third and fourth lumbar vertebrae into what's called the subarachnoid space. That's where they collect the cerebrospinal fluid sample."

"How long will the procedure take?"

"About thirty minutes. Then out comes the needle, and they'll have her lie flat for an hour before taking her back to the room."

"Why does she have to lie flat?"

"It lessens the headaches she might get following the procedure. Listen…" Beth reached out and touched his arm. "Don't worry, Max. Megan will sail through this test."

Max studied Beth's face as she spoke and knew instinctively that he could trust her.

"I hope so," he said. "She's my life."

Chapter 8

I
t was two o'clock in the morning, and Larry Drake was on the prowl in
the silent, dimly lit halls of the hospital. He felt a wild rushing lift of
euphoria courtesy of the powerful multi-drug cocktail he had injected into
his veins half an hour earlier. All of his senses told him he was brilliant,
unstoppable, and invincible. Probably immortal.

Drake's next victim was a man in his mid-thirties who had been in a car
accident. A heavily inebriated driver had crashed into his car after speeding
through a red light. The drunk had walked away from the collision unscathed,
but his victim's left leg had been broken in multiple places, and a surgeon had
to knit his femur together with two slender steel plates.

Except for his leg, the patient was in remarkably good shape. He had spent
three days in the hospital, and he was eagerly looking forward to being
discharged in the morning. His wife would be there to pick him up at eleven.
He expected this to be his last night in the hospital. What he didn't expect was
for this to be his last night.

Drake slipped into the man's hospital room, leaving the door slightly ajar
with just enough light spilling in from the hallway for him to see what he was
doing. The bed near the door was empty as he had confirmed earlier when
choosing his next target.

He glided over to the far bed and looked down at the man who was deep
in the shadowy folds of a murky dreamscape. His breathing was regular and
coarsely sonorous, interrupted by an occasional fluttering snore.

Drake glanced at the half-empty 100cc bag of D5W hanging from the
slender chrome hook of the IV stand. His eyes traced the tubing down to the
top of the man's left hand where the needle had been inserted into one of his
veins and taped in place. He followed the tubing back up and stared at the Y-

port an inch from the man's hand then shifted his gaze to the man's face.

Out like a light, Drake thought. *Dead to the world.* He grinned at his joke as he pulled a syringe out of his white lab coat and uncapped it. He stuck the needle into the rubber cap of the port and pushed the plunger with steady force, driving twenty ccs of cisatracurium besylate out of the syringe and into the tubing.

This won't take long, Drake thought as his mouth twisted into a smirk. *You're gonna be seriously relaxed in just a minute.*

Cisatracurium is an intermediate duration neuromuscular blocking agent used by anesthesiologists to paralyze patients' skeletal muscles during surgery. After it flowed through the tubing and into the vein on top of the man's hand, the drug traveled up the ulnar, axial, and brachial veins in his arm, traversed the loop under his clavicle, and converged into the superior vena cava which delivered it into the right atrium of the man's heart. From there it raced down the tricuspid valve into the right ventricle, up through the pulmonary semilunar valve into the pulmonary arteries to the lungs, and then returned to the left atrium of the heart via the pulmonary veins where it was pumped throughout the body.

Cisatracurium paralyzes by competing with a neurotransmitter called acetylcholine that is released from nerves that innervate skeletal muscle and initiate muscle contractions. The drug began working immediately after it reached the muscles, blockading the acetylcholine receptor sites and preventing the neurotransmitter from binding. Without the acetylcholine locking into the receptors, nerve conduction ceased, and the muscles failed to contract in the throes of absolute paralysis.

Because the heart is not made up of skeletal muscle, the cisatracurium had no effect on it; the man's heart kept beating as normal. The same could not be said of his chest diaphragm muscles.

Drake watched as the man's eyes opened and blinked once, twice, then locked in the open position. The total abject terror the man was feeling dwarfed the fearful expression frozen on his motionless face. He was fully conscious and fully paralyzed, prey to the unbearable, nightmarish horror of suffocation with complete awareness that he could not lift even a finger to save his own life.

With his eyes locked open, he could see Drake. He stared in silent horror for thirty seconds. Darkness clouded the perimeter of his vision as oxygen deprivation drove him mercifully into unconsciousness. In three minutes, irreversible brain damage would begin. In seven to ten, brain death would occur.

Drake looked at the syringe still dangling from the Y-port and grinned at the "azithromycin" label taped to the side of it. *Poor sucker. Looks like somebody gave you the wrong injection. Man, if I were your family, I'd sue the hell out of this hospital.*

He flashed back to that afternoon when Richard Berk had fired him. The familiar, seething rage began to churn inside him.

This hospital's going down Berk...and you're goin' down with it.

He slid out of the room, silent and unnoticed, leaving the door open. Once in the stairwell, he peeled off the thin surgical latex gloves he was wearing and stuffed them into his pocket.

Unstoppable. Invincible.

Chapter 9

The man in the Jeep Cherokee sat waiting in the parking lot of St. Andrews Medical Center. He looked up at the imposing ten-story edifice, sprawling side buildings, and medical heliport pad and thought, *Man, that's one big-ass hospital. It's ten times the size of that cracker box in Mammoth.*

He looked across the aisle and down three rows to where Max's white Suburban was parked and then checked the time. He'd been sitting here for almost five hours.

His cell phone rang, and he grabbed it off the seat next to him.

"Joe's videos," he quipped.

"What's your middle name, Joe?" the voice asked in a quiet monotone.

"That would be Raoul," he said.

"I assume you've located her."

"Snooped around first thing this morning and found her on the second floor. Room 238. Basic run-of-the-mill room with two beds."

"She alone?"

"So far. Nick's in place and reporting. He called me after sneaking a peek at her chart. Said there are clear orders for her to have a room all to herself. They think she's infectious."

"Where's her father?"

"Camped out in a chair at the foot of her bed."

There was silence on the other end of the line. Seconds passed. The man drummed his fingers on the steering wheel.

"Okay," the voice said, returning. "We need blood samples collected *tonight*. Two tubes. Make sure Nick waits until after seven o'clock to get them. Timing is critical. He has to collect them *after* seven o'clock tonight. Are we clear?"

"Got it. After seven o'clock tonight."

"For tonight's pickup, a runner will meet you in the parking lot right outside the main entrance at nine o'clock. Green Toyota truck. Guy's name is Sting."

"Green Toyota truck and Sting's the contact. Nine o'clock. I'll be waiting for him."

"Good. That's all for now. Call me tonight as soon as the samples are on their way."

"Will do. Schedule's still on as planned. Larry takes over for me in an hour and a half. Then I'm back at half past six for the night shift."

"Agreed," the monotone voice said. "Her father will probably spend the night in her room again like he did last night. I want surveillance maintained. Depending on the blood samples, we might need to snatch her and bring her in pronto."

"Just make sure I'm in on it. I'm major league pissed at the screw-up in Mammoth."

"Forget about it. It turned out it wasn't time to bring her in anyway. The tests on the samples we took from the Mammoth hospital showed that. We'll be damn sure she's ready this time around."

The man gripped the steering wheel in frustration. "As long as I'm part of it."

"*You will be.* One last thing. Make sure Nick reports anything strange going on in the hospital…even if it's just a little out of the ordinary. When we get ready to grab her, I don't want some glitch to blindside us and screw everything up."

"It won't," he said, looking at his watch. Nick was due to call him in less than twenty minutes. They made contact every three hours. "Nick's good at surveillance. I'll make sure he's on it. But now that you bring it up, he did report something strange this afternoon."

"What?"

"Probably nothing. Some scuttlebutt he overheard two nurses talking about…"

"Go on."

"Yesterday morning a woman went hysterical at the nurses' station up on the third floor. She was screaming at the top of her lungs and going ballistic. It seems she came by to pick up her husband. He was supposed to be all set to go home after having routine surgery on his broken leg. They found him dead in his hospital bed."

"What's that got to do with us? People die in hospitals every day of the week."

"Yeah, they do. But not like this guy. He was a total health nut. Ran freakin' marathons for fun. There was nothing wrong with him except his leg. The nurses found a syringe stuck in his IV line, dangling there. It was mislabeled. They think it had some kind of anesthesia drug in it. Guy was dead when they found him."

The voice on the line exhaled in a low huff. "Guess it could have been a mistake, but it looks suspicious. Maybe the poor sucker was offed by a business associate or someone he owed money to. His wife could have been after the life insurance. Who knows?"

"Anything can happen."

"Yeah. Could even be a wacko nurse running loose in the hospital killing people. I remember a couple of 'Angel of Death' stories like this in the newspaper a few years ago."

"Man…"

"It's a small possibility, but we're not taking a chance. Tell Nick to keep a super sharp eye on the girl's room. I don't want us finding her dead because we didn't think this could happen."

"I'll tell him."

"Good. We'll talk after nine."

Click.

Chapter 10

Beth put a stopper in the slender glass vial containing a clear liquid and lay it on a metal tray next to the procedure table. There was a second, nearly identical vial lying next to it completing a pair of cerebrospinal fluid samples.

"All done, Megan," she said. "You can relax now. That wasn't all that bad, was it?"

Megan quit flexing her back and let go of her knees as she extended her legs. "Not...too bad," she said in a halting whisper.

Max was sitting on the opposite side of the examination table, facing Megan and holding her hand. *Man, that needle was big*, he thought and felt a chill go up his spine. He forced himself to smile as he squeezed her hand.

"Megan, you were *so* brave, and now we're all through. I'm really proud of you!"

Megan squeezed back weakly. "Thanks."

"Your father's right," Beth said as she put the glass tubes in a plastic carrier tray for transport to the laboratory. "You're a very brave young lady." She smiled warmly at Megan and patted her shoulder.

Max sensed the unspoken trust that flowed between them. He was confident that his daughter could not be in better hands. He could feel Beth's genuine concern and empathy, and he was thankful for her comforting manner.

Beth turned, and he saw the caring expression that seemed completely natural on her face. Max felt another disorienting rush flutter through him. He was surprised again by the effect she had on him.

"She did incredibly well," Beth said, shaking her head. "I mean... exceptional. I've done dozens of lumbar punctures on both children and adults. Believe me. This was a breeze."

"Thanks, Dr. Collins," Max forced his eyes from hers to look at Megan. "That's my girl."

Beth picked up Megan's chart and wrote a note in it. Then she turned to Megan and said, "Your lower back area will stay numb for another half hour or so before the medicine wears off. It's kind of like when you get a filling at the dentist and he gives you a Novocain shot to numb your gums. Ever get a filling at the dentist?"

Megan nodded.

"When the medicine wears off, your back will start to tingle as the sensation returns, and then it'll ache for a while. The medicine we're giving you for your fever should help take care of the ache too. Understand?"

Megan nodded.

"Good," Beth said. She paused to write a final note in her chart.

Max stood up and stretched his hands above his head. "Are we all done for now?"

"Just about," Beth said, watching the muscles in his shoulders and arms flex. She glanced away when she saw him looking at her, but Max saw her cheeks flush.

Beth picked up the thermometer, swiped it across Megan's forehead, and recorded the temperature in her chart.

"Megan, one thing you *have* to do is lie flat the rest of the morning and afternoon..." She looked at the clock. "...until four o'clock. It's really important that you stay down, understand?"

"Uh huh," Megan said.

"Good," she said. "I'll have someone stop by in five minutes and take you back to your room."

Beth looked up at Max. A slight blush still tinged her face.

"I'll take these samples straight down to the lab," she said, holding up the plastic carrier containing the two tubes. "We should have preliminary results back from them sometime this afternoon. I'll stop by Megan's room around four, and we can go over what the results mean and what treatment path we should follow."

"Okay, Dr. Collins," Max said.

"Beth," she corrected him.

"Okay, *Beth*," he said with a smile. He could feel a wisp of electricity in the air between them. "Hey, I just want to say...thanks for taking such good care of my little girl."

"My pleasure, Max," she said. "It's easy when you have a wonderful patient like Megan."

She turned and headed for the door. "We'll see you at four."

"Yeah," he said. "We'll see you."

Nick watched as Beth left the room and walked down the hallway towards the elevators. He had hovered close enough to the examination room to hear parts of their conversation. Nothing unexpected.

He saw Beth disappear into one of the elevators. A lengthy stretch of hours yawned before him. A long, boring wait. Maybe he'd hang around for a few more minutes until they wheeled the girl back to her room.

Or maybe not.

Raoul had blabbered to him about being alert and on the lookout for anything out of the ordinary. Of course, Nick had brought that on himself after mentioning he'd heard those nurses gabbing about that man's weird death up on the third floor. But that was probably nothing more than a horrible nursing mistake.

And even if the "mistake" was intentional, someone likely had it out for that guy. No way was the girl in any danger. Her father was stuck to her like glue. Talk about a round-the-clock bodyguard.

He could take a couple of hours off as long as he was back in time to hear what the doctor had to say at four o'clock. He checked his watch again and calculated how many hours he could be away and still get back on the floor in time. Just to be safe, he'd call his replacement and see if he wanted to trade part of his shift.

An orderly wheeled a gurney into the examination room where Megan and Max were waiting, and Nick heard them talking. *Guess her ride's arrived,* he thought. He turned and headed down the hallway. *Absolutely nothin's going on till four. I'm calling him. And if he doesn't want to trade...Screw it. I'm taking off anyway.*

It was close to lunchtime, and the normally bustling nurses' station on the second floor was almost deserted. A single nurse stood by an unlocked cabinet at the back of the open and easily accessible station. She finished restocking her medication cart and then closed and locked the cabinet door.

Drake watched from a safe distance as she wheeled the cart out of the nurses' station and down the hallway away from him. He had been biding his time at different locations on the second floor. He knew which staff members on each floor would recognize him, and he made a point of avoiding them.

As he saw her disappear into a patient's room at the far end of the hallway, he rushed into the nurses' station and straight up to the locked cabinet. He fumbled in his pocket and pulled out a ring of keys. He selected the smallest key on the ring, inserted it into the lock, and opened the cabinet to a breathtaking pharmaceutical cornucopia. Row after row of powerful, delectable injectables, tablets, and capsules.

He fought the overwhelming urge to clean out the cabinet. He could reach in and sweep out all the contents into a bag and take them home for a perpetual drug orgy like he'd never experienced. His rational mind fought a raging battle to squash that impulse. *But they won't notice if I just take a few.*

Drake pilfered pills from several bottles and vials, burying them in the bottom of his plastic supply carrier beneath the lab tech paraphernalia. Then he locked up the cabinet and scanned the nurses' station. He moved to the perimeter of the station and looked up and down the hall. The medication nurse's cart was located at the far end of the hallway. The nurse closed a drawer on the cart and walked into a patient's room.

Drake crossed to the opposite side of the nurses' station to where a clipboard containing the roster of second-floor patients hung on a wall hook next to the rack of patient charts. He grabbed it off the wall and freed the sheets as he walked over to the copy machine sitting on the counter by the medication cabinet. Drake copied the two pages, replaced the roster and clipboard where he found it, and slipped out of the nurses' station. He scanned the list. This floor was completely full. Every room had a patient in it, and most of the semi-privates had two.

Ah...so many victims, so little time. A smirk curled up one side of his mouth, and he felt the familiar stirrings of the thrilling rush that engulfed him on his last two fatal excursions. He plowed through the door to the stairwell and stopped on the landing as the door shut behind him, smiling to himself as an idea flickered into his mind.

What if this time we do it right in front of the family members?

"Oops. I'm sorry. I was just gettin' a blood sample like the doctor ordered. I didn't mean to off your poor loved one. Guess Aunt Gertie musta thrown an embolism or somethin'. Lemme call the doctor."

Drake's smirk broke into a smile, and he laughed aloud. He couldn't believe how much fun he was going to have bringing this hospital to its knees. *It's payback time, baby. I'll teach them to fire me. And I've got special plans for butthead Berk.*

Holding the two-page patient roster up in front him, he closed his eyes. His finger darted around the page.

Drake let his finger drop to the bottom third of the page. Then he opened his eyes.

And the unlucky winner is…Paul Talbot, room 239, soon to leave the hospital in the worst possible way.

He looked across the row and saw a discharge date recorded with today's date and a time of ten o'clock. He shot a quick glance at his watch.

Damn. Lucky son of a bitch squeaked by with a couple of hours to spare. He oughta go out and buy some lottery tickets. Let's see…next lucky runner up is…

His finger moved up one line. Room 238. No discharge notation.

Megan Tyler, age 9.

Drake snickered to himself, thinking what an outrage this one was going to cause. He pictured killing her in front of her father, and it triggered twisted stirrings deep inside him.

Man, this is gonna be intense. Your parents are gonna sue this hospital for every stinkin' nickel and dime. This place is going down…way down.

He skipped down the steps, his mind whirling with the possibilities, a thrilling rush ascending in his core.

Chapter 11

Beth was sitting in the hospital cafeteria taking her last bite of sandwich when her cell phone vibrated. She tamed it with the push of a button and recognized the extension number on the text screen. *Fifth floor ICU...must be Carmichael again.*

She thought about the eighty-two-year-old patient, Levi Carmichael. He was teetering on the brink of death because of a fulminating varicella pneumonia infection complicated by a host of other physiological problems including the failure of one of his kidneys. She already had him on powerful IV antivirals and two different antibiotics. Hopefully, they would halt the damaging spread of his infection, but given the fragility of his condition, it was anybody's guess.

The intensivist, Dr. Everett Charles, was doing an excellent job managing Carmichael's overall condition. Beth enjoyed working with him. He was an analytic thinker who utilized state-of-the-art medical interventions, and he valued her infectious disease expertise and treatment leadership. But no matter how good a team they were, it was still going to be a miracle if they managed to pull poor Mr. Carmichael out of this alive.

Beth looked at her watch, surprised that it was already a couple of minutes past two.

Instead of returning a call to the number in the text, she decided to go straight up to the ICU nurses' station and talk to them in person. She had another patient to see there besides Carmichael and two more on the floor below. She estimated it should take an hour and a half to finish checking in on all four patients, barring any serious interventions Carmichael might require, and she'd be able to pick up Megan's CSF test results before four o'clock.

She thought about Megan, comparing her symptoms to those of all the meningitis patients she'd treated both bacterial and viral.

Viral...I've got a feeling about this one.

In five years practicing as an infectious disease specialist, Beth had lost two patients—an eighty-year-old man and a two-year-old boy—to bacterial meningitis. The two-year-old had been the worst. The emotional trauma of losing him and then having to break the news to his parents had ripped a jagged hole in her heart. The look on their faces had burned in her memory for months afterward.

She had lost no patients to viral meningitis, and she didn't plan to allow that to change.

Beth thought about her four o'clock meeting with Megan and her father as she left the cafeteria and headed toward the elevators. She visualized walking into Megan's room, discussing the results with Max and Megan, and taking them down the treatment path she would follow.

Max stuck in her mind, and for the first time, she allowed herself to confront the feelings she'd been avoiding for hours. She felt the same unsettling rush she'd felt when she was standing next to him beside Megan's bed.

What in the world's going on?

It was undeniable that there was a strong mutual attraction between them. The way he looked at her sent a fluttering cascade whirling through her. *It's like the crazy schoolgirl crushes I had back in junior high school. What's the matter with me?*

The elevator dinged, and the doors opened. She stepped inside and pushed the button for the fifth floor. She smiled to herself, thinking back to her last relationship that had ended almost a year ago. Not once had she come close to feeling like this.

It's a wild infatuation, she thought. *I just met him, and everybody knows there's no such thing as love at first sight. Right?*

Chapter 12

The tall grass undulated lazily in the breeze, buffeting Megan's legs as she ran toward the forest. The sky above her was deep azure. The grass at her feet was the lushest, most intense green she had ever seen, set in razor sharp contrast to the hills in the distance and the woodland she was approaching.

The rich springtime aroma of freshly cut grass filled her senses; every sight, smell, and sensation around her seemed richly complex and impossibly magnified. But she had no time to ponder the engulfing sensory paradise or soak in its wondrous magic. She was running for her life.

She looked over her shoulder and saw Sarah running close behind her. They were galloping through the grass as quickly as their legs would take them. In the distance, she could see the human predator chasing them. He was gaining on them.

"C'mon, Sarah! We've gotta hurry. He's getting closer!"

"I'm running as fast as I can!" Sarah squealed.

"You can do it," Megan said. "We're almost to the woods. He'll never find us in there!"

They raced across the last few yards. Megan looked over her shoulder one last time back before they disappeared into the trees.

The forest loomed above them, a towering, endless canopy of primeval foliage. The woodsy milieu and earthy smells of the forest engulfed Megan as she and Sarah scurried between the trees, deeper and deeper into the shady recesses of the arboreal shelter. Sun rays filtered through the high branches, and the soft warbling of birds resonated in the distant foliage.

She chanced a look back over her shoulder and saw their pursuer enter the forest through the same gap in the trees. He halted with a scowl on his face and scanned the terrain. When he spotted them, he broke into a run.

She grabbed Sarah's hand and tugged her to the right. The branches of shrubs scratched her arms as she hurtled through the trees. She heard Sarah whimper in fear and cry out in pain as the branches whipped the side of her face.

He was catching up to them. She was sure of it. Chancing another quick look over her shoulder, she glimpsed the man approaching at a furious pace. They weren't going to get away. He was closing in fast. And when he caught them...

Megan glanced down at the brown-haired girl at her side. Even in the midst of such terror, she felt overwhelmed with wonder.

It was impossible, of course. Completely impossible. The girl running alongside her was her exact twin, only three years younger. Her shoulder-length brown hair, her eyes and the set of her mouth, the way she ran. It was like Megan was looking at a picture of herself when she was six years old. How could that be?

Megan had the eeriest feeling while she was talking with Sarah that she was talking to herself. She seemed to know what the other girl was going to say before she said it. Finding out her name had sent Megan's mind spinning. Sarah was the name of Megan's best friend in the entire world.

"C'mon, Sarah! We've gotta get away! That man's going to hurt us really bad if he catches us. You've gotta speed up. As fast as you can!"

"I...I can't run any faster," she whimpered.

She stumbled over a large rock in the path. Her knees hit the ground for a second, and then Megan pulled her back to her feet and they were running again.

"Here, let's go this way," Megan said, cutting through an opening between the pine trees.

They zigzagged around the shrubs and trees in their way trying to get away from the man chasing them. Megan could hear him crashing through the undergrowth behind them. He was close enough now that she could hear his gasping breaths.

They darted around three large pine trees and were stopped dead in their tracks a moment later by an enormous outcropping of rocks. There was no way to climb the rocks and no way around them; a copse of trees bordered one side of the rock embankment, and a dense wall of shrubs bordered the other.

They were trapped. The only way out was the way they came in…and that wasn't an option.

Megan turned and looked over her shoulder. Her face drained of blood when she saw her pursuer crash through the shrubs and rush towards them. He had a scraggly, dirty brown beard and a maniacal look on his face. He held a large hunting knife high above his head, ready to slash down at them. Two steps and he would kill them.

Megan hugged Sarah close to her and opened her mouth to scream.

Max shook Megan awake. It took her half a minute before she was aware of her surroundings. Tears were streaming down her face; Max had never seen her look so frightened. She'd cried out in her dreams, a wordless scream of terror.

"Megan, wake up…wake up, honey. You were just having a bad dream. That's all. Just a bad dream."

Megan reached out for her father. He wrapped his arms around her. She burrowed her face in his shoulder and sobbed.

"I was so scared, Daddy."

"I know, sweetheart. Dreams can be scary sometimes. It's okay."

Megan buried herself in the warm safety of her father's embrace. It took a while for her sobbing to fade to nothing. Max could feel the tension in her arms and shoulders lessen as she started to relax.

They sat in silence for almost a minute before she pulled away from him and wiped the tears from her eyes. "There was a horrible man chasing us through the forest." Megan grimaced in fear at what she'd seen. "We were trying our best to get away, but I could hear him getting closer with every step. We ran around some huge trees, and we got trapped up against a bunch of big rocks. He ran right at us. He had this humongous knife. He was going to slash us."

Max squeezed her arm. "Bad dreams are funny, aren't they? Your mind was probably just replaying the thing that happened to us on our camping trip up in Mammoth."

"But this forest was different. It's like no place I've been before. And the man was taller...He was totally spooky looking."

Max nodded. He pushed damp hair away from her forehead and wiped a tear from her cheek. "Like we've talked about a whole bunch of times. When you dream, your mind takes things and twists them all around. Most of the time, normal sorts of things happen even though they're mixed up and kind of weird. But sometimes fun, happy things happen to you, and sometimes horrible, scary things happen. The worst nightmares you can imagine. It's all part of dreaming."

"I know. But this felt so real."

"I bet it did," Max said. "So...did I fight this guy off like I did in Mammoth?"

"No." Megan shook her head. "You weren't even in my dream."

"I wasn't? I thought you said he was chasing us through the forest with a knife?"

"He *was* chasing us," Megan said. "But...you weren't the one with me. It was this little girl...It was crazy strange."

"The little girl made it strange?" Max asked. "What about her?"

"Well..." Megan said, hesitating. "She looked six years old, but she seemed lots older. She was really smart for her age. I don't think we knew each other very long, but we were already best friends. And she was just like me."

Max grinned. "Doesn't sound too strange to me."

Megan had a serious look on her face. "No, you don't understand. She was *exactly* like me. My identical twin. But she was six years old instead of ten."

"You mean nine..."

"I'm almost ten," Megan said. "My birthday's in two months. It was like I was talking to myself. Like we could read each other's minds. She...she was trying to tell me about some awful things that were going on. And then she started to say something about Mom..."

Max gave her a quizzical look. "What did she say?"

Megan shook her head. A hint of sadness crossed her face. "She started to say something, but she didn't have a chance. That's when the man with the knife showed up and started chasing us into the forest. But she was talking about Mom like she knew her."

Max nodded and gazed past her for a few moments as thoughts of his wife drifted through his mind. A twinge of loss clenched and then released his heart as he pictured her. It was still hard to believe that she was gone.

"Well…I'm sure you'll dream about your little friend again, and I bet next time it'll be a happy dream."

"I hope so," she said. "I like her a lot. Her name's Sarah, and she's really nice."

"I'm sure she is," Max agreed. He glanced at his watch. A good chunk of the afternoon had already slipped by while Megan slept.

"You had a long nap. Do you want to try to sleep some more, or do you feel up to playing a game?"

"Depends," she said with a wispy smile. She looked weak, but a touch of color had returned to her face.

"On what?" he asked.

Megan's smile widened. "On whether you feel like getting whupped at *Skip-Bo* again!"

He chuckled. "You just *think* you're going to win. You're going down this time, girl. Where are the cards?"

Drake cruised the second floor, scouting the personnel who were on this shift. As usual, his reconnaissance was efficient and uneventful. He had worked as a hospital phlebotomist the past three years. He knew how to act and what to look for. A quick survey of the nurses' station and halls confirmed what he'd expected.

This afternoon would be the perfect time for his mission.

The nursing staff was coasting through the afternoon doldrums, and things wouldn't get busy again until it got closer to dinnertime. Today was an especially slow day.

Drake glanced inside Megan's room as he walked past it. He caught a glimpse of Max sitting by the far bedside dealing cards onto the bed table and could hear him joking with Megan.

No one else was in the room.

Drake passed several rooms that had been vacant since late morning. He reached the nurses' station and found it empty. Hurrying over to the rack, he yanked out the chart for Room 238 and opened it wide.

He had thumbed through Megan's chart a few hours earlier and read the orders for the spinal tap. Now he flipped to the lab section, read the results from her blood tests, and looked for any new orders for lab tests.

Nothin' here, he thought. *Guess I'll just have to fix that.*

He scribbled an order in her chart for a CBC and Serum Chemistry Profile—lab tests that would require drawing two vials of blood—and scratched today's date alongside the order.

Well, at least the order's in order. Too bad this simple blood draw's gonna turn into a horrible disaster.

Drake took out the lab section sheets, snapped Megan's chart shut, and slipped it back into the rotary chart holder. He peeled off the latex gloves he was wearing and dropped them in the trash before leaving the nurses' station.

Drake turned right and strolled down the hallway toward room 238. He slid past a nurse walking in the opposite direction. She had her nose buried in a medical chart and didn't notice him. He glanced over his shoulder and watched her turn into the nurses' station. Farther down the hall, he saw another nurse come out of a room, scribble something into a chart, and wheel a med cart to her next stop. She grabbed cups of medication from the top drawer and disappeared into another room.

The coast was clear. Time to go to work.

Chapter 13

Drake rapped twice on Megan's door with his knuckle. "Anybody home?"

"Sure. Come on in," Max said. He was sitting in a chair by the windows next to Megan's bed.

Drake smiled at them as he walked into the room and set down his plastic laboratory carrier on the narrow table by the empty bed next to Megan's. The test tubes in the carrier rattled with a barely perceptible tingling.

"Let's see," Drake said as he unfolded and scanned the papers he was carrying. "You're Megan Tyler, right?" he asked.

"Yes," she said almost soft enough that Drake didn't hear her. She glanced at the plastic carrier. "I don't have to get another shot, do I?"

Drake chuckled as he pretended to read his paper again. He looked up at Max and then over at her. "It says here you had a spinal tap today, so...man, I can see why you don't like needles." He shook his head and tried to look empathetic. "Problem is...I've got orders to get a blood sample for additional lab tests."

Megan winced. "They took some of my blood yesterday. Wasn't that enough?"

Drake shrugged. "Guess not. Tell you what though. I'll make this quick and painless. It'll all be over before you know it."

Max sized up Drake. In his years in the SWAT division, Max had been involved in countless hostage negotiations that exposed him to the darker side of the human psyche. His assessment of people was automatic and penetrating, honed by a degree in criminal psychology and years of police work. He sometimes wondered if he was too paranoid, but something about Drake rubbed him the wrong way.

"She has a good point," Max said, searching Drake's white lab coat for a nametag. "If they took blood yesterday Mr…Goldman…"

"Carl," Drake interrupted. "The C stands for Carl."

"Well, if they did lab work on her blood yesterday, Carl, why would they need another sample today?"

"It's pretty common," Drake said. "I see it all the time. They order a bunch of draws because they want to keep close tabs on the infection and screen the blood for bacteria and viruses. It's also to make sure that spinal fluid isn't leaking into the bloodstream. That can happen after a spinal tap. They usually order extra lab tests after a lumbar puncture."

Max's chest tightened in suspicion as Drake reached for his laboratory carrier. They hadn't even heard the results of yesterday's blood test yet. It was nothing more than raw instinct, but he trusted his instincts.

"Well, I'm sure the doctor knows best," Max said. He glanced at his watch, which read almost four o'clock, and remembered that Beth had said she'd stop by around this time with the results from the first blood test. He'd ask her about it.

Drake picked up the plastic carrier and put it on Megan's bed. The racing, skittering buzz of the drug cocktail he'd taken amplified the exhilarating rush of danger that coursed through him as he visualized what he was about to do. He couldn't believe how smooth he was at dishing out the crap and making it sound so damn good.

Even when this geek started asking questions, I was cool, calm, and in control. He suppressed a chuckle. *Man, am I the ultimate master of bullshit or what?*

Megan looked over at her father; Max could see a glimmer of fear on her pale face. She tried to act like she wasn't afraid, but he knew she had a strong fear of needles. He was proud of how brave she'd been through the blood draw yesterday and the spinal tap earlier that morning. "Megs, this is just a pin-prick compared to the test this morning. It'll be over in a second."

Megan nodded.

"Yeah," Drake said. "This will only hurt a little. It'll all be over before you know it." He reached into the lab carrier and pulled out a piece of small rubber tubing which he tied on Megan's upper right arm as a tourniquet. He dabbed the inner crook of her arm with an alcohol swab and then ripped opened another sterile packet containing a syringe.

He glanced up at Max, who was paying close attention to everything he was doing, and hesitated for a moment. He hadn't really planned how he was going to inject her with the lethal drugs with her father watching him like a hawk, but that was the thrill of it. It was the ultimate challenge. In his mind, he was smooth and powerful, so exceptionally superior at everything he did that no one could possibly touch him. *Watch this, Dad.*

Megan winced as Drake slipped the needle into the vein in her arm.

As he was drawing her blood into the syringe, it came to him how he could drug her without her dad knowing. He had decided against using a paralyzing agent this time since it would take effect immediately and he wouldn't be able to get out of the room in time.

Instead, he chose potassium chloride, which when injected into her bloodstream would stop her heart. It would take a few minutes for the drug to act. All he needed to do was draw the first tube of blood, change tubes to the one containing the five milliliters of potassium chloride, connect it to the needle cap remaining in her arm, and inject it as he prepared to draw another blood sample. Then he could change his mind, say one tube was enough for the lab tests, gather his stuff, and leave.

Both men watched in silence as the glass tube began to fill with Megan's blood. Drake waited until it was almost three-quarters full. He reached up and was about to disconnect it when a voice behind him spoke.

"What do you think you're doing?"

Beth had walked through the door seconds before. She'd taken one look at the man bending over Megan and prickled with suspicion.

"Just drawing blood…" Drake said, pulling the needle out of Megan's arm and pressing a cotton ball on her arm at the injection point. "Here. Hold this in place a couple of minutes," he said to Megan.

"Who told you to draw blood?" Beth asked.

"Got orders for a CBC and serum chemistry panel draw," Drake lied. He scooped his supplies back into the lab carrier. He tried to conceal the syringe with Megan's blood in his right hand.

"Who wrote the orders?" Beth said. Her voice had a sharp edge to it. She stood in front of the door with her arms folded. Beth had paid close attention to Megan and every page of her medical chart. She'd reviewed the chart less than two hours ago.

"The doctor did. It's Doctor…". His eyes raced over Megan's chart, trying to find the name of the physician on record. "…Collins. That's it…Dr. Collins wrote the orders."

Beth bridled at his words. She stepped forward and grabbed the papers out of his hands.

"Bullshit! *I'm* Dr. Collins, and I know for a fact there aren't any orders for a blood draw."

Drake's eyes dropped to her name badge then jumped back up to her face. He shrugged. "Beats me. The orders are right there in the chart. What can I tell ya?"

Beth flipped to the third page and read the instructions for a blood draw written there. She'd looked at this page less than two hours ago; there had been no orders for a blood draw. This wasn't her handwriting, and no one would have written these orders without her authorization. Clearly, this wasn't some innocent mistake.

"What you *can tell* me," she said through gritted teeth, "is your name. *And* show me your hospital picture ID."

Drake huffed in derision. "Yeah, sure…" he said, grabbing the handle of the lab carrier. "I'll tell you my name. It's Goldman. C. Goldman."

Drake started toward the door, but Beth grabbed his lab coat and yanked it hard. "You aren't going anywhere, mister. Stay right where you—"

Drake swung around before she could finish, pivoting to his left and raising the syringe he was still holding in his right hand. Beth couldn't block the attack in time. He embedded the needle in the left side of her throat and slammed down the plunger.

Beth let him go and grabbed the syringe. She yanked it out of her throat. Drake pivoted and hit her with the full brunt of a roundhouse punch. The blow landed squarely on her chin. She collapsed to the floor as he turned to run.

Max exploded out of his chair. He rushed toward Drake, diving onto the man's back and driving him through the doorway. It was a perfect open-field football tackle. Drake was slammed to the ground. He cried out when his face hit the hard linoleum. The contents of his lab carrier scattered across the floor. The vial of potassium chloride caromed off the wall.

Drake shoved Max with all his strength and scrambled to his feet. Max stumbled then regained his balance, squaring off against Drake, who pulled a knife out of his lab coat.

"Back off," he said. His nose was a bloody mess.

Max clenched his jaw. Every muscle in his body tensed. He ripped a Spyderco folding knife out of his pocket. His thumb found the hole in the top of the blade and drove the knife open with a resounding clack.

"Drop your knife!" Max commanded.

Drake's eyes fixed on the four-inch-long serrated blade, then darted back to Max's face. He took a step forward and jabbed with his knife, hoping to draw Max off balance. Max sidestepped the thrust and slashed down across Drake's right arm. The knife sliced through his white lab coat and drew a thick line of blood.

Drake jumped back in surprise and grabbed his arm. His face contorted in outrage at the blood seeping between his fingers. The wound was deep; it burned like acid. He couldn't believe he'd been cut. He lifted a hand to his nose. It felt like it was broken. He locked eyes with Max, who flashed his knife and set his stance with coiled intensity, battle ready.

"Drop your knife, or I'll cut you to pieces!" Max shouted.

Drake's rage exploded out of control. The gash on his arm and the sheer arrogance of this man standing in from of him—thinking he could ruin his perfect, glorious plan—sent him over the edge. He lunged at Max, his eyes unfocused, slashing with his knife like a sword-wielding pirate in a movie.

What an idiot, Max thought. He dodged sideways in a lightning-quick feint. As he darted back to the left, he brought his knife down in an arc. The razor sharp blade sliced a vicious gash across the top of Drake's right hand and thumb. Drake leaped back and dropped his knife.

Max pivoted and charged. With a powerful thrust, he embedded his blade into Drake's shoulder. The forward momentum drove them both against the wall. Drake cried out as Max's blade sunk deeper, burying itself up to the hilt.

Drake glanced up. A patient scurried back into her room several doors down. Two nurses standing at the other end of the hallway had frozen in shock when Drake and Max burst through Megan's door. They raced towards the nurses' station to call security.

Drake grimaced in pain as he wrestled with Max. He pushed him far enough to get his foot up waist high and then kicked outward with all his strength.

Max catapulted backward onto the floor, but he never let up the vise-grip he had on the handle of his knife. The serrated blade ripped out of Drake's shoulder with a sickening sound, widening the gaping laceration.

Drake swore as he slapped his hand over the jagged wound. Without wasting any time gathering his knife or the scattered supplies, he turned and ran down the hall towards the stairwell exit.

Max scrambled to his feet. He was about to run after Drake when he heard a noise behind him. He turned toward Megan's room. Beth was starting to wake up.

Megan looked on in horror, tears streaking her face.

Beth moaned. She lifted her head and brushed a hand against her jaw. It felt like a bruise was already forming. Pulling herself up onto her elbows, she looked over at Max. "Where...is he?"

"He just took off down the hall," Max said. He bent down and lifted her to her feet, then guided her over to the chair beside Megan's bed.

"After he hit you, I tackled him. He pulled out a knife. I pulled out mine. Things got bloody. He lost the fight."

Beth's eyes slid over Max's face down to his feet before focusing on the blood that covered his right hand. "Are you cut anywhere?"

"Not a scratch," Max said. He held up his hand. "This is all his blood." He glanced over his shoulder at the doorway then quickly back at her. "You okay? I might still be able to catch him if I go now."

"Go! I'll be fine. We've gotta catch this guy. I'm sure he's the one who murdered two patients here this past week."

As Max turned to leave, he said, "Call hospital security. They might be able to stop him before he leaves the building. And call 911. The guy's obviously a psychopath."

Beth watched him run out of the room. She grabbed the phone off the bedside table and punched in the code for hospital security. When they answered, she quickly described the emergency.

"That's right," she said. "Dr. Beth Collins. I'm on staff here...Head of Infectious Diseases. And when the police get here, make sure you send them straight up to room 238. In the meantime, send a security guard up here. I want him camped out in this room until the police arrive. I repeat. This is an emergency. Call 911 and send a hospital security guard to this room *immediately*. Is that clear?" She waited for the person on the other end to repeat her directions and nodded. "Fine," she said and hung up.

"Dr. Collins…?"

Beth turned to look at Megan. "What's the matter, honey?" Megan's eyes were wide with fear, staring at something behind her.

Beth started to turn around. A hand shot out and clamped a cloth over her nose and mouth.

She struggled violently, clawing at the hand and arm and trying to elbow her attacker. She felt him pull his fist against her stomach in a modified Heimlich maneuver, knocking the wind out of her. Her body screamed for oxygen. She inhaled the cloying, overpowering smell of chloroform. Darkness closed around her.

Chapter 14

Megan watched in horror as the man lowered Beth to the floor. Her mouth opened. The beginnings of a scream began to escape, but it froze in her throat as she looked up. The man was pointing a .45 caliber handgun at her face. From where she was sitting, the gaping black hole of the barrel looked like the mouth of a cannon.

"Shut up and don't make a sound," he hissed. "Not even a peep. Understand?"

Megan nodded slowly. "Yes," she whimpered.

"Good. We're leaving this hospital in *total* silence. You act normal and do *exactly* what I say."

He lowered the handgun and hid it away in a shoulder holster under his white lab coat. "Remember, I can yank this gun out in less than a second..." He let the threat hang in the air.

Megan's eyes welled up. A single tear rolled down her cheek.

"No crying either," the man said. He rolled a wheelchair over to her bed and motioned for her to get into it. Megan pulled the covers back, threw her legs over the side of the bed, and scooted into the wheelchair.

"You're gonna be okay," he said. "The guy who took your blood sample and attacked your doctor and father was trying to hurt you. We're gonna make sure that doesn't happen."

Megan stared at Beth's unconscious form on the floor. She took a deep breath, fighting the grip of fear tightening in her chest. Somehow, she mustered up the courage to speak. "What about Dr. Collins? You hurt her..."

"She's not hurt," he said. He picked up a white folded blanket off the foot of the second bed and covered Megan's lap and legs with it. He negotiated the wheelchair around Beth's prostrate body and rolled it towards the door. "I just put her to sleep for a little while. She'll wake up in a few minutes, good as new."

"But why did you knock her out?" she said, turning her head to look back at Beth. "And that gun…are you going to shoot me?"

They were almost to the door. "Shut up already! Keep quiet and act normal, or else."

"But what about my dad? He doesn't know where you're taking me."

The man huffed. "Look…we're going to another hospital. We'll let him know once we get you there. Now zip it. Not a sound."

He whisked her out of the room and down the hallway to the elevators.

Drake dabbed his bloody nose with his shirt and lunged down the stairwell two steps at a time. He kept his hand clamped over the wound in his right shoulder. His chest throbbed with a sharp burning stiffness radiating from his shoulder.

Damn it hurts. Blood from the gash in his shoulder trickled out between his fingers even though he was pushing hard on the wound. It was like sticking his finger in a leaky dike.

He dabbed his other wounds with his shirt to keep blood from dripping on the floor. He reached the first-floor landing and paused. A large linen closet was located not too far from the stairwell. He opened the hallway door a crack and checked the hallway. The coast was clear.

Drake ran to the closet, opened the door, and stepped inside. He eased the door shut behind him and waited for his eyes to adjust to the dim light.

He leaned against the wall and scanned the room. There were shelves full of bed sheets, pillowcases, bed covers, towels, water pitchers, and other patient room supplies. He found several rolls of bandage tape and boxes of gauze pads in a narrow cabinet.

He carefully slipped out of his bloodstained lab coat and bandaged up the smaller cuts that covered his arms and hand. He saved the shoulder wound for last. It throbbed in agonizing pain, and he fought from crying out as he covered it with gauze pads secured with tape.

He searched the room for anything he could use to cover up his arm and shoulder. An old lab coat was hanging on a hook on the back of the door. He slipped it on. Perfect.

He opened the door and checked the hallway in both directions before stepping out. A few minutes later, he left the stairwell on the ground floor and calmly exited the hospital. He kept his head down as he passed two police officers who were entering the building. They didn't notice a thing.

Max sprinted up the stairs, taking two at a time until he reached the second-floor landing. He had checked both lower floors and spoke with the security guards and the two police officers in the lobby. They had rushed to all the exits and stood guard looking for a dark-haired man in his late twenties, roughly six feet tall, with blood splattered on his shoulder and chest.

Can't believe he got away, Max fumed. He yanked open the door and ran down the hall to Megan's room where he found Beth getting to her feet.

"Beth!" He ran over to her and helped her walk over to the bed. She sat down on the edge and placed her head in her hands. The wispy scent of chloroform wafted about her.

"What happened?" Max asked. "Are you okay?"

"I'm...fine," she said in a halting whisper. "Somebody...held a cloth on my mouth...chloroform...knocked me out."

He looked over and was shocked to see that Megan's bed was empty. Rushing over to the console of the other bed, he grabbed a slender green oxygen tank with a single line of clear tubing and plastic mask attached. He brought the tank over to the bedside, turned on the valve, and held the mask to his face to feel the airflow. Then he held the mask up to Beth's nose and mouth and fitted the attached elastic band onto her head. "Oxygen," he said. "Breathe deeply."

Beth took several deep breaths in rapid succession. She shook her head, trying to clear out the cobwebs.

"Beth, they took Megan! She's not here."

"What!?" She exclaimed, turning to look at Megan's empty bed.

"She's gone," Max said. "Did you get a look at the guy with the chloroform?"

"Barely...he grabbed me from behind and held a cloth against my nose and mouth. Megan tried to warn me, but I couldn't turn around in time to get a good look at him."

Max bristled. "Whoever he was, he took Megan. Did you glimpse any details of him?"

Beth thought for a second. "Yeah, you know, I think I remember...He was taller than me. About your height, clean shaven, short brownish hair. Probably in his early thirties. And there was a wheelchair next to him."

"Wheelchair?" Max said. "Must've taken it with him. I bet he's wheeling Megan out of the hospital with it." He looked at his watch. "I wasn't gone that long. They couldn't have much of a head start. I'm going after them." He turned to leave.

"Wait a minute," Beth said. She stood up and took a shaky step forward. "I'm coming with you this time."

Megan sat quietly in the wheelchair, aware of the couple and their six-year-old son standing next to her in the elevator. The boy stood at eye level to her and stared unabashedly. A bright smile grew on his face as he held up the red Hot Wheels car he was holding and showed it to her. He moved it through the air as though it were driving on a bumpy road.

Megan glanced at the car and smiled back. She rolled up her eyes, motioning in the direction of the man behind her, and scrunched up her face in a grimace. The boy giggled. He grimaced back at her and giggled a second time but stopped when he realized the man was scowling at him.

Megan felt the elevator ease to a stop. The door opened with a ding.

The boy and his parents exited, and Megan watched them as they began to walk down the hall. The elevator door swooshed closed, and she was alone with the man.

"You came stinkin' close to getting yourself and that nice little family *killed*," he hissed. His voice sliced through the air like a shard of glass. "Don't even think of trying that again. Understand?"

"Yeah," she said in a terrified whisper.

The elevator started its descent again. Megan watched the button for the lobby light up as they slowed to a stop. The man wheeled her out into a long lobby. He maintained a calm, steady pace as he approached the hospital entrance.

Megan slumped against the back of the wheelchair, trying not to cry as the man wheeled her out through the big glass doors towards the parking lot. She prayed her father would find her.

Max and Beth flew down the stairwell and reached the lobby landing in less than a minute.

Max ripped open the door, and the two of them ran through, dodging people as they searched the lobby area.

"She's gotta be here somewhere," Max said in a harsh whisper.

"We'll find her."

They rushed toward the front of the lobby. Three patients were being pushed in wheelchairs toward the elevators. Max and Beth scanned their faces as they ran past. None of them was a child.

"He could have dropped off the wheelchair once he got to the lobby," Beth said. Her eyes frantically scoured every square inch of the lobby and admissions area.

"Look through the glass doors," Beth said, motioning to the hospital entrance. "There's a couple of empty wheelchairs sitting out there on the right."

Max started walking towards the line of wheelchairs.

He looked up and spotted something that made his stomach drop. In the distance, disappearing into the sea of cars that made up the hospital parking lot was a man leading a child. Max caught only a glimpse, but he was sure it was them.

"There they are!" he exclaimed.

Beth caught up to him as the doors opened, and they ran out into the parking lot.

"I got her," Nick said. "Where are you parked?" He tightened his grip on Megan's hand and pulled her forward, walking faster. The SUV he was headed toward—a black Ford Expedition—was still five rows over.

"Meet me at my truck in two minutes. After that, I'm headed straight to Viralvector. Orders are to bring her in." He ended the call and slid his phone back into his pocket.

They were within two rows of the SUV when Nick's partner walked over from his car that was parked in the adjoining row. He was a shade over six-three, dark-haired, and thickly muscled. He strutted as he walked with the swaggering gait of a bodybuilder with an attitude.

"You ready?" Nick said, pressing the button on his key chain car alarm remote. The Ford Expedition chirped in response and unlocked. He pressed another button on the remote, and the engine started up with a roar.

"Yeah. Why the change in plans? I thought tonight was only a blood drop."

"It was," Nick said. "Until some wacko med tech tried to off the girl right in front of her father. The doctor showed up in the nick of time, fought with the guy, and then the father beat the crap out of him. Cut him up pretty good, too, before he got away."

"And now it's too risky to leave her here," his partner said.

"Yep. Orders are to take her straight in. Don't pass Go. Don't collect two hundred bucks."

Nick hurried Megan along as they walked into the next row. Turning to his partner, he said, "Stick around here for a while and see what kinda commotion gets kicked up about the girl. Cops are already here. Her room's up on the second floor halfway down one of the halls. Room 238."

"Got it."

"Call me in an hour and let me know what's going on."

"Right."

They were less than a row away from his SUV when Nick heard someone yelling. He turned to see Max running towards him. Beth split off and raced down the next row over.

"Stop!" Max roared.

From thirty feet away, Nick could see the frenzied anger on Max's face. He motioned to his partner, who didn't need a signal to spring into action. He charged at Max. From the corner of her eye, Beth saw the two men collide and caught a glimpse of brutal hand-to-hand combat.

She forced her gaze forward, locking eyes with Megan, and pushed herself to run faster.

Nick reached out and opened the SUV's middle door. He shoved Megan up into the back, slammed the door, and circled around to the driver's side door.

Megan watched with wide eyes as Beth ran up to her side of the SUV. In a panic, she climbed into the front seat and turned towards Nick.

"Let me go!" she shrieked, flailing her arms and slapping his shoulder. "I want my Dad! Let me go!"

Beth smiled grimly when she saw Megan's distraction. She grabbed the back seat door handle, eased the door open, and slid inside onto the floor, disappearing from view.

"Knock it off!" Nick yelled, grabbing Megan's wrists and forcing them down onto the seat. He didn't notice the rear door opening and closing.

"If you want a backhand across the mouth, keep it up!"

Megan stopped screaming and struggling. She stared at him, her eyes wide with fear.

"I told you to shut up, and I mean it! Do you want me to tape your mouth shut?"

"No," Megan whimpered. "Don't…I'm sorry. I won't do it again."

"You'd better not," he said. He released her hands and pulled out his gun.

"You try anything—jumping out of the car, screaming, anything—and I'll kill you. No warning. No second chances. You're dead. You got that?"

"Y-Yes," Megan said, terrified.

He lowered the gun and placed it in his lap. "You're going to sit up front with me. Buckle your seatbelt and shut up."

Glancing over his shoulder at the battle that was still raging in the parking lot, Nick put the SUV in gear, tromped on the accelerator, and sped out of the parking lot.

Max unleashed his fury with controlled execution. He was an expert in three martial arts disciplines and knew every dirty street-fighting trick in the book. His opponent was strong and knew how to fight, but he was outmatched by Max's blinding speed and crushing blows.

He tried to tackle Max as he ran up, but Max sidestepped the frontal attack, grabbed the man's arm, and kicked his legs out from under him, using his weight and momentum to slam him into the ground. Max threw a crushing right cross, smashing the left side of the man's face. Bones crackled like glass under the impact of his fist.

The raging hulk kicked and shoved savagely at Max, finally breaking free of the powerful grip lock Max had on him. The two men scrambled to their feet and squared off.

Behind the man, Max could see Megan sitting inside the SUV, a gun pointed at her face. In the split second he glanced at her, he saw the driver put the gun away and turn to put the car in gear. He had to get to her somehow. He didn't have time to mess around with this muscle-bound thug.

Thinking Max was distracted, his attacker lunged at him, spewing loud, angry bravado. Max was unfazed and unimpressed. In a blur of powerful, lightning-quick kicks and punches, Max knocked his legs out from under him, breaking his left femur, crushing four of his ribs, and landing a skyrocketing uppercut that broke his jaw in two places and knocked him out cold. The attacker was unconscious before he hit the ground.

Max leaped over the man's body and bolted after the SUV. It was only twenty feet ahead, but the distance grew at a sickening pace. If he'd only been three or four seconds sooner…

Max chased after them until they pulled out of the parking lot. He stood there helpless as the SUV charged out of the parking lot and disappeared into traffic. He stopped and caught his breath, burning the details into his mind. *License number, color, model.*

He had to get Megan back. He would get her back.

And then they would pay. Oh, would they pay.

Chapter 15

Nick drove the Ford Expedition with the flow of traffic, gliding through unobtrusive lane changes as he approached the 91 freeway. As they neared the westbound on-ramp, he swerved to the right and pulled over to the side of the road.

Nick spun around in his seat, reached down, and shoved the barrel of his handgun into Beth's side. He had caught a glimpse of her during a lane change a few blocks back.

"Sit up."

Beth complied.

"I don't know how you got in here," he snarled, "but you won't be stayin' long." He tossed a roll of gray duct tape at her. It hit Beth in the shoulder and landed in her lap.

"Tear off a big piece and tape it across your eyes. Make sure you push it tight against your skin. You're comin' along for a ride."

Beth picked up the roll and looked at Megan, who was staring at her with a frightened expression on her face. It angered her that Megan was in the middle of this.

"Why are you kidnapping her?" Beth demanded. "She's just a little girl. A very sick little girl who has no business being out of the hospital."

Nick glanced at Megan then over his shoulder at Beth. "Nah, she doesn't look so bad to me."

"You moronic idiot!" Beth slapped the back of his seat. "I ought to know if she's sick or not. I'm her doctor, and it's extremely likely this girl you kidnapped has *infectious* meningitis."

"Yeah, yeah. Cool your jets," he said. "There are things goin' down you know nothing about. You just had to stick your nose in the middle of it all.

The girl's fine, and she's gonna stay fine."

Beth bit back another angry retort and dug her nails into her thighs. "Look. Why don't you let her go? She's really sick. *Please* let me take her back to the hospital."

Nick clenched his jaw. A brief image of him backhanding Beth across the face flashed in front of his eyes. Luckily for Beth, the picture was fleeting. Another plan popped into his mind.

"I got a better idea, Doc," he said. "Tear *two* big pieces of tape off that roll. Use the first one to tape your mouth shut and the second one to cover your eyes."

"Look," Beth said, "why don't we—"

Nick raised his gun and shoved the muzzle of the barrel against her forehead, causing a painful and audible crack.

"This *isn't* a discussion. *Do it!*"

After she finished, he made her put her wrists together, peeled a long piece of tape, and wound it around her wrists half a dozen times. He tossed the tape aside and pulled back out into traffic, accelerating up the westbound on-ramp and disappearing into the arterial flow of cars, trucks, and big rigs.

Max dragged the unconscious man to his Suburban and dumped him in the back cargo area. He grabbed a roll of nylon cord, cut off several feet, and formed a slipknot noose at one end. Yanking the man's arms behind his back, Max shoved his hands through the noose, tied his wrists together, and looped the cord around his neck before wrapping his legs with it and tying his ankles together.

Satisfied the man was immobilized, Max climbed into the front seat and peeled out of the parking lot.

Nick stayed on the 91 freeway headed toward Anaheim. He passed several off-ramps before spotting the one he was looking for, and then exited the freeway. He drove another ten minutes until reaching the large industrial park he had in mind.

The office industrial complex occupied four square city blocks and housed more than fifty single-story office warehouses of varying size and functionality.

There was a wide variety of small businesses mixed in with medium-sized distribution warehouses. Only a third of the buildings had been leased; most of the occupied suites were located in the front close to the main boulevard entrance.

Nick drove into the development and headed toward the back of the complex. They passed fewer and fewer occupied buildings until reaching the back section where none of the buildings had tenants.

He turned left down the last row and slowed to a stop in front of one building that was set apart from the others. Its warehouse was sandwiched between the buildings on either side and was somewhat sheltered from view.

Perfect, he thought and shut off the engine.

Leaning into the back seat, he grabbed the roll of tape off Beth's lap, climbed out, and yanked open Beth's door.

"Okay, let's go," he said, grabbing her by the arm.

Megan watched him lead Beth towards the warehouse door. Two four-foot metal posts stood to the left of it in front of a metal electrical connection box. He held her wrists against the first post and wound the tape around the post five times, pulling it tight and testing it as he went.

Forcing Beth to sit on the ground, he taped her ankles together and secured them to the opposite pipe column. He checked his handiwork one last time and bent down so that his mouth was inches from Beth's ear. "If you want the girl to live, don't even *think* of trying to follow us." He let the threat hang in the air. "And if I ever see you again…if I catch one glimpse of you…you're dead. That's a promise."

He turned and hurried back to the SUV. He swung himself into the seat, gunned the accelerator, and raced away from the warehouse without a backward glance. Megan watched as Beth, tied, bound, and struggling across two poles, grew smaller and smaller. Her last hope disappeared as they turned down another corridor and left the industrial park.

Max rolled to a stop at the end of a long dirt road. He had driven the back roads south towards Mission Viejo, searching out a remote fire road off the beaten track. He wanted complete solitude and privacy.

Nick's associate had come to ten minutes earlier. He hadn't quit complaining about the excruciating pain in his leg and throbbing in his jaw the whole time he'd been awake.

Max got out of the Suburban and ripped open the back door. He was keenly aware of how close he was to losing all control. He teetered on the precipice of uncontrollable rage and had to reach deep into his years of discipline to force himself back from the edge.

Channel the rage, he thought.

Grabbing the man by his unbroken leg, Max jerked him out of the Suburban and dragged him ten feet from the vehicle as the man swore in pain and anger. He let his leg drop in the dirt like a sack of cement.

"Ah, shit, that hurts!" The man writhed in the dirt with a rocking motion. "You broke my damn leg, you son of a bitch! And I think you broke my jaw too…"

His complaints faded away when he saw the deadly expression written on Max's face. Max reached into his beltline and pulled out his Glock. He gripped the slide and yanked it back in a fluid motion, seating a .40 caliber bullet in the firing chamber. *Ching-Chang.*

He cupped his left hand around his right and pivoted into a firing stance. He raised the handgun to eye level and lined up the front bead with the notch on the back sight, targeting the center of the man's forehead.

The man's eyes grew wide with fear. "Wait! Hold on a minute!" He raised his hand to shield his face. "Let's talk about this…"

An explosive boom ripped through the air. The 180-grain jacketed hollow point slug shrieked over the man's head less than six inches from his hairline. He could feel the powerful, distortive force as it zinged by, and for a split second, he was overwhelmed with the surreal feeling that he was already dead.

Then he realized he hadn't even been hit. He took a shaky breath and looked up at Max, who stood towering over him.

"Now that I've got your attention, listen very carefully." He took one step forward and trained his gun on the man's chest.

"I could've put that bullet right between your eyes. I guess that makes you lucky…at least for the moment. What I need is information, and you're going to give it to me if you want to get out of here alive. You get one chance. *Just one.* Are we clear on that?"

The man's eyes flitted to the gun pointed at him then shifted back to Max. His heart felt stuck in his throat. He nodded.

"Good. Otherwise, it'll get real messy. Firing a dozen .40 caliber hollow-point slugs into a man can ruin his whole day. First, where is your partner taking my daughter?"

The man glanced at the gun then back up at Max. "He's supposed to take her to a lab down in Rancho Santa Margarita."

"A lab? You mean like a clinic?"

"Lab, clinic...whatever. All's I know is it's some kind of lab."

"What's the name of the lab?"

"It doesn't have one."

"What do you mean it doesn't have one?"

"It's just a white building," the man said. "No signs or nothin' out front."

"What street is it on?"

"Canterbury Way."

"And the address?" Max asked.

"Uh..." The man scrunched up his forehead as though digging the information out of his memory was a painful excavation. "19607 Canterbury Way."

Max's patience snapped, and he fired a second round even closer to the man's head. The concussive roar of the gun, so loud and unexpected, made all the blood drain from the man's face.

"I don't have time to play twenty questions, *and neither do you!*" Max shouted. "Who do you and your partner work for?"

The shaken man looked at Max and knew that if he fired again, he'd shoot to kill.

"Okay. Don't shoot," he said. His voice quivered, and sweat was dripping off his face. "It's a company called Viralvector, Inc. They hired me and my partner to do special projects for them. We're like independent contractors."

"Viralvector. What do they do and where are they located?"

"They're a biotech company. Their headquarters is down in Rancho Santa Margarita, real close to the lab I was telling you about."

"Address?"

"24200 Spectrum Drive. It's all the way at the end where the road butts up against the hills. There's a complex of brand new buildings there with Viralvector in the middle of it...some kinda office technology park." He shook his head to fling the sweat from his eyes.

"What's any of this have to do with my daughter? Why did you and your partner kidnap her?"

"She's…she's part of one of Viralvector's projects. Our orders were to monitor your daughter and one other kid…make sure nothing happened to them either in or out of the hospital. Then when we got the signal, we were supposed to bring 'em down to the lab on Canterbury Way for more tests."

Max's mind spun with this new piece of startling information. "Tests? What kind of tests?"

The man shrugged. "I don't know. Blood tests, I think. They didn't tell me much more than that, and I don't think my partner knows any more than I do. We were supposed to stake out the kids and bring 'em in when we got the signal. Problem is…the second kid got away. Your daughter's it."

Max kicked the man's side and raised his gun. "You've got to know more than that. They hire you to kidnap my daughter and bring her to the lab. Why did they pick her to begin with? What the hell is going on here? Are they running experiments on her and the other kid?"

The man shook his head, squeezing his eyes shut against the pain in his side. "I got no freakin' idea. I'm just doin' what they told me to do."

Max glared at the man. A dozen questions jockeyed for first place in his mind.

"You said you were supposed to monitor the kids and make sure nothing happened to them. Earlier today, a bogus lab tech was taking blood samples from my daughter, and her doctor walked in right in the middle of it and broke it up. She thinks he's been killing patients. I fought with the guy, but he got away. Does he work for you?"

"No," the man said. "We heard there was a guy offing patients in the hospital, so we kept close tabs on your daughter's room. But the truth is with you there we figured she already had a bodyguard."

"What's the name of your contact at Viralvector?"

"Don't know. Some guy who calls himself 'Mr. B'. I think he's one of their execs. He calls all the shots and gives us exact instructions, but he only talks to my partner. That's all I know. My partner runs the operation. I just do what I'm told."

"Have you ever been to Viralvector?"

"Not inside. My partner and I stopped by one time, but I waited in the car."

"Then your partner must know who Mr. B is."

"I'm sure he does. I asked him once, but he said it was none of my business."

Max thought for a moment. "Do you know if they've run any tests on my daughter before? Injections? Blood samples? Anything?"

The man winced. He reached down and touched his leg which had swollen to twice its normal size in the area of the break. "Look, my leg is all busted to hell. It's killing me. Get me to a doctor, will ya?"

"Sure. Right after you finish telling me everything you know. What about any previous tests on her?"

The man grabbed his upper thigh. A bloodstain was spreading down his leg in a dark, oval circle. His femur was broken, and a sharp sliver of bone had jutted through the muscle, finally penetrating the skin when Max had dropped the man on the ground. Max eyed the compound fracture and felt no pity.

"You don't understand. That's all I know. I only came on board two months ago. As far as I can tell, they've just taken blood samples from her. But from bits and pieces I've picked up from my partner, sounds like they ran some tests 'bout two years ago. Somethin' about her being in a car accident."

"Car accident?" Max's thoughts ricocheted. "Are you sure that's what he said?"

"Positive."

"Have you got any details?"

"Nothin' more than they gave her an injection and ran their own tests at the hospital."

"Where'd they give her an injection?"

"I dunno. In the arm, I guess."

"That's not what I meant, you idiot," Max huffed. You said they gave her an injection and ran tests at the hospital. Did they give her an injection *before* she went to the hospital?"

The man thought for a few seconds and shrugged. "I think so. Sure sounded like they gave her a shot right there where the accident happened."

Scenes from that night flashed in Max's mind. Arriving at the crash site. Seeing the crushed, burning car. Realizing his wife Carol's body was inside. Then the miracle of finding Megan lying unconscious but alive on the ground several feet from the car. Unharmed.

"Know of any other tests on my daughter *before* the accident?" Max asked.

The man shook his head.

Max stood there in silence as the minutes ticked by, his eyes and gun trained on the man as he processed this information.

"Hey," the man whined, disrupting Max's mental analysis. "Can you get me to a doc or a hospital now? My leg hurts like a mother."

Max snapped out of his thoughts. "Yeah, we'll go. But first, three quick questions."

"Aw, shit," the man moaned. "I've told you everything I know. Gimme' a friggin' break."

Max ignored his whining tone and fixed him with an angry glare. "Number one: what's your partner's name?"

The man opened his mouth to speak then shut it abruptly.

Max took a step forward, raising the gun and aiming it at the middle of the man's forehead. "I won't ask again."

"Nick. Nick Todd," he gasped and shifted to his left, trying to take his weight off his fractured leg.

"Number two: that black, Ford Expedition he's driving…is it his? Does he own it?"

"I think so…It might be a lease."

"But it's not stolen?

"Nope."

"Third and final question: what's your name?"

The man hesitated a second but then shook his head in disgusted defeat. "Kyle…Kyle Horton."

Max grabbed the man by his tied hands and lifted him to his feet, never taking the gun off him.

"Well, Kyle, it's time for us to take a ride. Let's pay a visit to some friends of mine at the Yorba Linda Police Department. They'll take really good care of you and your leg."

Chapter 16

It took Beth nearly half an hour of scrunching her face and rubbing it against her shoulder, but she finally managed to loosen the duct tape covering her eyes and inch it up so she could see.

She rested for a few minutes before she began kicking and thrashing her legs, struggling to free them from the heavy, crisscrossed layers of duct tape that bound them to the pole. After several minutes of intense effort, her leg muscles burned, and she was breathing heavily through her nose.

Looking down at her ankles, she was stunned to see she hadn't managed to loosen the tape restraints even a little. She could move her knees apart, but her feet and ankles remained locked to the pole. *Complete waste of time,* she thought as she strained against the tape holding her captive. She leaned her head back on the pole and forced herself to calm down.

She pivoted to her right and stared at her palms. Leaning towards them, she stretched her shoulders and head as far as she could extend them. On her first try, she managed to brush her nose with her index finger.

C'mon, stretch further. You can do this.

She closed her eyes and tried to force all the tension out of her body.

Here we go. She took a deep breath and exhaled. She used to do Pilates regularly. She visualized the challenging stretches and motions from her exercise videos. *I'm good at this*, she convinced herself.

The muscles in her upper back and neck were loose as she leaned towards her hands, her eyes locked onto her right index finger and thumb. She leaned as far as she could then took a shallow breath, exhaled, and pushed her upper body forward further. She inched closer to her hands, and her finger and thumb found the edge of the duct tape securing her mouth. Clamping it in a pinscher death grip, she turned her head and pulled it sharply to the left, peeling the tape away. It was a small victory, but she knew the hardest part was coming up.

Closing her eyes and centering herself, she released all the tension in her muscles and imagined herself with unlimited flexibility, bending in any direction and as far as she needed.

Her eyes locked on the duct tape wrapped around her wrists. She leaned and stretched towards it, and her lips brushed the wide, gray tape. She tilted her head to the side until she found the top left corner. She teased it up so she could get a good grip on it with her teeth and tugged it sharply to the left, stripping the first layer of tape back from the layer below.

Thirty-five minutes later, sweating and sore-mouthed, she had ripped through all but the last layer of the tape. After chewing and stretching her way through one more layer, she twisted her hands and yanked them in opposite directions. The tape ripped, and with a final tug, she freed her hands from the pole.

Ripping clumps of tape off her hands, she leaned down and tore at the tape on her ankles. She found the edge, unwound the thick layers of gray sticky tape, and jumped to her feet.

She was free.

Max finished filling out the paperwork on Megan's kidnapping and dropped it on the desk of his friend, Detective Fletcher Stevens. He had described every detail of the events that took place in Megan's hospital room and the parking lot. It was no oversight that he omitted the rest of the story about the little episode out on the mountain road with Kyle Horton. He needed to confirm and act on that information independently.

"Okay, Fletch. I need a favor. A really big one. That son of a bitch took my daughter, and I'm getting her back without a scratch. I need to know who the black Ford Expedition belongs to."

"APB's already out, Max. No reports yet of a stolen vehicle related to this license plate number, but we're expecting something. The plate's registered to a green 2001 Honda Civic. Last known owner is a used car lot in Tustin, California. Looks like someone swiped the plate and put it on their Expedition."

"Figures." Max shook his head in disgust.

"We'll have to wait and see if whoever took the plate took the car too. We're contacting the dealer."

Max reviewed his options and considered how much to tell him. "Look, I know what I saw. This Expedition had to be brand new. It might have been last year's model, but I doubt it. I went shopping for an SUV a year ago, and I test drove a few, including that Expedition. How about running me a DMV owner's list of all the new black Ford Expeditions in the state? This year's model only?"

"We'll see what we can do," Fletch said. "Shouldn't be a problem. Give me a buzz in a couple of hours. I'm sure we'll have something by then."

"Thanks," Max said. "If you find out sooner, call me on my cell phone. I put it on the report."

"You got it."

The Yorba Linda precinct headquarters was a large, modern facility that served as the central hub and command center for police enforcement in Orange County. The surrounding cities—Anaheim, Irvine, Huntington Beach, and Mission Viejo—all had their own police forces, but the need for a centralized command center for the entire county had been recognized.

In the two years since it was built, the command center had successfully coordinated and handled more than two dozen county-wide police actions ranging from multiple high-speed freeway chases to SWAT team backup for hostage situations and even primary local security responsibility for a vice-presidential visit to Orange County.

Max knew the layout of the precinct headquarters like the back of his hand. The previous year, he had spent a four-month rotation here training a ten-member county SWAT team. Several of the SWAT team members had finished a weeklong advanced training course he'd taught two months ago up in L.A., and his good friend Mark Hunter was one of them.

As he headed down the hall and disappeared into a stairwell, Max mulled over asking Mark's help on the mission he was planning. He'd rather solve this himself, but there was no telling what he might run into, and Mark was trained to handle high-stake situations like this. He was as good as they came. Max would give him a call later and see if they could grab a quick beer tonight and talk about it.

Max had one more person to visit before he left for a reconnaissance trip to Rancho Santa Margarita. Her name was Tanya, and she was his buddy from way back. He had known her from his early days on the force and had attended her wedding years ago. He had also stood at her side at the funeral of her first husband, a police officer who'd been killed in action during a bank robbery chase.

He had been happy to learn that she was engaged to be married again. She was perky, positive, and full of life. And she was a geek-level wizard on the computer, especially when it came to searching for individuals on private and public databases. With unlimited access to all police work related databases, she could give him the name, address, phone number, vehicle registration, and police record of any registered driver in the United States, not to mention credit history, employment, and public financial records.

He only needed her to search for one person: Nick Todd.

With a couple of keystrokes, Tanya could generate a long list of California residents named Nicholas Todd, group them according to key individual demographics, and crosscheck that list with a national database. If anybody could find this guy and serve him up with a red bow on his head, Tanya could.

Beth pulled her iPhone out of the inside pocket of her white lab coat and looked at the indicator icons at the top of the screen. *Good. Plenty of power and a strong signal.*

She was about to push her Contacts icon when a sickening wave of dizziness washed over her. Her knees buckled. She grabbed onto one of the metal posts to steady herself hoping the feeling would pass, but it didn't. Instead it intensified and was joined by a nauseous free-fall sensation in her stomach, as though she had stepped off a cliff.

Beth dropped her iPhone back into her pocket and felt her forehead. It was sizzling hot. Much hotter than it should have been even after her sweaty escape.

Another powerful wave of dizziness engulfed her and darkness mixed with tiny sparks of light encroached on her peripheral vision. She knew she was passing out and managed to ease herself down onto her side before a wave of blackness overtook her.

It seemed like hours later when Beth woke but only twenty minutes had passed. Her transition from the netherworld of unconsciousness was a rapid, morphing slide across two dimensions. A pang of regret accompanied her return, a momentary wish that she could slip back into the crisp, highly charged world she'd just visited.

Beth had been immersed in the depths of a dream world that was intensely clear and fresh and real. Every breath she took filled her with penetrating, clarifying energy, and all her senses were impossibly magnified.

In her dream, she was chasing the black Expedition that was speeding off, carrying Megan away. She could see the SUV two blocks ahead of her accelerating down a street somewhere in the middle of Irvine or Mission Viejo. Her heart hammered in unison as her feet pounded the pavement. Her rapid breaths filled her lungs with bursts of cool air.

Her body felt powerful and sure, with a virtually unlimited capacity to accelerate. She unleashed her power and closed the distance between her and the SUV in a matter of seconds. As she reached for the door handle, she saw Megan looking back through the rear window and beyond her at the white two-story office building complex the SUV was racing toward. Her fingers closed around the chrome door handle. The surprising coolness of the metal sent an icy shock radiating up her arm.

The world vanished.

Beth's eyes flew open.

She shook the wispy fogginess from her head and pulled herself into a sitting position. Her hand was resting against the cool metal of one of the guard poles. *Well, here's the door handle.*

She rose to her feet, holding onto the metal bar for support, and felt her forehead. It was cool and dry to the touch. *Strange. No fever. And I don't feel even the least bit sick.*

She thought back to the sensation of burning up and the churning, nearly convulsive dizziness and nausea that had overwhelmed her right before she passed out. *What could have caused that?*

She came back to the most obvious answer as a vivid image of the struggle in Megan's room leaped to mind. Touching the sore spot on neck, she relived the med tech stabbing her in the neck with the syringe of Megan's blood and pushing the plunger.

I must be infected with Megan's virus. But why did the symptoms go away so fast?

She grabbed her phone and brought up Megan's information. She scrolled down to where she remembered entering Max's cell phone number. She pushed the call button and pressed the phone to her ear. It rang and rang. *Come on, Max. Pick up. Come on.* She ended the call and tried to type him an urgent text but fumbled the phone and barely caught it before it hit the ground.

Stop it! she thought. Her heart was pounding. *Okay. Send him a message. Then call him again.*

She was halfway through typing the text when her phone rang.

She looked at her screen. It was Max. Beth almost dropped the phone again as she tapped the screen and held it to her ear.

"Max? Yeah, hi. It's Beth. We need to talk…"

Chapter 17

The sleek building complex housing the headquarters of Viralvector, Inc. sat with imposing, high-tech prominence in the foothills of Rancho Santa Margarita, a thriving, well-heeled community southeast of Irvine, California. The six buildings that comprised the complex were individual masterpieces of ultra-modern architecture with stark white edifices edged in glossy chrome and gray metallic hues that jutted sharply up into the blue southern California sky. The buildings were interconnected with colonnades umbrellaed by artistic metal latticework cupolas.

Viralvector was a leading biotechnology company primarily focused on the discovery, development, and commercialization of innovative drugs for the treatment of cancer, immune deficiency disorders, and viral diseases. In its seven years of existence, Viralvector had built a pipeline of discovery research programs and drug candidates addressing major unmet needs in cancer and infectious diseases. It owned five compound and method of use patents and boasted a portfolio of promising experimental agents in various stages of development that represented significant commercial opportunities.

Wall Street valued the company's high upside potential. This was reflected by a substantially elevated stock price, despite the fact the company had yet to bring a product to market. Signed co-marketing agreements with several of the world's largest pharmaceutical companies buoyed expectations that the company was poised for explosive growth.

Forty-three-year-old business guru Blake Thornton was the brilliant but mercurial President and CEO of Viralvector. He had started the company with three partners. Over the years, they managed to build the company from the ground up into one of the most promising biotech firms in the industry. He held both MD and PhD degrees, but he had never practiced medicine. After simultaneously earning his dual doctorate degrees, he had gone straight into post-doc research in his mid-twenties, where he focused on gene manipulation and viral vector transmission. He had then worked in a series of startup biotech firms, climbing his way to Vice President of Clinical Research at the last one, which had gone public with an IPO and made him extraordinarily wealthy through stock options.

He was currently sitting at his desk in his private office. Its massive antique oaken desk, credenza, coffered ceilings, and walls of built-in bookshelves made it an imposing inner sanctum. The floor to ceiling shelves were loaded with scientific tomes, antique instruments, and arcane scientific gadgets, adding to the impressive aura of the room. The large bay windows looked out on the grassy hills and valleys that stretched for miles behind the office complex.

As he waited on the phone, Thornton leaned back in his chair and watched the grass in the distance undulate in waves as the blustery Santa Ana wind ebbed and flowed. He tried to make himself relax, but it was a losing proposition. He'd never been good at relaxing. He had lived his whole life driven by an edgy, unceasing intensity, never satisfied with his achievements or where he was at the moment. And the downward spiraling circumstances of late had just about pushed him over the edge.

C'mon! Let's go, he thought, tapping his pen on his desk. He hated waiting for anything.

He glanced at a picture on his desk of his seven-year-old son, Newt, and reflex pangs of regret gripped him as they always did. Thoughts of his soon to be ex-wife, Cassandra, flickered jaggedly through his mind, but he pushed them aside. That *gold-digging, world-class bitch,* he thought bitterly. *She should be terminated with extreme prejudice.* Goosebumps chased up his arms as he pictured her tripping into an untimely demise.

The negotiations for his upcoming divorce had so far been unbelievably rancorous, and he expected it to get worse. Greedy ex-wife. Greedy, parasitic lawyers. The word messy didn't even come close to describing the all-out war his divorce had become. *Two more months,* he thought. *Two more months, and then it'll be history.*

He was visualizing the appeal of life without his ex-wife when someone finally came on the line.

"Hello, Dr. Thornton?"

He snapped out of his daydream. "Yeah, I'm here."

"We've located Mr. Todd for you. He'll be on the line in just a minute. Please hold on."

Half a minute passed before the phone clicked and Nick's voice came on the line. "Hey."

"Looks like you're on time," Thornton said. "Everything go as planned with the revised plan?"

"Yep. As planned."

"Run this by me again. You were supposed to collect two vials of blood. That's it. A simple job. But major problems at the hospital made you bring her in. What the hell happened?"

"It was frickin' weird. That wacko we were talking about—the one who's been offing patients in the hospital—tried to nail her earlier today."

"Tried to kill her?"

"Yeah, about as ballsy as you can get. Cool as a cucumber, he walks in dressed up like a med tech and starts taking the girl's blood *while* her father's sittin' five feet away from him watching. Luckily, her doc walks in, figures out somethin' is seriously wrong, and scuffles with him. Dad jumps the guy, and they duke it out in the hallway. The tech pulls a knife on him. Good ol' Dad pulls out his own knife. He apparently knew how to use it. He carved the guy up pretty good. The wacko runs, and Dad takes off after him down the hall and out the stairwell. That's when I grabbed the girl."

"What about the doctor?" Thornton asked. "Did she do anything through all of this?"

"Naw. She was out cold on the floor. The tech coldcocked her with a punch to the mouth. She came to before I grabbed the girl and was on the phone with security. The second she hung up, I clamped a rag of chloroform over her mouth and dropped her like a rock. Took the girl and left."

"And after that, everything went smoothly getting her to the lab…right?"

"Well, not exactly…" Nick could hear the edge in Thornton's voice. Better to get it over with. He relayed the details of the scuffle in the parking lot, finding Beth in the car, and leaving her tied up at the industrial park. When he finished, there was an icy silence on the other end of the line. It went on for several long, uncomfortable moments.

"It's painfully clear she got a good look at you," Thornton said.

"Nope, not that good a look. Gassed her with the chloroform before she could turn around in the hospital room. And in the car I shoved a gun right in her face, and she only caught a glimpse before I taped her eyes shut."

"What about your license plate? Could she have memorized the number? They'll track you down in a heartbeat through the DMV if anyone—"

"Not a chance," Nick interrupted, bristling at the suggestion of incompetence. "I have a different car's plates on mine. Took 'em off a car on a used car lot. Whenever I work, I change plates every other day, and especially right after a 'retrieval.' There's no way I can be traced. I even stopped and changed them on the way to the lab."

"Okay. But what about your partner?"

"Like I said, he was fightin' with the girl's dad when I left the parking lot. Kyle's one bad-ass dude. I'm sure the girl's father wishes he'd never mixed it up with him. Probably a good thing they're in a hospital parking lot. After Kyle gets done with him, he's gonna need medical attention."

"Could be," Thornton said. "But that's assuming Kyle isn't the one needing hospitalization when they're through. The girl's dad used to be on a SWAT team."

"Believe me. Kyle took care of business. He's got orders to call me in an hour and let me know how things went." Nick looked down at his watch. "That's twenty minutes from now."

There was silence again on the other end of the line. Finally, Thornton spoke. "Okay. I'll assume that you and your hired associate took care of things. But I expect you to call me immediately after he calls you and confirm that that's the case."

"Right."

"You'd better lose this guy too," Thornton said. "I'm sure things are going to heat up considerably with the girl getting snatched, and we don't need any more complications or weak links. Just pay him well and tell him to disappear."

"Will do," Nick said. "I've already got him set up for a pay drop. I brought him in from out of state for this project. I'll tell him once he picks up his money, he's outta here."

"That'll work," Thornton said. "I'll expect your call in half an hour." He hung up and slammed his fist on the desk. *Damn incompetence. Why the hell can't people do their jobs right?*

Chapter 18

D rake sat on the edge of the examination table in the small room. The thin white paper crinkled under him as he shifted his weight and looked around at the dingy decor. The counters and sink looked clean enough, but the worn linoleum on the floor should have been replaced years ago. It curled up in the corners and was a puky green and brown color. He thought it looked like it belonged in a scuzzy tenement slum.

Not exactly what I'd call antiseptic.

An old poster with schematic sections showing the development of the fetus through the forty weeks of pregnancy hung on one wall, and a picture of a cutaway section of the digestive tract hung on another.

Great. Pregnant women, babies, and guts. Just what I want to see.

He reached up with his left hand and touched the skin near the gash in his right shoulder. It was throbbing so intensely he was sure he could see it pulse. *Damn this thing hurts.*

His hand drifted down to the slash on his arm and then to his swollen and stiff right hand. The hand and arm weren't all that bad; he knew they would heal okay. But his shoulder...that was another matter. The blade had pierced all the way through his shoulder.

He was sitting in the examination room of a neighborhood clinic in one of the poorest sections of East LA. It was a high crime area situated amid the abutting turfs of three rival gangs, a no-man's land where the wrong colors, clothes, or a wayward glance could get you shot and killed.

The clinic served a vital community service, and on average saw more gunshot victims in a week than all of Orange County did in a month. Drake was gently pushing on the area next to his shoulder wound, trying to lessen the throbbing pain when Dr. Javier Alberola walked in.

"Mister...Adams?" he asked, flipping up one of the sheets on his clipboard.

"Yeah," Drake said, sizing him up. He was five-ten with black hair, intelligent eyes, and a dark, closely trimmed mustache. Drake gauged him to be in his late thirties.

"I'm Dr. Alberola. I'll be taking care of you today. Says here you got attacked by a gang."

"That's right. Bastards cut me up pretty good. I don't usually come over to this part of town. I was on my way to visit a friend and stopped off to buy some beer. They jumped me outside the store."

"Unfortunately, that's pretty common around here," the doctor said. "Let's have a look and see what we can do about patching you up."

He took off the gauze bandages on Drake's hand and arm and probed the gash, careful not to exert too much pressure. He hummed to himself as he examined Drake's wounds. He saved the shoulder wound for last. When he pulled back the bandage and began probing the wound, Drake winced.

"Dammit! This hurts like a son of a bitch!"

"Sorry," the doctor said. "That's a nasty stab wound. Only good thing I can say is that it looks like no major veins or arteries were cut."

"Great. I'm freakin' lucky. But what can ya do about the pain?"

"Plenty. First, we'll clean up the three wounds, shoot them full of Xylocaine to deaden the pain, stitch them up, and then get you on painkillers. We'll start with the worst one—your shoulder."

An hour later, after paying for the medical services with a stolen credit card, Drake climbed into his car and started the engine. The bandages on all three wounds were clean, snug, and secure, and he felt pretty good. He was pain-free for the moment, but he knew the Xylocaine would wear off in an hour or two, and then he'd need to take the painkillers. *That's what drugs are for,* he mused.

He had a half hour drive ahead of him. He planned to think long and hard about Dr. Collins, the little girl, and the man who had done this to him. They were going to pay. All three of them.

Especially the man.

He was already dead. He just didn't know it.

Chapter 19

Megan looked around as she and a man in a white lab coat walked down a long corridor and into a bright room with a high vaulted ceiling peppered with islands of skylight panels. He gripped her hand as they passed several rows of tables loaded with laboratory glassware and electronic instruments with digital displays and blinking lights.

Moments before, she and Nick had walked into the lobby where the man was waiting for them. He and Nick exchanged a few clipped remarks. In the end, Nick handed her over to him, accepted a manila envelope in return, and left in a hurry.

The man in the white coat seemed friendly enough. He'd tried to soothe her with warm, calming words as he led her down the corridor and through the laboratory.

"I'm sure you're going to enjoy your visit with us, Megan," he said, smiling. "There are two other girls here around your age. Well, one of them is. The other's a couple of years younger. And there's a boy here who is exactly your age."

"Really?" she asked, staring up at him. He kind of looked like her family doctor—late forties, slightly gray hair—and he had the same quiet authority in his voice. But considering her ride over here at gunpoint, she knew better than to trust him.

"Yes, really. I'm sure the four of you will become good friends."

The man patted her hand and smiled again as they left the laboratory and started down another corridor.

"How do you know my name is Megan and how old I am?" she asked. Fear churned in the pit of her stomach. "Why'd that man kidnap me with a gun? What are you going to do to me? And what about those other kids? Did they get kidnapped too?"

"Megan," he said and chuckled. "Stop and come up for air!" He cocked his head to the right. His eyes twinkled as if she'd made a joke. "Everything's fine."

"No, it's not," Megan said, trying to pull away. "Everything's not fine. What are you going to do to us? Are you going to hurt us?"

The man kept a firm grip on Megan's hand as he leaned down. "Look, Megan. My name is Dr. Miguel Artal. I'm the guy in charge here at this clinic. You and the other three children are here for special medical attention you can't get anywhere else. That's all. We're not going to hurt you. We're going to take exceptionally good care of you."

Megan's face twisted in disbelief. She wanted to believe what he said. She'd always felt safe and protected by the adults in her life. But this was different. Her instincts told her that he wasn't telling her the truth.

"Then why did that man kidnap me with a gun and tie up my doctor?"

Dr. Artal shrugged. "I don't know all that went on during your trip over here, Megan," he said, "and I don't have all the answers. But believe me, we're going to take good care of you and the other children. You're safe here."

"But…"

"No more questions for now," Dr. Artal said. He turned away and began walking again, bringing her along in tow. "I have something I'd like to show you. Something I think you'll have a lot of fun with."

Megan thought the last thing she was going to have here was fun.

"When do I get to meet the other kids?" she asked.

Dr. Artal glanced at her out of the corner of his eye as they continued walking. They were almost to the end of the corridor.

"Soon. You'll meet them soon."

Beth watched her condominium come into view as Max turned the corner and drove down her street. The familiarity of her surroundings calmed her, dampening the rush of anger, fear, and helplessness that had collided inside her. Now all that was left was anger and outrage at Megan's abduction. And her abductor.

"No way is he getting away with this," she said as they rolled to a stop in front of a three-story condominium complex. There were two interconnected buildings nestled at the back of a spacious courtyard that was lushly and meticulously landscaped.

"He *won't* get away with it," Max said. "We're getting Megan back. Then we're going to get him. And I mean *get* him."

Beth read the grim confidence on his face. That was a promise he would fulfill no matter the cost.

"I believe you," she said.

Beth had learned quite a bit about Max and his background after their long drive over to her place. They had filled each other in on every detail of what happened to them since they split up in the hospital parking lot. In spite of all they had been through, she found herself enjoying being with him.

The subtle fluttering of attraction made her feel guilty, and she tried to push it out of her mind.

She opened her door and climbed out of the Suburban. "Come on in. I'm going to grab a super quick shower. Then we'll jump on the computer and find out everything there is to know about Viralvector."

Max was impressed by how gusty Beth had been standing up to Megan's abductor and then freeing herself when she'd been tied up. *Seriously impressive,* he thought. She was cool and controlled under fire, focused and unflinching even when staring down the barrel of a gun. Smart, tough, *and* beautiful.

Being this close to her sparked his feelings of attraction, and he fought to contain them. He'd sort out his feelings later when Megan was safe and this crisis was over.

"Well?" Beth said. "You coming in or not?"

Max snapped out of his daze. She'd caught him staring at her.

"Uh, yeah. I'm coming," he said, shutting off the engine and climbing down out of the Suburban.

Beth shot him a quizzical smile, and they headed up the walkway.

Megan had finished dinner and was lying on her bed flipping through a magazine when she first caught a glimpse of the girl. She zipped by in a blur in front of the partially open doorway. Someone in a white lab coat was hurrying her along.

Springing off her bed, Megan scrambled to the doorway and looked in the direction they were headed. The girl and her escort were moving at a fast pace down the hall. A strange sensation shot up her spine and gave her instant goosebumps. There was something eerily familiar about the girl.

As she opened her mouth to call out to them, the realization hit her and stopped her cold. From behind, the girl looked exactly like the one she'd met in her scary dream about the man chasing her through the forest.

"Hey, wait!" Megan called out. "Wait a minute!"

The person in the white coat turned around, and Megan could see it was a middle-aged woman with sharp features and gray speckled hair pulled back in a tight bun. She shot Megan a stern look. "Get back in your room," she barked. "It's eight-thirty. Time to turn out the lights and go to sleep."

Megan opened her mouth to say something, but nothing came out.

"I'll be back in a minute to check on you," the woman said. "You better be in bed, and your lights better be out."

Megan nodded in wide-eyed compliance. Her gaze shifted to the girl, who turned around and looked straight at her. A tiny smile grew on her face, and she kept smiling as the woman whisked her around the corner and out of sight.

Megan was stunned by the whirling dizziness of impossibility that hammered her in a clash of dream and reality.

It's her! The girl in my dream. The six-year-old who looks just like me.

Megan closed her eyes and focused on the girl's face, visualizing every line and feature. Hair. Eyes. Smile. *It was her. But that's impossible. It was only a dream.*

She opened her eyes and stepped out into the hallway, looking both ways to make sure the coast was clear. She hurried after them, finally breaking into a run as she approached the intersecting corridor where the woman and the girl had turned. Pressing herself against the wall, she leaned forward and peeked around the corner.

The woman and the girl disappeared into the second to the last room on the right.

That's gotta be her room. Curiosity tingled through Megan. She was tempted to sneak down the hall to have a look. *Boy, that'd be really dumb.*

Worried the woman would see her when she came out of the room, Megan backed away from the corner and scampered up the hallway and into the safety of her room. She hopped into bed and turned off the light on her bedside table. Then she laid down and pulled the covers up around her neck. She listened to the silence and thought about her dad. Thinking about him made her heart hurt. She missed him so much.

All she wanted to do was go home and sleep in her own room in her own bed. Back where it was safe and familiar. On top of everything else, she didn't feel very good. She felt hot and lightheaded, and her stomach hurt.

She was scared, but she knew she couldn't give in to her fear. She had to be brave. That's what her dad would tell her if he were here.

He'd find her somehow. There was no doubt in her mind that he would rescue her. But in the meantime, he'd expect her to be brave and try her best to escape. She wouldn't let him down.

Megan heard the soft clack of her door being locked followed by the sound of receding footsteps. She lay motionless and could hear a faint noise here and there in distant parts of the building.

In the dark stillness, the pounding of her heart and her breathing began to slow. Her mind drifted onto the surreal playground of sleep and into the deepest state of REM her brain had ever entered.

She floated amidst the quiver of swirling mists that fled before her and began to dream.

Beth stepped out of the shower and wrapped herself in a plush, over-sized bath towel. She had turned the water up as hot as she could stand it and set the shower nozzle to pulsate. The drumming of the water had soothed away most of her aches and pains. She felt clean and fresh and whole again.

Twenty minutes later, after getting dressed and drying her hair, she came out into the living room. Max was finishing a call on his cell phone. He was looking out through the sliding glass doors at her small, enclosed garden patio.

"Okay," Max said, looking at his watch. "Meet you in a little under two hours…half past eight sharp. Corner of Tustin and Chapman. Then we'll caravan down there. Like I said, night vision and reconnaissance gear. After we scope everything out, we'll grab Starbucks and plan tomorrow's action. Everything good to go?"

Max listened for a moment. "Thanks, Mark. Appreciate it. We'll get her back all right. And I want you to know how much your help means to me. I owe you, man. Yeah, see you at eight o'clock."

He turned around and saw Beth. A grin took over his face. "Don't you look all fresh and squeaky clean," he said.

She smiled back at him and struck an exaggerated fashion pose. "After all, I *am* the Queen of Squeak."

Max laughed. He couldn't take his eyes off her. "Well then, *your majesty,* I guess I should also tell you that you look great in street clothes."

Beth laughed. "Flattery like that won't get you far, but it will get you a beer. Want one?"

"Sure."

"Two icy ones comin' right up. I've also got loads of cold barbecued chicken and coleslaw left over from a dinner party I co-hosted night before last. Interested?"

"Absolutely," he said, following her into the kitchen.

"Hope you're as starved as I am. I plan to eat like a horse."

"You and me both."

They spent the next two hours eating and collecting every bit of available online information about Viralvector, Inc. They compiled multiple folders with over a hundred and fifty pages of printouts on the company, covering every aspect of its history, business structure, executive leadership, financials, collaborations, and research capabilities.

Beth accessed most of the major medical association membership databases. She searched ClinicalTrials.gov, Citeline, and other clinical trial databases, identifying multiple clinical studies Viralvector was involved in as well as the names of the investigators. A PubMed search yielded more than two dozen early science research abstracts and publications linked to the ongoing Viralvector studies.

"I think we've got everything we need," Beth said.

Max flipped through the stack, stopping on a sheet of paper that showed a picture of the corporate headquarters building. The next page was Google Map directions to the company's Rancho Santa Margarita address.

"So, let me get this straight," he said. "Viralvector is a biotech firm, and they've come up with a way to use viruses to carry genes into people."

"Right," Beth agreed. "Only they didn't come up with the basic biotechnology of using adenoviruses as vectors, or carriers, of genes into cells. Apparently, they've made some big advances in this field."

"And *why* would you want to do that in the first place?" Max asked. "I mean, I kind of know why. I read the mumbo-jumbo about gene repair, helping people with rare diseases, and all that."

"Some diseases are caused by genetic defects. The individual doesn't produce a particular protein or enzyme or produces defective versions of them. The hope and promise of gene therapy is to try to cure these people by replacing the damaged genes in their bodies with healthy, functioning ones." Beth leaned back and sipped her beer, realizing she was slipping into doctor mode.

"Sounds good," Max said. "But from the few news stories I've read, it seems like this gene therapy has mostly been tried on kids with that immune thing. What do they call it? The 'Bubble Boy' syndrome? And they even had trouble with that."

"True," she said. "Sometimes individuals have genetic defects that leave them with a weak immune system or, in the case of the 'Bubble Boy' syndrome, no immune system at all. The gene defect leads to a complete lack of white blood cells that can fight infection. Without treatment, most infants die during their first year of life."

"Scary," Max said.

Beth nodded. "If they can't get a bone marrow transplant, gene therapy is their only hope."

"If it works."

"There have been some spectacular successes with this therapy. Kids with literally no immune systems and no chance for a normal life are suddenly given that possibility."

"Amazing. But I read there were problems with it, right?"

"True." Beth said. "It turns out that in a few cases, the kids developed a leukemia-like syndrome around age three because of an error in the location of the insertion of the gene."

"What? The doctors made a mistake and put the gene in the wrong place?" Max asked.

"No," Beth said. "It doesn't quite work like that. You can't precisely control the placement of the genes inside the cell. In early studies, they used adenoviruses to carry healthy genes into the blood stem cells of these patients. The adenovirus injected its DNA and the new gene into the cell, the new gene got incorporated in the cell's DNA, and that corrected the genetic defect."

"So, it was just a crapshoot where the cell's DNA the gene got incorporated?"

"Pretty much," Beth conceded. She shrugged. "When the gene was inserted, it was a random process. In the cases you read about, it seems likely the gene was inserted near a flawed region of the DNA strand triggering the leukemia-like syndrome."

"That's not good. What happens to the three-year-olds with leukemia?"

"They're put on chemotherapy, and most go into remission," Beth said. "I don't know how the ones you read about are doing now, but childhood leukemia has a cure rate of around ninety percent."

"Okay." Max nodded, trying to process what she was saying. It was a lot of information. "What about the big advances supposedly made by Viralvector? They have any better luck?"

Beth flipped through several papers in the thick stack they had just printed out and scanned portions of them. "According to their PR releases and a whole slew of independent articles, it looks like it's been a huge success. Using a variant of the CRISPR-Cas9 targeted genome editing technique paired with modified adenoviruses, they've achieved extremely high location specificity in gene editing and insertion."

"Crispy what?

"CRISPR…It stands for *Clustered Regularly Interspaced Short Palindromic Repeats*. It's a highly sophisticated genomic editing technique that allows precision cuts to the DNA and replacement of specific genes."

"Okay…"

"But here's something that's a little odd," she said, holding out one page.

"What?" Max asked. He waited as she reread the text.

"It looks like they established themselves with breakthroughs in gene insertion technology. In fact, royalties from out-licensing deals and partnerships involving their gene insertion process make up a healthy chunk of their bottom line. It bankrolls the company and keeps investors happy. What's odd is that over the past couple of years, the majority of their primary and secondary research has been on dendritic, axonal, glial, and neuronal cell growth manipulation."

Max gave her a blank look. "I got the first part about the bankroll finances, but do you want to translate the second part into English?"

Beth looked up at him over the papers she was holding. "Basically, they're using their gene insertion technology to genetically alter and manipulate the growth of nerve cells."

"Growth of nerve cells...That's pretty exciting, if it works. I read an article in *Time* magazine a while back on some of the research going on to try to help quadriplegics and paraplegics with spinal cord injuries. If you could somehow get the spinal nerves of a quadriplegic to grow again and reconnect...it'd be a spectacular medical advance."

"Sounds like science fiction, doesn't it?" Beth said. "Actually, it might be closer to becoming a reality than you think. Parallel development of this process along with stem cell application advances could make it a reality in ten years. Or maybe even less."

"That'd be amazing," Max said.

Beth looked at her watch. "We're supposed to meet Mark in twenty minutes. Think we should leave now?"

"Yeah, we better head out."

They stood up, and Beth grabbed several folders of printouts.

"What's so odd about their research on nerves?"

Beth looked at the paper and squinted at the text. She picked up her purse and turned to Max. "They jumped immediately into nerve research with their new gene insertion process and excluded other critical areas, like immune disorders."

"They out-licensed their technology to a lot of companies," Max said. "They probably decided they'd let other companies use their process for immune disorder research while they focused exclusively on nerves."

"Well, that is what they did," Beth said. "But there's one bizarre thing that creeps me out."

"Creeps you out?"

Beth nodded. Her brows furrowed, and she stared at Max, and he could see she was serious.

"They aren't just doing experiments on spinal nerves," she said. "They're also inserting genes into brain neurons."

Max thought of Megan and cringed. "You mean...they're trying to grow *brain* cells?"

"Not trying, Max. They're doing it. They're using viral vectors and CRISPR-Cas9 techniques to insert genes into brain cells. And they're making them grow and replicate."

Max was silent for a few moments. He locked eyes with her, his expression a blend of outrage and grim determination.

"They are *not* going to do this to Megan." He grabbed his keys off the counter and stormed out the door. Beth double checked her folders and hurried out after him, locking the door behind her.

Chapter 20

Megan was back in the massive wooded forest with its towering, endless canopy of foliage and magnified sights and smells. An aura of familiarity enveloped her, and a crushing fear of danger gripped her chest.

She broke into a run.

Looking over her shoulder, she saw Sarah, her twin, running behind her, and further in the distance, their pursuer, the man with the knife. He stepped out from behind a stand of trees and looked around. A cold chill ran down Megan's spine when he spotted them.

The earthy smells of the forest filled her nose as she and Sarah scurried between the trees, deeper and deeper into the shady recesses of the protective woodland shelter. They ran until their legs ached and their breath came in short gasps, but just like before, the man was gaining ground.

Megan chanced another look back over her shoulder. Their pursuer was less than twenty feet away. He leered at her and swung his knife menacingly as he ran.

"C'mon, Sarah!" she screeched. Her young twin was falling further behind. "He's gonna catch us! Hurry!"

She turned to look forward in the direction she was running and collided at full speed with a tree branch that blocked her path. Her left cheekbone smashed into the unyielding mass of wood with a painful crunch. The impact knocked her off her feet, flattening her in midair and dropping her to the ground in a dazed heap. She fought unconsciousness but failed as she floated into the swirling vortex of perfect black and infinite silence.

Megan felt someone tugging at her as she drifted up out of the blackness. They pulled her sleeve in gentle, persistent tugs. She heard a voice whisper, "Are you okay?"

Megan opened her eyes, and for a few lingering seconds, she had no idea where she was. All she knew was she couldn't see out of her left eye.

"Are you hurt?" the voice whispered again with quiet urgency.

The room slowly crystallized into focus through her right eye, and Megan suddenly remembered where she was and everything that had happened. The left front side of her face was pressed against a cold linoleum floor. Her right eye revealed an angled, floor-up perspective, and she could see the dim light streaming in from the hallway. She must have fallen out of bed.

That was so real, she thought as the last wisps of the dreamscape dissipated from her mind. *I can't believe that was only a dream.*

She pulled herself up from the floor and took a deep breath. Her nose still held a hint of the earthy aroma of the forest. She wiped her face with her hand to see if any pine needles were stuck to it. Nothing was there.

"Guess I had a bad dream," she said to the girl, who had backed up and stood framed by the light of the doorway. Her face was shadowed; Megan couldn't see her expression.

Megan squinted and tried to make out her face. "Hi, my name's Megan. What's yours?"

Megan waited for her to answer, but the girl just stood there and looked at the ground. She gauged the other girl to be six or seven years old, and her hair was light brown, the same color and length as her own.

"It's okay. There's nothing to be afraid of. What's your name?"

The little girl glanced over her shoulder down the hallway, checking to make sure the coast was clear. She fingered the key she had used to unlock the door, and then she turned and leaned in towards Megan. "It's Sarah," she said in a conspiratorial tone.

Megan felt a whiplash of déjà vu surge as she gazed at the girl's face.

"Your name's...*what?*" she said, finally breaking the spell. Her voice sounded high-pitched and breathless.

The little girl looked at her with wide eyes. She leaned in close.

"It's Sarah. You..." She hesitated then blurted out the words they were both thinking. "You look just *like me.*"

The two girls stood inches apart. Megan reached out and touched Sarah's face, and Sarah did the same.

Megan shook her head in wonder as Sarah took a step back. She felt like she was looking in a mirror at herself in the past.

"How old are you, Sarah?" she asked.

"I'm seven," she said proudly. "Well, almost…I'm still six. My birthday's in a couple months."

"That's neat," Megan said, trying to sound upbeat. "I'm sure you're going to have a really fun birthday."

Sarah gave a non-committal shrug. "Guess so."

Megan tried to remember what it was like when she was six.

"How long have you been here?"

Sarah's face scrunched up in a frown. "I've…always been here. I live here."

Megan fought to keep the look of surprise off her face. "You…live here?"

Sarah shrugged. "Uh huh."

Megan forced herself to keep an even tone. Images of orphanages and the movie *Annie* flitted through her mind. "But what about your mom and dad. Do they live here too?"

Sarah's face dropped into a look of resigned sadness.

"I don't have a dad, and I only see my mother every once in a while. She's really, really sick…and she doesn't talk."

Megan felt an ache of protective empathy grip her heart.

"I'm so sorry, Sarah. Do they keep her here? Is she in a bed in one of these rooms?"

Sarah lowered her eyes and shook her head.

"Nope."

"Well, where is she then?"

Sarah looked up. "She's in a room at the other place. The one that's up in the mountains where you can see that pretty lake. They take care of her there."

"Up in the mountains…you mean by Lake Arrowhead? Or do you mean the other lake that's a little farther away. Big Bear lake?"

Sarah thought for a moment. "It must be the Arrowhead lake," she said. "I heard the men driving us up to the mountain say 'arrowhead' a few times on their cell phones. But they never said anything about 'big bears.'"

"How long has it been since you've been up there?"

Sarah tilted her head to the side. "I think it was about a week ago."

"Did you get to see your mom?" Megan asked.

Sarah let out her breath. "Not this time. They took me to a different building kinda like this one."

"What did you do there?"

"I played in the cool playroom they have there. It's got lotsa toys and games and stuff. And I walked around a lot and watched them move stuff in."

Megan thought for a minute. "Did it have a room like the one here with lots of glass beakers, test tubes, and instruments, and stuff?"

"Yeah, there's two rooms like that. One of 'em is even bigger than the one here."

Megan pictured the expansive high-tech lab she had walked through earlier.

"And there's a buncha rooms like this one," Sarah continued. "They also showed me where my new room is gonna be. And where Faith's room will be too."

"Who's Faith?" Megan asked. "Is she your age?"

"No," Sarah said. "She's older'n me."

"She is? How old?"

"Uh…I think she's about your age. How old are you?"

"I'm nine," Megan said. "I'll be ten in a couple of months."

"Yep. I'm right. She's your age. She just turned nine."

Megan looked at Sarah, and it hit her again how much they looked alike. She thought about Faith and wondered what *she* looked like. *This is all getting very weird.*

"Does Faith stay here all the time like you do?" Megan asked.

"No. I only see her every once in a while."

"Where does she go when she's not here?"

Sarah shrugged. "I don't know. When I ask her, she never tells me. She says she doesn't want to talk about it."

Megan couldn't help but stare at Sarah. "When was the last time you saw her?"

"It wasn't too long ago," Sarah said. "Last week, we…"

"Shh!" Megan hissed. "I hear somebody coming!"

Sarah gasped, and they both heard the loudening clackety-clack of approaching footsteps out in the hallway.

"Quick," Megan whispered. She grabbed Sarah's hand. "Get under the covers and hide!"

Sarah scrambled up onto Megan's bed and burrowed deep under the covers.

Megan slid into bed right after her, pulling the covers up around her neck and closing her eyes. The stern nurse who had passed by earlier charged into the room. She flicked on the light and walked up to Megan's bedside.

Megan lay with her head leaning to one side on her pillow, her eyes squeezed shut. Her mouth was open, and she forced herself to breathe slow and even.

"Where is she?!"

Megan jumped. She blinked up at the nurse. "Wha…What?" She propped herself up on her elbow, pretending to wipe the sleep out of her eyes.

"You heard me." There was an icy lethalness to the nurse's voice. "Where is she?"

"Where's…who?" Megan asked.

"Sarah. You know who I'm talking about. You saw me walking with her down the hall earlier tonight."

"I, uh…"

The nurse grimaced at her with an expression so harsh it looked like it hurt.

Megan's lower lip quivered.

"Sarah's missing from her room," the nurse said. "I locked your door two hours ago, and now it's open. It's obvious Sarah sneaked down here, unlocked the latch, and came in. Where is she?"

The nurse's eyes shifted from Megan's face down to the bed, and she noticed a suspicious lumpiness in the covers. She grabbed the top of the covers and ripped them off the bed revealing Sarah cowering in a fetal position.

"Sarah! Get back to your room this instant!"

Sarah scrambled off the bed and started for the door.

"I don't *ever* want to catch you wandering around at night again. Otherwise, we'll start locking *you* in. Do you understand?"

"Yes, ma'am," Sarah said in a timid voice. She glanced back at Megan before disappearing through the doorway.

"And you, young lady," the nurse said, turning her attention back to Megan. "From now on, you better be on your best behavior…and do *exactly* what you're told. Understand?"

Megan clutched the covers to her chest and nodded.

"Now get back to sleep! We leave early in the morning."

Megan watched the nurse storm out of the room and yank the door closed behind her. The latch of the lock snapped into place with a resounding clack.

Sweat beaded on Megan's forehead. She gasped for breath and placed a hand over her heart. It was pounding a drumbeat of rapid, powerful thumps.

Somehow, she had to escape this terrible nightmare. Somehow, she'd figure out a way…and she'd take Sarah with her.

Chapter 21

A full moon illuminated the clear starry night. Its stark luminescence framed the jutting, ultra-modern architecture of Viralvector, Inc. in razor outline against the surrounding hills. The lone streetlight at the end of the cul-de-sac cast an elliptical halo of light on the street in front of the secluded building complex. Spotlights illuminated the stark white edifices and groups of trees on the lawn that swayed in the breeze.

Max's Suburban was parked halfway down the block, hidden in the safety of darkness.

Max and Beth sat in the front seat sipping coffee and watching for any activity or movement from the buildings. They had been keeping tight surveillance on the complex for over two hours, continually scanning it with Max's high-resolution binoculars. He had also packed a powerful range-finding monocular sniper scope with night vision capability, but they didn't need it. The building was lit up like a Christmas tree. His gut told him that at some point it would come in extremely handy, along with the other gear he'd packed.

Mark Hunter was sitting in the back seat, his own binoculars trained on the complex. His car was parked across the street. They had decided that driving down separately would give them flexibility if events turned south.

Max and Mark went way back. They'd been friends for over a decade. Their friendship was built on a deep level of mutual respect that had grown steadily over the years.

Max had trained Mark for Special Weapons and Tactics. He'd spotted Mark's aptitude for this area of work from the get-go. His background comprised three rotations in the military, including Special Operations in Iraq and Afghanistan. He graduated at the top of his class at the Police Academy and was targeted for an array of Tactics Programs, but none had drawn his interest and captivated him the way Special Operations had. His application for the SWAT team had been immediately accepted.

Max turned and looked over his shoulder into the back seat. "Mr. Hunter, you ready for a perimeter recon?"

Mark lowered his binoculars. He nodded, all business. "We're good to go."

Max opened the console between the two front seats and pulled out a pair of micro two-way clip-on radios with earpieces. He placed one unit on top of the pile of papers on Beth's lap. She'd brought all the Internet printouts and had been reading up on Viralvector.

"Mark…is yours on?" he asked, putting the earpiece into his ear.

"I hear you loud and clear," Mark said, speaking into the miniature black device that he'd already clipped to the right shoulder of his shirt.

Beth looked the device over and slipped the earpiece into her ear. She pushed the transmit switch and whispered into the small black box. "Testing…alpha, beta, gamma…Do you hear me?"

Max grinned and spoke into his radio. "We hear you. But we don't know what you're saying. It's all in Greek."

Beth gave Max a wry look and slapped him on the arm.

"Just remember, when you two commandos are chattering at each other, I'll be listening in."

"Dang," Max said. "Guess we'll have to skip the off-color jokes this time."

"Guess so," Mark quipped.

Beth laughed. "Okay, boys. Get out of here and see what you can find."

"We're on it." He turned to Mark. "Got your night scope?"

"Ready to scout."

"Let's roll," Max said.

Beth watched them disappear into the night. She hoped they'd find Megan and bring her out safely. The odds seemed good. They were two determined, highly trained and heavily armed professionals. *Find her, Max.*

Megan woke up from another startling dream, heart pounding. She was shaking. She was sure that she had dreamt more in the last two weeks than she had in the last six months combined.

Closing her eyes, she tried to clear her mind and drift back off to sleep. She imagined sheep jumping over a fence and counted them. When that didn't work, she imagined lying on a raft in a pool watching clouds drift by overhead. But no matter what she tried, she couldn't get back to sleep.

She tossed and turned, tugging the sheets up tight around her neck as she curled up on one side then the other. Finally, she flipped onto her back and stared up at the ceiling.

Pictures of her dad played again and again in her mind like a streaming video. He was chasing after her, trying to rescue her, and he came close. It was the fiercely determined way he looked through the side and back windows of the SUV as it sped away from him in the hospital parking lot that gave her hope.

He'll come after me, she thought, convinced in her heart and mind that there was no single fact more certain in all the universe. *I know he will. He'll come.*

She looked around at the sparse room furnishings dimly lit by the soft outdoor light diffusing in through the window blinds. A thin line of light shone in from the bottom of the closed door to the hallway.

Yeah, he'll come to get me, she thought. *But I can't just sit here like a bump on a log until he does. I've gotta help him. I've gotta try to escape by myself.*

Megan threw her covers back and slid out of bed. A chill tingled up her spine when her feet touched the cold linoleum floor. She tiptoed as quietly as she could over to the door, turned the knob, and pulled.

The door didn't budge.

She examined the brass deadbolt lock above the door handle. It required a key to unlock it from the inside. Walking over to the desk against the wall next to her bed, she slid open the drawer and looked inside. She could barely make out the contents. She felt around and came across two paperclips.

Megan straightened them out and then hurried over to the door. She slid the first paperclip wire into the bottom part of the lock and the second in the top. She visualized the tumblers just as her father had taught her last year. She'd pestered him every day for two weeks to teach her how to pick a lock after she'd watched him pick a neighbor's car trunk lock in less than twenty seconds when the neighbor had locked her keys inside.

It took her several minutes of manipulating the wires in concert before the deadbolt slid to the left with a satisfying clack. Megan turned the doorknob slowly, placed a hand on the wall to steady herself, and opened the door just wide enough to stick her head out.

It was eerily silent.

She noticed a dim wedge of light emanating from a room with a partially open door at the end of the hall. She wondered if the mean, scary-looking nurse stayed in that room. That was one person she didn't feel like running into tonight.

Easing the door closed, Megan moved back across her room to the window and spread the blinds apart to peer out. From her vantage point, she had an angled view of the lawn and landscape at the front of the building. She could see about half of the planters and flowerbeds and most of the contoured lawn, but beyond where the spotlights were shining up against the building, everything was cloaked in darkened silhouette.

Megan scanned the grounds and the street looking for anything that might help her. She was about to turn away when a subtle movement caught the corner of her eye. She looked to her left across the grounds to the most distant edge of the property. A small black shadow was moving.

Megan put her hand up to shield her eyes from the glare of the spotlight that was aimed at the building. She focused on the shadowy figure that was running along the eastern perimeter of the building complex and taking obvious care to avoid the light.

She watched with rapt fascination as it crossed the end of the cul-de-sac, just out of range of the streetlight's field of illumination, and reached the opposite side of the street.

Who could that be? she wondered. She tried to make out the person's features, but whoever it was had dressed all in black and blended into the darkness.

Another shadowy form caught her eye as it emerged on the western perimeter of the property. It raced away from the building, keeping in the shadows until it reached the street and crossed.

Megan placed her forehead against the glass, putting both hands up to shield her eyes, and tracked the two shadowy figures as they sprinted two hundred yards further down the road and climbed into a parked vehicle.

Even from this great a distance, Megan felt a twinge of familiarity as she looked at the front of vehicle. Her chest clenched in hope and excitement as she realized it resembled her father's Suburban.

He's out there! It's gotta be him!

She whirled around and ran for the door, grabbing a sweatshirt hoodie that was draped over a chair. She paused when she reached the door and pulled the sweatshirt on over her head. She breathed in deeply to calm herself, then opened the door.

Looking up and down the hall, she could see the coast was clear. The lights were muted. She stepped out of the room and scurried down the hallway, making her way toward the exit sign that shone bright at the far end of the hallway. Her bare feet padded silently on the linoleum floor.

Halfway down the hall, she came to an intersection where a wide hallway on her left led to the corporate lobby and entrance. She stopped and peeked around the corner. A security guard was seated at a mahogany desk facing the door. He was leaning forward, his nose stuck in a book.

Megan kept her eyes locked on the guard as she tiptoed across the open corridor. She held her breath until she reached the other side and then stopped and listened. Her heart was pounding, but there was no sound from the guard.

She tiptoed down the side hall. She hadn't gone far when the murmur of voices stopped her cold. She backtracked to the lobby and peeked around the corner. The guard was talking with the scary-looking nurse, who was turned away from him staring at the front entrance.

Megan's stomach clenched in disappointment and fear. She hurried across the open corridor and raced back to her room. She locked the door and climbed under the covers.

Did she see me? If she looked back, even for a second, she would've seen me...

A few minutes later, her door opened, and the nurse stuck her head in the room. Megan pretended to be fast asleep. After a small eternity, she closed the door. Megan heard the flip of the latch and the clack of the deadbolt shaft sliding into place.

Trapped again. But I'll get away. Somehow.

Chapter 22

Max climbed into the Suburban and pulled the door shut. He glanced into the back seat as Mark climbed in and then over at Beth.

"How did it go?" she asked.

"Went well," Max said. "Standard recon."

"Ditto that," Mark agreed.

Max turned and dropped his gear into the back seat beside Mark. "Nothing out of the ordinary I could see. Just a garden variety high-tech building complex. I noticed the attached warehouse out back. Mark, you scoped that out. Anything unusual?"

"Nope. Lit up my night scope through a window in the walk-in door. Nothing but two long workbenches, storage shelves, and two late model SUVs. One silver and the other midnight blue. Neither of them was the black Ford Expedition, but I lucked out with the rear plates and snapped pics of them both."

"Good," Max said, opening the side view screen on the miniature camcorder. "I checked out all of the side windows and shot some video of the interior. There was a rent-a-cop in the front lobby, but the guy was oblivious."

Max rewound the video and watched it replay as he talked. "The rest of the building interior looked pretty upscale. State-of-the-art. They spent a lot of money on snazzy furniture and décor. I did get a partial view of a laboratory and a couple of rooms that looked like they were part of a clinic. But no one around except for the guard."

"Any sign of Megan?" Beth asked.

Max shook his head. "None. But I could only see a portion of the interior. They probably have her stashed away in one of the clinic rooms."

Beth looked out the window at the side street down from where they were parked. "There's one good thing at least," she said. "From where we're sitting, we've got a great view of both the headquarters and the lab building."

Max and Mark looked down the block at the clinical lab. It was housed in an unassuming office-warehouse building, fourth from the corner. It was virtually identical to the other buildings on the block.

"Nothing to do but wait and watch," Max said. They settled back in their seats and tried to get comfortable.

An hour passed in silence. Max scanned the building with his binoculars half a dozen times. Beth immersed herself in the papers she had brought along. The pile of printouts and folders was eight inches high. She painstakingly studied the information line by line using a penlight for illumination.

Max's gaze shifted from the building to Beth. "Find anything new?" he asked.

"Not really," she said. "I read the four research studies they published in the journals *Science* and *Nature*. I wanted to find out more about their gene insertion research on spinal nerves and brain neurons as well as ancillary biologic modifiers."

"What are the studies about?"

"It's esoteric stuff. Both *Science* and *Nature* publish cutting-edge, hard science research from all the different scientific disciplines. And I mean *hard science*."

She put the pile of papers on the floor but held onto the four studies.

"Two of the papers are on *in vitro* studies of human nerve growth factors and the synergistic effect of promoter region CRISPR-cas9 gene editing with insertions of signal transduction potentiators on nerve growth. The other two are *in vivo* studies in monkeys on homologous chromosome neuronal gene insertion. All four of the studies used modified viruses as vectors for the initial gene insertion."

Max cocked his head and raised his eyebrows. "Okay. No speaky the language. I somehow missed taking Greek in college. You want to translate?"

"Sorry," Beth laughed. "Basically, they tested their breakthrough gene insertion technique—modified CRISPR-cas9 gene editing combined with editor bases and biologic modifiers—on spinal nerves in the laboratory. This is the research we talked about back at my condo having to do with stimulating the growth of spinal nerves. The paraplegic stuff."

"Gotcha," Max said. "And it worked?"

"Yes, surprisingly well. And it could turn out to be a true breakthrough development—the critical advance that spinal cord nerve research needs. But the other two studies…" Beth's voice caught. "They were gene insertion studies on neurons—brain cells—in live monkeys."

Max shifted in his seat. "That was the stuff that creeped you out, right?"

"Majorly," Beth agreed. "And it creeps me out even more after reading the actual research paper. They took six laboratory monkeys and inserted genes directly into the neurons of each monkey's cerebral cortex. Ended up having major success in stimulating new brain growth."

"That's so bizarre," Max said, cringing at the thought. "How could they tell the brains were growing?"

"They ran tests on the monkeys using a series of PET scans. That stands for Positron Emission Tomography," she said. "The scans are used to measure changes in tissue function, uptake, and metabolism over time. They found increased cerebral metabolic activity."

"In all of them?"

"Yes," she said. "There was a significant increase in total metabolic activity of each monkey's cerebral cortex. It showed that either the brain cells were metabolizing more rapidly or there were actually more cells. After sacrificing the monkeys, they found microscopic pathologic evidence of significant brain cell growth in each of them."

"Unbelievable," Max said.

"Yeah," Mark agreed. "Seriously wacko. Who'd want to make monkeys' brains grow?"

Beth glanced at Max. He was gazing past her out the window.

"Sounds bizarre, doesn't it? In the first two papers on spinal nerve growth, they tout their results as a potential breakthrough for treating paraplegics and quadriplegics…helping them regain the use of their limbs. Then the next two papers are focused on growing new brain cells."

"But what do they say their goal is in the brain growth papers?" Mark asked.

Beth scanned the discussion section of the study. "Their claims are pretty grandiose. They hold up the promise their technique will one day help cure patients with stroke, epilepsy, brain injury, Alzheimer's disease, and even Down syndrome."

"What the hell?!" Max exploded. He whipped around to face Beth. "They've been injecting Megan with something for who knows how long, skulking around in the shadows and trying to abduct her to run tests and give her more injections. They're using her as a damn guinea pig for this brain experiment of theirs."

Beth reached out and grasped his arm. "I hate to agree, Max," she said, "but it sounds like that's exactly what they're doing."

He squinted and gritted his teeth, reining in his rage. A vein bulged on the side of his forehead. She squeezed his arm.

Max nodded and put his hand on Beth's. "There's gonna be hell to pay. The second we find out where Megan is, I'm going in and taking her. I'm getting her to safety. Then they're going down big time."

Beth looked out the window at the shadows beyond the dimly illuminated street. Max leaned back into his seat with a sigh. He held her hand as they sat watching, thinking, and planning in the midnight silence. Alone in their thoughts but connected.

Another thirty minutes crept by. There was no change outside, no sign of movement, nothing unusual.

Max rolled his neck from side to side and stretched his back. He looked over his shoulder at Mark, who was leaning his head back on the car seat. "Why don't you go home and get a few hours sleep? There's nothin' going on here."

"You sure?"

"I'm sure," Max replied.

Mark looked at his watch. "Okay, tell you what…it's twenty minutes to one right now. How about if I'm back here at six o'clock sharp with coffee and donuts?"

Max grinned. "How about Krispy Kreme donuts?"

"What do you think, Beth?" he asked. "You want to sleep in your own bed the rest of the night and then come back at six with Mark? I'm sure he'd be happy to give you a lift. It's not likely anything will be going on here tonight."

"Oh, I don't know. I think I'll just curl up in the back seat and snooze for a couple of hours. Then we can trade off…give you a chance to sleep too."

"Sounds good. See you at six, Mark. Smiling face, donuts, and coffee."

"I don't know about the smiley face part, but I'm up for the rest of it."

"Hey, one more thing," Max said. "Take your gear but leave your digital camera with the night scope. I want to check out the plates on those Suburbans and the other shots you took."

"Sure thing." He handed the camera to Max. Then he stuffed his gear back into the black duffel bag and zipped it shut.

"Later," he said, letting himself out of the Suburban.

They watched as he walked down the street to his car. A few minutes later, his car turned the corner at the far end of the block and disappeared from sight.

Beth climbed into the back of the Suburban and made her way to the bench seat in the far back. The seat was long and cushiony. "I'll have no problem stretching out here," she said. "I've got a couch at home that's not much longer than this."

"All the comforts of home," Max quipped. "There's a blanket under the seat you can use. Maybe even two if you want to use the second as a pillow."

Beth dug them both out from under the seat. "Thanks," she said. She glanced at her watch. "It's a quarter to one. How about you wake me at half past three. Then I'll take over."

"Sounds like a plan. Now get some sleep."

Beth covered herself with the blanket and got comfortable. It amazed her how good the makeshift bed felt. The weight of her fatigue rolled over the stresses of the day and began to envelop her in a satiny softness.

"Max?"

"Mmm?" It took him a minute to answer. He was busy studying the digital pictures Mark had taken on the reconnaissance. He'd just enlarged one of the license plate shots and was writing down the information.

"Whatever you do," she said, "make sure you wake me up at a half past three. I'm used to not getting much sleep, and you're going to need your wits about you. You've *got* to get some sleep."

"Will do," he said. He turned and looked at her. Her eyes were already closed.

"Sweet dreams," he whispered.

Chapter 23

Beth heard the voice come out of nowhere. It seemed to echo from the clouds, like God was calling her name. She awakened with a start from a cavernous dream. The wisps of its powerful reality disoriented her for a few seconds as she looked around. Then everything snapped into place, and she knew where she was.

"Beth, wake up!" she heard Max repeat. It was the voice from the clouds, only less thunderous, and definitely not from the Almighty.

"What a weird dream," she said. "I can't believe what…"

"Something's happening over at Viralvector." Max said.

Beth sat up and looked around. Max had his binoculars trained on the right side of the building where the circle driveway forked and one part coursed around the building, disappearing into the back. Her eyes flew to her watch. *Oh, man, I overslept…*

"What's going on over there?" she asked. "You know, you really should have woken me up an hour ago."

"Yeah, I know. Listen, I saw some flickers of headlights coming from the back. The garage that Mark checked out is back there at the right rear of the building."

"You think one of those SUVs is getting ready to leave?"

"I'd bet on it."

"What's the plan?" Beth asked, leaning forward. Max glanced over at her and then back at the building.

"First, we're going to keep our heads down and stay out of sight, so they don't see us when they cruise by. Stay exactly where you are. Then once they pass, I want you to pop up and use this night-vision video camera to film some shots of the rear of the SUV. You'll have clear access out the back window.

Just make sure you capture the license plate. And if more than one truck goes by, shoot them both."

He handed her the video camera but didn't take his eyes off the right side of the building.

"What are you going to do?"

"I've got this high-tech scope that's a combo x-ray/infrared telescopic camera. I can get heat images of all the SUV's occupants. If Megan's in the vehicle, I should be able to make out her image based on size. Even if they've got her lying on the floor."

"If she's in there, are we going to—"

"Hold it!" he interrupted. "Here they come."

Headlights appeared at the top of the cul-de-sac to the right of the Viralvector main building. The polished silver SUV glistened as it passed under the streetlights.

Beth flipped on the power to the night scope and slid open the digital camera's lens cover. She pointed the camera out the back of the truck and looked through the viewfinder.

The night looked strange, as though she'd stepped through a door into an alien parallel dimension. The landscape was bathed in the glow of a heavy green luminescence.

Beth pushed the toggle lever triggering the zoom lens, moving the field of focus to where the SUV would be when she shot the pictures. She dropped down on the seat and waited, her heart pounding an urgent cadence.

Max crouched down in the front seat, and the two of them waited in the silence. They could hear the muffled rumbling of the approaching vehicle.

The instant it raced by, Beth popped up in her seat just high enough to rest the video camera on the top of the backrest. She had timed it perfectly; the video camera captured the back of the SUV and the license plate with crystal clarity. *Snap.* She pressed the button for the zoom lens and took two more pictures. *Snap. Snap.* The SV sped off down the street, rapidly receding from view.

"Did you get a close up of the plate?" Max asked.

"Nailed it. This night vision attachment is pretty slick."

"Excellent," Max said. He turned the key in the ignition as Beth scrambled into the front seat.

"What did you see with that James Bond scope of yours? Was Megan in there?"

Max shoved the Suburban in gear and cranked through a sharp U-turn as Beth buckled herself in. She held the video camera in her lap clamped between her legs.

"She's in there," he said, tromping on the gas pedal. The Suburban accelerated with explosive force, surging down the street with an uncaged animal muscularity.

"I saw two adult forms in the front and two much smaller forms in the back, lying on different seats. One of them's gotta be Megan."

"Must be. I'm sure she's okay. They're probably making them lie down to keep them out of sight."

"She *better* be okay," Max hissed through gritted teeth.

They raced down the street. The speedometer zipped past eighty.

Beth reached into the front and picked up the x-ray/infrared camera Max had laid on the seat. "Did you shoot any pictures of the images you saw through this thing?"

"I had it in continuous shot mode."

Beth clicked through the digital pictures, enlarging and studying each of them.

"Too bad these aren't true X-rays, instead of these fuzzy glowing images." She held the camera closer and scrutinized the last image on the display screen. "If they were, I could positively confirm from the bone size and structure that the two smaller images in the back are children. They've gotta be considering the size difference. But, you know, there's one more thing that could ice this cake."

"What?" Max asked.

"Doesn't Megan wear a bracelet on her left wrist? I remember seeing one on her."

"Yeah, she does. Her mother gave it to her. It's a family heirloom handed down on my wife's side. Megan never takes it off."

Beth turned to Max. "The child in the very back is wearing a bracelet on her left wrist. The kid in the center seat isn't."

"It's her all right," Max said. He gripped the steering wheel tightly and negotiated a screeching right hand turn at the corner. The silver SUV was way up at the end of the next street, almost out of view. Max stomped on the pedal, and the Suburban surged forward.

"Could you take a quick look at the video you shot of the SUV and see if you can pair up the license plate number with one of these?" He handed her a slip of paper. "I copied these off the videotape Mark shot of the two SUV plates in the garage. The one on the left is the license of the silver-gray SUV in the garage. I'm sure it's the same one we're chasing."

Beth rewound the tape and compared the license number with the ones on the paper.

"Perfect match," she said.

"Okay, let's get her." Max glanced at his watch. He'd give Mark a call as soon as he caught up to the SUV and could tail it from a maintainable distance.

Slowly but surely, they started to gain on it.

Fifteen minutes later, after negotiating a serpentine pathway of surface streets through the heart of Rancho Santa Margarita, they were less than a mile from the 405 freeway. Max was trying to maintain an inconspicuous distance. He followed a block and a half behind the SUV, keeping it in view while blending in with the flow of traffic. He knew the freeway on-ramp this street led to and was sure the SUV was headed there.

Pulling out his mobile phone, he hit the speed dial number for Mark and waited while it rang. Mark picked up on the third ring.

"Hunter."

"It's Max. You awake?"

"I am now." He stifled a yawn and cleared his throat.

"Listen, they bolted with Megan. Remember the silver SUV in the garage? The one you shot video of?"

"Yeah."

"That's the one they took. We're trailing 'em. They're almost to the 405, and I've got a strong feeling they'll go north."

"Why's that?"

"Just a hunch. Beth researched the hell out of Viralvector on the Internet. She found a reference to some kind of office and lab they're building or have built somewhere up in Lake Arrowhead. My bet is they're taking her up there."

"Got an address?"

"No. The article only mentioned the general area near the lake where they're building the structure. It's a few miles north of the UCLA Conference Center, on the east side of the lake. How about if you print out a bunch of Google location maps of the streets surrounding that area then grab your gear and head up towards Lake Arrowhead Village. We can stay in touch by cell phone."

"Will do. I'm rolling in five minutes…but I'm still grabbing doughnuts and coffee for us on the way up."

"Great. Hey, can you do me a favor? Have Craig or Stan or whoever's working the night shift in Rialto run a full history on the license number for the silver SUV."

"No problem. Give me the plate number, and I'll squeeze it out of them."

Max read the number to him.

"There's something else," Max said. "When you talk to them, have them check to see if the SUV is packing a LoJack. With all the SUVs targeted by car thieves, lots of dealers are pushing it as an option you can't live without. I bet the majority of SUV owners have them."

"Good idea," Mark said. "If we activate the LoJack, we can pinpoint the SUV's location in a heartbeat."

"Give me a buzz on my cell phone when you're halfway up the mountain. I'll let you know where to meet us and—"

Mark heard a clunk as Max's cell phone hit the floor of the truck.

"Dammit!"

A few seconds passed, and then Max came back on the phone.

"Man! I can't believe this."

"What happened?" Mark asked.

"A stupid mutt ran out in front of us. I swerved and barely missed him. But that's not the problem. The SUV ran a red light at the intersection. I've lost them."

"Well, *that's* not good," Mark said.

Max gritted his teeth. "Tell you what…we're taking the 405 north to the 55, then east towards the 10 and up to the turnoff for Arrowhead. I bet they're going the same way. We may catch up with them. Or not. Get a hold of Craig or Stan about that plate and the LoJack. Let's just hope to hell the SUV's got one we can activate."

"Will do. I'll call you the minute I hear anything. Meantime, I'll head up to Arrowhead like we planned."

"All right. Stay in touch," Max said and hung up.

He clamped the steering wheel in a death grip and accelerated through the red light as soon as the cross traffic passed. Beth clutched the handle on her door with grim determination.

"We'll get her," she vowed.

Chapter 24

The first hint of dawn filtered through the surrounding forest as the silver SUV reached the top of the mountain. Megan looked out the window at the intersection they were approaching. The driver turned right, bypassing the short road that would take them into Lake Arrowhead Village. She gazed sleepily at the buildings and trees, thinking how pretty and strangely familiar they looked. She looked to her left down the road leading to the Village shops and suddenly realized she had been here before.

Megan thought back to a day six months before the accident that killed her mother. Her father and mother had brought her up here for a fun family outing on a warm spring day. They had spent the day wandering in and out of shops, eating lunch by the sandy park next to the water, and slurping ice cream cones. She remembered the gorgeous scenery and how her mother had loved the pine forests that surrounded the mountain lake. Vague images flickered in her mind of mansion-sized cabins nestled in the trees by the water's edge with private docks and boats.

She pictured her mother, bright eyes and warm smile, and her father, his deep belly laugh and the way he held her mother's hand, even while driving. That had been a wonderful day. Megan used to be able to recall every detail about her mother. It was getting harder, and the images were blurring, but this memory was crystal clear.

Since her mother's death, her father was doing his best to make up for her absence. He was loving and supportive, and he always made sure she felt safe and special. Megan missed him terribly and hoped he'd come for her soon. She was terrified, but she refused to think about it. Now was the time to be brave. He'd come for her, and she needed to be ready when he did.

They drove along the winding mountain road, weaving through the tall pine forest. Megan leaned her head back against the headrest and watched the cabins and towering trees clip by. They circled the lake through areas of scenery that seemed vaguely familiar, and she wondered where they would stop.

Megan felt a tug on her shirt sleeve and turned to look at Sarah. She was holding a stuffed Golden Retriever puppy.

"Hi," Sarah said, rubbing her eye with her other hand. "I just woke up."

"I slept a little on the way up too," Megan whispered. She smiled at Sarah.

"Where are we?" Sarah asked. She looked to the window at the evergreen trees zipping by.

"A minute ago, we passed the road where you drive that leads to the Village. You know…where all the stores and ice cream shops are and where you can take boat rides on the lake."

"I've seen it, but I've never been there. Sarah's expression grew downcast. "Whenever I ask if they'd take me there, they say no." Her shoulders drooped in a forlorn shrug.

Megan felt sorry for her. She glanced at the two men in the front seat and thought about Sarah's comment that she had "always" been at the Rancho Santa Margarita headquarters. She didn't really live there, did she? And if her mom was awfully sick and she didn't have a dad, who took care of her?

"Tell you what." She leaned in close so she could whisper in Sarah's ear. "When this is all over and we get out of here, I'll ask my dad to take us both to the Village. We'll have a lot of fun there. He'll want to take us to lunch and buy us ice cream cones and stuff."

"Could we go on a boat ride?"

"Maybe. But first, we need to get away. I hope my dad comes for me soon, but no matter what, you and I have gotta get away as fast as we can."

Sarah nodded, her eyes wide.

Megan looked out the window for a moment, nibbling her bottom lip. "Any idea how much longer it'll be before we get there?"

Sarah looked past Megan out the window. It took her a few seconds to recognize the area. "I remember that two-story cabin with the red door"—she pointed—"and I know that last time after we passed it, it still took a while to get there."

"How long do you think? Another half hour?"

"I don't know. I don't think it took *that long…* "

The two of them watched tendrils of sunlight filter through the trees, illuminating the forest and cabins nestled within. Daylight was coming fast; the clear blue sky canopied the crisp mountain scenery. Sarah leaned her head against Megan's arm. Megan glanced down at her. Her eyes were wide open but glazed. She looked afraid.

Megan's mind whirled. She had to stay alert. She had to remember everything.

The men drove the winding, curvy road three-quarters of the way around the lake. Megan heard the clicking of the turn indicator and felt the vehicle begin to slow. They turned onto a dirt road that led off to the right. She had made herself stay alert and concentrate during the entire drive from the Arrowhead Village turnoff, focusing on any landmark that stood out to her. She sat up straighter and searched both sides of the road for anything that would mark the turnoff.

There, she thought, looking down the road a ways to her left. A decorative, wrought iron gate marked the entrance to a driveway leading down through the trees to a cabin. Megan's gaze slid to the right of the gate, where an unusual wooden mailbox stood. A plank with the cabin owner's name, *Wolfe,* had been nailed directly below it.

The mailbox was a miniature replica of an A-frame cabin. It had rough-hewn log siding, a small porch, and a shingled roof with a tiny brick chimney. She memorized the look of the mailbox and the name using a memory trick her father had taught her. The image of a ferocious wolf crushing the mailbox in his jaws stuck in her mind.

The SUV gained speed as they climbed the sinuous mountain road toward the research facility. Sarah reached out and took Megan's hand. Megan squeezed it gently. Her eyes continued to skip over the road, searching out landmarks.

She had to know the way to go when they escaped.

And they would escape. She was sure of it.

Chapter 25

Beth pulled to a stop in front of Alexandra's Emporium shop and shut off the engine. It was peaceful in the empty parking lot of Arrowhead Village as dawn broke. Light began streaking through the surrounding trees, transforming the landscape of the mile-high mountain resort town. She looked over at Max, who was still asleep, and decided not to wake him. Mark would arrive in about an hour.

He had called earlier to let them know that his contact at the station had done a computer check on the license plate and confirmed the SUV had a LoJack on board. They had discussed the likely probability that the SUV was headed towards Arrowhead. Mark would call back only if he found out something different once they activated the LoJack. Otherwise, he'd meet them in the Arrowhead Village parking lot.

Beth had insisted Max let her drive while he rested on the drive up to Arrowhead. The commute had been long and quiet.

Beth glanced up the way at the shops that lined the open-air promenade. She hadn't been up here in years, and she was struck by how everything looked almost exactly the way she remembered it.

She looked down at Max, and her mind began to drift. She could see them wandering through the shops on the upper promenade, enjoying a bright Spring day...

Stop it! she chastised herself. *There you go again. California Dreamin'. Wait'll this is all over, girl. When Megan is safe and sound, and things get back to normal. Then see what happens. Maybe something...maybe nothing.*

Beth leaned her head back on the headrest. She looked down at Max sleeping peacefully and then gazed out the window to her left. Mark would be driving up from that direction.

Tiredness rolled over her like a thick, incoming fog. Her eyelids grew heavy. *Maybe I could close them. Just a little. Just for a minute.*

A sharp rapping on her window startled Beth awake. Seconds after closing her eyes, she had fallen asleep and straight into a vivid dream. She opened her eyes and saw Mark standing outside her window. He smiled and raised a box of Krispy Kreme donuts and a cardboard holder with three cups of coffee.

Beth fumbled with the keys in the ignition and pushed the button on the power window.

"Mark...Sorry, I must have dozed off."

He laughed. "Yeah, I was checking your window for nose prints and slobber. Guess you guys didn't get a whole lotta sleep last night."

"Amen to that," she said, arching her back and stretching. "And I got a lot more than Max. He took first watch and then didn't wake me up on time. All he got was a quickie nap on the drive up here."

"Quickie's too generous a term," Max said, sitting up in his seat and rubbing the sleep from his eyes. "Feels like I shut my eyes a minute ago."

"Aw quit'cher bellyaching," Mark quipped. "That's what my old Grandma used to say."

"Yeah? Well, you and your old grandma didn't stay up all night."

"Hey, leave my grandma out of this. And besides, when the goin' gets tough, real men get by on one hour of sleep as long as they've got donuts and coffee for breakfast." Mark raised the box again.

Max stared at the donuts for an exaggerated moment and then broke into a grin. "All right, dude. You win. Get in here. I'm starved!"

Mark filled them in on what he'd found out while they ate.

"After a bunch of phone calls, I nailed some key pieces of info down. We got a bulls-eye on the LoJack. Also confirmed the owner's name, address, age—the whole enchilada—off the plate number. The plate is linked to a vehicle with the exact description of ours."

"Great," Max said, handing Mark the box of donuts.

"Turns out this SUV is a 2015 Expedition and hasn't been reported stolen. Of course, no one answered when we called the owner's address so we couldn't confirm it. Anyway, the LoJack turned on clean as a whistle and is tracking like a mother. You know Kit Perkins, don't you?"

Mark squinted in recognition. "I think I met him a few years back at a SWAT shooting competition. Why?"

"He's one of my key contacts inside. He's a wizard at LoJack and a lot of perp ID tricks and procedures…knows who to go to and how to get what he's after. I had a hell of a time getting a hold of him this morning though. He got pulled into some early morning meetings, and I had to call around to even find him. Ten minutes after I talked to him, he called me back and had all the info on the Expedition. And he'd activated the LoJack."

"So, they're up here?"

"They're definitely up here. The Expedition was headed this direction from the get-go. When I checked in a half hour ago, Kit told me they were already halfway around the main lake past the turnoff for the community hospital and headed toward the north shore. Figure they've probably reached their destination by now."

Max took another sip of coffee. His mind was running ninety miles a minute.

"How are we going to follow where they're going without a map? You know the area up here really well?"

"No better than you do," Mark said. "But no problem. I ran a buncha Google maps of Arrowhead off the web with zoom-ins for all the street names and e-mailed them to Kit. We can coordinate the tracking location on our maps over the phone. Here are our copies."

Max flipped through the half-dozen sheets, tracing 173 around the lake and stopping to study the street names around Shelter Cove and off North Shore Rd. and North Bay Rd. on the northern side of the lake. He could visualize the gorgeous, heavily forested area, and wondered where Viralvector's lab was hidden away.

"How about if we call Kit again and see if they've stopped moving?"

"We can call while we're rolling. We know they're headed to the North Shore."

"Let's go," Mark said. "I'll grab the gear out of my car and throw it in the back. Time to turn 'n burn."

Chapter 26

They pulled to a stop at the end of the side road under a towering canopy of pine trees. Megan was surprised by the appearance of their destination. She thought they were going to another laboratory building like the one they had just come from, not the chalet-like complex before them. It looked more like a ritzy mountain resort than a corporate building.

The main building was two stories high with an upscale log cabin exterior. Finely cut logs and planks were notched and fitted with seamless notch and groove precision. A wrap-around porch with an elaborate but not ostentatious carved railing and a rugged shingle roof completed the look. The logs and planks were stained in a glistening golden brown.

Two additional structures stood behind the main building. They were similar in basic appearance to the first but slightly smaller in size. At the rear of the property was a metal shed big enough to house half a dozen cars. They entered the cool darkness of the cavernous metallic shelter. The driver stopped. An aluminum roll-up door descended behind them, closing off the doublewide entrance. Dim illumination framed the presence of three additional sport utility vehicles, a skip loader, and two snowmobiles.

Megan and Sarah were hurried out of the SUV, which was left idling in a parking space, and shuttled through a side door into the brightness of the burgeoning dawn. The man and the nurse held their hands as they rushed them diagonally across the property, down the driveway, and into the main building.

The ultramodern interior of the building was as much a surprise to Megan as the exterior of the building, and it made her think she was back down in the Viralvector headquarters building in Rancho Santa Margarita. The man walked off down another corridor; the nurse continued to herd them down the hallway, through several connecting corridors, past offices and laboratories, to a room that had been outfitted and decorated to be their living quarters.

"I don't want to hear a peep out of either of you. Understand?" The nurse's voice was cold and harsh. "You know the routine, Sarah. Make sure your new friend here learns it real quick."

Sarah stood there with her head down and her hands clasped in front of her. "I will, Miss Creade."

"I *know* you will," she said. The unspoken threat hung in the air.

The two girls looked at each other. Sarah's eyes were wide, and Megan's eyebrows climbed upward.

"The two of you've got tons of toys, games, books, and movies in here to keep you busy, but you will be *silent*. Nothing louder than the TV turned down low. Breakfast trays come at seven. Tests have been scheduled for both of you today. I expect you to be quiet and fully cooperative."

The nurse turned and looked directly at Megan. Her focused stare gave Megan the creeps.

"Simple rules," she rasped. "Do exactly what you're told or you get punished. *Severely.* Are we clear on that?"

Megan gulped. She met the nurse's stare and held it for a moment before nodding.

"Remember. No noise. Not a squeak." She turned and left, slamming the door shut.

Megan turned to Sarah with a hint of resigned disgust on her face. "Geez, whatta witch. What happened? She lose her broom?"

Sarah giggled.

"I know I asked you this before," Megan said, "but is she always this awful?"

Sarah shrugged. "Guess I'm used to it. She's pretty crabby most of the time, but she's been nice to me before…well, at least once."

Megan looked around the room. "So, here we are, up in the 'mountain place' you were talking about. Is this the room you stayed in last time?"

"No. My room's way in the back." Her eyes trailed from one wall to the next. "They must've fixed this room up. It had mops and storage stuff in it."

"I don't think we're going to sleep here. There aren't any beds. Could be we'll end up in your room. Does it have two beds?"

Sarah's eyes grew wide. "My old one didn't. But last time they showed me where my new room is going to be. It's bigger than this one. They might have put two beds in it!"

"Maybe," Megan said. She walked over to the door and tried the doorknob. She kept looking around the room as she talked. "You said they showed you where the other girl's room is. What's her name again…Faith?"

"Mmhmm."

"Is her room right next to yours?"

"No. But it's close to my new room. Just down the hall."

Megan tried to gaze through the door's peephole and then walked over to the window and looked out. There was a reinforced screen mesh with eighth-inch steel rod grating covering the window. No burglars could get in. No little girls could get out.

"What's she like? I mean, you told me a bit about her before, but is she nice?"

"Yeah, she's nice. She's kinda quiet. And she won't answer when I ask her where she came from."

"Do you get to see her or play with her much?"

"Not really."

Megan put down the toy VW she was fiddling with and lifted the cardboard lid to a game of Candyland. She started tracing out the pathways with her finger, following Lollipop Lane through its curves to the Finish Zone.

"What about the boy?" she asked.

Sarah stared at her with a bashful expression. Megan didn't look up from the game board until the silence became obvious. She returned Sarah's stare, her eyes squinting quizzically as she broke into a smile.

"What's the matter? Cat got yer tongue?"

Sarah was silent a few seconds longer. A smile blossomed at the corner of her mouth. "No. My tongue's right here in my mouth. No stinky old cat's got it. See?"

She stuck her tongue out and blew a slobbery raspberry.

Megan laughed. "I can see that." She looked expectantly at Sarah and waited for her to talk.

"Which boy?" Sarah asked.

Megan gave her another quizzical look. "What do you mean…which boy? The one you and I talked about at the other place. Remember? I told you that the man in the white coat…Dr. Art…"

"Dr. Artel."

"Yeah, Dr. Artel said there were two girls there—you and Faith—and then he said there was a boy there too. He was supposed to be my age."

"You mean Eddie. He's ten. But there's another one too."

"There is? Wonder why the doctor didn't mention him. Who's the other one?"

"His name's Newt. I've only seen him once."

"Know anything about him?"

"I think his dad owns the company or something."

"Why do you think that?"

"He's got his own nurse who came with him, and I heard her talking to the other nurses. She was telling them about the really big house Newt lives in with all kinds of servants and rich stuff. Then she said something about his dad running the company and being the president."

"So, what's Newt like?"

"He's kinda strange. They said he's older than me, but there's something weird about him. We played together one time. He talked dumb and acted like a little crybaby."

"He could be one of those kids who's slow in the brain."

"You mean, like he was born that way?"

"Maybe," Megan said and shrugged. She walked over to the couch and sat down. There was a pile of movie DVDs stacked in the corner of the couch. She picked them up and started flipping through them. They were mostly Disney films mixed with a few Harry Potter movies. She picked one up and stared at the cover. It was *Moana*.

"Tell me about this guy named Eddie."

"He's really neat," Sarah said.

Megan smiled. She could tell Sarah liked him. "*And...*" she prodded.

"And he likes to play games, and he makes me laugh, and he's a lot of fun. I think you'd like him."

"I bet I would," Megan said. "You said he's what...ten?"

"Yep. He had a birthday a couple of weeks ago."

"Do you see him often...any more than you see Faith?"

Sarah scrunched up her brow. "No. About the same," she said. "He's definitely a lot more fun than Faith is. He always wants to play games...and he talks a lot and tells me jokes and funny stories."

"Sounds like he's lots of fun to play with."

Sarah grinned and energetically nodded her head.

"Did you get to go to his birthday party?"

Megan regretted asking the question the moment it left her mouth. She watched Sarah's cheerful expression plummet into glum resignation. Her face telegraphed the answer before she spoke it.

"No. They didn't have a party for him here."

"Did they even celebrate his birthday?"

Sarah sat down on the couch, but she didn't look at Megan. "All he said was he got a couple toys and books. I asked him if he had a party, but he said no and didn't want to talk about it."

"What about his parents? Does he ever get to see them? Does he live here like you do?"

Sarah shrugged. "I don't know. I ask him about all that stuff. He never answers."

Megan looked down at the pile of board games and thought about everything Sarah just told her. Nothing made any sense.

Her mind skipped through the events of the last twenty-four hours.

This is totally weird. First, they kidnap me so they can run a bunch of tests and experiments on me. Then I meet Sarah, who looks exactly like me and says she's "always" been here...like this is her home. And now I hear about the son of the company president who's kinda strange, and Faith and Eddie, who supposedly are nice but won't talk about their families or where they live. What the heck's goin' on here?

Megan glanced over at Sarah, who was staring at her with a quizzical awe. "What?"

Sarah blinked. "I don't get it," she said. "How can you look so much like me? Are you my twin sister or something?

"I can't be your twin, silly," Megan said. "I'm older than you. Twins are born at the same time. And I can't be your sister either. We have different moms."

Sarah thought for a few seconds then her eyes grew wide as another question bubbled up. "Where's your mom? Mine's here in one of the other buildings. She's awfully sick, and they don't let me see her, but she's here. Where's yours?"

Megan felt a pang stab at her heart like a sharp knife. It was a feeling that never seemed to go away completely. The pain was always there, ready to cut and slice even after all this time.

"She died two years ago," Megan said in a half-whisper.

Sarah gasped. "Your mommy…died?"

Megan squeezed her eyes shut and nodded.

Sarah stood there looking at her, mouth agape in disbelief.

"But…what happened?" Sarah asked. She scooted closer to Megan. "Mommies aren't supposed to die…least not till they get really old. What happened to her?"

"Car accident," Megan said in a dull monotone. We were driving home, just her and me, and this car ran us off the road. At least they told me that's what happened. I don't remember much from that night. All I know is I woke up on the ground. Our car was crashed into a tree twenty feet away, and it was all on fire. My mom was still in the car. That's where she died."

Megan teared up as the knife twisted in her heart. Her mouth opened in a silent cry of pain. She wiped her eye. Sarah leaned over and threw her arms around her. She buried her face in Megan's dress.

"I'm sorry your mommy's gone," Sarah said through a muffled sob.

Megan hugged her back. "I really miss her."

They held each other for a long time. When they finally pulled apart, they sat nose to nose, staring at each other.

"Hey, you want to play a game?" Megan asked, smiling through her tears. "They've got *Sorry!*"

Sarah grinned back at her. "Yeah! That'd be fun. But you're gonna have to teach me. I've never played it before."

"You haven't? It's a lot of fun. Let's play!"

They both sat down on the floor. Megan opened the box and set up the board as she told Sarah the rules of the game.

"Okay, here we go. You first!"

Chapter 27

The coffered walls of the boardroom were paneled in deep, rich cherry wood that stretched from floor to ceiling. Built-in bookshelves filled with scientific tomes both ancient and new lined the walls, and archaeological artifacts and century-old instruments lay scattered in archival displays on the shelves.

Blake Thornton, the president and CEO of Viralvector, Inc, sat behind a formidable desk at the far end of the room. His back was turned to a man in a white lab coat seated across the desk from him, immersed in a medical chart. It was his top research scientist, Calvin Lynch.

Thornton listened impatiently to the voice on the other end of the phone as he looked out the windows at the expansive pine forest that stretched down the mountainside. It was a scene of verdant beauty that on most days calmed his anger and enveloped him in tranquility. But this was not one of those days.

"What the hell do you mean they activated the LoJack on the SUV?" he barked. As he listened, his face swelled red, and a vein near his temple bulged.

"How could anyone know we brought them up here?" he shouted into the phone. "And who has the authority to activate a LoJack device without the vehicle being reported stolen *and* without the owner's approval?"

The voice on the other end of the phone sped through a possible scenario.

"Someone must have staked out the corporate office and seen the Expedition leave with the girls in the back seat. But what about the LoJack activation? Yeah, I know he's got connections with the Police Academy and a bunch of guys on the force. His contacts must have helped him out. Give me ten minutes. I'll call you back and tell you what we're going to do." He hung up.

What the hell are these clowns doing? He gritted his teeth, fighting the urge to throw his cell phone across the room.

Thornton swiveled around in his chair and looked across the desk at Calvin. "There's been a change of plans," he spat.

The tall, slender scientist's demeanor and movements were decidedly crane-like. He looked up, head tilted to one side, and glared at Thornton. His aquiline features and penetrating blue eyes supplemented his avian nuances, giving anyone who spoke with him the unsettling sensation of interacting with a bird of prey.

"What now?" he asked.

He was never one to defer to the power of higher management, and he had a clear perception of how indispensable he was to this project. "Are we going to have to move them *again*?"

Thornton was in no mood for complaints. "*Yes.* That's exactly what we're going to do."

Lynch gritted his teeth and stared at him with impatient resolve.

"Fine," he said. "But remember the detailed status report I gave you yesterday and the key points. One…" He flicked his index finger up in the air. "The boy and girl are showing a startlingly accelerated intellectual development and cognition enhancement at a rate that's nothing short of *spectacular*. Two…"

Another finger flicked up. "Their blood titers are precisely where we want them, and the PET scans show maximal hippocampal assimilation. Three…"

His hand closed into a tight fist. "We need to do the surgery *now*."

Thornton stared at him in focused silence. Eyes penetrating. Mind racing. Anger contained but simmering.

"All your points are well taken. I don't disagree. The critical timing of our situation is obvious, and nobody feels the pressure of this more than I do. My son is involved, remember? You'd better believe I'm feeling an overwhelming urgency to—"

"All the more reason to expedite the surgery."

"Yes, and have the police storm the place in the middle of the procedure," Thornton shot back. "We're not taking that chance. Surgery's on hold until after we move."

"And how long's *that* going to take?" Lynch made no effort to hide his anger and frustration.

"We'll leave early this afternoon. Surgery will take place the day after tomorrow."

They stared each other down, the silence between them filled with bristling tension.

A small eternity passed. Lynch exhaled audibly and was the first to speak.

"Fine. We operate the day after tomorrow. Which facility are we going to? Dallas or the place in Colorado?"

"Colorado," Thornton said without hesitation. "We'll transport via helicopter to Ontario International Airport and fly out on the corporate jet."

Lynch drummed his fingers on the chart. "What about the business with the LoJack activation? What's to stop them from finding this place and storming us before we leave?"

Thornton glared at him. "I already gave Derek and Ted strict instructions to lose the SUV after they dropped off the kids. They're miles away from here by now, somewhere down the mountain."

"They could've pegged this location already."

"The SUV dropped the kids off and started moving again in the less than a minute. To anybody tracking the signal locator, it would barely look like a stop."

"Granted," Lynch agreed. "But they could also have easily researched that our company has a facility up here and figured out where the SUVs—"

"I know that," Thornton interrupted. "That's why I'm having the kids shuttled over to the chalet on the other side of the lake. They'll be packed and rolling in ten minutes. The rest of us need to go there immediately. Logistical arrangements are being made for all of us to fly to Colorado late this morning. Grab the stuff you'll need and go. I'll meet you there in an hour."

Chapter 28

Drake waited for the nurse to turn the corner of the long hall before entering the nurses' station. The other nurse on graveyard shift had already left for her break, and with her partner on late-night rounds, the coast was clear. But only for a few minutes.

He rushed over to the center island and scanned the partitioned shelf that housed the patients' charts. His eyes chased the room numbers up to the 230s. He felt a sharp but not altogether unexpected smack of anger when he saw the chart for room 238 was missing.

Shoulda figured, he thought as he searched every countertop, chair, cart, and cabinet. *No way they'd leave a kidnapped girl's chart hanging around. Gotta go to plan B.*

He raced out of the station, down the hall, and into the nearest stairwell. Looking nonchalant but purposeful in case anyone noticed him, he exited on the first floor and strode down the hall until he reached the room that served as an adjunct of the business office. He glanced over his shoulder as he pulled a keyring out of his pocket. He slipped the largest of five keys into the door lock, turned the knob, and let himself in. The door locked behind him as it shut with a muffled clack.

Drake had been in this office several times before. He had sporadically dated a mousy data entry clerk named Tina who worked there. She was gullible enough to think he was actually attracted to her, and he'd strung her along, taking what he wanted from her but never quite letting her know where she stood with him. Their somewhat heated physical relationship was nothing more than a mildly amusing sport to him, a means to an end.

The second time she asked him over to her apartment, he'd managed to get ahold of her work keys, fabricated a sudden need to make a quick run to the store, and had copies made of all the keys. He'd found what a treasure trove he'd scored later that week when he tried out the keys and found they opened doors to most of the hospital administrative offices, including the locked filing cabinets of patients' records.

Mousy Tina had also unwittingly provided him access to the hospital's password-protected electronic database. Here, with a few keystrokes, he could access any patient's personal information and medical records, and as a major bonus, track the quantities, storage locations, and floor delivery times of his favorite narcotics and psychoactive pharmaceuticals.

Drake walked over to the computer workstation, turned on the unit, and sat down in front of the flat screen. The computer booted up rapidly, and he entered the password he'd stolen from Tina. After a minute of processing, the screen filled with the main Patient Records menu.

Drake had used this database many times. He knew exactly what he was after, but even so, that familiar illicit thrill rushed through him. He gripped the mouse tighter and scrolled down to the last names beginning with 'T'. *Tanner...Tosk...Tyler, Megan.* One click, and her medical record materialized on the screen.

Drake printed out the first two pages of her record, which included her home address, phone number, and emergency contact information. Max's work information and his cell phone number were also listed.

"No wonder he was such a pain in the ass when we mixed it up. Guy's a cop." He scanned the reference to the Police Academy then locked on the words 'Special Weapons and Tactics.'

"Not just a cop. He's some bad-ass SWAT dude," Drake muttered under his breath. He fingered the bandage on his shoulder. The wound throbbed painfully in spite of the dampening effect of the painkillers he was taking. *Son of a bitch is gonna pay big time.* Graphic pictures of attacking and stabbing Max filled his mind. *I'll teach him to cut me up...give him what he deserves. But right before he dies, he's gonna watch me off his daughter.*

The thought gave him grim satisfaction. He smiled when he imagined killing Max's daughter in front of him. Bullet, knife, bat to the head—there were so many choices. He visualized Max's face wracked in horrified anguish as he placed a gun to the girl's head, pulled the trigger, and watched her head explode in a blur of red.

"Now how do I want to set this up?" he whispered out loud. His mind shifted into planning mode. He'd have to make this his best plan *ever*.

Before exiting the system, he pulled up the medication inventory program and printed out the current levels and locations of the hospital's entire stock of narcotics and controlled substances.

Need to make a quick stop for some goodies...

He shut down the computer and turned off the monitor. After checking the desk area to make sure everything was just as he'd found it, he flipped off the light switch and slipped out of the office.

Chapter 29

Blake Thornton opened the door and stood in the doorway. His seven-year-old son, Newt, was busy stacking blocks on the floor in the far corner. He had already assembled nearly a hundred of the colorful wooden cubes into a triangular-shaped tower that stood almost three feet tall. Newt didn't look up when Thornton approached. He could hear the boy muttering to himself. He listened for a moment and realized his son was repeating the numbers and letters on the blocks as he set them in place, pronouncing them with clarity and precision.

Newt had Down Syndrome. When Newt was born, Thornton's first reaction was rage and denial. He'd been sure there must have been some mistake when the nurses told him. He demanded that Newt be retested a second and third time. He took his anger out on the doctors, nurses, and the diagnostic lab technicians, convinced that somebody had screwed up the test results.

By the next day, he had calmed down and forced himself to analyze the medical reality of his son's condition.

He researched the genetic disorder and talked to several experts to confirm what he'd always thought, that there was a range of capability and potential among those born with the syndrome. Different genetics rendered those with trisomy 21 a different potential level of functioning in society, and all of them benefited by an enriched environment and attention-filled upbringing.

Thornton had made sure Newt had every possible enrichment from his first day of life, but Newt had not been on the high achieving end of the Down spectrum. The possibility of him living alone and making it on his own when he grew older was slim.

He'd had deep suspicions about his wife, Cassandra. He wasn't known for his fidelity to his wife, but the possibility that Newt wasn't his child plagued his psyche and continually flared his anger.

After they returned home from the hospital, he demanded a paternity DNA test on Newt. He had samples sent to two different companies. Both results had been identical. With a probability of error of less than one in two billion, he was absolutely and certifiably Newt's father. From that point forward, he'd detached himself from Newt, viewing his son as a scientific challenge, a test subject and nothing more.

The first two years of Newt's life he'd remained distant, burying himself in his work, spending late nights at the office and many weekends away. During that time, he successfully negotiated the very lucrative sale of his first biotech company and founded Viralvector, Inc.

It wasn't long after this that Cassandra decided she wasn't cut out for motherhood—especially the mothering of a Down syndrome child. She began to rely more and more on the nanny and the educational therapist they'd hired to take care of Newt. She was rarely at home, and when she was, she paid little attention to her son. To get back into hard-body shape, she hired a trainer and slaved through intense aerobics classes and gym workouts. Then she insisted that Thornton pay for plastic surgery enhancements, dermatologic face treatments, and beauty and fashion advisors. The result was a stunning transformation.

It didn't take her much time to rejoin the exclusive social circuit of high society parties and events that had filled her days prior to her marriage. With her husband continuously out of town or working late, Cassandra had plenty of social opportunities to flirt and seduce at will.

She had several tempestuous affairs over the next few years. Thornton caught her on one occasion, but he was sure it was only a drop in the bucket. It was all over when Cassandra landed the big fish, a Silicon Valley billionaire who had gained his vast wealth by selling three disruptive technology start-up companies. The man was completely smitten with Cassandra. He left his wife and three children for her. After his vicious and prolonged divorce, Cassandra moved in with him and filed her own proceedings against Blake. Their divorce, now close to being final, was proving to be every bit as vicious. Ever since she'd moved out, Cassandra hadn't even bothered to see Newt. It was if he didn't exist.

Newt lost both parents the day his mother discarded him and set off on her new childless life. She disappeared completely, and Thornton remained detached and nothing more than a cold scientific investigator.

Fixing Newt became Thornton's biggest scientific challenge. His all-encompassing obsession. He was driven by the prospect of achieving a scientific breakthrough that would gain him international acclaim in both the scientific and lay community, not to mention a vast fortune since the process would be patent-protected. Venture capitalists were already lining up trying to induce him to spin off this area of research into another company so they could launch a second IPO. But he didn't need their money and didn't want them sharing in his profile. He held sixty-five percent of Viralvector shares, and once this breakthrough was announced and commercialized, the stock price would quadruple, making him a billionaire.

Thornton had concentrated his entire research platform and all of his company's resources on developing and perfecting the use of viral vectors and CRISPR-Cas9 for gene transfer, alteration, and neuron growth stimulation. He was certain the tens of millions he'd spent were about to pay off. The final stage was about to begin.

He watched with clinical detachment for a minute longer and then fired off a quick assessment test.

"Newt."

The little boy turned around and faced him. "Yeah?"

"What's three times four?"

"Twelve," Newt said.

"How about six plus eighteen minus nine?"

"Fifteen."

"Who were the first three presidents of the United States?"

Newt didn't even need to think about it. "George Washington, John Quincy Adams, and Thomas Jefferson."

"Good," Thornton said. "We're going to be leaving here in a few minutes, so pick out a couple of toys you want to take with you."

"Where are we going?" Newt asked, tilting his head. Thornton noted that his facial expressions had become more focused and defined.

"To a house on the other side of the lake."

"What are we gonna do there?"

Thornton had no time for this. "Look, just get ready. We're leaving right away. You'll find out when we get there."

He turned and left in a hurry.

"D...Daddy...?" Newt asked as Thornton disappeared. He waited for a response, but none came other than the sound of steps receding down the hall.

Next collected four of the colorful blocks—his four favorite numbers—and stood in the middle of the room, waiting for his dad to come back.

Chapter 30

Max accelerated through the winding curves, pushing the Suburban to the limits of its cornering ability. The tires squealed in the sharper turns but gripped the road throughout, negotiating the turns surprisingly well. The high center-of-gravity Suburban was a rollover risk, and Max was compensating as best he could, but there was no time to spare. His heartbeat ticked like an oversized clock.

Sunlight streamed through the towering canopy of the pine forest. The sunrise was breathtaking, but the beautiful scenery whipped by unnoticed.

"You're seeing *what*!?" Mark barked into his cell phone. "C'mon, Kit. You're kidding, right? They turned around and are heading back *towards* Arrowhead Village?"

Max glanced at Mark in the rearview mirror and saw a look of surprise on his face.

"And you've been trackin' them the whole way?"

Mark took a quick look at the scenery and then studied one of the map printouts he'd brought along.

"They stopped somewhere near Shelter Cove off North Shore Road on the northeast side of the lake? That's right about where we figured they were headed. We've got an approximate location up here for a secondary Viralvector facility they're building. It's gotta be where they stopped."

He traced his finger on the map along highway 173 to the location then back down along the east side of the lake and around the southern loop toward the west side. He stopped at their approximate location.

"What? Yeah. We're movin' fast toward the south side of Lake Arrowhead. Current location about three-quarters of the way to Papoose Lake from Arrowhead Village. You said the target's where?"

Mark gulped down another bite of donut.

"Geez, no kidding! We gotta be comin' up on them. Hold on a minute." He held the cell phone face down on his leg. "Max, listen to this. The SUV is headed back toward us. It's just made the looping turn at Papoose Lake coming towards the Village. ETA's two to three minutes. Two ships passing…"

"Hang up and get the scanner scope ready," Max said. "I bet they dropped Megan off and now the SUV's scattering. Cab service."

Mark raised his phone. "Hey Kit, gotta go. Do me a favor, will you? Keep an eye on the SUV's transit for another hour and let me know where it ends up. We got a feeling it was a limo ride up here to drop Megan off. I'll buzz you later. Thanks."

Mark pocketed his cell phone and raised the scanner scope digital recorder.

They were accelerating out of a long turn when the SUV came racing towards them in the opposing lane. The polished silver SUV glistened in the radiating sunbeams. Beth squinted against the glare and pointed. "Incoming at eleven o'clock."

Mark raised the scanner scope and pointed it at the oncoming vehicle. He pushed the record button as he locked onto his target.

"Say 'cheese' and gimme a smile," Mark said.

The image in the viewfinder morphed into an iridescent, surrealistic x-ray image when he pushed another switch. The skeletal outline of the driver appeared in sharp contrast to the vehicle's interior. It was a head-on view.

"Bad guys comin' around the curve…captured on film by a CNN news crew…"

The SUV raced past them at maximum speed, the driver oblivious to their presence.

Beth strained to see if there were any other occupants besides the driver. As far as she could see, he was alone. The middle seats, back seats, and back cargo area looked empty, but that didn't mean Megan wasn't lying on the seat or the floor, forced down out of sight.

Mark scanned the vehicle with the scope. The driver was alone.

"All's clear," he said, scoping the back of the SUV as it sped away from them and disappeared around a curve. "Just like we thought. They dropped off Megan and scattered."

"License plate check out?" Max asked.

Mark rewound the recording and toggled a modal review switch on the side of the scanner scope. He played back the last few seconds in standard view and slowed the action down to a near standstill. He zoomed in on the vehicle's rear license plate.

"That's a big affirmative. Vehicle and license are identical to what I filmed down at Viralvector. Same SUV you chased up here. Silver-gray Ford Expedition."

"Okay," Mark said. "Let's get to Viralvector's second office. It's in the Shelter Cove area, right?"

Beth flipped through the pile of map printouts and stopped at one showing an enlarged view of the northern half of the lake. She traced the path of road 173 into the area and studied the street names around Shelter Cove.

"It's off North Shore Road and North Bay Road. We're on 173. We'll take this up and turn left onto North Shore Road."

"It's right on North Shore?"

"Just off it."

"The asterisk marks the spot where Kit said the SUV stopped," Mark interjected. "He said it was on a street off North Shore. I scribbled the name down on the map. Pine something…"

"Yeah, here it is," Beth said. "Pine Hollow."

"That's it. There was something else too. When Kit checked out the street on an expanded map, he said it was pretty squirrelly. Basically a private road with no other addresses on it. The boys at Viralvector must have had the street put in when their building was built. They could own the street too."

"Doesn't surprise me," Max said. He looked over at Beth and then glanced in the rearview mirror, catching Mark's eyes.

"We're close," he said. "We'll be there in less than ten minutes. Chow down the rest of your donuts and get ready."

Pine Hollow Drive was not quite what Max expected. He turned onto the road, drove down a ways, and pulled over to the side, leaving the engine running as he surveyed the surrounding area.

The road had been carved out of the forest. It stretched a quarter of a mile down a corridor lined by a towering, verdant canopy. The forest around them was dense with intermingled Douglas fir and cedar trees. A main building and a second shorter structure could be seen at the road's end, but to Max, it didn't look at all like the setting for a corporate office.

"You sure this is it?" Max asked.

Beth flipped through the papers on her lap and found the one she was looking for—an enlarged map of the area on the driving directions printout.

"It's gotta be," she said, looking up from the map. Max handed her a pair of binoculars. She zoomed in on a fleck of white in front of the building to the right of the entrance.

"Here, check out the numbers on that sign by the front steps. It's hard to see, but it matches the address we're looking for."

Max took the binoculars from her and scanned the road all the way to the building a quarter of a mile away. No sign of people or any activity.

He centered the field of view on the steps that led up to the front of the building and then focused the powerful Zeiss 12x56 binoculars on the sign.

"This is it. Gear up and get ready to jump. We're going in."

Chapter 31

Max pulled to a stop at the right rear side of the building near the towering shed. Mark opened the door and bolted out of the back seat. He held the digital camcorder in one hand and darted inside the structure. He quickly checked for people as he took in the contents of the spacious warehouse. Switching the digital scanner to x-ray mode, he scrutinized the entire interior. No signs of anyone.

He was sure his surroundings were clear, but he wasn't taking any chances of being detected. He crept through the warehouse, weaving between storage boxes, vehicles, and machinery. When he reached the far end of the shed, he whispered into the tiny microphone transmitter attached to the collar of his shirt.

"Nobody around. Nothing in here but two trucks, a tractor, a couple of snowmobiles, and a bunch of tools and construction equipment. And no SUVs in sight…"

"Okay, move on," Max said. "We're sticking with Plan A. Cover the back of the building and gain entry. Beth and I are going in according to plan. I'll contact you as soon as I've secured my area."

"Will do," Mark confirmed. "I'll be in position in three minutes and inside in five."

Max and Beth checked their gear and their collar transmitters and then climbed out of the Suburban.

They fanned out. Beth approached the front entrance while Max darted to a metal, window-less, double door on the side of the building that appeared to be used for stock deliveries.

Max tried the turn handle, but as he expected, the door was locked. He bent down and assessed the make and model of the deadbolt, a higher-end, industrial-grade Schlage. A picture of the inner lock mechanism and the complex alignment of pins and tumblers appeared in his mind.

As a teenager, he'd spent three summers working with his uncle, a master locksmith, and had mastered the inner workings of virtually every major type of lock. He'd handled hundreds of locks over the years, dismantling, studying, and reassembling them. He'd never come up against a lock he couldn't master.

He pulled out a leather wrap case and selected a thin, ultra-narrow blade and a slivery, needle-like rod, both of which resembled short dental instruments.

He slid the blade into the lock and lodged it against the tumbler pin. Holding down the pin cam with the needle pick, he used the blade to depress the multiple tumbler pins and felt the muffled clack as they slid into position, releasing the locking mechanism.

Max twisted the handle down and pushed the door open, stepping through into the darkened room. He turned around and examined his surroundings. He was standing in a delivery storage room filled with stacks of moving boxes, office furniture, and laboratory equipment. He slipped through the maze of obstacles and reached the door to the hallway, where he paused for a full minute, listening for any sounds of activity on the other side of the door. Then taking a deep breath, he opened the door and stepped into the brightly lit hallway.

He walked swiftly down the hall towards the reception area at the front, glancing through every doorway and pausing at the closed doors, ears straining to pick up any sound.

Most of the rooms were offices, but two of the rooms he explored were laboratories, and he came across a surgical suite with an attached recovery room.

He unlocked the front door and let Beth in.

"Anybody here?" she whispered.

Max shook his head. Beth sensed his unease. His eyes shifted, sweeping over the reception area. "And I checked all the rooms on my way up here."

"Seems a little odd."

"More than a little."

He spoke into the microphone clipped to his collar. "Mark, you read me? Are you in?"

"Sharp and clear," Mark said. "And Elvis is *in* the building."

"Where?"

"Just inside the hallway in the back. Doesn't look like anyone's around."

"Same here. We're standing in the main reception up front. Place looks deserted."

"Rooms secure?"

"Partially," Max said. "I cleared the rooms up the main hallway from the side entrance to the front. That's about three-quarters of the way back. There were two doors left to check back in the hallway at your end."

"I'll get 'em cleared. Where do we meet?"

"Back where you are. We'll quick check the rooms on our way back there and meet you in five."

"Five it is. Over."

Max and Beth made their way down the hallway, stopping to re-examine several of the rooms. Beth shot pictures of the reception area, offices, laboratories, and surgical suites. She paid particularly close attention to the laboratory equipment instrumentation and the surgical suites outfitted with state-of-the-art instruments and monitoring technology.

They met Mark as he was coming out of a meeting room halfway down the hall.

"Nothing?" Max asked.

"Zero-mundo." Mark shrugged. "Nobody home…".

"That's *not* what I expected."

"What now?" Beth asked. "I didn't expect us to walk into an empty building."

Mark opened the door of a hall closet. "And we're sure this is the right place…" he said, examining the supplies on the shelves.

"Positive," Beth said. "On the desk up front, I saw corporate headings on the stationary, and then there's this little item."

She clicked the review button on the back of her digital camera and looked through the pictures. She found the one she was after and turned the camera around for Mark to see. "Take a look at this."

On the screen was a clear picture of the wall behind the reception desk in the front lobby with the corporate logo and company name, Viralvector, Inc. in shiny chrome bas-relief.

"Okaaay…Looks like positive confirmation." Mark's face conveyed mock resignation, and he raised his hands in surrender. "Now what?"

Max glanced up the hall, reviewing the options that were popping into his mind. He turned back to Mark.

"Call up Kit and see where the SUV is. They must already be at the bottom of the hill. Have him send someone out to pick up the driver for questioning and impound the vehicle."

"Way ahead of you, buddy." Mark pulled out his cell phone. "We'll locate them in no time." He pivoted and took a few steps down the hall.

Max touched Beth on the arm. "Let's check out that first office again and see what we can dig up. I saw a file cabinet on the back wall we can go through. There's gotta be something in there that'll help us figure out where they went."

"Good place to start," Beth said. "And when we're through with that one, I want to look at the third office. You know, the one with the side hallway leading to it."

"The plush CEO's office we spotted?"

"That's the one. Rich cherry wood paneling, huge desk, built-in bookshelves, and wood file cabinets. There's bound to be confidential corporate files in that office."

"Let's go."

They hurried up the hall and turned into the office. Max headed straight over to the file cabinet and slid open the top drawer. Beth went to the plain desk in the center of the room and sat down. The flat computer screen on top of the desk was dark, and stuck to its base were several sticky notes with call reminders scribbled on them. Beth read the notes and dismissed them.

After checking a short stack of papers neatly stacked on the right side of the desk, she went through the two desk drawers, paying close attention to the bottom one that was packed full of manila folders. She flipped through the files and found nothing more than standard business correspondence, form letters, vendor account records, and current utility statements.

She looked around the spartan office; there was nothing else to check besides the desk and the file cabinet in the corner.

Max was going through the last files in the third drawer. He finished, pushed the drawer shut, and opened the fourth and the bottommost drawer.

"Find anything?" Beth asked.

"Nada. How about you?" He started opening files and skimming them for key information.

"Zip."

Max took a few minutes to finish checking all of the files. With a frustrated groan, he stuffed the last one back into place and slammed the drawer shut.

"Well, that was basically worthless," Max said. "Time to hit the CEO's private office."

Beth was already halfway out the door. She turned and shot him a look. "Hopefully we'll have better luck there."

Beth walked to the center of the CEO'S office and turned in a circle, her eyes taking in the palpable richness of the cherry wood paneling and coffered walls. An august aura of importance permeated the room and hung suspended like a fog.

Someone's inner sanctum, all right, Beth thought.

She looked at the floor to ceiling built-in bookshelves that lined the back wall, her eyes shifting from the dusty books on the top shelf to the newer scientific texts, to the archaeological relics and antique instruments that lay in posed in various locations on the shelves, giving a formidable museum quality to the room.

Max walked into the room and stood behind her. "Okay. This is seriously impressive," he said. "What is this Viralvector CEO's name? Thorn-something?"

"Thornton...Blake Thornton."

"Yeah...well, it's obvious he's into power decorating. This place is dripping with intimidation. I'm sure it's just the way he likes it."

"This is definitely Ego Central," Beth said. "I bet Thornton's a self-obsessed tyrant. Must be loads of fun to work for him."

She walked over behind the massive cherry wood desk in the center of the room. Three papers were stacked to one side of the immaculate desk alongside an expensive Mont Blanc desk pen set with matching letter opener and notepad holder, a multi-line corporate speakerphone, and a large flat screen computer monitor.

Beth reached under the middle of the desk and slid out the computer keyboard tray.

"I knew I remembered this being on," Beth said, pointing to the computer screen. The words *Viralvector—Discovering Tomorrow's Medical Advances Today* undulated across the screen in a ceaseless Moebius circuit.

Beth moved the mouse, and the screen saver disappeared. A white password box materialized in the center of the bluish gray screen.

"Figures," Beth said. "Too much to hope for that the screen would be unlocked."

She sat down in the desk chair and surveyed the drawers on the front of the massive desk.

Max walked over to a built-in file cabinet next to the bookshelf.

"Let's see what we've got," he said, sliding open the top drawer and pulling out the first file folder.

Beth opened each of the desk drawers on the left side and worked her way through the contents of the top two drawers.

In the bottom drawer, underneath some empty folders and a pile of old *Time* magazines, she found a folder with the words *Newt—pictures* scrawled on the tab.

She opened it and found a full name written out: *Issac Newton Thornton.* Next to the name were the date and time of his birth along with his weight and length.

This must be Thornton's son, Beth thought. *Newton. Newt.*

The folder contained a small stack of pictures of a newborn in the hospital. Beth flipped through several that showed Thornton's son in the baby ward and cuddled in his mother's arms in the hospital room. One picture jumped out at her. It showed a man posing at bedside with the mother and baby.

Beth instantly recognized Thornton from a picture she'd seen in one of the Viralvector, Inc. annual reports.

She set the photograph aside before thumbing through the remaining dozen or so pictures. There were a few shots of Newt being brought home from the hospital, and the rest were of him from three months old on up to his first birthday party.

There were no pictures after that.

That's odd, Beth thought, calculating Newt's age from his birth date. *He's seven now. Why no more pictures?*

She dug through the bottom of the drawer, but there was nothing there but a scattering of half-blank papers. She pushed it shut and searched the top two drawers on the right side of the desk, which only contained office supplies. Then she tried the bottom drawer.

Locked.

Max was leafing through the folders in the top file cabinet, searching the titles for anything that could point them in the right direction.

"Find anything?" he asked, slamming the top drawer shut. He opened the second and began thumbing through the folders. "So far, all that's here are boring employee records and some files on competitors."

"Nothing yet," Beth said. "But can you come over here? I have a lock I need you to pick."

"Somehow I think I can manage that," Max said, walking over to the desk. He pulled out his leather case and opened the flaps. Sizing up the lock, he selected two ultra-fine, curved wires and slid them into the opening. He manipulated them briefly and rotated the mechanism to the left. There was a soft clack.

"Open sesame," Max said, sliding the drawer out.

"That sure wasn't much of a challenge," Beth said. "Remind me never to feel safe behind a locked door anymore."

Max grinned. "Yeah, well keep feeling safe. Your average street thug can barely tie his shoes. Put him up against a good dead-bolt and he's not going to—"

"Hey, guys…" Mark interrupted, rushing into the room. "Bad news."

"What is it?" Max stood and spun to face him.

"I just hung up with Kit. The SUV never made it to the bottom of the hill."

"Never made it? What do you mean? It pulled off somewhere?"

"It didn't make it. Less than halfway down the hill, somewhere around the Crestline turn-off, it took a dive off the side of the road. Tumbled four or five hundred feet to the canyon floor below, lit up, and burned to a crisp."

"And nobody was on board, right?" Max said.

"Don't know," Mark said with a shrug. "It'll take them another couple of hours to get to the wreck and go through it."

Max's face tightened with determination. He glanced down at Beth, who returned a look of steely resolve.

"Buried in these files or on this computer is information that will tell us where they're taking Megan," Max said. "There could be a third facility. And it could be anywhere."

"Then let's find it," Beth said. She picked up the first file in the drawer and began to read.

Chapter 32

The Bombardier Learjet 45 XR began its initial descent into the Denver International Airport. The downward pull of the executive jet was noticeable but not unpleasant to most of the ten passengers on board. Most, but not all.

Sarah reached over and took Megan's hand as the jet hit a patch of mild turbulence. It thumped sporadically as the plane dropped in altitude.

"Are you scared?" Megan whispered.

Sarah squeezed Megan's hand and gave her an anxious look.

"Don't worry," Megan said in as comforting a voice as she could muster. "There's nothing to be scared about."

"But what if we crash?" Sarah squeaked.

"We aren't going to crash. I've flown a couple of times. Sometimes it gets bumpy, that's all. It's no big deal."

Megan's brave words belied the butterflies fluttering in her own stomach. Sarah's eyes begged Megan to lessen her fear, so she smiled and tried to put on a brave face.

Twenty-five minutes later, the Learjet landed smoothly and taxied for several minutes before coming to a stop near their landing gate.

"Okay, kids. Grab your backpacks and let's go," Nurse Creade barked in her usual gruff tone. "And I want all four of you to stay together and close to me."

Megan, Sarah, Faith, and Eddie stood up and made their way up the aisle to the front of the plane. With no luggage to pick up at the baggage claim, they moved through the airport in record time.

A caravan of three SUVs was waiting for them in front of the airport. The third vehicle was full of Viralvector security personnel. As instructed, Megan and the others marched silently out to the curb and climbed aboard the second SUV.

When they were buckled in and underway, Megan felt Sarah take hold of her hand again. She leaned over and whispered in Sarah's ear. "Have they brought you here before…to Colorado?"

"No," Sarah whispered back. "I've never even been out of California."

"Me neither. Wonder where they're taking us."

"Probably another lab or something." Megan felt the heavy weight of Sarah's head rest on her shoulder. They were both exhausted.

Megan looked out the window wistfully. *How's my Dad supposed to find us now?*

Sarah tugged on Megan's shirtsleeve. Megan bent her ear close to Sarah's mouth. "Do you think your dad's really gonna come rescue you?"

"He'll come. I know he'll come for me," she said with absolute certainty.

"Do you think…" she started to say then hesitated.

Megan waited as several moments passed. Just when she decided that Sarah wasn't going to finish her question, she did.

"Do you think…I could come with you? And, uh…maybe even…live with you?"

Megan felt a wave of empathy wash over her. She squeezed Sarah's hand. "Sarah, I swear I'm getting out of here somehow, and I promise I'll take you with me. When this is all over, I don't know if my dad will let you come live with us…but I'll sure ask him."

Sarah looked at her with bright eyes and a wide smile. "You mean it? Really?"

"Yeah, I do. I can't promise what he'll say, but I'll ask."

Megan's expression became serious as she looked into Sarah's eyes. The eerie sensation of looking into a mirror of her younger self flitted inside her.

"Listen to me, Sarah," she whispered. This is so important. No matter what, we've got to be super alert and ready at any second to get away."

"I'll be ready," Sarah whispered.

They drove out of the Denver metropolitan area and made their way west and then southwest, passing through Silverthorne and Frisco and on through Leadville and Rios, a trip that would take two and a half hours. Beyond Rios was a highway 82 turnoff they would take at Twin Lakes that would lead them close to their destination. If followed for an additional thirty miles, the highway wound through the heavily forested mountains all the way up to Aspen.

Sarah dozed for an hour, but Megan couldn't contain her thoughts enough to sleep. When Sarah woke up, they played a memory game that Megan devised.

"We've got to remember *everything* we can about where we've been and where we're going…"

"…so we'll know where to go when we get away."

"Right," Megan said. She looked over her shoulder at Faith and Eddie in the back seat. They were talking about a picture Eddie was drawing on a note pad.

"Boy, with all the signs and buildings and stuff you remember, you sure have a great memory," Megan said. "Anybody ever tell you that?"

"Yeah, they tell me all the time that I've got an amazing memory. That's one of the things they keep testing me on."

Megan looked at her quizzically. "Who keeps testing you?"

"The doctors and some other people in white coats who work for them."

"But why would they test your memory over and over?"

Sarah shrugged. "I don't know. It's some kind of experiment. They always make me take a bunch of tests the day after I get my shots."

"Shots?" Megan winced. "I hate shots. They really hurt."

"I'm kinda used to it now. The needle's pretty big."

"Ow!" Megan said, cringing. "Needles totally creep me out. How often do they give you the shots?"

"Once a week."

"What?" Megan exclaimed and then slapped a hand over her mouth. She leaned over and whispered, "Oh, man, Sarah, every week? But I don't get it. Why would they give you shots and then test your memory?"

"Well, they don't *just* test my memory. They have me read really complicated stuff and then see if I understood what I read. Pages out of textbooks, science journals, that kind of stuff. I heard one of doctors talking to his assistant, and he said the shots were helping make me super smart."

"The *shots* were making you smart?"

Sarah nodded. "The doctors keep saying I can remember things better than ninety-nine people out of a hundred, and that I'm getting smarter every day. They're excited that I'm already reading and doing math at junior high school level."

"Geez, are you serious?" Megan couldn't hide her surprise. "But you're six years old. You should be in, what…first grade?"

Sarah shrugged. "I guess so…"

"What do you mean, you guess so. Don't you go to school?"

"Not to a real school. They bring a teacher in to teach me. Her name's Miss Peoples. I like her a lot."

Megan tried to imagine what it would be like not going to school.

"What's she like?"

"She's nice and funny. She makes learning stuff interesting and fun. And she's so pretty. You ever see the movie *Matilda?* "

"Yeah."

"Remember the teacher, Miss Honey, in the movie? Miss Peoples kind of reminds me of her."

"Boy, she must think you're some kinda genius or something if she's teaching you junior high school level classes."

Sarah smiled. "She says that the reason she's tutoring me is because I'm very smart and I need special attention. But the neat thing is she talked to the doctors, and she got their okay to take me on field trips to play with kids my own age."

"Sounds like fun," Megan said. "How often does she take you?"

"Not very often. About once a month. But it's always lots of fun. We go to the playground a lot, and sometimes they take me to the park or a museum. I've even been on a couple of field trips with a real first-grade school class."

"Sorry you can't play with them more."

Sarah looked away. "Yeah, me too."

Megan squeezed her hand and felt pangs of regret for the little girl sitting next to her.

"Sarah, keep your eyes open and remember everything you see, and I will too. We'll need it for later."

"Don't worry. I will. I'm taking pictures in my head," Sarah said.

Megan laughed at Sarah's impish expression and the sparkle in her eyes.

They drove another hour and a half, passing through gorgeous mountainous terrain and expansive valleys. Megan and Sarah stopped talking and paid more attention to the road, memorizing every sign, building, and natural landmark along the way.

Megan made ridiculous and exaggerated mental pictures of the names of towns and roadside landmarks and linked them in outrageous actions in her mind. She had no idea that memory experts had been using this mnemonic technique for years.

Megan was amazed at how easily she could remember things. She had consistently been a good student. Learning new information inside or outside of school had never felt like a chore. But something seemed different now.

Her mind was crystal clear and felt lightning-quick. She was convinced that she could learn anything effortlessly.

They eventually turned off the main highway. Sarah squeezed Megan's hand. "Remember..." she whispered.

"Everything..." Megan whispered back.

They drove another thirty to forty minutes along a weathered two-lane road that wove a sinuous path through a mountainous pass and descended into a heavily forested valley. A quarter of the way across the valley, they turned off onto a narrower road that meandered through an expansive grove of Aspen trees. Their passage cut through a thick sea of white trunks. High above them, an undulating canopy of oval leaves shimmered in flecks of green and silver in the afternoon sun.

The sparkling, wavy motion lulled Megan and Sarah with the feeling of entering a fairy tale forest replete with elves, pixies, and deep woods magic. Megan basked in one of the most beautiful sights she'd ever seen. "Wow, I can't believe it...it's so..."

"...pretty," Sarah said.

Megan nodded, at a loss for words.

They finally emerged from the towering arbor into the sunlight and continued along the road that skirted the perimeter of the forest.

It was another twenty minutes before they arrived at a building complex that was similar in look and feel to the one in Lake Arrowhead. It could easily be mistaken for a large cabin estate nestled in the protective shroud of a pine forest.

"Here we go," Sarah murmured.

"We won't be here long," Megan whispered. "We know the way out."

Chapter 33

Max jerked the second file cabinet drawer out as far as it would go and flipped through the files. He was working hard to contain his emotions. If he had any chance of rescuing Megan, he had to focus. He had to stay calm. Stay cool.

But man, were they going to pay.

Beth finished looking through the first file in the large bottom drawer and set it aside. She felt a hollow sense of dread when she read the section separator labels that partitioned the rest of the files. There were three main tabs: *Project—VIQ, Medical Records,* and *Future Projects.*

But it was the smaller tabs in the *Medical Records* section that sent a shiver skittering up her spine. The first tab read: *Newt Thornton.* Then *Faith Pearce, Eddie McClure, Sarah X.,* and finally, *Megan Tyler.*

Her eyes froze on Megan's name, and her heart skipped several beats as her chest clenched.

She sat there for a moment, frozen in her seat. Her mind refused to process the information. Then a wave of outrage shattered her paralysis. She grabbed her digital camera and snapped two close-up pictures of the open file drawer with the captioned tabs clearly visible.

A sickening void gripped her stomach as she lifted Megan's file out and began to read.

Three minutes later, she abruptly stood up, scooped all the file folders out of the drawer, and rushed for the door.

"I'm copying these. I'll be back when I'm done."

"What did you find?" Max asked, looking up just in time to see her race out of the room. She didn't hear him.

He turned and continued examining the countless files stuffed full of mind-numbing documents: scientific papers, US Patent office documents, construction invoices, and ancillary financial records.

He knew what he was looking for, and none of this was it.

He slammed the drawer and opened the next one, plowing into another folder filled collection of minutiae. Then the next.

After thoroughly searching all the folders in the next two drawers, he opened the final one, braced himself, and began looking through it.

C'mon...Something's gotta be here... He was three-quarters of the way into the drawer when he found it.

The files in the bottom drawer were partitioned alphabetically, and Max had just started the 'R' section. The first was a thick folder labeled *Reagents/Surg & Lab Misc.* It was filled with nearly a dozen files of different supplier companies containing nothing but brochures and transaction paperwork for lab chemicals, surgical instruments, and miscellaneous supplies.

The next section was labeled *Real Estate,* and it contained only three folders labeled *Rancho Santa Margarita, CA, Lake Arrowhead, CA,* and *Rios, CO.*

Rios, Colorado.

The name jumped out at him. *Is this it?* he thought. *Could they have taken Megan to a third location?*

He pulled out the thick manila folder and opened it. The first document was a copy of the Title Deed with a legal description of the property and its location. Behind it was a location map, a series of real estate transaction papers, and a few photos of a building under construction. The final photo showed the completed building complex, an expansive main building with an architecturally appealing wood exterior, and behind it stood two large ancillary wood structures. Both were cabinlike in structure, but the similarities stopped there. The main building looked identical to the one in the Lake Arrowhead complex in which Max was now standing.

This has to be it.

He flipped through the remaining papers in the front half of the folder, stopping to scan the project contract and invoices from the general contractor, and traced the chronology of construction from groundbreaking to turnkey completion. It had been completed in record-breaking time—less than four months.

A divider separated the last document from the next section, which contained a thick pile of invoices for office furniture and supplies, laboratory equipment, surgery suite furnishings, and miscellaneous items. All of the shipping invoices listed a remote address on the outskirts of Rios, Colorado.

Max grabbed the Colorado folder and left the room. He turned toward the front of the office and followed the soft humming of the copier machine.

He found Beth sitting on a folding chair. She was reading a file, deeply immersed in thought. A Xerox machine was swooshing behind her, churning out collated and stapled copies.

"Beth," Max said over the din of the copier machine.

She looked up but didn't seem to acknowledge him, staring straight past him at the wall. Her expression was a pained mixture of astonishment and outrage. She glanced down at the paper she was clutching then turned toward Max.

"Oh, those *sick* bastards…They're really doing it, Max."

"Doing what?" he asked. Fear and anger gripped his gut. The look of disgust she projected was palpable. He knew what she was going to say.

"The gene insertion experiments we talked about…not the ones using that technology to genetically alter and manipulate the growth of spinal nerve cells. I mean the ones where they're inserting genes into brain cells and making them grow."

Max gritted his teeth. *Stay Cool. Channel the anger.*

"And this time they're not experimenting on monkeys," he said in a steely monotone. His face looked as blank as his voice sounded. "They've already started doing this to Megan…"

Beth nodded. "It's all documented right here in her medical records. They're keeping a detailed file on her injection history. And they've got files on several other kids. I haven't had time to read them all yet, but I'm sure they'll be similar to Megan's."

Max dropped the files he was carrying and clenched his fists.

"I'll get her back," he vowed, looking through Beth at a distant, future battlefield. Conflict executed with extreme prejudice. "I'll get her back. And then I'll crush them into the ground."

"Max, I'm so sorry," Beth whispered. She reached out and touched his arm. "This is so evil and twisted. We'll find her. We'll rescue her."

"Yeah, we will." He bent to pick up the files. "And I think I know where they're taking her next."

Beth looked surprised. "What? Where?"

"I found a pile of information on all their properties in the file cabinet. It turns out they had files on three properties: the main headquarters in Rancho Santa Margarita, this property in Lake Arrowhead, and a third building complex in Rios, Colorado."

"Rios, Colorado?"

"Looks like a small town southwest of Denver…about a two-and-a-half-hour-drive down from there."

"What's in the Rios file?"

Max opened the folder. "Everything we need to know about the place. It's brand new. They just built it. The file's got a record of the construction timeline. There's a stack of pictures showing their progress all the way up until they finished the three buildings a few months ago. Then there's a thick file of receipts for furnishings like office furniture, lab equipment, and surgical suite supplies."

"Then that's got to be it," Beth said. "With a lab, surgical suite, and all that other stuff, it sounds like a mirror image of this place. They had to have taken her there…especially if I'm reading the medical records right."

"What do you mean?"

"I only had a chance to read Megan's file and scan the other kid's files. Hold on a minute." She opened Megan's folder again and re-read the last two pages. Then she opened Newt's and studied the last few pages of his file. She moved quickly through Faith and Eddie's files. When she got to Sarah's file, she slowed down. Her brow tightened and her eyes locked on the page. She picked up a pencil and underlined several sentences.

"Outrageous!" she exclaimed. "I thought I saw something about an operation and plans for more surgeries. The file on Newt, Sarah, and the other kids confirms it."

"What? Max asked, perplexed. "What do you mean *surgeries*? I thought you said they were doing gene insertion experiments. You know, like injecting them with something that traveled up their bloodstream and inserted genes into their brain cells."

Beth was staring at the last page of Sarah's file, oblivious to what Max was saying. Then she reread the medical record page in Newt's file.

"That *is* what they were doing…at first," she said in angry disbelief.

"Guess it was just phase one of the experiment." She looked up at Max. "What a sick perversion of medical ethics. How could they? I can't believe they're even thinking of doing this!"

Max stared at her. "*Surgery?*"

Beth opened Newt's file and ran her finger halfway down the next to last page to where the medical history and future treatment plans were detailed. "Multiple simultaneous surgeries," she said, looking up from the file, "beginning with Newt, Megan, and Sarah.

"They're planning to operate on their *brains…*" she said. "The medical charts are pretty skimpy on the rationale for the procedures. All that's listed are some clinical lab results and mechanical and logistical details of the upcoming surgeries."

"Like what?"

"Timing and order of the surgeries, references to the general neuroanatomical areas they'll be working on, planned anesthetics, estimated recovery times, scheduled PET scans post-surgery. The one thing the files *do* have are detailed records of the multiple viral vector gene insertion injections the kids were and are being given. Some of them have been getting them for a really long time. Years even. Newt in particular."

"*Years* of injections?" Max inhaled audibly. "What about Megan?"

Beth flipped open Megan's chart and ran her finger down the page.

"When did your wife die in that car accident? Didn't you say it was about two years ago?"

"That's right."

"Okay, let's see. Two years ago would put it here. That makes it…" She looked up at Max with a wary glance. "Megan's injections started a year before the accident."

"*Before…before* the accident? A year…before?"

"That's what her chart says. Looks like she had two injections before the accident spaced a few months apart. Then several around the time of the accident."

Max shook his head and started pacing. His mind scrambled to make sense of this information. Megan hadn't been to the doctor often. She was almost never sick. No accidents, no trips to the emergency room, no stitches. She had a booster immunization shot, but that had to be at least three years ago.

He stopped and turned to Beth. "That's impossible! It can't be true. There's no way they took her and gave her injections. We would've known about it."

Beth piled up the charts and the stack of copies she had made. "Maybe," she said, standing. "Just like you would've known about the *five* injections they've given her since the accident, with the last *three* being given during the past week?"

Max stared at her as she turned and headed for the door.

She stopped in the doorway and looked back at him. "Max, I know this seems totally impossible, but the record in her chart says it happened. I don't know how they pulled off the first series of injections, but the last three are easy to figure. Anybody could have sneaked into her hospital room and injected something into a port in her IV line. In fact, one of them could have been like that guy who slammed the syringe in my neck right before you beat him to a pulp."

"Yeah, well we know that guy was a psychopath killer who *wasn't* working for them. But you're right. That whole thing up in Mammoth…shooting her with the tranquilizer dart and trying to kidnap her. And then at the Yorba Linda Hospital, I wasn't in her room every single minute…"

"Could've happened," Beth said. "And now that they've kidnapped her, they can give her all the injections they want."

Max's expression shifted as another realization suddenly came to mind. "You know that hospital psychopath I fought with was planning to inject Megan with something to kill her. But when you came in, he'd just finished drawing blood from Megan, and he didn't have time."

"Right," Beth said. "He had lab tech gear and vials in his tray, and I saw the syringe half full of her blood."

"When he stuck you in the neck, you got injected with Megan's blood. I remember seeing the syringe on the floor, and it was empty. Plunger pushed all the way down."

Beth shrugged her shoulder up to her neck and began rubbing it.

"It's likely I've got some of Megan's viral stuff swimming around in my bloodstream."

Max looked at her with concern. "So much has been going on, I haven't even asked…how are *you* doing? Are you feeling okay?"

Beth half-smiled. "I'm fine, I guess. Other than the bizarro dreams I had when we snoozed in the SUV in Arrowhead Village."

"Hopefully, you didn't get exposed to too much viral stuff."

"Hopefully. But who knows?" She walked over to Max. "Sit down for a minute," she said, taking his hand. "There's something else I need to tell you."

"About Megan?" Max asked uneasily as he sat down on a nearby chair.

"No. It's not about Megan," Beth said. "At least not directly. This is about Sarah."

"Sarah?" Max's eyebrows rose in surprise. "What about her?"

"Her file doesn't give many details about her background. Another file that supposedly contains her complete history is referenced. It basically tells us she's six years old, gives her injection history, and lists the plans for her surgery—"

"Yeah, so?"

"—and the fact that she was created by in vitro fertilization using a donor egg that was embedded as an embryo into a surrogate mother."

"What's that have to do with—"

"Max. The egg donor was your...your wife, Carol."

Max stared at her in stunned disbelief. "What? No!" He jumped to his feet. "That can't be. Let me see that."

Beth opened the file, and Max grabbed it from her, reading the sparse sentences that included the mention of Carol as the egg donor.

"What are 'cryogenically preserved' eggs?" Max asked.

"'Cryogenically preserved' means frozen," Beth said, as Max handed the file back to her. "Women can donate eggs that can be used right away for in vitro fertilization, or they can be frozen—cryogenically preserved—and then thawed and fertilized later. Sometimes years later."

"So, Carol donated eggs at some point?"

"Or had eggs harvested for some reason. Did she ever mention this to you?"

Max shook his head. "No, but she had a cancer scare the year after she got out of college. That was way before I met her. Looked like she was going to need a complete hysterectomy. We talked about it once, but the memory was painful. She didn't want to bring it up again."

"That's terrible," Beth said. "What happened?"

"She was days from having the hysterectomy when a third opinion determined that she didn't have cancer after all. And a fourth opinion with retesting at a top cancer center confirmed the good news."

"So, she could have had her eggs harvested," Beth said.

"Yes. It's possible."

"The question is…what happened to the eggs?" Beth said. "She could have donated them to an egg bank...or maybe they were forgotten or stolen."

Max wrestled with the possibilities.

"What?" Beth asked. Her eyes searched his face for a hint of his thoughts.

"I've been wracking my brain ever since this thing started trying to figure out why they would've picked Megan to experiment on in the first place, and now we've got this link to her mother and this girl, Sarah."

"There are still so many details we don't know anything about. Look, I'm going back into Thornton's office to put these files back and see if I can crack his computer password. I'm sure the whole rationale for this project is in a file there somewhere."

"Really think you can crack his password?" Max asked.

Beth gave Max a coy look. "Well…I found a solid hint in one of the files, and I'm a bit of a tech geek with computers. Let's see what I can do."

Chapter 34

B eth sat in front of the computer screen and wiggled the mouse. The undulating screen saver banner dissolved into the blue background with nothing but a password entry box in the center. A cursor flashed next to the words "Enter Password."

Flipping open Newt's file, she turned to the second page of his medical record where she'd seen a pale green sticky note in the lower corner. There was a pencil scribbling on it that had caught her attention the first time she'd gone through the file. The cryptic letters read *pwnbdtIQ*.

"PW…password," she whispered out loud. She thought for a moment, staring at the first two letters. "It's gotta be…"

She typed *nbdtIQ* and pressed enter. Nothing happened.

She tried *pwnbdtIQ,* and again, nothing happened.

Beth had loved puzzles her whole life. She had possessed an uncanny sense for identifying patterns since she was seven and began working thousand-piece Charles Wysocki jigsaw puzzles with her mother. Her father introduced her to word search and acrostics when she was eight, and in later years, she'd advanced to crossword puzzles, Sudoku puzzles, and extreme Mensa riddles.

"PW…password," she whispered again, as she wrote down multiple versions of the acronym. She hyphenated the letters in every combination she could think of, keeping the first two letters, *pw,* at the beginning. After studying the list, she circled her top three possibilities. Her number one choice was *pw-n-bd-tIQ.*

The note is in Newt's file…The 'n' is probably Newt or Newton or Newtie or something like that.

She wrote down several variations of Newt's name before moving on to the acronymic letters *bd.* She scribbled down a list of possibilities.

BD could stand for lots of things. Birthday, begin date, bold decision, brain deficit, big dream, boyhood dog.

She felt drawn to her first choice. *Birthday…birthdate…that's got to be it*, she thought.

Beth flipped through the file to the first page of Newt's medical history and found a box labeled *Date of Birth: October 23.*

Next to the *bd* on her pad she scribbled *1023, 10-23, October23, 23Oct and Oct23.*

Now, what in the world could 'tIQ' stand for besides some type of IQ?

Beth stared at the 't', clicking the ballpoint pen she was holding and thinking of options. She ran her finger down Newt's medical history page and didn't have to go far. Halfway down the page was a box marked *Target IQ: 125.*

Her eyes jumped to the line above it where she had just seen another IQ listed.

Newt's Initial Intelligence Quotient is 62…Thornton's trying to double his IQ.

She prioritized her top choices and lined them up under each of the letter segments of the password acronym.

Okay, first choice for the password…n-bd-tIQ…name-birthdate-target IQ.

She looked at her list and thought about what she'd learned of Thornton's character and personality traits from his interviews. He was a driven man with an enormous ego who couldn't stomach the mental impairment of his own offspring.

There was only one possible choice from the name variant for Newt.

Thornton would never call him by a nickname, she thought. *He seems too cold and detached.*

Below the 'n' she circled *Newton*. She circled *1023* for the birthday and *125* for the Target IQ."

She rewrote the password in its entirety: *pw = Newton1023125.*

Let's give it a try, she thought, swiveling in the chair to face the computer screen.

She wiggled the mouse, clicked on the password box, typed in the test password, and hit the enter key.

The screen flickered, and then a message box appeared. *Incorrect password.* Dang! Wrong.

She looked at the second choice she had written on her list: *Newt1023125*.

After clearing the message box on the screen, she typed in the revised password and pounded the enter button.

Incorrect password.

She made two more attempts. Both failed. All of her prioritized choices were out of the running.

"What's going on here?" she muttered, looking at the remaining choices on her list. A disturbing suspicion entered her mind that she might get locked out of the computer if she made too many more password attempts.

Thornton would choose something simple. Something he could remember. But he'd want to make it seem complex.

Beth considered the next five choices on her list and made a few changes. *All letters should be lower case, for easy entry,* she thought. *And I'm sure Thornton wouldn't use a nickname.*

newton23oct125. Worth a try.

Beth held her breath as she typed in the new password and hit the enter key.

"Yes!" she exclaimed.

She scanned the thirty icons that filled the screen. The folder in the upper left corner of the middle section was labeled *Newton*.

She double-clicked on the folder and read the captions of the four files. She opened the one labeled *Medical*. It contained Newton's complete medical history and an exhaustive record of the treatments and medical interventions he had undergone.

She scrolled down the sidebar on the right side of the screen. Tables. Charts. Graphs. Microscope digital images of biopsy sections.

The medical record was twenty-eight pages long; the last entry was dated yesterday. She scrolled back up to the beginning of the document and read the first ten pages. She glimpsed snippets of the rationale for the experiments, Newt's injection history, results of a minor exploratory surgery, and tracking of his improvement on IQ tests.

Beth clicked out of Newt's medical file and opened a file titled *Adenovirus/CRISPR rationale*.

The screen filled with text. Beth studied the details on the theorized mechanism of action of the bioengineered adenovirus, its use as a vector to enter the neuronal cells of the brain, transform the physiology of the axons, and generate pools of neuronal 'stem' cells that could migrate and stimulate axonal multiplication. Additional paragraphs detailed the CRISPR-Cas9 genomic editing mechanism and its synergy with the adenoviral vector utilization.

She read aloud the last sentence of the section. "…Resulting in dramatically heightened neuronal complexity and resultant enhanced potential for association and memory."

Max walked into the room. "What are you muttering about?" he asked.

Beth looked up with a start. "Geez, Max," she said. "You really know how to scare a girl. You always appear out of thin air?"

Max grinned. "Excusez-moi. Next time, I'll cough or knock or something. What was all that scientific mumbo-jumbo you were entertaining yourself with?"

"Got in!" she said triumphantly.

Max looked from her to the screen and back again, his eyes narrowing. "Excellent. You find anything?"

Beth nodded. "We hit the mother lode."

"Like what?"

"I've been going through Newt's file. Here, take a look."

She closed out the document and brought up the list of the files in the folder.

"I scanned his medical file, and it's the real deal. Every detail and record about the experimental treatments they've been giving him: injections, surgery, biopsies, scans…"

She clicked on another file. "But there are other files—like this one—that should give us everything we want to know about the research project and the experiments they're doing."

She brought up the My Documents directory. "Look at this. Files on Megan, Sarah, Faith, Newt, and a second boy named Eddie."

Max leaned over her shoulder and stared at the screen. "Unbelievable," he said.

"I'm capturing this entire My Documents directory on my flash drive," Beth said. "I've got to read these files."

She slid the 1 Terabyte flash drive she'd brought into the USB port. It took less than ten seconds to copy the files onto the drive.

"Breaking news!" Mark abruptly entered the room.

Beth jumped in her seat. "Man...what is it with you guys?!" she exclaimed. "You startle me every time I turn around."

Mark laughed. "Jittery, are we? Sounds like somebody had a few too many cups of coffee today."

"Yeah...stuff it, Mark. What's the breaking news?"

"Glad you asked," he said with a clipped smile. "My contact at the Ontario International Airport gave me the flight itineraries of all the private jets taking off and landing there today. And, lo and behold, whataya know...*three* of them have scheduled flights from Ontario to Denver International Airport."

"Three?" Max asked. "What are their departure times?"

Mark glanced at his watch. "Two of them left already. The third is probably taxiing down the runway as we speak."

"I'll bet one of the three is our boy, his crew, and the kids." Max looked back at Beth, who had inserted a second flash drive into the USB port. "Making another copy?"

"Redundancy. I'm going to mail the second drive to my office. I'll use the first one to load the files onto my laptop so I can study them and figure out what we're up against."

Max turned back to Mark. "You've got the alphanumeric identifiers for each of the jets?"

"Right here," Mark said, handing him a piece of paper. "All the info we need to trace these planes is right on this sheet. Have we got the serial number of Thornton's company jet?"

"Here, give me that," Beth said. Mark handed her the paper. She removed the flash drive and clicked open a file that had the word 'jet' in it. A full portfolio of information about the Viralvector, Inc. corporate jet filled the screen.

Beth scrolled down to the registration information and compared the identification numbers.

"Looks like we have a winner," she said, handing the paper back to Mark. "Jet number two is a perfect match."

Mark checked his notes. "In that case, they took off from Ontario two hours ago."

Max gave him a questioning look. "You able to miss a few days of work? I need your help."

"Yeah…but you're gonna owe me big time. I had some vacation days planned for this week—a four day weekend—and now I see that fading fast."

"Thanks, man."

Mark grinned. "Don't mention it. Well, don't mention it, but don't forget it either. I may want to borrow your cabin up in Telluride sometime soon."

"Any time you want," Max said. "We're going to need to bring our gear with us, so someone'll have to drive the Suburban."

"Guess that would be me," Mark said. "I've driven to Vail, Colorado in thirteen hours flat before. Figure I can do that again if I don't make too many stops."

"Good. We'll print out hard-copy directions to Rios, that town just outside of where their office is located. Let's meet at one of the gas stations there. We can stay in contact via cell phone once Beth and I land in Denver."

Beth was already on the web, punching in the address. She printed out driving directions for Mark and two copies of vicinity maps. She handed Mark his copies and gathered up her files.

Max looked at her. "Ready?"

She tilted her head and squinted. "Born ready."

Chapter 35

The narrow living area offered all the warmth and ambience of a sterile dormitory room. Two basic twin beds with plain white bedspreads lined the long opposing walls, splitting the room in mirrored symmetry. Two pinewood tables were aligned side by side against the far wall. Each had its own lamp and a white lazy Susan with a pencil holder and compartments stocked with school supplies.

Megan and Sarah sat together on one of the beds and looked around the room. There wasn't much to take in.

"Oh, brother, look at this place," Megan said. "Is this boring or what?"

Sarah glanced around the room again. "Boring." She slipped off the bed and walked over to the closet door. She tried to force the door open, but it wouldn't budge.

"Pull harder," Megan said. "Put some muscle into it."

Sarah braced herself and grabbed the knob with both hands. Putting one foot against the wall, she yanked as hard as she could and kept the pressure on. After a moment's hesitation, the door flew open, sending Sarah tumbling backward to the floor.

Megan and Sarah looked at each other and burst out laughing.

"Good move, Sarah!" Megan exclaimed. "You outta try out for the Olympics. You could get a gold medal in door-opening gymnastics!"

Sarah giggled. "Yeah, well I've been practicing a lot. Can't you tell?"

"Sure can, and you've got *great* form landing on your butt!"

Sarah scrambled to her feet and ran over to the main door. Megan had picked the deadbolt lock ten minutes earlier, but when they'd checked, there were people at the far end of the hallway. Sarah opened the door and stuck her head out.

"Nobody's out there now. How about if we go exploring and see what kinda place this is?"

"Let's go."

Megan took Sarah's hand, and they took one step into the hallway.

"You two, come here immediately!"

Sarah tried to stifle a gasp. "It's cranky Miss Creade," she whispered.

"Oh, great," Megan muttered. "The Wicked Witch of the West fell off her broom."

They turned and shuffled up the hall. Creade was standing in front of an open office door with arms akimbo, a frown on her face.

"I was just coming to get you. How did you get out of your room? Darryl was supposed to lock your door when he put you in there."

Megan and Sarah both shrugged.

"Well, anyway…you girls need to pick up the pace. When I call you, you should come running."

"Yes, ma'am," Sarah said.

Creade turned her stern expression to Megan.

Megan stole a quick glance at Sarah then looked up at the towering woman. "Yes, ma'am," she said politely.

"All right. The two of you come with me. We're going to pick up Eddie and Faith, and then I want to talk to all four of you."

They walked down the hall and turned left down a lengthy corridor. Halfway down the hall, they stopped in front of a room. Creade put her key in the door lock and turned it, then clenched her fist and launched a thundering attack on the door.

"Eddie, get out here!" she barked.

A few moments passed, and Creade raised her fist again. She cocked her arm back, ready to pound, when the door opened.

A boy with sandy blonde hair stepped out. Megan remembered him from the plane flight and car ride. He was slightly older than her and a few inches taller. His mussy hair framed an all-American boy face, and he looked lean and athletic.

"It's about time! What took you so long?" Creade asked.

Eddie shrugged. "I was reading a really good book, and I wanted to finish the paragraph."

"Not acceptable. Next time, you jump when I call you. Do *not* make me wait. Understand?"

Eddie gritted his teeth. "Yeah. I got it."

Creade fixed a scrutinizing glare on them that left no question that she meant business.

"Okay then. All three of you follow me. And don't dawdle."

Megan looked at Eddie, and he smiled at her. She couldn't help but stare. He had the bluest eyes she had ever seen.

"Hi, my name's Eddie," he said. "What's yours?"

Megan blinked. "Uh…it's Megan," she said. "Nice to meet you. I can't believe how blue your eyes are!"

Geez, did I really just say that? she thought.

"Um…nice to meet you too," he said. "And, yeah…I guess they are pretty blue. That's what people tell me."

Creade frowned at them. "Quit the socializing and let's get moving," she barked.

Megan rolled her eyes and shrugged. He flashed her another smile as they hurried to catch up to Creade, who was walking at a fast clip.

They stopped by Faith's room. She came out immediately after Creade unlocked the door and yelled.

"Listen up," she barked. The children's murmuring stopped, and they looked at her.

"I want all of you to pay attention. Eyes front, no talking. First of all, I think you've all noticed we're in a new place and a new location. Where we are is not important. What is important is that you follow *all* the rules and do *exactly* as you're told when you're told it. If you don't, you will be punished severely. And I mean *severely.* Are we clear?"

They all nodded.

"Good. Now what I expect from each of you is—"

"I have a question," Megan said.

Creade's brow furrowed, and she shot Megan a look that could kill a small animal. "What?" she growled impatiently.

Megan braced herself. "I want to go home. When are you going to let us go home?" She glared at Creade. Fear bubbled in her stomach, fragile bravery tossed about like a dingy adrift in a storm. Her nails bit into her palms as she took a defiant step forward. "I want to call my dad. Right now!"

Creade forced her expression to soften, a strained effort that was decidedly unnatural. Equally disturbing on a number of levels was her attempt to assume a soothing, less gruff tone with her voice.

"Megan…I'm sorry. You're probably scared about all this. But don't worry. There's nothing to be afraid of. This will all be over in a little bit. You'll be seeing your father soon."

She paused. Her eyes trailed from Eddie to Faith and Sarah.

"I guess I should tell you all at least something of what's going on. All of you have an illness, and what we're trying to do is make you better. We're trying to cure you."

Megan cocked her head. A skeptical look spread across her face.

"What do you mean, make us better? We're not sick. Do you guys feel sick?"

"Not me. I feel fine," Eddie said.

"Me too," Sarah agreed, glancing over at Faith.

"That's…nice," Creade said with crocodile sweetness. "Glad you all feel so healthy and chipper. But, you know, things aren't always the way they seem. There's something I need to tell you."

"Like what?" Eddie said.

Creade tried to mold her face into a concerned expression and shot him a tight smile. "The doctors have informed me of some bad news. All of you are infected with a virus. A very nasty virus."

"You mean like a virus you have when you've got a cold?" Megan asked.

"Yes. Exactly."

Megan looked at her skeptically. "Then why don't we feel sick? Shouldn't we have a fever or something?"

"I know. But this is a rare and deadly virus," Creade said. "It's already killed dozens of people, and we don't want it to spread out into the community and across the country. That's why we're keeping you here with us. We've quarantined you to prevent it from spreading."

"I still don't get it." Megan took a step forward and flailed her arms. "Why don't we feel bad?"

"You may feel good now, but when this virus builds up to a high enough concentration in your bloodstream, it can kill you in a matter of days. Unless you're treated."

"Is that what happened to my mom?" Eddie interjected. "That's why she's so sick?"

Creade nodded. "But we're trying everything we can to save her."

"And what about my mommy?" Sarah asked.

Creade's gaze slipped to the floor for a moment. Megan held her breath.

"I'm sorry, Sarah. Your mother is extremely sick. We don't know if she's going to get better."

They all stared in silence at Creade. Seconds passed.

"What about us?" Megan asked. "Is this virus going to make us sick and kill us too?"

Creade exhaled loudly. "Actually, we're pretty sure the answer's *no*. It's not going to kill you. But it might make you sick. That's why you all need to cooperate with us. We need to treat you for this sickness. You know all the shots you've gotten and the blood samples we've been taking from you?"

They nodded in unison.

"We're giving you an experimental version of a medicine that kills the virus and keeps it from multiplying in your bloodstream. And we do lots of lab tests to check to see how much virus is still in your blood. We've hardly found any virus when you have the shots. But without the shots…the virus comes back."

Eddie opened his mouth to say something, but Megan spoke first. "Is this experimental medicine going to cure us?"

Creade shrugged. "The medicine seems to be knocking out the virus. We think that with a half-dozen or so more injections, we may be able to get rid of it for good."

"Oh, great," Faith moaned. "Just what I wanted. A buncha more shots."

"Well…if it cures you…" Creade retorted.

"Yeah, I guess so…" Faith agreed reluctantly. Megan and Eddie nodded.

Creade looked up the hall and then back at the four of them.

"Speaking of that," she said, looking at her watch. "Tonight, a couple hours after dinner—maybe nine or so—we're going to be coming around to your rooms to give you another shot. Because this one will be a bigger dose than usual, we're going to give you a little light medicine to help you go to sleep. That way the shot won't make you feel nauseous or sick. You'll wake up the next morning feeling great. Any questions?"

"What about my dad? You still haven't told me when I can see him."

"You'll see him soon enough, Megan. Remember what I said about how infectious this virus is? We'll let you talk to him soon…most likely in a few days."

"Really?"

"Really. Now, it's time to get back to your rooms," Creade said.

Creade led them down the hall towards their rooms, marching as though she were leading a contingent of military students. Eddie scribbled something on a piece of paper and folded it into a tight square. Sidling up close to Megan, he reached out and stuffed the note into her hand. He edged away from her, his eyes fixed on Creade's back.

Megan closed her fingers around the note. Her hand tingled where Eddie touched it.

They reached the turn-off for Eddie's room, and Creade turned around.

"Into to your room, Edward. Dinner's in two hours."

Eddie nodded and then turned to Megan and the others. "See you later," he said, giving Megan a look. He turned and headed for his room.

"Bye, Eddie," Megan, Sarah, and Faith chirped in unison.

Creade locked the door. They continued up the hall and around the corner. They dropped Faith off at her room.

"Night," Megan said.

Faith looked back over her shoulder and mouthed the words, "Good night."

Creade walked Sarah and Megan's to their room. She paused in front of their door and fixed them with her usual glare.

"Sarah, be sure to go over the rules with Megan one more time. Make sure the two of you keep things quiet. Be ready for dinner in two hours."

"We know…" Sarah sighed.

Creade stepped aside, and the two girls shuffled into the room. She closed and locked the door behind them. Megan waited for the door to clack shut and then ran up and pressed her ear against it. She heard the clop-clop of Creade's footsteps fade down the hallway.

Looking down at her right hand, Megan unfurled her fingers. Eddie's note was curled safely in her palm. She unfolded it and began to read.

"What's that?" Sarah asked.

"Shhh! Keep it down."

"Sorry…"

Megan glanced down at the note, then back at Sarah. "It's a note from Eddie."

"A note? When'd he give it to you?"

"He snuck it in my hand while we were walking back to his room. Right under Cranky Creade's nose."

"What's it say?"

"He wants us to wait ten minutes then sneak out and meet him at the top of the hallway by his room. He says it's urgent. There's something important he wants to talk to us about."

"Something important? Like what?" Sarah asked.

"I don't know, but I'm going. What about you?"

"If you're going, I'm going. But how can he get out of his room? He's gotta be locked in just like we are."

Megan was busy working on the lock with her paperclip wires. The deadbolt slid back with a soft clack.

"Beats me," she said. "Maybe he can pick locks like I can."

Ten minutes passed in a blink.

Megan turned the knob and opened it. She leaned out, glancing down both sides of the hall.

A lab technician disappeared from view around a corner. Megan waited and watched. The hallway looked deserted.

"I don't see anybody now. Come on."

They slipped out of the room. Megan eased the door shut behind them.

She took Sarah's hand and hurried them down the hall, checking over her shoulder twice before they reached the intersecting hallway on the left where they had dropped off Eddie.

Nobody was there.

Megan looked back up the hall in the direction they had come and then in the opposite direction.

"C'mon, Eddie," she whispered. "C'mon…"

She felt sure they were going to be seen. Then she saw him step out of his room. Faith was with him. "There he is," she sighed in relief.

Eddie and Faith started up the hall in their direction. Eddie gave Megan the thumbs up when he saw them watching.

"Sorry we're late. Anybody see you leave?"

"Nope," Megan said. "The hall was deserted."

"Good," Eddie said, nodding in approval.

Megan found herself staring at his azure blue eyes again.

"Faith and I just got back. We've been out exploring already."

"You have?" Megan asked. "Where'd you guys go?"

"Kinda all over," Faith said. "After Eddie unlocked my door and let me out of my room, we did a little scouting around."

"We've gotta find out what's really going on around here," Eddie said. "There's more to it than that infection story Creade tried to scare us with."

"Is that the reason you wanted us to meet you?"

"Yeah. That and how I think we need to plan how we're gonna escape...today."

"Escape? So, you don't believe what Creade said about the virus and the deadly infection and all that?"

Eddie shrugged. "I don't know. Part of it's probably true, but a lot of things don't add up, and I get real suspicious when things don't make sense."

"Like what?" asked Megan.

"Like the situation with Sarah's mom, and them not letting you see or even talk to your father. They said the same thing to me about my mom over a month ago, and I still haven't been allowed to see her. It's the same thing with Faith's mom."

Megan turned to the other girl. "Faith, they're still keeping you from seeing your mom too?"

Faith looked down, crestfallen. "I haven't seen my mom in weeks."

"Sure seems like they're holding us prisoners," Eddie said. "If things are the way they say they are, then why can't we see our parents?"

Megan nodded. "You're right. I keep asking Creade that."

"And what about you, Sarah?" Eddie said. "I don't want to upset you, but how much have they told you about your sick mother?"

Sarah looked down at the floor.

"Sorry. I shouldn't have brought that up. Guess what I'm trying to say is there are lots of questions, and we don't have answers to any of them."

"So, what do we do?" asked Megan.

"We *find* the answers. C'mon."

Eddie led them into a part of the complex they hadn't seen before. A laboratory was down at the end of a long corridor, and they could see that someone in a lab coat was entering it. They tiptoed past the hallway to the end of the corridor. Eddie shot his arm out and brought them to an abrupt halt.

"Okay. See that door down there on the left?"

Together, the girls said, "Yeah."

"That's Newt's room. When Faith and I were out exploring, we saw Blake Thornton, the top guy, go in there. You guys know that Newt's his son, right?"

Megan glanced at Sarah. "He's the one who's kinda slow?"

"That's him," Eddie said. "But the strange thing is Newt seems like he's a lot more with it lately. Like he's gotten smarter. Weird. Anyway, we saw Thornton go in his room. We headed down there to try to listen in to what he was saying, but somebody started coming out of another room. We ducked into a closet in the nick of time, or they would have seen us."

"What do you want to do now?" Megan asked.

"Same thing. Let's go down and listen at the door. We can find out what he's saying to Newt and—"

Eddie was interrupted by the sound of Newt's door opening.

"Hide," Eddie whispered urgently.

Megan and Sarah scrambled around the corner of the hallway and tried the first door they came to. Luckily, it was unlocked. They closed the door behind them and flipped on the light switch. They were in a medical examination room.

Megan grabbed Sarah's hand. "We've gotta leave the lights off. You stand over there, and I'll stand over here. If somebody opens the door, they won't see either of us. Especially in the dark."

Sarah's eyes were wide. "Okay," she whispered. She sidestepped behind a rack of shelves and crouched in her hiding place.

Megan flipped the switch. The room went black.

Eddie and Faith were hiding in a storage room diagonally across the hall from Newt's. The room was dark except for a sliver of light where they had left the door partially open. Eddie stood with his eye pressed against the opening.

Thornton stood in the doorway of Newt's room.

"Newt, quit crying," he barked impatiently. His voice lacked even the slightest hint of empathy. "It's a tiny procedure…just like the last one you had. Remember? That wasn't bad at all. You went to sleep for a little while, and then you woke up, and it was all over. We're trying to help you here. This quick procedure tomorrow morning is going to make you better."

Eddie heard another muffled cry.

"I said quit crying. You're not a baby, so don't act like one. Dinner will be here in an hour, and after that, you can watch a movie. Then our nurse will be around to give you something to help you sleep."

Newt mumbled something, but Eddie couldn't make it out.

"Quit your whining! Now settle down and play. I'll see you tomorrow."

Thornton closed the door and sped off down the hall.

Through the slit in the doorway, Eddie watched him zip by and disappear around the corner. Eddie pushed open the door, and he and Faith hurried down the hall after him as quietly as they could.

Megan heard footsteps approach then pass by and fade. She eased the door open and saw Thornton disappear into an office at the far end of the hallway.

She pushed the door wide open and motioned for Sarah to follow her. The two of them stepped tentatively out of the storage closet and nearly collided with Eddie and Faith, who were scurrying by.

Megan choked off a gasp of surprise. "Eddie, you guys scared me!"

Eddie put a finger to his lips. "Sorry," he whispered. "We're following Newt's dad. He went that way…down there."

"Yeah, I know," Megan said. "I saw him go into the last room on the left."

"I'm going down there," Eddie said, squinting his eyes. "We've gotta find out what's going on. I heard him tell Newt he's going to have a procedure tomorrow. They're giving him something after dinner to 'help him sleep.' I wonder if they're planning something like that for us?"

Megan's skin crawled. "I'm coming," she said. "What about you two? You want to wait here until we get back?"

"No way. I'm goin' with you guys," Sarah insisted.

"Me, too," Faith said.

"Look for a hiding place on the way down in case Newt's dad or somebody else comes out of an office. And *keep quiet,*" Eddie said. He mimicked zipping his mouth closed.

He tiptoed toward the office, and the others followed single file keeping to the left side of the hall.

When they reached the room, Eddie and Megan crept towards the closed door. Sarah tiptoed up next to Megan and motioned for her to bend down so she could whisper in her ear. "The room down there on the right is a storage room," she said, pointing down the hall.

Megan nodded and brought her finger up to her lips. Sarah mimicked her and stepped back.

Megan leaned forward and placed her ear against the door. She was facing Eddie, who was little more than a foot away from her. His eyes were unfocused; he was listening intently to the murmuring. Megan found herself getting lost in his eyes as she strained to hear the voices behind the closed door.

"No, we don't need to wait," Thornton insisted.

"I'm just saying I think it might be wise to give it another week. The primordial population would be even larger than it is now."

"Let me say this one more time." Thornton's stern voice raised goosebumps on Megan's arms. "All the injections to date have generated almost twice the anticipated result. The viral vector has performed flawlessly. It is doing exactly what it was designed to, inserting the trigger fingerprint genes in the neurons of the hippocampal region. The primordial population of CRISPR-Cas9 modified neuronal stem cells is significantly more than enough to ensure a strongly positive outcome. The most recent CT and PET scans confirm this in all of the kids."

There were a few moments of silence followed by a rustling of papers. It sounded like someone was flipping through a folder.

"I suppose I am being too conservative," the second person said. His voice was unsettled. "I'm just trying to magnify our chances for success."

"That's all fine and good," Thornton said dismissively. "But let's proceed."

"Okay. We're sticking with the original plan. The surgeries are scheduled for first thing in the morning. We'll stagger the surgeries beginning with the boy and that Faith girl first since we'll be harvesting them in the deep cerebellar region. That's going to be tricky. We'll immediately infuse those stem cells into Newt's cerebellum."

"How long start to finish?" Thornton asked.

"From cranial prep through harvesting and transplant…about two hours."

"Then the twins."

"Right. Then the sisters. We'll prep them simultaneously, harvest the hippocampal stem cells, and transplant them into Newt's hippocampus."

"Newt'll be under the entire time."

"Yes, but from prep to his final suture is a max of three and a half hours."

"Good. The team's assembled and ready?"

"Assembled and ready for a six o'clock start. I'm lead surgeon. I'll be driving the stem cell harvesting aspirations and transplant deliveries. Eric will be steering me via real-time stereotactic CT imaging. Carla will be assisting with surgical support and closing, and Devon will handle the anesthesia."

"Excellent. Looks like we're all set. Proceed."

"One last thing…"

"What?" Thornton snapped impatiently as he turned to leave.

"About the post-surgical logistics…the kids…"

Thornton waited a long moment before responding. "What about them?"

"Have you decided…?"

"Yes. It's going to be the Southeast Asia 'adoption' plan. All four of them will bring an extremely attractive price, and no one's around to accuse or ask questions about the project. Contact Mary to initiate plans for their departure. When will they be ready? Two days post-surgery?"

"Two full days is the minimal amount of time. They should be fine leaving on the morning of the third. Glad to hear you chose that option."

"Indeed. Option two would've been messier."

"And crueler."

"Quit trying to be my conscience! This project is monumentally important, and not just for Newt. It's a quantum advancement in medical science and neuro-regeneration. When we succeed tomorrow—and I mean *when*—our modified CRISPR-Cas9 genome editing technique and quantum advancement in adenoviral vector technology will blaze a major trail in medical history. This will change the landscape of medicine. We'll become masters of what used to be our genetically predestined fate."

"Agreed. I wasn't questioning the importance of this project. It *is* monumental."

"Fine. I'll see you in the morning. I'm going to gown-up for the surgery. I want a front row seat to watch history being made."

"See you at six."

Thornton turned and headed for the door.

Megan's eyes held Eddie as she mouthed the word, "Run!"

They pivoted and rushed away from the door. Eddie grabbed her hand and rushed her down the hall. As they passed Sarah, Megan grabbed her hand, almost yanking her off her feet. Faith followed close behind. They scrambled to reach a perpendicular hallway before Thornton pushed open the door and stormed down the main hallway in the opposite direction.

"C'mon, we gotta hurry," Eddie said.

He pulled them down the hallway at a half-run.

"Man, we're in luck," he whispered as they reached the exit door at the end of the hall. A tiny green light was shining brightly on the digital control pad to the left of the door.

"The door alarm system is off. The coast is clear. Were out of here."

He pushed open the door, and they rushed out into the late afternoon sunlight. A light breeze greeted them as they ran for their lives.

Chapter 36

*L*ike the wind.

Megan heard her father's voice echo in her mind, urging her along as the four of them sprinted away from the complex.

Run like the wind.

She'd heard him say it countless times over the years, infusing her with confidence and embracing her with his words.

A memory from last spring leaped into her mind. The final big game of the soccer tournament was about to begin. He'd grasped her shoulders, looked her in the eyes, and lifted her spirits with these words of encouragement.

She'd run her fastest and scored two goals. Her team had won the game. And through it all, she'd run like the wind. Just like she was doing now.

They sprinted down the long dirt and gravel private drive. They followed it halfway down before cutting to the right and disappearing into the trees. The drive continued off to the left where it connected with a rugged fire road that curved jerkily another seven to eight miles down the mountain to the two-lane county highway.

Megan led them into the trees at a full run. She'd always been good at running. She was faster than all the girls in her class and most of the boys. Faith was next. Eddie was close behind her. He held tight to Sarah's hand, pulling her along as swiftly as she could run.

They darted through the trees, passing further into the shelter of the wilderness. After running at full speed for ten minutes, they stopped, out of breath, and rested on a tree stump next to an enormous fallen tree and a group of moss-covered boulders. The forest was quiet and still.

"Just…a couple minutes," Megan said between gasps for air. "Gotta…gotta keep going…"

Eddie, Faith, and Sarah nodded as they huffed and puffed.

A few minutes passed in near silence, but Megan's eyes never stopped darting around, searching their surroundings and the direction they were headed. Off to the left, she saw an opening that appeared to continue down the mountain.

"C'mon," she said, standing up and heading over to the opening. The others followed.

"Look, it's a trail!" Faith exclaimed.

The path weaved in and out amidst the trees, disappearing in the distance with the downward slope of the mountain.

"This'll make things a lot easier," Megan said. "Let's go!"

They scampered down the narrow path that carved a loosely defined, serpentine trail through the forest. They were unmindful of the forest canopy that loomed overhead and the redolent scent of pine that engulfed them. Oblivious to all but the urgency of their journey to freedom.

High above them, securely bolted in the branch nook of a massive Ponderosa pine tree, a video surveillance camera switched on. Dual weather-resistant motion detectors aimed at the trail triggered the camera to life, and it automatically radioed its video capture back to a control station receiver in the cabin complex. A red light began blinking on the front of the receiver, and a crystal clear picture of the trail and four receding kids appeared on one of the monitors.

"How much longer until we land?" Beth asked, gazing out the window of the airliner. It was a clear day, and the blue sky panoramic view from thirty-three thousand feet was breathtaking.

"Just under two hours," Max said. "It's a perfect time to catch some zzzs. No telling when we'll get the next chance." He leaned back, crossed his arms, and closed his eyes. He was asleep in thirty seconds.

"Uh huh," Beth muttered as she went back to studying the piles of documents she had copied from the file cabinet at the complex. She'd read through most of the thick stack of papers on the drive from Lake Arrowhead to the Ontario International Airport and during the two-hour wait at the airport before their flight departed.

"Unbelievable…" she muttered to herself. She flipped back to a long section she had flagged with sticky notes and read the dozen or more pages slowly and carefully. The horror and disgust she'd felt the first time she read them returned full force.

The pages were written like a clinical trial publication in a medical journal with a background summary of chronological neuronal research experiments leading up to the current state-of-the-art science. Next was a detailed discussion of the combined CRISPR-Cas9 and viral-vector mediated gene-insertion techniques and neuronal stem cell development breakthroughs Blake Thornton and his team of research scientists had achieved.

It was a dizzying manipulation of biological processes. In theory, if the biotechnology was further explored and developed, paraplegics and quadriplegics might have a very real chance of complete recovery from their permanent injuries. But the potential promise of the first set of breakthroughs had deliberately been shelved and stalled in development. It had been superseded in priority by an equally startling breakthrough: a process that enabled the controlled generation of neuronal stem cells.

As Beth read further, her stomach tightened with revulsion. She learned about Newt's congenital mental impairment, Thornton's plan to enhance Newt's cerebral capacity, and the injections of these engineered viruses into Megan and the other four children who were involved in the study.

"Thornton's a psychopathic Dr. Frankenstein," she whispered under her breath. *And these poor kids are his guinea pigs.*

She returned to the last paragraph she'd read. Her fingers gripped the page. She finished the remaining pages and closed the folder, mentally drained and disgusted. *How could he do this to these kids? And to his own son?*

She knew there were no answers that could justify the enormity of Thornton's twisted plan, no matter his intent or rationale.

Beth's eyes drooped as a wave of exhaustion crashed over her. She shook off the drowsiness long enough to tuck the tall pile of papers back into her carrying bag and shove it under the seat in front of her.

Leaning her seat back, she slipped a thin airline pillow under her head and closed her eyes. And stepped off a ledge into an uncontrolled free-fall down a slumberous abyss.

The darkness lightened and the willowy sheets of mist dissolved, revealing a dense expanse of forest filled with Douglas fir trees and towering cedars. She was moving through the trees. She looked down at the scantly delineated trail before her that was zigzagging around trees and boulders. Her muscles ached at the exertion, and she strained to catch her breath.

Muffled voices buffeted her from behind, but she couldn't make out the words. She turned to look over her right shoulder and saw a sandy blonde-haired boy, a girl nearly his age, and a second smaller girl who looked like a younger version of Megan following her.

She watched as the boy picked up a stick and tossed it into the trees. He turned and faced her. His lips moved like he was speaking, but all she could hear was a buffeted, moaning noise coming from him, like a person talking underwater. He pointed down the path and motioned off to the right.

As she turned and looked at the trail ahead of her, the view tunneled and shortened, telescoping toward her. She began moving down the path again, looking back and forth between the trail and the forest area where the boy had pointed.

Before long, she came to a partial clearing. She veered off the path and headed into it, walking twenty or thirty yards to where the forest became denser. Then she turned to look back over her shoulder. The boy motioned her to continue. She walked further in, through the closely bunched trees to a point where a second clearing opened.

She stopped in the middle of the open, grassy area and rotated three hundred sixty degrees, taking in a panoramic view of their protected enclave. It was surrounded by dense, virtually impenetrable forest, walled like a castle fortress. The towering canopy allowed scant glimpses of the darkening sky above. Dusk was rolling into twilight. Night was arriving.

Beth turned toward the hollowed-out area on her left. As she watched, the boy walked over and stood in the middle of it, pointing to the exceptional density of cover in the lower ceiling of branches. The natural tent of trees, with its protective cover and thick carpet of pine needles, offered a cozy shelter in the middle of the wilderness.

The boy pulled out a flashlight out of his pocket and switched it on, motioning for her and the two other girls to join him in the shelter.

The smaller girl who resembled Megan ran into the hollowed-out enclave, turned, and spread her arms wide. She smiled as she hopped and spun in place. Her lips began to move, and the same eerie, underwater moaning sound that the boy had made came out of her mouth, only higher pitched.

Beth scrunched her forehead, trying to make out the words. It seemed like she was saying, "Look at this! Isn't this cool?" Her face and body language signaled her next question. The words fit the shape of her lips as she spoke. "Really...isn't this so cool?"

A background noise came out of nowhere. A shoveling, clunking sound followed by a popping spritz that permeated the entire enclosure. The others were oblivious to the noise. The smaller girl turned toward the boy and continued talking, but the sound repeated, drowning out the girl's voice.

The edges of the forest clouded and darkened, and the scene dissolved into a swirling, receding darkness as the shoveling, clunking sound grew louder and clearer.

Beth opened her eyes and sat up. She glanced past Max to the aisle. A flight attendant was filling a cup with ice on the beverage cart. She pulled a Coke Zero out of the middle drawer, popped the tab, and poured it into the cup.

The attendant looked over at Beth and asked, "Would you care for anything to drink?"

Beth stared at her blankly. "Uh, no thanks."

She turned to her right and tried to get into a comfortable position. She tried to go back to sleep, but her mind raced, playing back every minute detail of the dream she had just experienced. She could picture the little girl's face as clearly as if it were right before her. Every feature stood out with razor sharp clarity. An exact but younger version of Megan.

Replaying the dream several times in her mind, she discovered she could slow down the action and focus on any part of it she wanted.

The girl...she had looked so much like Megan. She squeezed her eyes shut and focused on the girl's face again. She took in the shape of her nose, her smiling demeanor, the liveliness of her bright blue eyes.

What did it all mean?

Eventually, Beth's exhaustion caught up with her. Just before drifting off to sleep, the words that the little girl spoke in her dream echoed through her mind, loud and clear.

"Isn't this *so* cool?"

Chapter 37

Nurse Creade looked at her watch as she approached Megan and Sarah's room. There were far too many things left on her to do list for tonight.

Quarter to six, she thought. *Damn meeting went on forever. Gotta get dinner over with, shoot up the kids, set up all the prep stations for tomorrow's surgeries, check the surgical computer assist software on the CT scanner...When the hell's it ever gonna end?*

She paused before the girls' door with her hand on the latch and listened.

The *Let it Go* song from the movie *Frozen* blared through the door.

She unlocked the deadbolt and shoved the door open, bursting into the room. She loved to shock the girls.

There was no yip of fear or surprise. No startled gasps. No scramble to turn down the sound.

Creade stood in the center of the room and looked around, suddenly aware of the emptiness, which stunned her even more than the song blaring at a teeth chattering decibel. She walked over and turned off the TV.

"Sarah...Megan?"

Her eyes paused on the closet door. It was the only possible hiding place in the small room. She crossed the room in three long strides and ripped open the door. Her stomach dropped. Nothing but clothes, hangers, and air.

Where the hell are they? she thought in a panic.

She stormed out of the room and down the lengthy hallway toward Eddie's room. She could hear the TV blaring through the door, but this time she didn't stop to listen. She scrambled to unlock the door and burst into the room. She found herself alone in the middle of the room.

She took a deep breath and exhaled in a loud huff. *Okay. I came from the meeting rooms and through the play area and the lunchroom. Nobody there. And they're not in Sarah's room or Eddie's room. What's left...Faith's room? Newt's?*

She all but dismissed the last option. The other children tolerated Newt, but none of them would think about hanging out in his room with him.

It's got to be Faith's.

She fought to keep her galloping sense of alarm under control as she raced out of the room and down the hallway. She popped her head into Newt's room and saw him sitting alone on the floor, building a Lego contraption.

She ran down the hall to Faith's room, knowing even as she heard the TV blaring through the door again that they weren't in there.

Unlocking the deadbolt and crushing the door latch down, she charged into the room, scanned it in a glance, then grabbed her push-to-talk phone and switched it on.

"Ted! Meet me in the control center. Now! The kids are missing."

She rushed down the hall, her thoughts blurring in a storming rage.

"Look at this. Isn't this cool?" Sarah spread her arms wide and twirled around in a breezy, carefree pirouette. She stopped and looked up at the overhand of pine branches that formed a low canopy above her. She turned and smiled at Megan, Faith, and Eddie.

"Really, isn't this *so* cool?"

Megan and Faith stole a look at each other and stifled a giggle.

"Definitely cool!" Faith said with a grin. "And you're a great spinner!"

Eddie walked into the hollowed-out enclave and stood next to Sarah, who was leaping up as high as she could, trying to touch the dense thicket of interlocked branches above her. He looked all around the natural shelter.

"What do you think?" he asked, glancing at Megan. "Is this hideout sweet or what?"

Megan and Faith scurried in and stood next to Sarah as Eddie walked past them and began scouting around the area in front of the shelter. He walked off to the side and began pulling down low hanging branches from a tree.

"What are you doing?" Megan asked.

"Just checking things out," he said. "Seeing if I can make this place invisible."

He dragged a branch over and leaned it upright against the front left side of the shelter. Going back to where he broke off the branch, he looked around and found two more long, bushy branches on the ground. He dragged them over and leaned them up next to the first one, tucking them together so that the branches interlocked.

He stepped back and smiled at his handiwork. "Perfect."

Megan walked out and stood next to him. "Looks pretty good. Add another ten or twelve branches, and our hideout will disappear completely."

"Yeah," Eddie agreed. "We'll have ourselves a perfect little camouflaged fort."

Megan looked around at the surrounding forest. It had been fairly light only minutes before, but dusk was skipping into twilight.

"We've been walking for almost four hours," she said. "It's going to be pitch black here in just a couple of minutes."

"You're right," Eddie said.

Megan glanced at him. "I think we ought to spend the night in this hideout and then leave early in the morning."

Eddie nodded. "That's exactly what I was thinking. You want to help me get some more branches and finish covering it up?"

"Sure," Megan said.

"Us too! We want to help!" Sarah and Faith chimed in.

Ten minutes later, they had covered the front of the shelter with pine branches. They left one opening barely big enough to squeeze through on the right side.

The four of them crawled in and bedded down for the night on soft piles of pine needles they had scooped into mounds. Before she drifted off to sleep, Megan thought about her father. She pictured him walking into the clearing, calling out her name, and throwing his arms around her.

Soon, she thought.

As the mists of slumber enfolded her, the image of her father was replaced by Dr. Collins. She stared down at Megan and reached out to brush the hair from her forehead. A calm feeling stole over her, and she drifted close to the edges of sleep.

Chapter 38

Creade slammed the door shut and stormed up the hall in a seething rage, a one-woman, level-five hurricane fully capable of wreaking death and destruction on anything in her path.

At that precise moment, Ted the guard had the unfortunate bad timing to be racing around the corner. He ploughed right into her, knocking her completely off balance. She staggered back, arms flailing, narrowly managing to catch her balance.

"Watch out, you idiot!" she barked. "Are you trying to kill me?"

"Sorry. I didn't see you coming. Really, I'm sorry. I…uh…"

"Just *zip it*! We don't have time for half-assed shenanigans. You find any sign of the kids outside?"

"No," he said. "Checked all over."

"Well, where the *hell* are they? You sure you checked everywhere? All around the grounds *and* in the garage *and* the two big sheds?"

"Damn straight I checked everywhere!" Ted fired back. He'd had enough abuse from this maniac nurse. "I combed every square inch with a fine-tooth comb, and I'm tellin' you, they ain't out there."

"Okay, okay already. So, we've already checked every room and closet in the building *twice,* and they're not here. *And* they're not anywhere on the grounds. They must have run for it."

"That's how I'd size it up."

Creade scowled. The lines on her forehead and around her eyes deepened into jagged canyons as she chewed on her thumbnail, calculating her next move. There weren't many. In fact, there was only one.

This was not going to be pleasant. Not pleasant at all.

She dropped her hand and fixed Ted with an unblinking glare. "Round up

Darryl and Sam and go to the control room. Dale is probably already there, checking the remote video surveillance camera reads. See if any of the cameras captured the kids on tape. We'll be damn lucky if they did."

"On my way," Ted said.

"Wait there for me. I'll be there in a few minutes. If I'm still alive. I've gotta go tell Thornton his pet project just walked out the door. *Man* is he going to be pissed! Get ready to have your asses chewed and handed to you on a plate."

Ted watched Creade storm off down the hall. He exhaled in a huff of anger, grabbed his phone, and called his partners.

Megan lay on her back and stared up at the canopy of overlocking branches above her. Stars twinkled through in a few scattered places, and Megan thought to herself that if it were raining, this shelter might keep all of them dry.

The events of the past two days spun around in her mind, a kaleidoscopic mélange of images. She scrunched her eyes closed even tighter and imagined floating in perfect, peaceful darkness. She listened to the sounds of the forest and the murmuring noises of her sleeping friends. Someone was snoring. Probably Eddie. Or maybe Sarah.

She slipped further into the darkness. A wonderful, weightless floating sensation enveloped her and carried her adrift across a soothing Neverland sea.

Images floated toward her out of the darkness, an entire world materializing with impossibly real sights, sensations, and sounds.

They were back on the path in the forest, the one they had traipsed down for two hours earlier that day. Megan could hear the branches crunch beneath her feet, smell the heady aroma of pine in the air, and feel the breeze that rustled through the trees.

She heard her friends talking around her and looked over her shoulder at Eddie. He was joking around with the walking stick he had picked up, pretending to be Gandalf in *Lord of the Rings*. Faith gave him a playful shove and tried to grab the walking stick away from him.

Megan turned back around and looked forward in front of her. She wasn't the least surprised to see herself leading the group down the path. A thought wafted lazily across her mind. *There's Megan, my best friend.*

In that moment, she realized she was seeing through Sarah's eyes, hearing through her ears, feeling what she felt and experienced. She heard the other Megan speak, and the words were familiar. They had been spoken earlier that day. She had spoken them.

As real as everything seemed, she had the disorienting sensation that the entire reality she was walking through was only a dream. A dream she was seeing through Sarah's eyes.

A branch snapped off a tree and fell in the distant forest. The noise jolted her awake. The incredibly palpable dreamscape dissolved in a splintering array, and a new reality took its place.

She sat bolt upright. Pine needles fell out of her hair and off her arms as she looked around. Her friends were all fast asleep, unaffected by the noise.

She leaned towards Eddie. He lay facing her. His eyes were closed, and his mouth hung open. She determined he was the source of the snoring. No surprise there.

She took in the sounds of the forest. Somewhere off in the distance, an owl hooted a soft, soulful refrain. High above her, tree branches rustled in the intermittent breeze that filtered through the forest.

She leaned to her right and stared at the slumbering form of the other two girls.

Faith was closest. Megan watched her shift in her sleep, her peaceful expression undisturbed.

And next to Faith was…

But that's impossible. That's…me. Megan. But that can't be. The dream ended. I'm already awake.

Shock jolted her completely awake. The second dreamscape disintegrated into a thousand slivers as Megan opened her eyes. She was staring at the forest again from an entirely different vantage point.

Megan sat up. She brushed at the pine needles that covered her arms. A shower of them fell out of her hair again, but this time, she could truly smell the forest. She felt a soft breeze buffet her face and the grittiness of the pine needles beneath her hands. She gripped and raised a handful, then opened her hand and let them filter between her fingers to the ground.

Looking to her left across Faith's sleeping form, Megan saw something that sent a chill up her spine.

Sarah was sitting up, looking at her with eyes wide, her mouth agape. Time stood still as they stared at each other.

Megan was the first to speak.

"Sarah…I just had the *weirdest* dream in the world. It was, like…totally unbelievable."

Sarah nodded slowly. It took a moment for her to speak.

"Me too. It was *really* freaky." She hesitated a few seconds then took a deep breath. "What was yours about?" she asked.

Megan shook her head. "It was so…bizarro, and so…I don't know…real and crazy. We were walking along the trail, like we were earlier today, but the spooky part was that I was *you*. I could see everything through *your* eyes—"

"Yeah, I know," Sarah interrupted.

"And if that wasn't strange enough…I thought I woke up and sat up like I'm doing now but…but I was *still* seeing through your eyes."

"Yeah, I know."

"I mean, I just can't believe it. The dream was…" Megan stopped abruptly and narrowed her eyes at Sarah. She could just make out her face in the moonlight. "Wait a minute…what do you mean *you know*?"

"I had the same dream."

Megan opened her mouth, but the words wouldn't come.

"You…did?" she asked finally.

"It was exactly the same…only it was me seeing through your eyes."

"But that can't be!" Megan exclaimed. She glanced at Eddie and Faith. "How could you have the same dream as me?"

"I don't know," Sarah said, "but I did. And somehow, I knew you were seeing what I was seeing. I could kinda feel you inside my head, looking through my eyes."

"Oh, man…That's what I felt too. This is just *too* strange and creepy and…and neat at the same time."

"Yeah," Sarah said. She stood up, stepped around Faith, and sat down next to Megan. She scooted closer to her until their noses were only inches apart.

She looked deeply into Megan's eyes, which glimmered in the filtering moonlight. Megan stared back, the two of them silenced in wonder, trying to read the mystery that bound them.

Sarah blinked. "Are you my twin? Or my older sister? Or…something?"

Megan pulled her close and hugged her.

"I don't know, Sarah," she whispered. Her arms tightened around the smaller girl. A fleeting image of Dr. Collins zipped across her mind's eye along with the wispy sensation that she had somehow been in the dream too.

"I have no idea." Megan drew back and brushed a strand of hair out of Sarah's bright, hopeful eyes. "But as impossible as it seems, maybe we are. I sure hope we are. I'd really like to be your sister."

"Me too," Sarah said.

"I promise we'll find out," Megan said, squeezing her arm. "But the first thing I promise is we're going to get out of here. My dad will come for us, and nothing's going to happen to you or me. Tomorrow we've got to make sure that we escape. I'm going to protect you, Sarah. I promise."

"I know," Sarah said. "And I'm going to protect you."

Megan smiled. "Now let's get back to sleep. I'll try to keep out of your dreams."

Chapter 39

Nurse Creade hadn't been kidding when she said that Thornton would not take the news well.

He had gone ballistic. Creade and the four members of his security team stood before him as he ranted and cursed for five minutes straight and then stopped abruptly. He glared at them in soundless rage.

The silence and unspoken tension stretched on until it grew unbearable. Creade cleared her throat and started to say something.

"Silence!" Thornton barked. "I'm still thinking."

A full minute passed, masquerading as an hour. All eyes avoided looking at Thornton, who was staring out the window at the forest that stretched to the horizon.

"Okay. Listen up. I'm only going to say this once." Thornton's eyes darted from one face to another. "You're going after them *right now*. And you're not quitting until you find them...no matter how long it takes." He paused, his eyes resting on his security team leader. He let the words hang in the air for a moment before continuing.

"Two things are absolute non-negotiables. You *will* get them back here tonight, and we *will* do the surgical procedure tomorrow as planned but later in the day. Am I clear?"

Creade glanced at the security team members, who nodded in unison.

"One small detail," she said. "How are we supposed to find them in the miles of wilderness that's out there? They could be anywhere. Four little needles in one big-ass haystack."

"Come, come, Nurse Creade. Where's your positive attitude?" Thornton sniped with a viper smile and shifted his piercing stare to his security personnel. "Dale, I assume you and your men spotted them on the remote digital surveillance tapes."

Dale was a taut, physically imposing man in his late-forties with chiseled facial features and short-cropped hair speckled with gray. His appearance mirrored the extreme conditioning he'd experienced as an ex-Army sergeant; everything about him emanated an aura of discipline.

He locked eyes with Thornton and cleared his throat.

"That is correct. We captured video footage of them in three separate locations. Recordings from quadrants two, five, and seven show the four subjects walking down the path. The time is recorded on each segment. Ted, roll the tapes."

Ted walked over to the digital video recorder, rewound the tape, and punched the play button.

"Have a look, sir," Dale said. "This first one is from quadrant two, about two and a half miles from here where the path heads east down the mountain."

Thornton leaned forward as the first video began playing and stared at it with intense concentration.

The picture had remarkable resolution, courtesy of the million-dollar surveillance system Thornton had had installed. If it had been in the middle of the night, the motion-activated video camera would have automatically switched to night vision and recorded in green-hued illumination. This recording was captured in the late afternoon, and Megan, the latest addition to their research project, could be seen walking down the path away from the camera. Sarah followed close behind, and the other two—Eddie and Faith—tagged along further back.

The tape continued until the four of them disappeared from sight. The lack of motion and infrared signature had toggled off the power and shut down the surveillance camera.

Thornton rewound the first video capture and replayed it several times. He scribbled something down on a pad.

"Is this first camera location *exactly* two and a half miles from here?" he asked.

"Close to it," Dale said. "If we look at the overall reconnaissance alignment"—he pulled a spiral-bound notebook out of a drawer and scanned the first two pages—"it's slightly more than two miles from here to the first quadrant. Each quadrant is marked on a tree next to the path and is measured off half a mile apart, starting at quadrant one. We have fifteen quadrants between the first and highway 82, and there are remote cameras positioned every three quadrants or one-point-five miles apart."

"Okay," Thornton interrupted. "So, looking at the time recorded on the tape, they crossed this point over two and a half hours ago. Quite a head start…"

"Yes, sir. But we're—"

"Show me the next tape."

Dale motioned to Ted. "Bring up the tape from quadrant five."

Thornton's eyes never left the screen. Sarah skipped into view, and behind her, Megan and the others.

Thornton scribbled down the time registered on the screen and some additional notes.

"And you've got one more video capture?"

"Third and final," Dale said. "Ted, put on the quadrant seven tape."

This time the picture was dark and grainy. Dusk had slid into twilight, and the shadowy figures that appeared were barely identifiable. Thornton recognized the light blue hoodie Megan was wearing and the colorful backpack-purse Sarah had strapped to her back.

Megan was in the lead again, but all four of them were moving slower than in the previous tapes.

Thornton replayed the tape two more times. He clicked the Pause button and looked up, training his penetrating glare at Dale.

"It's almost dark in this tape. They look exhausted."

"I agree," Dale said. "It could be that after this, they stopped for the night. Or at least for a few hours of rest."

"I've got one question," Thornton said in an icy tone. "Why the *hell* isn't the time recorded on this tape?"

Dale gritted his teeth. "Recording error, sir."

"What do you mean *recording error*?"

Dale cleared his throat and braced himself. "The surveillance camera at quadrant seven was set to record the time and date on the tape but malfunctioned. We tested it remotely, and we can't get the time and date function to activate."

"Well, isn't that just perfect," Thornton said. "Right when we need the camera to work…" He exhaled in frustration and glanced again at his notes before continuing. "This is from quadrant seven?"

"Yes, sir."

"What about quadrant…eight? Did that camera activate?"

The other three security men stole a quick look at Dale.

"Yes, it did," Dale said. "There's a short blip of tape—three seconds or less—that didn't show anything but a very dark glimpse of the forest, then the camera shut off. Likely just a deer or small animal triggering the motion/infrared sensor."

"And you think that's what it was?"

"It could be, but we aren't sure. We tried to activate the camera; it didn't respond. We believe the quadrant nine camera is also malfunctioning."

Thornton clamped his jaws shut. A vein above his right eye pulsed in time with his heartbeat.

"Glad to see my million-dollar surveillance system works so well. What an asinine fiasco."

"We'll have it checked out and corrected, sir," Dale said.

"It *better* be." Thornton exhaled his frustration. A frigid tension filled the air as he processed the information and his anger.

"We've got to play the cards we've been dealt," he said after a full minute of silence. "What three things do we know. *First,* we taped them at the quadrant-two camera over two and a half hours ago. *Second,* they passed the quadrant-five camera over an hour later. It took them an hour to go a mile and a half. *Third,* when they passed the quadrant-seven camera it was dark, but we don't know the exact time."

"Right." Dale nodded once. "By this time, night's fallen, and they're tired. Could be they stopped in quadrant eight or nine."

"Maybe, but the quadrant eight camera fired," Thornton said. "We don't know if it was them."

Dale looked at his watch. "True…the few seconds of footage on the tape were pitch dark."

Thornton stared right through his security team leader. "So, the question is: would they stop somewhere for the night or would they keep walking through the forest in the dark?"

He mulled it over a minute, and his thoughts slid together and assembled into a plan.

"Here's what we're going to do. All of you leave now and meet at the quadrant-seven camera as fast as you can make it there. Dale, can the ATVs get us there quicker than hiking the trail? Any shortcut roads or paths to quadrant-seven?"

Dale sprang into action. "Absolutely. A couple of fire roads crisscross all over the mountainside. I'll double-check the map, but I know one of them passes within half a mile of quadrant seven."

"Excellent," Thornton said. "We've got five ATVs, so double up. Drive the entire way on low throttle to keep the noise down. When you get close, shut them off and walk the last half mile."

"On it," Dale said. He turned to his men. "Grab the night vision scopes, flashlights, and duffel bags of gear. Meet us out at the big shed in five minutes. I want the ATVs gassed up and ready to go. Move it."

His men scrambled out of the room.

"One more thing," Thornton said. "Get ahold of Carl. Tell him to drop everything and meet you at quadrant seven with his tracking dogs. Tell him he'll get three times his normal rate for however long it takes to find the kids. If he doesn't come now…he won't work for us again. Keep me in the loop."

"Right," Dale said. He turned on his heel and started for the door.

Thornton turned to Creade. "Get him something from each of the kids with their scent on it. The dogs will need it for tracking."

"Will do," Creade said.

Chapter 40

It was dark by the time Max and Beth had driven their rental car over two hours southwest of the Denver airport. They were approaching Leadville, and once they passed through it, they would arrive in Rios, about twenty minutes further south.

Beth accessed the Internet with her iPad and looked up the numbers of a few hotels in Rios to call.

"The Starlight Motel it is," Beth said. "I booked us two rooms."

"Perfect," Max said. "You want to get hold of Mark?"

"Yeah, I'm dialing now."

It rang a few times. Then he answered. "Joe's Texas Hold'em Poker Parlor."

"Mark?"

"The one and only. How're you doing, Beth?"

"Good," she said. "But how did you know it was me?"

"Caller ID. I've already got your number stashed in my phone."

"How are you?" she asked. *Where* are you?"

"Way out in the middle of Egypt somewhere. Been cruising pretty fast the past few hours though. Should be coming up on Cove Fort, Utah in about an hour. Then I'll rip across I-70 to Grand Junction, Colorado in a shade under four hours."

"You're making great time."

"That's my plan. Flyin' low, flyin' fast. When I hit Grand Junction, it'll be another three hours to Vail and then an hour or so down to Rios."

"Excellent. Looks like you're about…nine hours away," Beth said. "I called and booked us two rooms at a place called the Starlight Motel. It's right on the main drag through Rios, Highway 24. The same road you'll be taking south through Leadville. The guy told me it's on the west side of the road across the street from a Burger King."

"*Great. So*unds like a hooker hangout," Mark quipped.

"It's not the Ritz, but the pictures on the web looked semi-passable. You'll be staying in Mark's room."

"Doesn't matter if it's the 'No-Tell Motel' as long as I can crash for a few hours. Figure I'll get in between four and four-thirty, Rios time."

"Good. Sleep in until nine, then we'll grab a quick breakfast and head out."

"Roger that. We've got a plan," he said. "In the meantime, I'm glad Starbucks owns a chunk of real estate in every town I drive through. They're making some serious money on me tonight. Later."

"Bye, Mark."

Megan was running through her dreams.

She heard the faint, distant baying of hounds. An English fox hunt in full progression materialized out of thin air. British gentry atop tall white horses galloped after a pack of yapping and howling beagles in frenzied pursuit of a fox. They were closing in on their prey, and the scene was growing bigger than life, every smell and feature starkly clear, the thrill of the chase visceral and real.

The hunt zipped by, disappearing from view in a blanket of mist that whirled across the dreamy panorama. The sounds faded gradually into the distance, and all was perfectly silent.

Then the baying resumed. Louder. Closer.

Megan burst through the surface of consciousness and opened her eyes. She sat up, a feeling of dread constricting her chest. Her eyes darted over the sleeping forms that lay beside her and paused on Sarah, who bolted upright and stared directly at her.

Megan was buffeted by a strange mix of expectation and déjà vu.

"Don't tell me," she said. "You just had a dream of some English guys riding white horses with a pack of howling dogs chasing a fox. Right?"

Even in the dark Megan could see Sarah's jaw drop.

"How did you know?"

"Because I had the same exact dream."

"*Again?*"

"Look, I don't know how this works," Megan said. "Or why we're connected. We just are."

Sarah scooted towards Megan, a worried look on her face. "Do you think it's because of the shots they've been giving us?"

"What do you mean?" Megan asked. A wave of anger and protectiveness surged inside her. *What did those doctors do to us?*

Sarah hesitated.

"We already look like twins. Maybe the shots make us have the same dreams."

Megan's eyes drifted upward. "Yeah, like something out of a scary movie. All I know is they're not giving me any more shots."

Her gaze sharpened on Sarah's face. "No way they're even getting close to me again."

"Me either," Sarah agreed. "And I wonder if…"

A sound broke the silence of the night.

Sarah stopped suddenly. She jerked her head around and looked out into the blackness of the dark forest. The sound could have come from anywhere.

It happened a second time. They both heard it. A baying of hounds off in the distance that was every bit as loud as it was in their dreams.

"What would dogs be doing out in the middle of the night?" Megan asked.

The sound faded as if the dogs were moving away from them. The two girls waited in tense silence for a minute, two, three. Megan sighed in relief. And then the baying resumed. Closer.

"They're looking for us," Sarah whispered. She reached out for Megan, and the older girl pulled her close. "They used the dogs before. Eddie told me about it. Six months ago, he tried to escape and run away into the forest. They sent out a search party with these dogs that are really good sniffers and can find anybody they're looking for."

"Bloodhounds?"

"That's what he called them. He almost got away, but the dogs followed his trail and found him."

"We better get out of here!" Megan scrambled over to Eddie and Faith and shook them awake.

"C'mon you guys! Wake up! They're coming after us. We gotta go!"

Eddie and Faith scrambled to their feet with dazed expressions.

"Uh…whaa…what's goin' on?" Eddie shook his head. His eyes darted around the campsite.

"Who's coming? Where are they?" Faith said.

"Shh! No time to talk," Megan said. "Follow me!"

She grabbed Sarah's hand and took off down the trail. Eddie and Faith followed close behind.

Megan ran into the dark line of trees, trying to stick to the crooked path in the dim moonlight. They stumbled several times over the patchwork of gnarled roots that crossed the path.

The hounds were getting closer, louder. Their baying sent chills up and down Megan's spine. Megan stopped in her tracks when she realized where the sounds were coming from.

She swung her head around and faced Eddie and Faith, who came running up, huffing and out of breath.

"Why…are we…stopping?" Eddie asked.

"Did you hear the dogs howl that time?" Megan asked.

"Yeah," Eddie said. He bent down, his hands on his knees, and tried to catch his breath.

"Sounds like they're getting really close," Faith said.

"They *are*," Megan said. "And I think we're running right towards them."

"Do you think they're on the trail?" Eddie asked.

Megan grabbed his arm, forcing him to look up at her. "Eddie, Sarah told me you tried to run away once, and they used the dogs to track you and finally catch you."

"It was scary. Those dogs are gigantic, and they've got huge, gnarly teeth."

"Eddie, try to remember. When they tracked you, did they come *up* the trail as you were going down the trail?"

Eddie thought for a second and shook his head. "I don't know. I didn't take the trail when I tried to escape. I tried running down the mountain through the thick part of the forest. I thought it would be a lot harder for them to find me."

"Okay," Megan said, "but when they did catch you, were they coming up or down the mountain?"

Eddie's eyes widened. "Oh, man…they were definitely coming *up* the mountain."

"Everybody follow me," Megan said. "We're going back up the trail. I saw a place where we can leave the trail and head out into the forest. We'll split up and go sideways across the mountain. Then when the dogs sound far enough away, we'll head down the mountain towards the highway. C'mon, we've gotta run our fastest!"

They scrambled up the trail a ways before veering off and heading into the trees. They cut a lateral path across the mountains. The branches whipped them as they scurried across the thick pine foliage of the primeval forest.

In the near distance, a team of three men with night scopes made their way up the trail accompanied by three bloodhounds. The dogs fell silent, noses to the ground as they tried to pick up the kids' scent again.

Twenty minutes later, the bloodhounds caught the scent. They raised their snouts to the sky and let out a blood-curdling howl. The chase was on.

Chapter 41

Megan winced as she shoved aside another pine branch that scratched her arm. She gripped Sarah's hand as she pulled the younger girl across the rough terrain of the thick forest, trying to hurry while keeping her footing in the darkness.

She looked up at the sky through the trees and was able to find the constellation Orion, just like her father had taught her, and use its position to get her bearings and orient their direction. Seeing the three stars of Orion's belt brought a warm, fleeting image of her father to mind, and with that, a small glimmer of hope. He'd come for her, or she'd find him, and he'd make this bad nightmare go away.

Megan pushed a branch out of the way and held it until Sarah passed before letting it go. It slapped back, almost catching Eddie in the face. He held it back as Faith went by, then let it fly.

They scurried across a clearing and entered the trees on the other end. Sarah slipped on a pile of rocks and cried out. Megan grabbed her arm and held her up.

"Careful, Sarah," she whispered. "The rocks are slippery."

Sarah regained her footing, and they raced into the trees. A dog howled in the indiscernible distance.

In spite of the partially clouded moon in the sky, it was difficult to see the forest floor or much more than twenty feet in front of them. It was easier to make out their surroundings in the clearings, but the ambient light grew dimmer the farther into the forest they went.

Branches crunched beneath their feet as they ran, and they continually had to climb over fallen trees or skirt around the much larger ones.

Megan tried to keep them going in a straight direction and had rechecked Orion's position in the sky when they were in the clearing. She knew they were going in the right direction, but as she scrambled through the trees, she hoped they were running fast enough to escape. If only the dogs wouldn't find their trail.

The forest opened up, and Megan pumped her legs harder, keeping a tight grip on Sarah's hand. She could hear Eddie and Faith huffing and puffing behind her; they were drifting farther back.

"Keep up, you guys," she said. She didn't have the time to look back.

They weaved through a copse of trees that gradually thinned out, becoming sparser as they entered an area of older growth. The Ponderosa pine and Douglas fir trees in this part of the forest were massive.

Megan tried to take advantage of the easier terrain by picking up her pace. Sarah stumbled a few times trying to keep up, but Megan helped her hurry.

The dogs howled again, an unnerving, haunting refrain.

They were close. Way too close.

Megan stopped and turned around. Eddie turned back to Megan, his face contorted with shock and fear.

"They've got our scent, and their closing in on us," he said. His voice broke slightly.

"Follow me," Megan said. She took a deep breath, squared her shoulders, and took off through the trees with Sarah in tow. Her heart pounded explosively in her chest, making it difficult to breathe.

They dashed through the forest, zigzagging through the trees until they came upon an enormous fallen Douglas fir that blocked their path. The trunk was over three feet in diameter, and the tree had crashed its way through the dense surrounding foliage and wedged itself against two other trees, its top coming to rest ten to twelve feet off the ground.

Megan scanned the inclining length of the trunk to her right and saw it disappear into the dense branches of the trees holding it up. She turned and began to run to the opening where they could pass under it but halted as the dogs bayed again. They were just too close.

She looked down at Sarah. "Can you be brave? Braver than you've ever been in your whole life?"

Sarah nodded. "I can be brave."

Megan looked up the length of the sloping trunk.

"I'm going to lift you up on this tree, and I want you to climb all the way up there and hide behind those branches. See?"

Megan pointed up the tree. Sarah's eyes followed her finger.

"Think you can do that?"

"I know I can do it," she said. "I'm one of the best climbers ever! Lift me up."

Megan boosted her up onto the trunk. Sarah paused for a moment, then gained her balance and began to crawl up the tree.

"Wait a minute," Megan said, stopping her. "Listen. You need to hide out up there for at least an hour. Maybe more. Until it's light and you can't hear the dogs anymore."

"Okay," Sarah said. She looked at Megan with expectant eyes and her bravest face. "Then what?"

"Only then, climb down and make your way *down* the mountain as fast as you can. Make sure you go straight down, not sideways, and keep totally hidden. When you reach the main highway, hurry over to the gas station we saw on the drive in here and ask to use someone's phone to call the police to help us. Remember where the gas station is?"

"Of course," Sarah said with a forced smile. "Remember how good my memory is?"

"Yeah. Probably the best in the world."

"Probably."

"Now get up there and hide."

Megan watched Sarah as she scurried up the sloping trunk. "One more thing! Tell 'em my Dad's a SWAT police officer in Southern California. His name's Max Tyler."

"I will," she said

Megan watched her climbing.

Canine bellowing broke the silence, shocking in its proximity. Five minutes away. Maybe less.

Megan spun around and grasped Faith's arm. "C'mon, you guys. We've gotta get out of here."

She took off to the right, down the length of the trunk, then ducked under it to the other side and ran into the forest with Eddie and Faith on her heels.

They ran for several minutes, dry forest debris snapping beneath their feet. Pine needle branches whipped them in the face as they dodged through the trees, but they ignored the stinging pain.

They sprinted at top speed for another five minutes, but Megan knew they couldn't keep up this pace for long.

The dogs howling grew more fervent and frenzied as they closed in on their prey. The stronger scent proclaimed proximity.

Megan expected them to appear at any minute. She halted to let the others catch up to her.

"We've...got to...split up. That way...they can't catch...all of us."

"Right..." Eddie exhaled.

Faith struggled to catch her breath. "That's...the only thing...that'll work," she said. Her eyes tightened in determination. Adrenaline raced through her veins. "We've gotta do it."

Megan forced herself to take a couple of deep breaths, in through her nose and out through her mouth. "Whoever gets away...get down the mountain...call the police and send 'em up here..."

"Yeah..." Faith huffed. She locked eyes with Megan and nodded once.

"Okay..." Megan said. "Now!"

She darted and disappeared into the trees, running ten steps forward before changing direction and racing diagonally down the mountain.

Eddie and Faith fanned out to the left, heading in diverging paths as they ran for their lives.

The search team—three men, one bloodhound, and two Arkansas coonhounds—reached the spot where they'd separated a few minutes later. The dogs circled around the area, yelping and baying.

"Musta split up," the first man said, scanning the area in a full circle rotation with his night scope.

"Don't see nothin' out there, dammit. Back the dogs up ten feet and find the split, boys."

He yanked hard on the leash and circled his bloodhound around and back up the direction they had come. The other two men did likewise. The dogs surged against their leashes, eager for the hunt.

"We'll split up where we need to," the first man said. "Three dogs...we'll cover two or three trails. Whatever we find."

"What if there's a fourth?" asked the second man.

"Then we catch three of 'em and come back here to start tracking the final one."

He took a paint canister out of his jacket and sprayed a large orange X on a tree.

"Keep the talkies on, and radio when you've caught your kid. Otherwise, silence unless it's important. Got it?"

"Yeah," both men said in unison.

"I'll take the first trail. When they're locked on the scent...unleash 'em. Dogs'll chase 'em down."

He yanked the thick leather leash and pulled his dog back. "Sit!" he commanded.

The bloodhound sat, and the man put his hand on the back of the dog's muzzle. He slid it back to the crown of his head and held it there five seconds, calming the dog and directing his focus.

"*Conan.* Search!"

The bloodhound charged forward, nose to the ground. He reached the point where the kids split up and angled to the left, locked onto a scent that was strong and fresh.

The trail was Eddie's.

The second man repeated this with his coonhound. The dog picked up Faith's trail that diverged off to the left at a sharper angle.

When the third man came to the split point, he had to yank his Arkansas coonhound off the other two trails. He sat down the large, gray-speckled dog, took hold of his head with both hands, and looked him straight in the face.

"Calm!" he commanded. He held the dog still for half a minute then released his grip and moved to the dog's side. He pulled the leash taut.

"*Striker.* Search!" the man commanded and yanked him to the right.

The coonhound picked up Megan's scent and bayed as he surged down the invisible trail she'd left.

With a chilling smile, the man reached down to unleash the coonhound. "Go get 'em!"

Chapter 42

Eddie heard the deep guttural bellowing of the bloodhound that was closing in on him. He tried to pick up speed, but the forest, already thick with new growth, had grown even denser. It was a labyrinthine maze, an arbor gauntlet of living wood.

His mind flashed back to the last time he'd escaped the lab and run free. He replayed the moment when the snarling dog had chased him down and clamped its jaws on his leg in a wickedly painful vice grip. The dog had run him down like a rabbit and caught him.

His leg pulsed with a ghost pain in the spot where the dog's teeth had penetrated his skin.

He couldn't let it happen again. He had to get away.

He dodged through the trees and felt a glimmer of hope when he saw the trees thinning up ahead. He jumped up onto a fallen tree and ran along its trunk for twenty feet before hopping off the opposite side to the ground.

Running through the trees, he clung to the hope that his little maneuver would confuse the dog, or at least slow him down.

The bloodhound reached the trunk a few heartbeats later. He spent all of ten seconds deciphering where the trail continued. He circled the trunk, calling out his excitement. Then he locked on the trail and took off again.

The pursuit ensued. Tempus fugit. Then Tempus stopped. Inexorable hope gave way to the inevitable.

Eddie didn't dare stop to look over his shoulder. He heard the growling seconds before the dog pounced.

With a cry of fear, Eddie launched himself at an overhanging tree branch. He managed to grab hold and swing skyward, pulling himself up out of the way a second before the dog's snapping jaws would have closed on his ankle.

The bloodhound stood on two legs with his front paws leaning against the tree and howled at his treed prey. The canine song of a successful hunt.

Eddie scrambled halfway up the tall tree and sat on a branch with his feet dangling. He waited there, out of breath and trembling in fear, until a man walked up.

"Good job, Conan." He yanked on the leash, pulling the dog back and down. Then he unholstered a Taser pistol and held it up for Eddie to see.

"Your choice," he said in a gravelly voice.

Eddie stared wide-eyed at the man and the weapon. He remembered his last escape attempt and the horror of the taser—the prongs piercing his chest, the jolting, incapacitating electrical shock paralyzing his body and short-circuiting his brain, the sickening smell of the hair all over his body crisping.

And last time he'd been shot with his feet on the ground, not perched on a branch twenty feet up in the air where gravity is most definitely not your friend.

His resistance evaporated along with all glimmers of hope.

Eddie held up his hands in a sign of defeat then turned and began to climb down. The man kept the taser pointed at him and grabbed his arm when he reached the ground. He secured Eddie's hands and marched him back to the path.

Faith felt like she was making incredible progress running through the forest. Her hopes of escape rose with each passing minute. She had picked up her pace, pushing herself to the limit as she zigzagged amongst the trees. She was running a slalom that could take her to freedom if only she could go fast enough and far enough.

She ran through a grassy glade, not stopping to look around but increasing her speed and entry back into the forest. The trees on the other side were spaced farther apart than the section of forest where she'd been running. She could feel the fierce pounding of her heart pummeling in her chest as she sprinted. Focusing on the loud, chopped patter of her breathing and the trees before her, she blocked out all other thoughts and rode the excitement of her pending escape.

Her physical motion and the terrain before her enveloped her senses, so it stunned her when she heard the dog howl nearby.

No! A voice shrieked in her mind as daggers of icy panic stabbed her chest. *How'd they get so close?*

She sped forward to an outcropping of rocks, leaped onto the first small boulder, and hurried up the next one and the next, all the way to the top.

For a fraction of a second, she looked around. Then she scampered to the top boulder, where she stood and hesitated for few seconds before jumping off the opposite side of the outcropping.

It was a long drop to the forest floor, but Faith landed solidly on her feet and sprinted into the trees. She zigged and zagged through the forest, rapidly picking up speed and keeping her eyes locked on the trees ahead. But she missed the rocky depression covered in a tangle of branches and pine needles.

She stepped on it at full speed, her right foot breaking through a sparse pile of twigs and hitting a sharp angular rock. Two of the bones in her foot fractured and a tendon in her ankle twisted and tore.

Faith stumbled forward and began sprawling to the ground. She cried out in pain and reached for her ankle as excruciating pain shot up through her entire body. As she fell, she didn't see the splintery branch shard until it was too late. It jutted up like a jagged, twenty-inch spike from a branch buried in the leaves.

The shard impaled her, piercing through her upper right side, then through the right and left lobes of her lungs, deflating them both. Faith struggled to inhale and found she couldn't breathe. Panic consumed her as she fought for air, and she convulsed in sheer terror as she tried to lift herself off the pointed shard.

"No, no, no..." she rasped as clouds of darkness closed in from the perimeter of her vision.

Three minutes later, the coonhound reached her. He nudged her hand with his cold nose. When she didn't respond, he sat down near her head and stood guard until the tracking team arrived.

Megan ran like the wind.

This was it. Her best chance. Her one chance.

Branches scraped and scratched at her as she penetrated the pine foliage, but it felt like she was moving in slow motion. She hoped the density of trees would thin soon, or another clearing would appear, anything to let her open up full bore and run at top speed.

Her wish was soon granted. A few yards up ahead, the forest grew sparser, and beyond that a clearing yawned before her.

She bore down and accelerated, streaking across the clearing and then reentering the trees. She darted among them, managing to slow her pace only slightly as she negotiated the terrain.

An enormous Ponderosa pine, felled years earlier, blocked her path. It lay propped at a thirty-degree angle, supported by another downed tree it had toppled when it fell.

Megan slowed as she approached the obstacle. Without stopping, she jumped onto the sloping trunk, scampered up its length, and hopped onto the trunk of the second tree. She hurried down its length to where it intersected a shorter tree that had collapsed onto a rugged outcropping of rocks. She shuffled down the branches of the shorter tree onto the rocks, jumped to the forest floor, and hit the ground running.

She picked up speed, dodging the trees and branches in her way. Her best option wouldn't be outrunning the dog tracking her but keeping him confused. She hoped her convoluted detour on the fallen trees would throw him off her trail. At least long enough for her to get away.

Five minutes passed before Megan heard the coonhound howl. The fevered keening sent a chill up her spine and stopped her dead in her tracks.

Is he howling because he can't find my trail or because he did? she thought.

She burst into a run and pushed herself to the top limits of her speed.

Fifteen minutes later, she had her answer.

The tree where Megan stopped was a primeval giant, an enormous Douglas fir that stretched a hundred feet or more into the sky. She leaned hard against it, struggling to catch her breath, buckled over from the sharp, relentless pain in her side.

She'd been sprinting for what seemed like forever. Her heart thundered violently in her chest as she gasped for air. Never in her life had she been so completely out of breath.

Just a few seconds. Can't...breathe...

She gulped air, fighting a panicky sensation that she was suffocating. It wasn't until her breathing had finally returned to normal that she heard it.

A low guttural growl that raised the hairs on her neck and sent a quiver snaking up her spine.

Her eyes darted around the forest behind her. She didn't spot anything out of the ordinary at first. Then ten feet away, she saw the coonhound's eyes and snout poking through the low pine branches.

He stepped out of the cover of the branches, and Megan's heart caught in her throat. He was the largest, meanest looking dog she had ever seen. His upper lip curled into a vicious snarl, revealing enormous white incisors and a fierce complement of numerous jagged teeth.

Megan knew there was no way she could run for it. He'd be on her in seconds, shredding her with his razor teeth.

As abject fear pulsed through her, an eerie wavering appeared in the periphery of her vision, at once transparent and morphing. An unfamiliar view of the forest encroached on the edges of her visual field. It overlaid itself on the scene before her, like the views from two different windows in a house layered on top of each other. Both were clear and transparent but separate and distinguishable, like a see-through picture within a picture.

The second forest view was changing perspective, rotating as though a video camera were shooting panoramic footage of the forest. The main scene underneath it—Megan's terrifying reality—didn't change, and she found she could focus on it, keeping the secondary view on the periphery.

Before her, the growling coonhound was all too real and terrifying.

The vicious canine stepped towards her, his growl intensifying, his fangs glistening.

Three miles away, Sarah stopped suddenly and turned to look at the forest behind her. After waiting thirty minutes, she had scampered down the trunk of the fallen tree she was hiding in and had just started heading down the mountain when strange ripples appeared in the perimeter of her vision. It transformed into an unfamiliar scene of the forest. The transparent overlay of two different views of the forest disoriented her, and it took her a minute to realize what she was looking at.

She shook her head from side to side and watched the forest in the center of her visual field shift. The peripheral picture of the second forest grew clearer and moved on its own.

Sarah closed her eyes and shook her head, thinking her mind was playing tricks on her, like she was dreaming but awake.

She scrunched her eyes closed one last time, hard enough to see stars, and then opened them wide.

The simultaneous forest views were still there. Both were crystal clear. Both seemed equally real.

She focused on the forest before her and found that she could keep the second image on the side of her visual field. The more she focused, the more muted the second image became.

Then, even though it scared her a little, she tried the reverse.

As Sarah concentrated on the peripheral image, it grew in intensity and clarity, enlarging and shifting more to the center as the first image muted into the background. The overlay allowed her to see the second forest view clearly but still be aware of the view directly before her.

Two realities. Two different places in front of her eyes at the same time.

The transparent picture on top of another picture fascinated Sarah, and she wondered how fast she could switch between them.

She flipped views again, and the image of the forest before her quickly became dominant.

She flipped back, and just as quickly the peripheral image enlarged.

Sarah concentrated on this image. *Where is this part of the forest?* she wondered.

As she watched, the perspective of the second forest image shifted, and a terrifying scene unfolded.

She saw a large dog step out of the cover of some low tree branches, snarling and vicious. It stared directly at her. She could see the hairs on its back standing up and the flash of its enormous teeth as it stood poised to attack.

Sarah held her breath as she watched it take a step forward.

Then the image shifted, and she saw something that made her gasp in surprise.

The view angled toward the ground, feverishly scanning back and forth. A hand reached down out of nowhere and grabbed a rock.

Megan tore her eyes from the snarling dog and frantically searched the ground below her for anything she could use as a weapon.

She saw a good-sized chunk of granite laying on the ground near a small outcropping of rocks about two feet away. She reached out and grabbed it and then squared off to face the dog that had taken another step closer.

The view on the periphery of her visual field had muted considerably as she focused all her attention on the snarling dog before her. He stalked forward and crouched at the base of the tree, coiled for attack. His growl intensified.

An image of her father teaching her to pitch on her Little League team flashed in front of Megan's eyes. He'd worked with her for months, and although she was the only girl on the team, she'd become the starting pitcher in her second year. Hundreds of windups and pitches. Good form. Full power. Good follow-through. She was the strikeout queen. She had taken her team to eleven and two for the season, including one shutout.

Now all she needed was one strike. Just one.

The rock in her hand was heavier than a baseball but not too big to control. Her eyes narrowed, and she squared her shoulders. One shot. One strike.

She went into a full wind up just as the snarling dog attacked. It sprung into the air a fraction of a second before she released the rock. The chunk of granite hit the coonhound squarely in the mouth. The impact snapped off half of one of his upper incisors and the impact wrenched his head around, stopping him in mid-leap.

Megan watched him crumble to the ground with a yelp, stunned and momentarily immobilized.

He shook his head and tried to scramble to his feet. Megan didn't stick around to see if he'd be able to. She took off like a streak through the trees. Seconds later, she heard the dog chasing after her, gaining on her with every second that passed.

She spotted a fallen spruce tree with a medium-sized Douglas fir tree growing next to it. She sped towards it and took a running leap, spring boarding off it like a trampoline and jumping as high as she could toward the lowest branch of the fir tree.

Her fingers clawed the bark, and she locked her arms around the branch, her legs dangling for a few terrifying seconds as she struggled to pull herself up.

She managed to hook one leg over the branch just before the coonhound jumped onto the fallen tree and into the air, snapping at her feet.

He clamped onto her tennis shoe, ripping it off as she yanked her other leg up to safety. With his trophy firmly in mouth, he plummeted to the ground in a jumbled heap.

He scrambled to his feet, dropped the shoe, and began barking ferociously as Megan climbed higher and wedged herself in the nook of the tree.

She looked down at the agitated dog and noticed that the second forest view at the periphery of her vision had narrowed and grown smaller, minimized by her adrenaline-charged escape.

The two men tracking her showed up not long after that. One of them put a leash on the dog and gave him a harsh yank.

Megan's awareness of them faded as she concentrated on her second-sight image, which she had managed to stretch and clarify by pure will power.

Something odd was happening.

Chapter 43

Sarah was stunned by the image of the hand darting in and out of the picture in her peripheral view. She also caught a glimpse of a pink sweatshirt sleeve that seemed familiar. *Wasn't Megan wearing a pink sweatshirt today? I'm sure she was…*

Sarah focused on the changing picture, and as it heightened in size and further crystallized in clarity, she watched the drama unfold: the rock smashing the attacking dog in the mouth and him crumbling to the ground, the dizzying change of view shifting to the tree branch, a glimpse of the dog pulling a white tennis shoe off a foot, a view of more branches as the scene panned up the tree.

Megan was wearing white tennis shoes today too.

The image panned down and centered on the dog. Chills shot up Sarah's spine when she realized she could hear a dog barking in the distance. The sound was in perfect synchrony with the image of the dog barking in her peripheral view.

As she stared in wonder at the creepy image, it shifted upward and aligned on two men who had walked into view.

The one in the forefront was a gruff-looking, bearded man in a hunter's jacket. He had something in his hand, but at first, Sarah couldn't make it out. He looked like he was shouting at her. She watched as the view shifted and he walked up to the dog and snapped on a leather leash. As he yanked the dog back and into a sitting position, the dog in the image appeared to stop barking.

Sarah gasped in surprise as the barking in the distance stopped at that exact moment. An eerie wave of chills tickled down her spine.

The second man, who was wearing a gray security uniform, stepped up next to the first. Sarah felt another shock of surprise as his face came into focus.

That's Darryl, the jerky security guard! He and that man with the dog are trying to catch us. But this is so weird. How can I be seeing them?

She thought about the hand and the pink sweatshirt sleeve she had seen in her second image. Her mind shifted back to the weird identical dream she and Megan had both had earlier that night.

It's Megan. It's gotta be. They've caught her, and I'm seeing through her eyes.

A sudden revelation clicked in her mind. *Can see through my eyes?*

Sarah held her hand up and stared at her palm. She waved at herself. Then dropping her hand, Sarah concentrated on the picture in her peripheral view and watched as it expanded and sharpened.

A moment later, a tentative hand came into view, palm forward, blocking the view of the two men and the dog on the ground. It waved back at her.

Sarah gasped in stunned amazement. *What?!...is this for real?*

She held her left palm in front of her face and with her right index finger traced out her name in capital letters, *S-A-R-A-H*. Then she held her breath and waited to see what would happen next.

Three miles away, Megan stared in fascination at the letters being traced on the palm in the image before her. A surreal surge of wonder made her heart skip and the breath catch in her throat.

"Sarah," she whispered in disbelief. A few seconds passed as Megan tried to grasp the impossible. Her hands clenched and unclenched in unbridled awe. She held her palm up to her face and traced out her name in block letters, *M-E-G-A-N*. Then she wiggled her fingers in a wave.

She held her breath, her gaze locked on the expanding peripheral image, which refined into sharper focus. Then she saw it. The hand slid into view. The palm opened, and the index finger appeared and traced two letters: H—I. Then the letters: I—T—S M—E.

Megan felt a dizzying rush of eeriness and wonder.

Sarah! It really is you.

Megan held her hand up in front of her face to respond but was startled by a loud shout from the two men on the ground.

"I'm *not* going to say this again!"

Megan looked down at the gruff man in the camouflage jacket. She tried to zero in her split vision on the device he was pointing at her.

Is that a gun?

"Get down here *now*, or I shoot you with the taser."

At this distance, he could hit her with his eyes closed.

"You got three seconds to start moving before I zap you with fifty thousand volts. One…*two*…"

Megan flung her legs over the branch and started climbing down the tree.

In her frenzied descent, she barely noticed the peripheral view of the forest and Sarah's palm shrink down to a pin-sized dot and vanish. As soon as her foot touched the ground, the men grabbed her and began leading her back toward the building complex.

"Sarah?" she whispered to herself.

She tried squeezing her eyes closed and opening them again and again, but the image wouldn't return.

Sarah saw the palm appear again.

She waited for another message to be traced out, but the hand dropped from view. In its place was a crystal sharp view of the two men. One of them shook an odd-looking weapon menacingly at her.

They've got her now, she thought.

The edges of the image began to collapse inward and the window of second sight telescoped down to a pea-sized circle and then a pin-size dot before disappearing. Sarah's breath caught in a sob as she shut her eyes tightly and reopened them. The image wouldn't return.

"No! Megan! Wait! Come back!"

Tears pooled in the corners of her eyes. She gritted her teeth in defiance and willed herself to stop.

No way. I'm not gonna be weak. How can I help Megan escape if I sit here and cry like a baby?

She gripped her hands into fists and began running straight down the mountain.

Down to the small town on the highway. Down to help.

Chapter 44

Max drove out of the café parking lot and pulled onto the main highway heading south. He floored the gas pedal, and the powerful V8 engine roared to life.

Dawn was breaking with a vibrant cascade of color as red-orange iridescent tendrils streaked the eastern sky. In half an hour, the rich colors would fade to a pale ghost of their current grandeur.

Max, Beth, and Mark had grabbed a quick breakfast and finalized their plan of attack.

"You dreamt what?" Max asked as they rocketed down the highway.

Beth looked up from the map she was reviewing. "I know how strange it sounds, but it was so real."

"And you saw Megan again?"

"Even clearer than last time. I was running down a path with three other kids. Megan was gripping my hand, and we were so close, I could see her blue eyes in the moonlight. She opened her mouth to say something, and then all of a sudden, my perspective shifted, and I was seeing through Megan's eyes...like I dissolved right into her."

"That *is* weird," Max said.

"I could sense how scared Megan was. It was like...like I was feeling what she was feeling. And I'm looking at this girl who looks exactly like Megan only younger with longer hair. She's wearing an aqua Aeropostale hoodie, blue jeans, and white tennis shoes. Behind her is another girl, older, probably nine or ten, and a boy the same age."

"Wait a minute..." Max said. "The first girl looks just like Megan?"

"Right."

"Okay. Then what?"

"Then I hear myself tell the little girl—her name's Sarah—that she's got to be brave and climb way up this sloping tree and hide behind the branches until it's light and she can't hear the dogs anymore."

"Dogs?"

"Yeah. Some kind of search team. Trackers or something. I tell her to hide up there until it's light and there's no sound of the dogs, then climb down, head down the mountain to the gas station, and call the police. I even told her your name and said to tell the police that you're on a SWAT team in Southern California."

"Did she make it up the tree?"

"All the way up. The dogs howled, and the other girl and boy and I took off running. I could hear the dogs gaining on us. I told them we had to split up if we were going to escape, and for any of us to call for help if we made it down the mountain."

"Any of them get away?"

Beth thought for a second and shook her head. "I don't know. I didn't see what happened to the other two kids. My perspective kept shifting back and forth between Megan and Sarah. First, I was one…then I was the other."

"Either of...you...get away?"

"Well, Sarah climbed that tree, and then things started getting garbled. I think Megan climbed a different tree. I kept seeing her hands coming in and out of view. My view constantly shifted between the two of them and I lost track of who was who. I saw two men and a dog catch one of them…me. Then the scene dissolved. That's about it."

"You weren't kidding," Mark piped in from the back seat, "That was a *seriously* strange dream.

"I told you," Beth said.

Max glanced at her and grinned. "You can't see through my eyes, right? Or can you?"

"Never can tell." Beth winked. "Maybe I can."

Beth's gaze slid to the side and she stared out the window at the passing Colorado scenery. Max sped down the highway and left her alone with her thoughts.

They reached the turnoff from the highway fifteen minutes later and had driven nearly a mile up the road when they spotted her.

She emerged from a field of grass on the left side of the road. She hopped off a small dirt berm onto the pavement and took a few steps forward before turning and looking straight at them.

Beth felt an overpowering rush of disbelief course through her.

"I can't believe it," she whispered in breathless awe. "That's her. That's Sarah from my dream...Megan's friend."

Max stared at Sarah and felt the shock of impossible recognition. She was a younger version of Megan, identical to how she had looked four years ago.

"She's wearing an aqua hoodie and blue jeans," he said. "She looks...just like Megan..."

Beth climbed out of the SUV, walked around in front of it, and paused. She stared across the road at the girl, who was staring right back at her.

"Sarah?" Beth asked tentatively. She stood perfectly still, not wanting to spook her.

Sarah stood motionless, ready to run at the slightest provocation. She stared warily at Beth, but Beth thought she saw curiosity in the girl's eyes. Curiosity and, as hard as it was to believe, a glimmer of recognition.

"I think I know you from somewhere," Sarah said. Her voice conveyed her mental grasping. "It's like I saw you in one of my dreams. Who are you?"

Beth tried her best to smile and appear friendly. "It's not easy to explain. And I saw you in my dreams too. You know Megan, right?"

"Yeah..."

"Well, I'm Megan's doctor from California. My name is Dr. Beth Collins. And that's Megan's dad, Max Tyler." She turned and pointed at Max, who put his hand up.

"Max Tyler?" Sarah blurted in surprise. "But Megan said I was supposed to call him if I escaped..." She clamped her mouth shut, afraid she'd said too much.

Beth swallowed and forced herself to talk calmly in the midst of this surreal vortex.

"I know," Beth said. "I had a dream about you and Megan last night. And in my dream, Megan told you to hide in that tree until the men with the dogs left. Until it was safe for you to make your way down the mountain to call the police."

"How can you possibly know that?" Sarah said. She looked at Beth in astonishment. "Megan said that to me last night. There's no way you could know—"

Beth cut her off. "And to tell the police that Megan's dad, Max Tyler, is a policeman and a member of a SWAT team in Southern California."

"*SWAT team*," Sarah repeated. She stood open mouthed, her eyes filled with amazement. "That's just what Megan said."

Beth took a step forward and raised her hands. "Sarah, you can trust us. We're here to rescue you. And we need your help to find Megan."

Sarah looked at Beth, studying the strangely familiar woman and trying to decide if she should trust her. She sure wanted to. *But what if this is a trick?* a voice in her head said. *What if they work for the lab?* She wavered in doubt for a small eternity. Then an idea flashed in her mind.

"So, he's Megan's dad," she said, pointing at Max.

As if on cue, Max rolled his window the rest of the way down and stuck his head out.

"Hi, Sarah! That's right. I'm Megan's dad. My name's Max Tyler."

Sarah stared at his face, her eyes searching for a reason to believe. "Then I guess you have a California driver's license with your name on it…"

Max smiled. "And my picture and home address in Southern California. Did Megan tell you the name of the street we live on?"

"Yes," Sarah said.

"Good." Max slipped his driver's license out of his wallet. "Here," he said, flinging it like a Frisbee towards Sarah. It landed on the road at her feet. "Have a look."

Sarah picked up his license and studied it, her heart racing as she read the details. His name was there, as well as the street address and the name of that funny sounding city Megan had mentioned, Rancho Santa Margarita. The license also identified him as a police officer.

"Do you believe us now?" Max asked. "Will you help us find my daughter, Megan?"

Sarah glanced up from the license at Beth before slowly turning to face Max. He saw the hesitation on her face, the fear, and he didn't say a word.

Finally, Sarah's expression relaxed. "I think I believe you."

"I'm glad," Max said.

"But there's one way I know I can be sure. If you're really Megan's daddy, then only you will know the answer to this question."

Max nodded. "Fire away, Sarah."

"She told me that she was totally scared last year about something she was going to do. I mean scared out of her wits. You put your arm around her and calmed her down. And then you said something to her. You looked her right in the eyes and told her just what she needed to do. She told me as long as she lives, she'll never forget it. What did you say to her?"

Max felt a pang grip his chest as the memory of that day flooded in. He looked away for a moment, grappling with his composure. Looking back, he locked eyes with her and said, "That's easy, Sarah."

"It is?"

"Easy," Max said. "It was a sunny day in May, and it was the last playoff game of the soccer tournament. Megan was nervous. She was worried about letting her team down. I hugged her and told her I loved her. I told her to do her best and that, no matter what, her best was good enough. Then I squeezed her shoulder and looked her right in the eyes. And that's when I said: *Run like the wind.*"

Sarah felt a rush of excitement wash over her as she stared wide-eyed at Max, all doubt evaporating when he uttered those last four words. She scurried across the road to him and stopped inches from his door, a wispy smile on her face.

"Here's your license back," she said, reaching up and handing it through the window to him.

"Thanks," Max said. "Why don't you get in back?"

Sarah opened the rear door and climbed in next to Mark. Beth got back into the front seat and closed the door.

"We've gotta hurry," Sarah said. "Megan's in horrible trouble."

"What do you mean?" Beth asked, looking back at Sarah as Max started up the engine.

Sarah's eyes welled up. "They're gonna operate on her. And they're gonna do it as soon as they can."

Chapter 45

Megan lay flat on her back. She was strapped to her bed. She could move her head and wiggle her fingers, but the straps around her chest were so tightly fastened she had trouble breathing if she struggled at all.

Nurse Creade stood by while they bound Megan. She made it painfully clear that if she cried or made even a squeak of noise, she would storm right back in and tape her mouth shut. So Megan stayed quiet and still.

As she looked at the sparse furnishings in her room, she relived every minute of the last several hours. The entire night seemed like a horrible dream.

She almost got away. Almost.

What she didn't know was if any of the other kids had escaped.

And what about Sarah? she thought. She closed her eyes, and the image of the mysterious hand darting in and out of her field of view came back vividly. Along with it came the shock of realizing it was Sarah's hand and that she was seeing through Sarah's eyes.

It wasn't a dream. It was real. I was hanging onto the branches and wide awake.

Megan rubbed her thumbs against her fingertips. They were sticky with sap. *If only the dogs hadn't been able to find my trail and track me there…I would've gotten away.*

Where is Sarah now? she wondered. *Did she get away?*

With her eyes closed and surreal images wafting across her mindscape, Megan felt the full weight of exhaustion from the exertion of the chase and from staying up all night.

A soothing, enveloping wave of darkness washed over her, carrying her off to the realm of REM.

And there, once again, she dreamt.

Chapter 46

"What do you mean you can't find her?" Thornton shouted into his push-to-talk phone. He listened for a long, painful moment, clenching his jaw with rage.

"I don't give a rat's ass how hard it is to find her trail! You've got the best damn tracking dogs in the state, the most powerful infrared night scopes in existence, and I'm paying you more money for this one project than you'll make in a year. You *do* still want to collect that fat paycheck, don't you?"

He listened for half a minute, fighting the urge to throw the phone out the window. The other people in the room were sure they could hear him grinding his teeth.

Thornton forced himself to ratchet down his anger. This was getting nowhere. It was time to go to plan B.

"Yeah, yeah," he said, cutting off the caller's blabbering voice. "Carl, will you shut up a minute?" he barked. The voice on the other end of the line fell silent.

"You already tracked down three other runaways with no problem, right? Caught them pronto. What's the big deal with Sarah? Even if they did split up and run, she's younger and weaker. She should have been easier to catch than the older kids, not harder. If you and your team are worth the money I'm paying you, you'll—"

"Ahem." Calvin Lynch cleared his throat loudly and rolled his eyes at Thornton.

Thornton covered the mouthpiece. "What is it?"

"Aren't we all forgetting a little something with regard to Sarah?"

"Like what?"

Lynch raised his eyebrows and gave Thornton a smug look.

"Cut the crap. Spit it out."

Lynch squinted, and his aquiline countenance looked decidedly predatory. "I seem to recall that Sarah was the first and only one of the kids we outfitted with a subdermal transponder chip. Inch-long silicon wafer, barely detectable under the skin? A few years back we injected, it in the hollow of her left shoulder blade. Out of reach."

"And?"

"And if memory serves me, once we activate it, she'll be sending out a traceable signal good for a three-mile radius."

Thornton's expression lightened noticeably. "Now that's a useful piece of information. Hold on, Carl. We're checking something out. I'll come back on in a minute."

Turning to Dale, he said, "Bring us the transponder."

Dale rushed off and returned in less than two minutes with the unit.

"Activate the transponder," Thornton said. "Then grab an ATV and take the signal receiver out to Carl. Call him when you're on your way."

Dale pushed the toggle switch on the hand-held tracking unit. "Unit's on and powered up. Dr. Lynch, what's the code for the transponder?"

Lynch glanced dismissively at the security chief. He directed his gaze and comments at Thornton.

"Before we activate Sarah's embedded transponder, we might want to activate a second one right here to make sure the tracking device works properly."

"Good idea," Thornton agreed. "Why don't you activate one for us?"

Lynch turned and tapped out a password on the computer keyboard. The desktop appeared on the screen, and he clicked on one of the files.

"Enter this transponder code," he said to Dale. "S-39-40110."

Dale tapped the touchpad buttons on the book-sized GPS electronic device.

The screen went blank and then lit up, showing the location of the Viralvector complex and the roads leading up to it. A small blinking red dot appeared where the building was positioned.

Dale enlarged the map, and it clearly showed the rectangular outline of the Viralvector building. The red dot blinked in the exact location of their room.

"We're up. It's blinking away."

"Deactivate it," Lynch said. "Let's test another one."

Dale entered the number again and pressed delete. The red dot disappeared.

Lynch read off another code, and Dale repeated the process. Another red dot appeared.

"Perfect," Dale said. "Just like the last one."

Lynch glanced at Thornton then back to Dale. "Clear it," he said.

Dale deleted the number. Lynch punched some keys on the computer keyboard. "Get ready," he said. "Here's the code for Sarah's transponder: M-607-90402."

Dale tapped in the code on the touchpad and hit *Enter*. The screen went blank and then lit up. But this time there was no blinking red dot.

Dale hit the command key to zoom out, but nothing happened. There wasn't even a location map on the screen.

"Damn. We got nothin'."

Thornton grabbed the phone. "Okay, Carl, listen up. We've got a transponder tracking unit that Dale's going to run down to you. He's grabbing an ATV and leaving right now. He'll raise you on the talkie when he's underway."

Thornton motioned to Dale to get moving. "That last girl you're after has a transponder chip embedded in her shoulder, but it's got a range of just under three miles. Her tracking signal doesn't show up on the screen here. When you get the unit and locate a signal, call me immediately."

He listened impatiently to Carl's response. He yanked the phone away from his ear with a scowl and just as quickly put it back to his ear. "No. Will you shut up for two seconds? I said call me after a signal shows up on the tracking unit. Then again, once you've got her. Dale will radio you in the next minute or two for you to guide him to where you are. Get it? Got it? Good."

Thornton ended the call and turned to Lynch. "His team should be able to find her in no time."

Lynch's mouth screwed into a wry smile. "Just peachy. And if she's out of range and they can't locate her?"

"Then we operate without her. It's a go in three hours no matter what."

"I see," Lynch said through clenched teeth. "You know why I'm insisting on both girls. We need a guaranteed threshold of neuronal stem cells for Newt's operation. I want the biggest chance of success. I'm sure you agree."

"Of course," Thornton said. "And we've been over this several times. One of them should be adequate. A second is a guarantee. I did choose the most talented surgeon in the world for the job, didn't I?"

Lynch bristled and stared him down. The silence stretched on.

"Of course you did. One will be sufficient."

Chapter 47

Sarah gulped the last of her orange juice and handed the empty container to Beth.

"Get enough to eat?" Beth asked. She stopped herself from staring at the younger version of Megan sitting in the back seat.

"Yeah, thanks," Sarah said.

She had devoured every food item they'd bought her at a convenience store without stopping to take a break. In between bites, she filled them in on everything that had happened since she'd met Megan, including their escape and the upcoming surgeries. Mark and Max asked her a lot of questions about the layout of the Viralvector complex. Sarah responded with detailed descriptions and locations of the rooms and offices.

"Sarah, you are one very smart girl!" Beth said.

"Really smart," Max agreed. "I can't believe what an amazing memory you have!"

Sarah just shrugged and smiled.

"Ditto from me," Mark said. "What a brainiac!" He looked down at the paper he'd been working on and drew one final line. "Okay, I think I've got it," he said. He handed Max a detailed sketch of the building floor plan based on Sarah's description with all the rooms labeled and the approximate dimensions shown.

Max stared at the page, matching up the pictures in his mind with what he saw on the paper.

"Looks good," he said. "That's how I pictured it."

Max got out of the Suburban and climbed into the back seat next to Sarah and Mark. He handed Sarah the sketch and said, "Sarah, take a good look at this and see if we've got all the rooms and halls positioned in the right locations."

She studied it carefully, trailing her finger along the hallways, counting under her breath as if measuring relative distances between the rooms.

"You missed the lab that's next to the operating room," she said. "That's where they take blood samples from us and give us our shots. It should be right here." She put her finger on the diagram. "There are two doors. One to the hallway and one that goes into the operating room."

"Good," Max said. "Anything else?"

"Uh…I think it's more like fifteen feet from the front entrance door to the secretary's desk. And Carl the security guard's office is ten feet down the hall from that on the right side."

"Good," Mark said. He took the sketch back from her and made the changes on it. "How's that?" he asked.

She looked at the laboratory room he'd added and checked the changes he'd made in the dimensions at the entrance.

"I think it looks..." She stopped in mid-sentence, opening her mouth in a gasp.

"Wait a minute. I just remembered something. There's a storeroom down at the end of this hall at the back of the building. Here," she said, tapping the sketch. "Eddie and Faith and I got in trouble one time for playing in there. The thing is, it's got a door to the outside. When we were in there, I unlocked it and peeked outside. All that was out there was a bunch of gravel on the ground around the building, and then thirty feet away, the forest starts."

Mark reached over and sketched a room where she pointed. "So, the room's here? And about this size?"

"Pretty close...maybe a little longer on this end," she said. "And don't forget the door to the outside. I don't think anybody uses it at all, but it's there."

"Is it a walk-through door or one of those big warehouse truck delivery doors?"

"It's just a people door."

Mark finished the sketch. "How's that?"

"Looks good," she said.

"Thanks, Sarah. You've been a great help. I think we nailed it." He handed the revised sketch to Max.

Max looked it over, focusing on the new room.

"Sarah, tell me something about this storeroom. When you opened that door to the outside, was the forest back there packed with trees? I mean, could someone hide there without being seen?"

Sarah thought for a moment, her brow furrowed, and then nodded. "There's a buncha of trees back there, and I don't think there's anything but the forest beyond that. The only road is the one in front of the building, leading down the mountain."

"Thanks," Max said, returning to the driver's seat. He studied the sketch for several minutes as the final pieces of a plan clicked into place. The others waited in silence.

The early morning sun was just beginning to send streamers of light filtering through the branches of the pine forest when he turned to Beth and Mark.

"Okay. Here's our plan of attack. This is how we're going to get Megan back…"

Carl and his partner, Jake, sat smoking on a flat boulder as the muffled growl of an ATV engine grew closer. They'd been on their feet all night, crisscrossing up and down the mountain for hours after they'd captured and returned Megan. As tired as he was, Carl was seething that they hadn't been able to track down Sarah.

Their speckled coonhound, Striker, lay on the ground before them, resting after an exhausting night of searching. His ears pricked up as Dale rode into view on the four-wheel all-terrain vehicle and pulled to a stop a few feet from them.

Dale switched off the ignition of the red Honda TRX450R sport ATV, and the growl of the engine died instantly. He dismounted and slipped the backpack from his shoulders.

"Here's the transponder tracker," he said, walking over to them.

Carl stood up and dropped his cigarette, crushing it out with his boot. Striker stood up, stretched, and halfheartedly sniffed Dale's cuff.

"It's about freakin' time," Carl said. He was in no mood for small talk or formalities. "Gimme the unit."

Dale pulled a black case out of the backpack. Carl grabbed it, zipped it open, and yanked out the tracking device, dropping the black nylon case to the ground.

"Okay, show me how this damn tracking gizmo works."

"There's a toggle switch on the left edge towards the top. Push it, and it'll power right up," Dale said.

Carl slid the button, and the screen lit up. Roads and topographic landmarks populated the screen.

"Wait a minute," Carl said. "This looks just like a Google map on my iPhone. Where's this Sarah girl's tracking signal?"

"We have to punch in her transponder code," Dale said. "She's gotta microchip embedded under her skin. Problem is, we already tried entering her code back at the complex and got nothing. Course the signal's only good for up to three miles max. Probably out of range."

"Yeah. Thornton barked all about it. Let's see what happens down here. Punch it in."

Dale tapped in Sarah's code on the touchpad and hit *Enter*. After a quick flutter, the map reloaded with the topographic landmarks again. A blinking red dot appeared in the middle of the screen.

"Bingo," Dale said. "There she is."

"You sure that's her?" Carl asked, squinting and bringing the unit up to his face. The red dot was located a hundred yards off the turnoff toad, a mile up from the main highway.

"Positive," Dale said. "Can't be anyone else. Her transponder is the only one connected to that code."

"Let's move out. Dale, you drive. Jake and I'll hitch a ride on the back. Keep Striker on the long tether. He'll run alongside."

They piled onto the ATV and sped down the bumpy mountainside. Carl radioed Thornton and gave him the news.

"Yeah," he barked into the mouthpiece. "Got her transponder signal on the tracker. We'll pick her up and have her to you in about an hour. What? Yeah, you can thank me when I get there. Just have my big-ass check waiting. Over."

Max watched as Sarah came bounding out of the forest with Beth in tow. Their urgent nature-call excursion into the trees had only taken a few minutes.

"Everything okay?" Max asked as Sarah and Beth climbed back into the Suburban and pulled the doors shut.

"Now it is," Beth said. She glanced over at Sarah, who was looking down at the seatbelt she was fastening.

"Good." He shifted the Suburban into gear and inched back onto the turnoff road. "So, what do you think, Beth? Another six or seven miles to the complex?"

Beth looked at the map printout that was lying on the console. "Close. Seven and a half."

"Not too far," Max said. "What's the distance to the turnoff road leading up to the complex?"

"A little over two miles."

"We'll be there in no time," Max said. His hand gripped the steering wheel. Beth reached over and squeezed his arm.

Sarah sat with her nose pressed to the window, staring at the passing trees as they reached the turnoff and started up the road. Her lips moved as if she was whispering something to herself, the same phrase over and over.

Beth noticed how tense she was, and she reached back and patted her on the leg.

"You all right?"

Sarah glanced at her and then turned back to the window. "Uh, huh."

"I can tell you're scared," Beth said. "But don't worry. You're safe with us."

"I…I know," Sarah said. Her lips trembled. "It's just that those men who chased us are terrifying. And I'm really worried about Megan and…and what they're going to do to her with the surgery and stuff. I saw them catch her in my second sight thing. If we're too late…"

Beth patted her on the arm. "Don't worry, Sarah. We'll rescue her. And then we'll take both of you far away from here."

They drove a while longer through the heavily forested terrain. They rounded a curve, and Max slammed on the brakes.

"Damn it!"

Beth looked up, and her heart plummeted. An ATV blocked the road a quarter of a mile ahead.

"Hey, Mark. Check this out," Max said. "Looks like we've got ourselves a welcoming committee."

Mark leaned forward in his seat. "Let's have ourselves a closer look."

He pulled out a pair of powerful rangefinder Zeiss binoculars and scoped in the figures in the distance.

"We've got three gruff looking men, an ATV, and a big old slobbery hunting dog."

"What!" Sarah unlatched her seat belt and scooted up next to Mark. Her eyes were like saucers.

"Take these and have a look," Mark said, handing her the binoculars. "Could be your friends from last night."

She grabbed them, leaned forward, and brought her worst fears into focus.

"Oh, no…" she whimpered.

Beth watched the blood drain from Sarah's face as terror gripped her. "Is it them?" she asked.

Sarah sat immobilized in stunned silence.

"Sarah?"

Sarah snapped out of her paralyzing terror. "Oh, geez…it's them all right. Those are the two tracker men and their dog from last night. And the third guy wearing the uniform is Dale. He's the head security guard at the building, and he's really mean."

Beth took the binoculars from her and looked through them. "That Dale guy keeps staring down at an iPad or some kind of instrument he's holding."

"Listen up, everybody," Max said. He started the SUV rolling forward at 5 miles per hour. "Sarah, I want you to get down on the floor, behind the bench seat. Don't make a sound or come up out of hiding unless I tell you to. Understand?"

Sarah nodded, too scared to speak. She slid to the floor and scrunched herself down, partially wedging herself under the back of the bench seat.

"Beth, you and I are vacationers from California, and we're cruising along this road looking for a good hiking trail we were told is up here."

"Got it."

"Mark, there's a dense clump of trees coming up in the slight curve on the right that'll give you good cover," Max said. "Grab some firepower, slip out the back, and circle around. There's likely going to be trouble. Keep your shoulder talkie open."

"On it," Mark said, grabbing his gear.

Max increased the speed of the SUV. As they approached the denser grouping of trees, Max pulled closer to the right side of the road, providing cover for Mark to exit out the back and disappear into the forest.

They continued up the road and rolled to a stop in front of the three-man blockade.

Max turned his head away from the ATV and spoke into his concealed shoulder walkie-talkie. "We're stopped in front of them," he said. "You in place?"

"Affirmative. I'm wicked close and ready to move."

"Here he comes. It's show time."

Chapter 48

Thornton smiled as he clicked off his radio unit and shoved it into his lab coat. Crotchety old Carl was going to come through for him one more time and deliver Sarah in an hour. The gruff, belligerent mountain man was always a pain to work with, but he was the best tracker in the business, and he kept his mouth shut. Worth every dollar he charged.

Thornton sped down the hallway. The preparations needed to be finalized and the surgical team suited up and ready before Sarah arrived.

"Creade!" he barked as he stormed into the laboratory next to the surgical suite.

"Quit your shouting. I'm right here," she said. She walked out of a storage closet holding a small pile of surgical gowns, caps, blankets, and sterile gloves.

"Get everything ready and assemble the team. Full op-room prep…everything," Thornton ordered. "I've already talked to Lynch. We'll operate in an hour and a half."

"They found Sarah?" Creade asked. She plopped the pile of surgical supplies down on the counter.

"Picking her up as we speak. Signal showed up on the tracking unit. They know exactly where she is."

"Great."

"It will be when they deliver her. I want the procedures started thirty minutes after they bring her in."

"I'll get Newt, Eddie, and Megan gowned and in pre-prep," Creade said. "When Sarah gets here, I'll have all four fully prepped, in the surgical room, and ready to go." She intentionally didn't mention Faith's death. Thornton had exploded into a tirade when he'd found out.

Thornton squinted. "You do that. The neuronal stem cell harvesting and transferring procedures should take three and a half hours. Then we bandage

241

up the three of them and let them recoup for four days before shipping them off to Southeast Asia and their new lives. The buyer is already waiting."

"Preps are coming up," Creade said and started to turn away.

"Remember," Thornton said, catching her arm. "You'll get your bonus check when the three of them touch down in Asia and our buyers take delivery."

"And it's four times my annual salary," she added.

"That's right. So Creade"—he pulled her arm and squeezed it harder—"make sure nothing goes wrong. Or else."

Dale walked over to the driver's side of the SUV. He stopped about four feet from the vehicle and motioned for Max to roll down his window.

"How are you folks this morning?" he asked. His eyes darted between Max and Beth.

"Fine," Max replied. He sized Dale up, taking in at a glance the forty-plus-year-old man: medium height, reasonably fit, square chin, brown eyes, leathery outdoorsman skin, and wearing a rent-a-cop security uniform.

"Are you a policeman?" Max asked.

"Nope. I'm head of security for a research company whose headquarters is a few miles up the road."

"What company is that?"

"Just a scientific research company," Dale said. "This is a private road, and it dead ends, so there's no outlet. Where are you two headed?"

"We were told there's great hiking trail up here. I think it's called the Maroon-Snowmass trail or nature hike. Something like that. Supposed to be an incredibly beautiful five-mile hike."

Dale stared at Max blankly. "Hiking trail, huh? I'm not sure I know about any Maroon-Snowmass…"

"I heard of it," Carl rasped as he stepped forward and stood next to Dale. He took a deep drag from the cigarette he was holding and exhaled a cloud of smoke. "But it ain't anywhere near here. You gotta trek about thirty-five miles up Highway 82 to Aspen and then about another mile or so past it. Trail starts there…winds along south an' southwest for quite a ways."

"Thanks for the heads up," Max said. "Looks like we've got some backtracking to do."

Max noticed that Carl was looking past him, scoping out the back of the SUV. He caught Dale doing the same. Their eyes darted back and forth, scanning the back seats, then focusing on him again.

"Listen," Dale said. "We've been out most of the night looking for a missing girl. She's six years old, a little under five-foot tall, with brown hair. It's a runaway situation. She's got a medical condition. It's real important we find her fast so she can get her medicine. Any chance you folks have seen her?"

Max glanced at Carl, who was looking down at the handheld electronic device he was carrying. A jolt of realization suddenly hit him. *It's a tracking device. They tagged Sarah, and they're tracking her.*

"Haven't seen her," Max said, "but we'll sure keep our eyes open. If we spot her, who should we call? You?"

Dale looked back at Carl, who gazed down once more at the GPS unit. He looked up at Dale and gave him a subtle nod.

Turning back to Max, Dale gripped the butt of the revolver in his holster and said, "Mister, I need to ask you to get out of the car."

Max's calm expression morphed into stony resolve.

"What do you mean get out of my car?" he said, gripping the handle of the taser on his lap and resting his finger on the trigger.

Dale drew his Smith & Wesson .44 caliber revolver and pointed it at Max. "I said, get out of the car."

Max reacted in surprise and anger. "You've got to be kidding. What the hell is going on here? Get that gun out of my face!"

"Mister, I said get out of the car."

Max locked eyes with him, staring him down for a long moment before speaking with icy resolve. "And I said…why?"

Dale gritted his teeth. This wasn't going exactly how he'd planned.

"Because," he said finally, "we're going to search your SUV. You do know where this girl is…in fact, you're hiding her in your car. Now get out!" He cocked the hammer of the handgun and took a step closer.

"Okay," Max said, holding both hands up briefly before dropping them back into his lap, out of sight. "Hold your horses, and don't shoot anybody. I'm getting out."

He started easing the door open, continuing to talk in a more submissive tone. "But you're wrong. We haven't seen this girl. Take a look in the back. There's nobody there. We're the only ones in the car." He flicked his head in a quick snap over his left shoulder.

Dale's eyes followed the motion. It was all the distraction Max needed. He threw the door open, smashing into Dale's outstretched arm and deflecting the powerful handgun that discharged with a booming roar, sending its lethal projectile whizzing over the hood of the SUV.

Dale stumbled from the door's impact. Max leaped out of the vehicle in a blur, clenching the taser in his right hand. He raised it to a chest-high aim, reflexively tracking his moving target.

He squeezed the trigger, and two wired, stainless steel prongs exploded from the taser at a muzzle velocity of 630 feet per second and penetrated Dale's shirt, burying their barbs in the skin of his chest.

The instantaneous pulse-wave delivery of 50,000 volts electrified Dale's body, overloading the neuronal synapses in his brain and the neuromuscular junctions of his muscles. He dropped to the ground in a convulsive heap and spasmed uncontrollably. His eyes rolled back in his head, and spittle ran down the side of his mouth.

The handgun had scattered away on the rocks during the fall, but Max wasn't looking at Dale or his gun. Max dropped the taser and ripped his Glock .40 caliber handgun from its side holster, raising it as he raced toward Carl, who was raising his own handgun to aim and fire at Max.

Two wired barbs hit Carl in the chest, and he collapsed to the ground in a writhing mass.

Mark dropped his taser and pulled out a .45 caliber Hoechstel as he ran up. He looked past his neutralized opponent for their third and final target, Jake.

The guttural snark of the ATV engine fired up a second before Mark locked on his target.

Jake gunned the engine to full RPMs, and the ATV bolted away from them. It kicked up dirt and rocks as Jake sped to escape, the coon dog running close behind him.

Max and Mark, both certified expert marksmen, drew a bead on the retreating target. It was an easy shot that either of them could have made with their eyes half closed.

"Hold it," Max barked. "Let him go. No one's dead yet. We'll try to keep it that way if we can."

"He'll go back and warn them."

"We'll deal with it," Max said. "Give me a hand cuffing these guys and tying them to a tree. Then we'll blitz straight up there and execute our plan."

Chapter 49

Megan wiggled and squirmed, straining against the strap that held her to the bed. She couldn't just lie there and do nothing. She needed to move.

There had to be some way she could free herself.

She stopped her frenzied struggling and focused her attention on the nylon straps that bound her wrists to the bed. The one on her left wrist was somewhat looser than the right, and it allowed her freedom to rotate her hand.

Megan studied the left strap, wiggling her fingers as she turned her left hand back and forth, testing to see how far it would go. Scrunching her fingers and thumb together as tight as she could, she pulled her hand toward her with increasing force.

The strap inched along, digging into her wrist and grinding to a halt as it reached the padded base of her thumb. She pulled harder, but the strap wouldn't budge. Her thumb turned red, and pain lanced up her arm. She gritted her teeth in pain as the strap dug into her skin.

Just when it seemed hopelessly wedged and immobile, just when the pain was at its most intense, the strap began edging up over the base of her thumb. The shift was imperceptible at first. Megan held her breath as it gradually gained momentum until it slid over her knuckles. Her left hand slipped free with an audible plop.

Megan bit her lip to keep from crying out in agony. The intense pain continued for a full minute, and then she held her throbbing hand up in front of her face. She turned it this way and that, wiggling and bending her fingers. A small gasp of pain escaped her lips as she rotated her wrist.

It hurt, but nothing was broken or torn.

She grasped the tie on her right hand and yanked at it, scrunching her fingers. Ten minutes later, both of her hands were free.

She scanned the room, making sure that she was still alone, before sitting up and freeing her feet. She slid off the bed, retrieved the paperclip wires she'd seen in the desk, and tiptoed to the door.

Megan held her breath and listened. There was no sound but the thunderous pounding of her heart. She pressed her ear against the door, but all she could hear was a pair of muffled voices and the padding of footsteps fading down the hall. She waited until she couldn't hear them anymore and then used the two wires to pick the lock.

She eased the door open a crack and peeked out into the hallway. She could see all the way down to both ends of the hall. There was nobody in sight.

Before she could change her mind, she swung the door open, stepped out into the hall, and closed the door. She hurried up the hall and around the corner. Megan spotted another door at the end of that hallway and fixed her eyes on it. She raced toward it, heart pounding.

She flung the door open, and her heart sank. It was a supply closet, not an exit door.

She turned and sprinted back down the hall. She stopped at the intersecting hallway to peer around the corner.

She remembered seeing another exit door when they'd taken her to the lab for bloodwork the previous day. It was located at the far end of a short hallway by one of the offices near the lab. She only hoped she could find it.

She passed first one office and then another, her panic rising as she drew closer to the lab.

Where is it? I know it's by the lab, and there's the lab coming up. So…where is it?

Her eyes darted up and down the left side of the hallway. *C'mon, where is it?*

She sped past the lab, certain she was about to be caught, and darted down a side passage.

Wait a minute…I saw it on the way back from the lab, not the way there. It's on the wall across from the offices.

She poked her head around the corner. There, less than ten feet away, was the short hall, just as she remembered. Megan's panic soared into ascending hope. She was able to take two promising steps towards a chance at freedom before freezing in shock.

Straight ahead, Creade came rushing out of the lab and stopped not six feet from her with a look of surprise on her face. Her expression quickly slid into outrage.

Behind Megan, a powerful, authoritative voice boomed in disapproval. She looked back over her shoulder and saw Thornton walking toward her from the open door of his nearby office. He stopped a foot away from her, towering and angry.

"Creade! What the hell is she doing up and around? I thought you had her strapped to her bed until the procedure."

"*I did*," Creade snarled through gritted teeth.

"Well, handle it. Newt and Eddie had better be prepped and ready."

"They are. Ready to go."

"Then I assume you can handle getting Megan prepped without her running off again."

"Of course," Creade fumed. She stepped forward and grabbed Megan by the shoulders.

"Good," Thornton said. "Sarah should be delivered to us any minute, and I don't want any delays. We start exactly thirty minutes after she arrives."

"She'll be ready."

"She'd better be," Thornton uttered in a menacing tone as he turned and stormed off down the hall. His push-to-talk crackled to life as he stepped inside the surgical suite. He grabbed it. "What?" he asked.

Creade clamped Megan's arm a in painful vise grip and yanked her along towards the lab.

Megan's wisp of hope evaporated in the blink of an eye.

Chapter 50

Thornton clenched his jaw in blistering outrage as the person on the other end of the phone informed him about Sarah's escape.

Stupid, incompetent fools.

He took a deep breath and exhaled, loosening his vise grip on the crackling talkie unit.

"All right…so it was a white SUV with no license plate in front. The driver was a man, and there was a woman in the front passenger seat. The GPS tracking unit positively confirmed the girl's signal was coming from the SUV, but since none of you actually saw her, you assumed she was hiding in back."

Thornton listened as Jake began repeating his muddled, excuse-filled explanation.

"That's what you said the first time. What I want you to do now is circle back around to where they were taken down. Park your ATV and go on foot. Be quiet about it. They might have tied up Carl and Jake and left them behind. Call me back when you find out anything."

Thornton ended the call and pulled a memo pad out of the inside pocket of his lab coat. After scanning the page, he dialed one of the numbers.

A man with a gruff voice answered. "Yeah?"

"It's Thornton. Who's this?"

"Nick."

"Good. Where are you and Raoul, and when are you getting here?"

"About fifteen miles from your complex, plus or minus. Should be there in twenty to thirty minutes."

"Well, step on it. I need you here in twenty."

"I'll see what I can do. What's the rush?"

"We've had a development. And it's negative. I want to make sure we still move according to plan."

"What development?"

"I'll let you know in a second. But first, tell me about Xavier. You check with him in the past hour to see when he's going to arrive?"

"He's already here."

"He is?" Thornton asked, surprised.

"Yeah. Made good air time and landed the chopper at the Colorado Springs airport half an hour ago. He's fueling up as we speak."

"Finally! Something positive. How fast can he get here from Colorado Springs once we call him?"

"If he jams it…probably twenty minutes. Maybe less."

"Is he any good?" Thornton asked. "Last guy we had was barely mediocre."

"Guy's a pro. He can land a chopper anywhere. Drop it right in your backyard with no clearance. I told him to be ready for our call. He said he could be in the air in ten minutes."

"Excellent," Thornton said, looking at his watch. "The surgical procedures are starting soon. We should be calling him in about two and a half hours. But if the situation implodes, I could need him immediately. Tell him to stay primed and ready to go."

"We'll tell him," Nick said. "What's the development?"

Thornton summarized the escape and recapture of Megan and Eddie and the botched capture of Sarah.

"Sounds like a couple of pros," Nick said. "Taking your boys down like that."

Thornton scowled. He hated it when things didn't go according to plan.

"Bottom line is this," he snapped. "Jake's circling back to see if they left Carl and Dale behind. We don't have Sarah, but we're going ahead with the procedures without her."

"What do you want from us?"

"Just get your asses up here *now*. No telling if the guys in the SUV have Sarah and are headed straight this way. I need you and Raoul to stand guard out front to stop them. And I want to make damn sure we're not interrupted. If you spot the SUV, intercept them and take them out."

"What about the girl?"

"We want her back, so do everything you can to grab her."

"And if it gets messy and that's not an option?"

"Erase her with the rest of them."

"Understood."

"Call me when you're up here and in position."

"You got it," he said, clicking off the line.

Max pulled off the road two hundred yards from the complex and drove into the trees. Diffuse morning sunlight filtered through the upper branches of the overarching canopy. The Suburban, while partially hidden by the trees, was still visible from the road leading up to the complex.

Max rolled to a stop and shut off the engine. He unfolded the floor plan they had sketched with Sarah's help and spread it open on the console. His eyes traced the perimeter of the building, locking in on the unsecured entrance Sarah had identified.

"Okay, so our targeted point of entry is the door leading to…"

He stopped in mid-sentence as he glanced toward the back seat. Mark was motioning toward Sarah, who was staring blankly at the seatback in front of her. Her eyes were unfocused, and her mouth was slightly agape. Max saw that her eyes were moving as though she was watching a slow-motion video clip. *Or*, he thought, *like she's dreaming with her eyes open.*

He turned to say something to Beth. She had the same dazed expression on her face. He looked back and forth between Sarah and her. Something strange was going on.

Looking back at Mark, he motioned that Beth and Sarah were acting the same way, as though both were entranced under the same spell.

"Mark?"

"I don't know," Mark said after leaning to the left and peering at Beth's profile. "What do you call this? Stereo zoning?"

"Guess so," Max said. He reached out and gently shook Sarah's shoulder. "Sarah?"

She snapped out of her daze and blinked.

"W-what?" she stammered, sitting upright in her seat.

"I think you were asleep," Max said.

"Yeah…with your eyes open," Mark piped in.

Max glanced over at Beth, who was rubbing her eyes.

"I think both of you were," he said.

"Actually…I wasn't," Sarah said. Her eyes darted back and forth between Max and Mark.

"I wasn't asleep at all. It's just that…"

Max waited. "Just what?"

"It happened again."

Max looked at Mark and Beth then back at Sarah.

"It?" he asked. "You mean that weird thing where you see through Megan's eyes?"

Sarah nodded. "We've gotta get her out of there. She's in her room. They just made her change into green surgery clothes, and then they stuck a needle in the top of her hand. It was attached to some tubing and a bag of clear liquid."

"They started her on an IV," Beth said.

Max looked at her.

"I saw it too."

"What do you mean? You saw the same thing Sarah did?"

"Yes. I was looking through Megan's eyes, and it was as clear as I'm seeing you and Mark right now."

Max gave her a surprised look. "You're kidding?"

Beth looked him in the eye, dead serious, and shook her head. "Do I look like I'm kidding?"

"But that's—"

"C'mon, you guys. We've gotta hurry," Sarah said. She leaned forward, her hands fisted in urgency. "The last thing I saw was they were starting to wheel Megan out of her room. I know they're gonna do something really bad to her."

"She's right," Beth said. "We've got to get her out of there."

"Okay, people. Let's roll!" Max said. "Mark, you set with your gear?"

"Good to go."

"Beth, how about your front door diversion?"

"All set."

"Good." He turned to Sarah and saw the wide-eyed, worried look on her face.

"Are you…gonna be able to rescue her?"

Max smiled and spoke with warm confidence. "Trust me. We'll get her out of there. Do you remember what we talked about?"

"You want me to stay here until you get back with Megan.'

"That's right.'

"But I know that place inside and out…like the back of my hand. I could help you." Her eyes pleaded with him even more than her words.

"Sarah, we've been all through this. Your input on the floor plan we sketched is so valuable. You've already given us a huge advantage."

"But I could help you more. What if you—"

"Sarah, Mark and I are trained police commandos. We're going in with guns and attack gear, and we'll be taking Megan back by force. The biggest help you can be to us is to wait here where it's safe."

"Okay."

"Good," Max said. He patted her shoulder.

He looked at Beth and Mark.

"Okay, people. Let's turn and burn."

Chapter 51

Megan winced as Nurse Creade slid the needle into the vein on the top of her hand, attached the IV tubing to it, and taped it securely in place. She looked up at the hanging IV bag of 5% normal saline dripping into the enclosed reservoir and watched Creade twist the turncock, increasing the flow of drips into the line.

"What are you're giving me?"

"Just some IV fluid," Creade said. "We need to keep you hydrated for the surgery."

"But why do I even need an operation? What are they going to do to me?" Megan's voice wavered as tears began trickling out of the corner of her eyes.

"Quit your whimpering," Creade snapped. "It's a short procedure. Nothing to get all worked up about. Now *hold still* while I get you ready."

Creade opened a surgical prep kit on a metal tray stand next to Megan's bed and put on sterile latex gloves. She picked up a pair of scissors, held Megan's head down with the side of her wrist, and began snipping the hair off a silver dollar-sized area on the right front side of her head.

They had tied Megan to the bed again. This time she couldn't even move. She tried to struggle, straining her head and neck against Creade's hold, but the older woman leaned down with her whole weight, holding her in place.

"Please don't!" Megan cried out. She began sobbing.

"Hold still, dammit," Creade barked. She picked up a disposable razor and flicked off its plastic blade cover. "I've got to shave this dinky little area with a razor, and I'm sure you don't want me to cut you."

Megan squeezed her eyes shut as Creade shaved the area on her head.

"Much better," Creade said, tossing the razor onto the prep tray. "See…that wasn't so bad."

Megan's breath hitched in a sob. Creade hummed to drown out the noise while she gathered up and disposed of the prep tray debris, then unlocked the wheels on the gurney.

"All right. We're ready to go," Creade said. She grabbed the railing on the end of the gurney and wheeled her out of the room.

Megan gripped the sides of the bed. Silent tears crept down her cheeks. They turned the corner and sped down the hallway towards the operating room.

Her throat clenched shut, and an escalating panic overtook her. Her stomach plummeted in a free-fall as terror gripped her heart, squeezing out all hope.

"Daddy…help me…please…"

Chapter 52

Max was the first out of the trees, darting low and fast across the thirty-foot clearing to the back of the building. Mark was right behind him. They flattened themselves against the wall and waited. There was no sound or movement except the soft rustling of the trees in the breeze.

Before leaving the safe cover of the trees, they had done a quick reconnaissance of the building and discovered two surveillance cameras at the front of the building and a third by the large equipment shed.

But there were no cameras watching the back of the building.

Scattered piles of lumber scraps, construction debris, and scrap metal were strewn haphazardly along the wall; the entire rear of the building appeared abandoned.

Max stood motionless, listening, then edged his way towards the door. He stopped when he reached it, looking up and down the back of the building before motioning over his shoulder to Mark that they were set to go in.

It took Max less than a minute to pick the lock.

He gave the door a shove. It hesitated before smoothly gliding open. With a glimpse back over their shoulders, the two of them disappeared into the storeroom.

Max scoped out the confines of their surroundings while Mark scanned the length of the inside doorjamb and the edges of the door, looking for small, opposing contacts that would indicate the door was protected by an alarm system.

"Door's clean," he whispered. "No wires, no sensors."

Max nodded and motioned for them to head deeper into the semi-dark room. Mark was careful not to make a sound as he shut the door and followed

Max, who was weaving his way through the cluttered maze of stacked boxes, storage bins, stepladders, and janitorial supplies.

Max reached the door to the hallway and motioned for Mark to stop. He pulled out the sketch of the floor plan they'd made and clicked on a high-intensity flashlight that he kept on his keyring.

"Okay, we entered right here." He tapped the sketch on a spot at the back of the building. "And over here's our target." He traced a path up the hall, sharp left turn, then three-quarters of the way down on the left.

"The OR," Mark said.

"And we've gotta move. You heard what Sarah said…what she just saw." Max folded up the sketch and put it away.

"So, you think she's really seeing through Megan's eyes?" Mark asked.

Max looked at him and gave a sharp nod. "Sounds insane, but…yeah, I do. What do you think?"

"It seems like something out of a sci-fi movie. But I tell you…the way she described it…I gotta buy it. I've got no idea how this is supposed to work."

"Same here. It's gotta be something to do with the shots they've been giving her and Megan. Beth thinks they've been giving them an engineered virus."

"Virus…" Max repeated to himself. He clenched his jaw. "They're never touching her again. We're getting her out of here."

Beth opened one of the twin glass doors and entered the lobby of Viralvector, Inc. The spacious layout and strikingly modern décor of the lobby surprised her—a rich mix of metal and burnished woods. Spartan simplicity. Business efficiency.

It seemed odd to her that they would build an office research facility like this, up in the mountains, miles away from any big city, and outfit it with décor that was more suited for bustling Orange County in Southern California or Silicon Valley in Northern California.

Beth knew from her internet research on Viralvector that the facilities in Rancho Santa Margarita and in the mountains at Lake Arrowhead were prominently showcased in the corporate reports and PR news releases. This facility, however, was intentionally hidden. It wasn't mentioned anywhere in the corporate reports. She only discovered it by chance while pouring over reams of snippets and disparate information that she'd found in the file at Lake Arrowhead.

Beth walked across the foyer with confidence. A receptionist was sitting behind a desk, busy chewing gum and reading the latest issue of *People* magazine.

She looked up as Beth approached. She dropped the magazine and smiled. "Can I help you?"

"Yes," Beth said. "I'm Dr. Elizabeth Collins, from the NCI...the National Cancer Institute in Bethesda, Maryland. I have a nine o'clock appointment with Dr. Blake Thornton."

The receptionist slid the *People* magazine out of the way and opened a black appointment book.

"Sorry. I'm a few minutes late," Beth said, looking at her watch. "This place isn't easy to find."

The receptionist was in her twenties, attractive, and clearly new on the job. Beth watched her fumble with the appointment calendar before locating today's entry page and running her finger down it.

"Uh...I'm sorry," she said. "I don't show an appointment for you today at nine."

"What?" Beth said with just the right mix of shock and incredulity. "Of course, I have an appointment. Are you sure you're looking at Tuesday the eighth, nine o'clock?"

"Y-yes. There aren't any appointments on the calendar today. It's all blocked out as a research day." She flipped back through the previous two to three weeks and then forward a week, scanning the time slots and scattered entries as quickly as she could.

Beth watched her slightly panicked effort. She let the tension rise in the lengthening silence. Finally, she spoke.

"This is *completely* unacceptable," Beth said with a razor edge in her voice. "I know my administrative assistant made this appointment over a month ago. And I've just traveled over *two thousand miles* to meet with Dr. Thornton about a very important research project the NCI is interested in doing with him. I suggest you go tell him I'm here."

"I'll...I'll be right back," the receptionist stammered. She jumped up and hurried down the hall.

Beth looked at her watch and smiled to herself. *Shouldn't be long now.* She walked over to one of the comfortable reception area chairs and sat down.

Max put his hand up, motioning for Mark to stop. They had edged their way down a side hall and were about to move out into the main hallway. The approaching rat-a-tat of the receptionist's shoes caused both of them to scramble back a few feet. They hid behind an open closet door as the frazzled young receptionist hurried past them down the main hallway.

"Beth's in place," Max whispered.

They didn't have to wait long for a response. They could hear Thornton's booming voice from the far end of the building followed by the opening and slamming of a door and the sound of hurried footsteps clattering up the main hallway.

Max peered through the crack between the door and the doorjamb and saw Thornton in surgical greens and the young receptionist walk past. He heard Thornton hiss under his breath, "You're *sure* she said the National Cancer Institute?"

"Yes, Dr. Thornton," she answered. Her voice quivered with fear. "From the…National Cancer Institute in Bethesda, Maryland. That's…that's what she said…"

Their hushed voices receded down the hallway.

Max and Mark slid out from behind the door and crept up to the intersection of the hallways. Max peered around the corner and saw Thornton and the receptionist disappear to the left into the reception area.

When he heard Beth's voice a few seconds later, he signaled Mark. They pulled out their handguns and headed down the main hallway towards the operating room.

Chapter 53

"Dr. Collins?" Thornton asked. He strode up to Beth and reached out to shake her hand.

Beth grasped his hand and looked him directly in the eye. "Hello. Are you Dr. Blake Thornton?"

"I am," he said with a forced smile. His eyes scanned her head to toe and lingered on the folder she was holding in her left hand. She felt disturbingly like an insect under a microscope.

"I'm sorry for the misunderstanding about the appointment," he said. "My receptionist said you're from the NCI. What can I do for you?"

"First of all, thank you for seeing me even with the appointment mishap. I can tell by the way you're dressed that this is an obvious interruption."

His shoulders belied undercurrents of tightly restrained impatience although he answered with a pleasant voice. "Yes, but it's...fine," he said.

"I'll get to the point," Beth said. She opened the folder she was carrying and pulled out the latest scientific study Thornton and his research team had published in the journal *Nature*.

"This paper you published last year on vectoral transfection and genetic transmission is an impressive piece of work...a real advance of the science."

"Thank you. That *was* the general consensus in the scientific community."

Beth ignored his haughty response and continued. "As you're probably aware, research teams have recently done whole exome sequencing of several cancers, including breast, melanoma, lung, and colon, and have—"

"Yes, I'm familiar with that work," he said, cutting her off. "I know several of the primary investigators personally."

Beth nodded as if she were impressed. "Then as you well know, the result of the sequencing was the discovery of one hundred eighty-seven previously unknown genes that are likely involved in the cancer process. Other investigators determined through DNA microarray analysis that up to a quarter of these could potentially be mutated tumor suppressor genes. My team and I at the NCI would like to adapt your methods to systematically investigate a number of these."

"What are you planning?" he asked with detached interest.

"Essentially, we'll use your vectoral transfection techniques to transfer iterative combinations of these tumor-suppressor genes into variant nude mice and map the functions of these genes. This will help us identify potential targets for cancer drug development or possibly gene replacement targets."

Thornton squinted at her. "Fairly interesting. Of course, our methods are proprietary, and we'll need you to sign legal releases protecting our rights for future potential commercialization."

"Understood. I'm sure our contracts people at the NCI will come up with an agreement that's mutually acceptable."

"I'm sure they'll do just that," Thornton said.

"Well, what we'd like to have," Beth continued, "is the schematic of your transfection protocol so we can get pre-lab preparations lined up while we're waiting for the contract to—"

A loud boom cut her off in mid-sentence. The ear-splitting roar of close proximity gunfire. Thornton whirled around and looked down the hall where the sound had originated.

He flinched and turned back as two more shots were fired in rapid sequence, their concussive explosion rattling the windows in the lobby.

"Get out of here!" he shouted.

Beth pivoted and rushed for the door.

Thornton turned and ran down the hall towards the gunfire.

He grabbed his push-to-talk phone. "Nick! Where are you guys? We're under fire…"

There was silence for a moment. Then the phone crackled to life.

Max looked across the main hall at Mark, who was wedged against the corner wall of the perpendicular hallway.

After Max had gotten into position, Mark had started moving down the main corridor. That's when guards at the end of the hallway caught sight of him and ordered him to halt. When he'd retreated instead, they'd opened fire.

There were two bullet holes in the wall near Mark. The third shot had flown wild.

All the shots had been fired at Mark, and Max was sure his partner was the only one they had seen. The element of surprise was back on their side.

Inching closer to the corner, he locked eyes with Mark and nodded. "Scope them," Max whispered into the microphone attached to his lapel.

Mark flashed a thumbs up and slipped a telescoping canister from his belt. The device was a high-tech version of a child's toy periscope with high-resolution digital magnification and infrared capabilities. It collapsed down into a cylinder the size of a small Maglite flashlight and could be snapped onto a utility belt.

Mark extended the scope to its full half-meter length and eased the head of it beyond the edge of the corner.

"Two of them," Mark whispered into his lapel mike. "Crouched in the third and fourth doorways down the hall on my side. Shade under fifty feet away."

"Okay, here's the plan. On my signal, let them glimpse you then dive back behind cover. I'm loading up with a mag of tranks. A quick two-shot, and I'll take 'em both out. Then we'll close in and storm the OR."

"Got it," Mark whispered. "On your signal."

Max unsnapped a magazine holder on his belt and withdrew a ten-shot magazine loaded with high-velocity dart cartridges. He switched out the magazine in the Glock and slid back the top glide of the gun, chambering the first shot.

"Signal on count of three. One…two…*three!*"

Mark sprung out from behind the corner, looked straight at the two guards, and then dove back deep behind the corner. He hit the ground just as both guards unleashed a fusillade of bullets.

Max stepped partially out, wrapping himself around the corner and planting himself in a solid crouch with his right upper arm wedged against the wall. He took instant aim and squeezed off two shots in rapid succession at each guard.

All four darts hit their targets, and both guards dropped unconscious to the floor.

"Targets down," Max said. "Move it!"

Mark scrambled to his feet and met Max in the middle of the hall. They rushed down the hallway, past the prostrate guards, to the door of the operating room.

It was locked.

Max took a step back and charged with a powerful thrusting kick, splintering the door and jamb. He kicked the door again, and it crashed open. Two deafening booms roared simultaneously from behind and beside him.

Max turned to look, and a bullet whizzed by within inches of his face, burying itself in the wall beyond him.

He spun around and saw Mark crouched in a braced shooting pose. Further down the hall, near the two fallen guards, a third guard lay face down on the floor, his gun scattered a few feet from his outstretched hand.

Max looked over at Mark and tipped his head.

Mark nodded once in return.

Max switched out the magazine in his Glock for the one filled with .40 caliber ammunition.

"Advance," he said, charging into the operating room. He stopped short.

The room was empty.

Chapter 54

Max took in the surgical suite in a glance with its meticulous set up of monitors, computer video screens, anesthesia equipment, sterile drapes, and stainless tray tables with surgical instruments laid out and ready for use. The monitors and anesthesia equipment were all on, and Max's eye caught the green phosphorescent screen of the heart monitor blipping steadily. The unit's connected chest leads were lying haphazardly on the surgery table that was covered with disheveled sheets and surgical drapes.

It was clear the surgical team had left in a hurry.

"This way!" Max shouted and rushed across to room toward a set of twin doors. He burst through the twin doors and emerged in time to catch a glimpse of two people rolling a hospital gurney around a corner.

"There they are!"

He sprinted down the length of the hall, skidded to a stop, and peered around the corner.

"Halt! Police!" Max shouted as he closed to within thirty feet of them. Alongside the gurney were a nurse and a man both dressed in surgical greens with surgery face masks dangling from their necks.

Beyond them, further down the hall, another security guard turned and was hurrying back towards them, drawing his gun as he approached.

Max slowed to a fast walk and raised his Glock in a two-fisted grip.

Megan sat up on the rolling gurney and saw Max. Her eyes widened in surprise as she lifted her arms to him. Hope filled her eyes.

"Daddy! You came! I knew you would!"

The hardest thing in the world for Max was to look away from her. He locked his gaze on the approaching guard, who was raising his gun as Megan screamed.

Max blocked out all other thought and drew a bead on the center of the guard's chest.

"Police! Drop your gun. Now!"

The man swung his gun toward Megan. "No! You drop your gun or I'll—"

In the handful of milliseconds it took Max to react, a flood of adrenaline rushed through his body, generating maximum nerve conduction velocity. Impulses raced down the radial and ulnar nerves of his right arm to the fingers of his hand in less than two hundredths of a second. Faster than the blink of an eye. With precision accuracy honed by hundreds of practice hours on the shooting range, Max squeezed the trigger.

An ear-splitting roar filled the hallway as his gun fired. The slug slammed into the guard's chest, ripping through lung tissue and sinew, severing a major nerve trunk to his right arm, and blasting out through a large exit wound in his back. The impact drove the guard back, and he dropped to the floor in a crumpled mass. His gun bounced off the floor and skittered harmlessly up against the wall behind him.

As Max swung his aim towards the man and woman, Mark stepped up alongside him, his gun trained on them also.

"Don't shoot!" Nurse Creade pleaded. She flung her arms up.

The man, a surgical assistant, held his arms straight up in the air, palms out.

"Yes…pl…please don't," he stammered. His face blanched white as a sheet, his eyes unfocusing and rolling upwards as he fainted. His head smacked against the linoleum tiles with a resounding crack.

Max trained his gun on Creade. "*Move away from her.*"

Creade scurried away from the gurney, her arms still high in the air.

"Lie down on the floor, next to him," Mark ordered. "Face down, arms behind your back."

Creade did as she was told. Mark clacked a set of cuffs on her wrists and bound her ankles together with plastic ties. He repeated the same steps on the unconscious surgical assistant.

After checking the body of the wounded guard, he kicked the guard's handgun down the hall. He continued to the intersection up ahead and then turned and scanned the hallway in the opposite direction.

"Daddy!" Megan cried out. She was kneeling on the gurney, arms outstretched towards Max. Tears streamed down her cheeks.

Max ran over to her and swept her up off the gurney, enveloping her in a bear hug. She clung to his neck, gripping with all her might and sobbing.

"It's okay, princess," Max whispered into her hair. "You're safe now. Daddy's here. Everything's going to be okay."

Max scooped her up and turned toward Mark, who signaled with a thumb's up.

"Let's go," Max said. They retraced their steps through the corridors back to the storage room where they had entered.

They didn't meet anyone else on their way. Everyone had fled when they heard the first round of gunshots.

Mark pulled open the door to the storage room and flipped on the light as he entered. Max was about to follow him when Megan lifted her head up off his shoulder.

"Stop! Wait a minute!" she cried.

Max stopped and looked in her eyes, which were wide open and glazed. Her pupils were oddly dilated.

"What is it?" he asked.

"They've...got her," she said, slowly turning to face the wall. Her body stiffened as she struggled against his grip. "They've got both of them."

Max put her down and crouched in front of her, looking into saucer eyes that stared right through him, through the walls, to something beyond.

"They've got who?" Max asked.

She didn't answer for several seconds, and then her eyes came back into focus and she looked at Max,

"They've got Sarah!" she shrilled in alarm. "And Dr. Collins! They've got them both!"

Chapter 55

"What?" Max asked. "You saw them? Both of them?"

"Yeah," Megan said, blinking twice. "I could see through Sarah's eyes, and I saw everything when they caught her. Sarah was walking up the road towards the front of the building. Dr. Collins ran up to her and said something. Then she took Sarah's hand, and they started hurrying back down the road. But then these two scary guys with guns came running out of the trees and grabbed them."

"Did they hurt them?"

"No," Megan said. "But they pointed their guns at them and made them walk over and get into a black SUV. Then it drove away, really fast, starting back down the mountain."

"Did this just happen?" Max asked.

"I'm...not sure." She squeezed her eyes tight. "I think it happened a few minutes ago, but it could have been longer than that. It's really weird...I was seeing two pictures at once, and both were looking out different windows of the SUV."

"Two *different* pictures?" Mark asked. He was standing just inside the storage room. "You mean like a picture-in-a-picture screen on a TV?"

"Kinda, I guess," Megan said. "I think the really clear picture is from Sarah and the other's from Dr. Collins."

"Whoa...stereo ESP," Mark muttered under his breath. "Beyond weird."

Max took Megan's hand and pulled her through the storage room in a hurry. He opened the door to the outside and stepped out. In the distance, he thought he could hear the faint whisper of a receding vehicle, but it could be his mind playing tricks. He wasn't sure.

"Megs, this is important. When you were seeing through Sarah's eyes, did you by any possible chance—"

"—see the license plate?" she interrupted.

"Yeah. Did you see the number?"

Megan gave two quick nods. "Sarah must have been thinking the same thing, because she stared at the plate for forever as they were walking up to the SUV."

"So, you got a good look?"

"Better than that...I memorized it."

"That's my girl," Max said, giving her a smile.

"Excellent," Mark said. "Got my pen out...let me have it."

Megan read off the number. Mark repeated it to her after writing it down and compared it to the previous plate number.

"Damn," he said. "Different SUV. We got lucky with the last one because it had a LoJack tracking system we could activate. I can try to call my buddy and see if we luck out again with—"

"Hold on." Max stepped back inside the storage room. "What about that thing they implanted under Sarah's skin?" he asked Mark. "Think we can figure out how to use it?"

Mark's eyes lit up. "I bet that nurse or the other guy we left back there would know how to track her. Let me have a few minutes alone with them. I can be very convincing."

"I'm sure you can," Max said. "Megan and I'll get the Suburban and wait for you right outside this door. Get us some tracking info."

"Comin' right up," Mark said, turning and heading back up the hall where he'd left Creade.

Max drove up to the rear of the building and pulled to a stop in front of the storage room door with the engine running.

He had held Megan's hand the entire way down to retrieve the Suburban and the entire drive back. And he was still holding her hand. He couldn't dwell on how close he'd come to losing her. He locked those impossible thoughts away in the dark recesses of his mind. Later, when all of this was over, there would be time to let them surface.

Megan was with him now, alive and safe, clinging to his arm in the cab of his SUV. One crisis over.

He focused on their current crisis. Tactical scenarios swirled in his mind as they waited for Mark. Ten minutes passed in relative silence. Max was about to radio Mark on his shoulder walkie-talkie when he saw him burst out of the door holding a black backpack.

Mark ran over to them and climbed into the back seat, slamming the door shut.

"Got it! Let's go."

Max put the Suburban in gear and gunned it. The tires kicked up spraying fantails of gravel as they sped away from the building.

They raced down the sinuous road towards the main highway and town.

"So, what'd you get?" Max asked, glancing at Mark in the rearview mirror. "I'm assuming one of them talked."

Mark flashed a grin. "Yep. I got the nurse to sing like a songbird. Chirpity-chirp. Amazing how convincing I can be when I need to be."

"No surprise. What have you got in the duffel bag?"

Mark reached in and started pulling out a transponder tracker receiver.

"Well, this just happens to be a seriously cool, high-tech toy," he said, running his fingers over the device controls. "But first…listen up. Here's the quick debrief."

"Fire away."

"So Brunhilde starts singing like a canary when I showed her my gun. She gives me the Reader's Digest version of the grand plan, and it turns out, Beth nailed the bull's-eye. The CEO of Viralvector, this Blake Thornton dude, has got only one kid…a son with Down Syndrome."

"His name's Newt," Megan interjected.

"Yeah, that's it," Mark said. "Anyway, she confirmed what Beth found out in the computer files. They've been injecting Megan, Sarah, and two other kids with this genetically modified virus that supercharges connections in the brain. Thornton and his surgical team were about to operate and transfer virus-enhanced brain cells from Megan and Eddie to his son. Called them 'modified neural stem cells' or something. They would've used Sarah's cells along with the other kids' if they'd been able catch her. But instead they had to go to plan B, hoping Megan and Eddie would have enough of a supply."

"And we got there in the nick of time," Max said.

"Barely," Mark agreed. "A few seconds before the gunfire broke out,

Thornton's men radioed him and said they'd grabbed Beth and Sarah. After the guards started firing at us, Thornton left through the second room with his surgeon, some guy named Calvin Lynch, and his anesthesiologist. They grabbed Newt and Eddie, who were closest to the door, escaped outside, and took off in the SUV that was waiting outside with Beth and Sarah on board."

"So, they were driving away before we even caught up to Megan."

"Looks like it."

"What else?" Max asked, doing a mental calculation of the elapsed time. He slowed as they entered a sharp curve and accelerated out of it.

"Couple of things," Mark said. "This nurse—Creade's her name—got fired up after getting past her fear. She wants to cooperate with us. She says she'll do anything it'll take to keep her ass out of prison. Even testify against Thornton."

"Good."

"She said Thornton owns a house and some other real estate up here, but all she knows is the house is in the hills somewhere north of town. No clue about the other properties."

"What about where they're headed. Any idea?"

"Nothing. Her best guess is the house. Said she doesn't know of any other company-owned facilities. The two in California and this one are it."

"You believe her?"

"I think so. Her story jives with what Beth found out on the internet, and the threat of prison's got nurse Creade spooked. Before I even asked her, she brought up the transponder they implanted under Sarah's skin and then proceeded to tell me how we could use it to track her."

"She did?"

"Yeah. Volunteered all kinds of info about it. I freed up her ankle ties so she could take me down to the control station, get me this thing, and show me how it works. Took me through it step by step."

Mark held up the tracking device.

"Nice," Max said. "Where'd you leave her?"

"Cuffed to the metal desk in the office. I unhooked the phone and chucked it, but I told her I'd be putting in a call to the police before I left, and they'd be coming for her."

"Who'd you call?"

"Ed Manning back at SWAT headquarters."

"He'll move on it."

"Definitely. I gave him the rundown on Megan's kidnapping and Sarah and the other kids. He's going to handle the calls to the local police and regional FBI office for us and get out an All-Points alert."

"Good. So how does this thing work?"

"It's pretty cool. You power it on by sliding this toggle switch," Mark said, pushing it with his thumb. "Once it's fired up, the screen looks like this."

Max glanced at the screen, which showed a high contrast white and phosphorescent blue flied marked with roads and topographic landmarks.

"Nice," Max said. "High-def GPS mapping."

"Like Google maps on steroids."

"Okay, how do we get this thing to track them?"

"It's like we thought. Nurse Creade confirmed that Sarah's got a microchip transponder embedded under the skin of her left shoulder blade. All we need to do is punch in her transponder code on this keypad and hit *Enter* to activate the transponder. She demonstrated it for me with a spare transponder. Looked up its code in this notebook and then punched it in."

"Did it work?"

"Like a dream. Signal showed up as a bright blinking red dot."

"Did you try Sarah's transponder code?"

"Sure did," Mark said. "The notebook listed codes for all the transponders, including Sarah's. But here's where the caveat comes in."

"What caveat…?"

"If she's in range, Sarah's tracking signal will show up on the map. But the range is only three miles."

"Three miles? That's it?"

"Right. Pretty wimpy. But that's for high resolution, pinpoint accuracy. The good news is that if you flip this switch on the back to lower resolution, the range expands to around ten miles." He turned the receiver over and slid the switch. "Of course, you lose resolution and accuracy."

"*Not* a big deal," Max said, relieved. "We track them at low resolution until we get close and then flip the switch."

"That'll work…providing we can stay within ten miles of them."

"Did you punch in the code and try it?"

"Yep, back in the control room with my new buddy Creade. Sarah and Beth are outside high-resolution range, but still show up on low res. Problem is, the red dot was already at the five to six-mile range. They're were moving fast. They might almost be out of tracking range."

Mark unfolded a piece of paper with some numbers on it. He tapped in Sarah's code on the keypad and hit *Enter*. The screen fluttered and then went dark and lit up again. The roads and topographic landmarks reappeared. The red dot began blinking at the top edge of the screen.

"Bingo," Mark said. "There they are. About ten to eleven miles from here as the crow flies. They've moving up Highway 82 on the way to Aspen."

"You sure it's them?"

"Positive. Only Sarah's transponder sends out the signal for the code we entered."

"Then we better gun it before they get out of range."

"Damn!" Mark exclaimed, as the red blip suddenly disappeared from the screen. "We lost 'em."

"Hold on tight," Max said. He reached over to check Megan's seat belt.

"Daddy?" she said. Worried distress crossed her face.

"Don't worry." Max slammed the gas pedal down, and the Suburban lurched forward, soaring through the turns on the winding mountain road.

"We know the direction they're headed. We'll chase them down until they get back into range. Then we'll catch them."

Chapter 56

Max sped down the serpentine mountain road. They reached highway 82 fifteen minutes later and made a sharp squealing right turn onto the highway that would take them through the mountains to Aspen.

"How many miles up Highway 82 were they when the transponder signal disappeared from the screen?" Max asked.

"Let's see." Mark studied the screen and put his finger on the spot where the red dot had disappeared. He scrolled the map down, positioning the location in the center of the screen. He opened a folding map of the area and used the mileage scale legend at the bottom of the page to measure the distance.

"It looks like they were three to four miles up this road on their way to Aspen. Then add to that about seven miles from here up to the Viralvector building, and we're at ten or eleven miles. Out of signal range."

"What are the next few towns coming up?" Max asked.

"No towns until we reach Aspen in about twenty-eight miles." Mark looked closer at the map. "Beyond Aspen—staying on Highway 82—there's Woody Creek eight miles out, as well as the turn off to Snowmass. Next up is Basalt eleven miles from there, then El Jebel—another five miles—and Cattle Creek eleven miles beyond that. At that point, we're almost up to Interstate 70."

Max lined up the towns and their distances in his mind.

"So, they couldn't have reached Aspen yet. They must still be on this road. I'm thinking they're headed toward 70."

"Seems likely." Mark looked up from the map and scanned the road.

"If we keep gunning it at top speed, we're bound to gain ground on them and recover the signal."

Max pushed the SUV to its maximum safe speed around the countless curves in the heavily forested mountain road. Fifteen minutes passed.

"Stop dreamin' and start believin'!" Mark exclaimed. "Houston…we have a signal!"

"Yes!" Max pumped his right fist. "Where are they?"

"About four miles this side of Aspen."

"Excellent," Mark said. "We've got to do everything we can to keep the signal on our scope."

Mark continued navigating the SUV through the turns and switchbacks with urgency, accelerating in the short straightaways and then slowing only as much as needed in the curves. They reached Aspen fifty minutes later and continued on past Woody Creek, all the while gaining on the Suburban with the signal they were tracking on the scope.

"That's weird," Mark said.

"What?

"The red blip on the screen's not moving."

"What do you mean? It's just sitting there?"

"Stationary and blinking away," Mark said. "Two miles or so north of Basalt. It's like they stopped."

"How far are we from them?" Max asked.

"Looks like a little under eight miles. We've cut their lead and we're closing in."

"Let's hope the signal keeps blinking. Are they still on Highway 82, or have they pulled off on—"

"Oh, no!" Megan shrieked.

Max and Mark both turned their heads and looked at her. She was staring straight ahead through the windshield, locked in a trance.

"Megan, what is it?" Max asked, shock and worry lacing his voice.

"It's Sarah. There's a syringe with a needle coming towards her. They're giving her a shot. She's starting to cry."

"Megan," Max said urgently. "Listen to me. "What else do you see? Are they still inside the vehicle…the SUV?"

"Yeah, it's the inside of an SUV. Looks kinda like ours. Sarah's sitting in the seat behind the driver, but all she's looking at is the needle stuck in the inside of her left arm. The man's pulling it out now, and…the picture's starting to get blurry all of a sudden."

"It is? Can you see anything else?"

"Um…She's looking up at a man sitting next to her. He's got wire-rimmed glasses on and a white doctor's coat. He's lifting another syringe up towards her. She's looking back at her right shoulder…it's bare, like they made her take her t-shirt off or something."

She watched the scene unfold in her mind with mesmerizing alarm. Her fingers dug into the seat rest. "Now he's giving her a shot in the back of her shoulder. I can't see…it's getting blurrier. She's looking up at somebody in the back seat…"

Max waited. Megan stared speechless, mouth agape, at the vision before her.

Moments passed. Her expression morphed into joy and surprise.

"Megan?" Max asked. His voice softened, and he took her hand. "Who is she looking at?"

Megan gulped and then spoke. "It's…it's…Beth…Dr. Collins! She's holding Sarah's hand. But the picture's breaking up and growing dark. I can't see her face anymore."

Megan stopped talking and slouched back in her seat.

Max watched her out of the corner of her eyes as she closed her eyes and sat in silent dejection. A few minutes passed. Suddenly, her face brightened.

"I…see something again."

"You do? What?" Max asked.

"It's hard to make out. The picture's fuzzy, but now I'm…"

She stopped talking and stared out into infinity. Immobile and entranced.

"Now you're what?" Max pushed, glancing between her and the highway.

"I'm looking through Dr. Collin's eyes." Megan's face was scrunched, her eyes shut tight, and her voice seemed to come from farther away. "She's watching the guy who gave Sarah the shots. He's wiping the back of Sarah's shoulder with a couple of cotton balls and some kind of dark liquid. Oh, geez! He's got a scalpel in his hand. He's putting the point of the blade right there on the skin on her back. He's starting to cut."

Max waited for her to continue.

A few seconds later, she jerked in surprise and turned her head to the left.

"Wha…What?!" she cried.

She blinked and shook her head. The haze cleared from her mind.

"Megan, what is it?"

"Beth was watching him make the cut when all of a sudden she turned to her left and looked out the window. Like something surprised her."

"What was it?"

"I don't know," Megan said. "Maybe a truck or a car honked as it drove past them. They're parked right off the highway. I think they're in the parking lot of some old boarded-up motel. When Beth looked to the left, I didn't see anything strange. Just a buncha' cars zipping by. And across the highway was this broken-down old gas station with a strange name...Terrible Herb or Herbs..."

"Terrible Herbst?" Mark asked.

"That's it!"

"Do you still see it?" Max asked.

Megan shook her head. "It's gone. I can't see anything anymore. Sarah's gone, *and* Beth's gone."

"Why don't you give it a rest for a bit," Max said. "Maybe something will come back in a little while. In the meantime, we'll try to close in on them. Terrible Herbst..." he muttered to himself. "Wait a minute. I think I remember passing that old abandoned place on the drive I made to Aspen a few years ago. I'm pretty sure I know where that is."

"Well, hurry up and get us there," Mark said, looking down at his scope. "Signal's still blinking...and it's not moving."

Max pushed their speed past one hundred.

Six minutes later, they pulled into the desolate parking lot of the boarded-up motel that Megan had seen. The shattered remains of a neon sign out front read *Mountain View Motel*. In the past, it might have been a welcome respite to weary travelers, but now it was just a deteriorated, graffiti-marred building. The crumbling blacktop of the parking lot was buckled and pocked with potholes, and weeds and sagebrush had reclaimed the area in scattered patches.

Max looked over his left shoulder at the decrepit gas station/mini-mart across the highway.

"Terrible Herbst." Turning back, he scanned the empty parking lot.

Mark smacked the side of the transponder tracking scope and shook the device.

"What the hell's the matter with this thing?" He said. "It's still blinking, and the signal hasn't moved an inch. Either the scope's malfunctioning or Sarah's here somewhere."

"Let's find out," Max said.

He drove the entire length of the parking lot, creeping along at 2 miles per hour, studying the windows and doors of each room as they passed. The glass in all of the windows had been smashed out, and most of the windows were covered with weathered plywood, nailed sloppily into place. An irresistible canvas for itinerant graffiti artists.

Max reached the north end of the building and executed a sharp U-turn. They rolled back to the way they came and continued looking for anything out of the ordinary.

"Keep going," Mark said. "Past that end unit and around the corner of the building."

Max edged the Suburban past the building's edge then swung left and stopped.

"There," Mark said, pointing to the side of the motel. "Lower right window."

Max narrowed his eyes and spotted what Mark saw. The glass panes were shattered like they were in the rest of the building, but on the lower right side, a large hole had been smashed through the plywood covering the window.

Mark checked the scope. The signal was blinking strong and steady. He put it back into the duffel bag on the seat next to him.

"Let's have a look," Max said.

They climbed out of the Suburban with handguns drawn, rushed over to the window, and flattened themselves against the wall next to it. Mark stood on the left side of the door. He holstered his gun and dropped the duffel bag to the ground. Kneeling, he retrieved a three-pound sledgehammer from it. He stood, gripping the wooden handle with both hands, and looked at Max.

Max gave him a countdown with his fingers. Three...two...one...then a fist.

Mark swung the sledgehammer, aiming for the vertical midframe of the window. The brittle plywood shattered into jagged pieces, imploding en masse into the decrepit motel room and kicking up a cloud of dust as it landed on the bare concrete floor.

Max was the first one through the window. He held his handgun before him and scanned the room, fanning his gun from right to left. The high-intensity Mag light on his shoulder harness illuminated sections of the room with daylight clarity.

The dusty room had long ago been stripped of all furniture, carpeting, and wall décor. The floor was strewn with wood scraps and shards of drywall. Even the closet door and the door to the bathroom were missing, and Max could see that the sink, faucets, toilet, and other fixtures had been removed for salvage.

Max stepped further into the empty room and heard a muffled crunch and buzzing crackle beneath his right foot. He backed up and shined his light at the floor. A gallon-sized Ziploc bag lay there. It contained bloody gauze, surgical gloves, two used syringes, bandage wrappers, and a bottle of brown solution.

Max bent down and nudged the contents with the muzzle of his gun as Mark climbed through the window.

"Room's secure," Max said. "But completely abandoned. Nobody's here."

"Kinda figured that's what we'd find," Mark said.

"Take a look at this." Max pointed to the Ziploc bag.

One of the syringes was crushed. Next to it was a dime-sized, translucent glass wafer with a smear of blood on its shattered surface. Microelectronic circuits were partially visible in its interior.

"Remember what Megan saw? The guy starting to use the scalpel on Sarah's back? I bet he cut the transponder out, and this is it. Looks like I crushed this bug when I stepped on it."

"Let me check the scope," Mark said, hurrying off to the SUV. He rushed back with the unit, smacking the side of it as he had done before.

"I can't believe it. The signal's gone," he said. "Guess you're right. You must've crushed the bug."

Mark nodded. "How are we supposed to track her and Beth now?"

They stared at each other and then turned and looked back through the broken window at the Suburban. They could see Megan was sitting in the passenger seat, staring back at them.

"Megan's got to see something again," Max said.

Mark thought for a moment. "In the meantime, all we can do is keep cruising down the highway in the direction they were headed."

Max picked the Ziploc bag up by its corner, and they turned and headed back.

Chapter 57

Max climbed into the driver's seat of the Suburban and pulled the door shut. He looked over at Megan, who was staring straight ahead through the windshield.

"She wasn't there, was she?" Megan asked.

"No. She wasn't."

Megan turned and looked at her father, smiling wanly. "Before the picture in my mind disappeared, I saw them cut something out of the back of Sarah's shoulder. Maybe it was that tracking signal thing."

Max nodded. He held up the bag. "This was lying on the floor in the hotel room. I stepped on it. Signal disappeared from Mark's tracking scope right after that."

Megan's face fell. "So how are we going to find her now?"

Max shook his head. "I don't know. I told Mark we'll keep driving the same direction for a while and hope we can spot them. Maybe they're headed to Denver to catch a plane. We're really hoping you have another vision episode and see something that might help us."

"Me too. I wish I could control when I …"

Megan's face went blank. She tilted her head back as her eyes grew glassy. Max watched her turn and direct her gaze through the front windshield.

"Megan?" he asked tentatively after a few moments. He didn't expect her to respond right away.

He watched her eyes moving REM-like, observing a separate reality unfolding before her on a canvas only she could see.

Another full minute passed, and then Max asked louder, "Megan…what do you see?"

She remained silent, her brow furrowing as she stared out the windshield with rapt attention. She raised her hand, palm facing Max, silencing him.

Max waited. Seconds stretched into minutes. He was getting ready to ask her again when Megan broke the silence.

"Sarah's back," she whispered. Her unblinking gaze didn't falter.

"Good," Max said. "What do you—"

"She's walking outside their SUV, towards the back of it. She's stopping and bending over next to the rear tire, looking at the ground. She's…she's…"

Beth patted Sarah's back as she convulsed in a racking dry heave. She'd thrown up twice before this, emptying the contents of her stomach.

Sarah coughed and snurfed, trying not to whimper. She looked back over her shoulder at Beth.

"You're okay," Beth murmured. "You're just having a bad reaction to the sedative the doctor gave you. Happens sometimes." She continued rubbing Sarah's back in big, soft circles.

Sarah leaned over and spasmed in a partial dry heave.

"Here, wash your mouth out with this," she said, handing Sarah a bottle of water she'd grabbed earlier. "I've got some tissues you can use too."

Beth reached into her right jacket pocket and pulled out a travel-sized packet of Kleenex tissues. Her keys came out with it. Beth stared at her keyring and felt the tingling stab of opportunity.

On the ring was the small, stainless steel Leatherman Micra that her younger brother had given her years ago. She rarely used it, but she'd always kept it on her key chain in case of emergency. Ten useful tools were packed into this compact device, including scissors, tweezers, screwdrivers, a nail file, and the one tool Beth was looking for: a knife.

She dug her thumbnail into the slot of the slender blade, swinging it out and locking it in position. The razor sharp, stainless steel blade reflected a brief glitter of light as Beth shifted it in her hand and tightened her grip. Now was the time to be quick and neat.

Reaching beyond Sarah and using the girl as cover, she plunged the inch-long blade into the tire, between the thick treads. She pulled it out and rapidly plunged it in again near the first puncture. Barely audible hisses began emanating from the tire in stereo sibilance.

"Sarah…are you okay, honey?" Beth said loud enough for the others in the SIV to hear. She folded the blade back in, collapsed the tool, and slid the keyring back into her pocket. Sarah blew her nose and wiped it with the tissue.

"We've got to go now," Beth said, starting to rise. She gripped Sarah's arm and helped her stand.

She turned around and saw that the man sent outside to guard them had been scanning the horizon instead of watching the vomiting sideshow. He was only now turning back to face them. He glared as she and Sarah walked to the open door of the SUV. He climbed in after them and slammed the door shut.

The engine had been idling. The instant Beth and Sarah sat down, the driver shifted it into gear and gunned the accelerator, thrusting them back in their seats. Beth slipped her hand into her pocket and closed her fingers around the multi-tool, her mind racing.

Several miles down the highway, she heard the telltale sounds begin with alarming immediacy.

The pitchy thumping grew more intense at the high speed they were traveling. It heightened in force and intensity until the entire vehicle shook in pounding convulsions.

The driver leaned on the brakes, dramatically slowing the SUV down under 30 miles per hour. The high-pitched thumping devolved into a rhythmic lub-dub.

"What the hell's wrong?" Thornton barked.

"Must have a flat," the driver grumbled. He pulled the car over to the side of the road and rolled to a stop.

Thornton looked at his watch and slapped his leg. "Dammit! One of you get out there and change the tire. And make it fast. It better be a damned speed record! We've got twelve minutes to get to the rendezvous point for the pickup. We are *not* going to be late!"

The driver and the man in the back seat scrambled out of the SUV.

Three minutes later, the SUV kicked up dirt and gravel and accelerated onto the highway, speeding northward.

"They're driving again," Megan said. "They pulled back onto the highway, and they're headed the same direction as before."

"Can you see any road signs or landmarks that stand out?" Max asked. "Anything that'll give us a hint where they are?"

"They passed a bent and faded green sign on the right side of the road that said *El Jebel Diner: Breakfast, Lunch, Dinner. Next Exit.*"

"How far do you—"

Mark lowered the pair of binoculars he was looking through and pointed. "You mean like this gnarly old green billboard coming up in mile and a half?"

Max looked up the road at the distant sign. Megan blinked out of her introspective vision and glanced over at her father.

"Is that it?" he asked. "Same sign?"

Megan nodded. "That's the one I saw."

"So, you think they just passed it? Or do you think it was a while ago?"

"I'm pretty sure it was now," Megan said. "I think I'm seeing what Sarah sees right when it happens."

Max checked his speedometer, which was tipping seventy, and looked up the highway ahead. The closest vehicle was a Honda Accord, several hundred yards in front of them. Half a mile beyond that was a white pickup truck, and a few car lengths ahead of it, a bigger vehicle. Black. Boxy.

"I bet that's them, way up there," Max said. "looks like a black SUV ahead of the pickup truck."

Megan stared at the black vehicle, then closed her eyes and sank into her mind. A distant, entirely different perspective filled her mental landscape.

"It *is* them," she said.

"You're sure?" Max asked.

Megan opened her eyes and tilted her head to the left. She met his gaze then looked away from him and stared off into the distance, her eyes locking on the SUV.

"Yes. I'm sure. I'm looking through Sarah's eyes…and a little bit through Dr. Collins' at the same time. It's that split-screen thing all over again. Sarah's looking at Eddie. And now she's looking back through their rear window, way back down the road…right at us. I can tell she knows we're here."

"Any way you can find out from her where they're headed?" Max asked.

Megan smiled uncertainly. "I can try," she said.

Grabbing a legal pad and a pen out of the holder slot in the passenger door, Megan wrote in large block letters: *DO YOU KNOW WHERE THEY'RE TAKING YOU?*

She held the pad close to her eyes and stared hard at the words.

The larger of the two images wafting in her mind shifted. A palm of a hand appeared, filling the breadth of her visual field, and a finger began tracing out a word in capital letters: *H-E-L- I-C-O-P-T-E-R.*

Megan could see the hand shaking as it paused, and then the finger traced out: *5-M-I-N.*

Suddenly, the finger pulled out of the picture. The hand and the rest of the image dissolved. The window of Sarah's perspective vanished completely.

Megan turned her attention to the smaller image through Beth's eyes and watched as it began to flicker and fade. Its perspective shifted direction from the rear of the SUV to the right passenger side window as the vehicle slowed down and eased into a right turn.

The last vestige of the dissipating image was a glimpse of a gravel road stretching several hundred yards into the distance. Then the image disappeared.

Megan turned to her father. "The pictures are gone."

"What did you see?"

"Sarah traced out the word *HELICOPTER* on her hand. She traced five minutes. I think that's when the helicopter is picking them up."

"Helicopter?" Max asked, only somewhat surprised.

"The last thing I saw was them turning right onto a gravel road that—"

"And that must be it," Mark said. He was looking through the binoculars at the black SUV again. "They turned right when you said they did…and it looks like they're on a gravel road."

"Where's it lead?" Max asked. "See anything down the direction they're headed?"

Mark scanned the entire length of the gravel road and studied two run-down buildings where the road appeared to end.

"Looks like some rickety old barracks from an Army training camp or whatever. Probably dates back to World War II."

Max looked up the highway.

"There's another gravel road coming up fast," Max said. "Scope it out. Possible back door option?"

Mark turned and zoomed in on the gravel road coming up and traced its length to where it T-boned into another gravel road running parallel to the highway they were on.

Switching to this road, he traced its path as it stretched northward in a slightly angled straight line, ultimately dead-ending at the old barracks.

"That's an affirmative. Looks like a backdoor."

He scanned over to the black SUV that was headed toward the barracks then slid his view to the right, past the barracks and all the way back up the second gravel road.

"Hold on a minute," Mark said, lowering his binoculars. "What we've got here is another *front door* option, not a back door. They'll see us coming a mile away. Literally."

"Then they'll just have to see us," Max said, hitting the brakes and easing them into a right-hand turn onto the gravel road. He stomped on the accelerator again, kicking up gravel as they sped down the road parallel with the one the black SUV was on.

They reached the second gravel road, and Max swerved through the left turn. They were now headed north, directly toward the barracks. He leaned on the accelerator and searched the length of the gravel road that stretched ahead of them a mile-and-a-quarter to where the barracks stood.

"Mark, scope the rock outcropping about two thirds the way up on the right."

"I'm already on it," he said. "And let me tell you…a mighty fine Mt. Olympus it is. Perfect elevation and angle for flinging lightning bolts…if we need them."

"We'll need them," Max said. "We'll execute option one exactly as we set it up. You're Zeus. Full line of sight and deadly. Get ready to exit on the roll. I'm slowing down but not stopping."

"I'm ready now."

"Good. Implement encrypted radio contact through our collar mikes the second you're set up. Don't wait for my signal for fire cover."

"Roger that."

Chapter 58

Megan stared out the window at the black vehicle racing almost parallel with them in the distance. She knew beyond a doubt that Sarah and Beth were both on board. She could feel the physical reality of their presence in her mind.

Closing her eyes and focusing inward, Megan felt the sensation magnify. The feeling of their proximity was overpowering and visceral, churning inside her. She could picture the two of them looking out their window at a car in the distance, the one she was riding in, and knowing that she was near.

Megan embraced the sensation for a several seconds before looking down at the yellow legal pad on her lap. She deepened her concentration, blocking out her surroundings. Picking up her pen, she began to write an urgent message.

"Do you see it?" Sarah whispered.

Beth glanced at her and nodded once. The barest tilt of her head, and then she turned to look back out the window.

Sarah focused on the back of the driver's seat in front of her and let the window in her mind stretch wide open. A writing pad pixilated into view followed immediately by a hand and a pen.

The pen hovered over the pad for a moment. Then it began to write.

Sarah took in the message, reading and rereading each word as it appeared. When the writing stopped, she looked up at Beth, wide-eyed and questioning.

Beth's eyes softened. She reached out and grasped Sarah's hand. "I saw it."

Sarah raised her eyebrows.

"Tell her yes. We'll do it…"

Sarah hesitated a few seconds.

"Go on. Tell her."

Sarah bent over and uncurled her left hand. She focused on it as hard as she could, concentrating with all her might, and then traced out the letters: *O-K W-E W-I-L-L.*

She looked up at Beth, who gave her a reassuring smile. "I—"

They both whipped their heads toward the front of the SUV, startled by the loud chopping sound above them.

The Bell 206B3 Jet Ranger III helicopter slowed its rapid descent, swooping down with a moaning roar to within fifteen feet of the ground before leveling off. It hovered like a huge black dragonfly, its blades slicing through the air with a muscular, whumping cadence, stirring up a swirling dust storm.

Sarah watched out her window as the helicopter hung in the air for over a minute before it descended and touched down. Its rotor and blades decelerated but continued to swirl at a fast clip as the engine idled.

"Okay, everybody out," the driver barked. "Move it outta here and keep your heads down. Those blades can slice you into sushi in the blink of an eye."

Eddie exited the SUV and was hurried along by one of the men. Sarah and Beth climbed out and shot glances over their shoulders to the south. Max's Suburban was a quarter-mile away, racing towards them now, leaving a swirling contrail of billowing dust in its wake.

One of Thornton's men grabbed Sarah by the left arm and yanked her towards the helicopter. Sarah glanced back and saw Beth being strong-armed along by another man. She caught her eye, and Beth gave a sharp, unmistakable nod in return.

The countdown began.

Sarah let the man pull her along as she counted off the seconds under her breath. "One-one thousand, two-one thousand, three-one thousand…"

When she reached ten seconds, she pivoted to the left and sank her teeth into the hand of the man gripping her arm. She bit down with all her strength and felt a satisfying crunch as two of the man's finger bones cracked.

"Ahhhh!" The man dropped Sarah's arm and yanked back his wounded hand, trying to free himself from her vicious shark bite.

Sarah let go and sprinted away from him. She spat out the sickening coppery tasting blood as she ran. Her eyes locked on Max's white Suburban.

"You stinkin' bitch! Come back here!" Thornton's man roared, sprinting after her.

He caught up with her and gave her a powerful shove from behind, throwing her off balance and sending her tumbling forward.

Sarah tripped and fell into the dirt and brush, skinning her forearms, nose, and cheeks as she skidded face down in the dirt.

Dazed and in searing pain, she still managed to spring onto her feet to face her pursuer. He backhanded her across the face, sending her reeling and crumbling to the ground, and drew a black handgun out of his shoulder holster. Sarah cried out in terror as he pointed it at her. She faced the gaping black hole at the end of the barrel, certain she was staring at her own death.

"I ought to shoot you right here! I'll teach you to bite me, you little—"

Sarah watched as the man jerked and staggered backwards. He stumbled a few steps and collapsed to the ground, his gun scattering on the rocks.

A second later, she heard the echoing report of a rifle gunshot in the distance.

She watched a circle of blood appear and spread on the front of the man's shirt, dead center in the middle of his chest.

He wasn't moving.

Sarah turned and ran in the direction of Max's rapidly approaching vehicle, pushing herself to the absolute limits of her speed. She heard another loud crack of a rifle shot followed by a reverberating echo. The gunfire came from somewhere ahead of her.

She glimpsed over her shoulder to see if anyone was chasing her and spotted Beth off to her left, running parallel to her. The man who had been pursuing Beth lay sprawled in a crumpled heap on the ground behind her, the victim of the second rifle shot.

Sarah and Beth raced towards Max's Suburban. Max slammed on his brakes and brought the speeding vehicle to an abrupt stop in the midst of a billowing dust cloud. He jumped out and opened the rear door just as Sarah ran up and scrambled in. Beth ripped open the front passenger door and rushed in, slamming it shut as Max climbed back aboard.

Max put a hand on Beth's shoulder. "Are you okay?"

She launched herself into his arms, and he embraced her in a hug.

"I am now," she said.

Max held her tight for a few moments before they released. "How about you, Sarah?"

Megan had scampered over the console into the back seat when they'd stopped and was hugging Sarah, who was gasping and sobbing in relief. All Sarah could do was nod.

Max put the Suburban in gear and accelerated into a sharp U-turn headed back towards Mark.

With Eddie already on board, Newt climbed into the Jet Ranger helicopter ahead of Thornton, his bodyguards, Calvin Lynch, and three surgical associates.

As soon as the doors shut, the roar of the engine intensified, and the rotors accelerated rapidly with a whining pitch. The helicopter shifted sideways and began to lift off.

Seven hundred yards away, Mark peered through the 10x42 Leupold Ultra M3A telescopic sight mounted atop his M24 bolt action military sniper rifle. He lined up the intersecting crosshairs of the mil-dot reticle on the center of the helicopter's fuel tank. After making several quarter MOA adjustment clicks on the rifle scope to compensate for the distance, he slipped smoothly into an altered, deepened consciousness of precisely controlled breathing and slowed heart rate.

The helicopter rose a foot off the ground. Between heartbeats, he squeezed the trigger with constant, even pressure. The M24 rifle recoiled as the .300 Winchester Magnum cartridge fired, its 180-grain bullet exiting the muzzle of the rifle at 2,960 feet per second, over two and a half times the speed of sound.

The shot hit the exact center of the helicopter's fuel tank.

Mark fired off two more rounds in rapid succession, grouping both within a six-inch circle of where the first shot hit. Fuel began leaking from the tank in pulsing streams, cascading from the helicopter that was rising into the air.

Mark made a final minute-of-angle click adjustment on his scope, tracked the helicopter as it rose, and fired one last shot when the helicopter pivoted to head north towards Denver. The shot hit the lower rear quadrant of the tank on the opposite side, putting a fourth crippling hole in the fuel tank.

Through his scope, Mark could see the wispy, windblown streams of fuel sputtering behind the helicopter as it sped northward in the blue Colorado sky.

Nailed it. Four for four, Mark thought, pleased with himself.

He gathered up his rifle and gear and walked over to Max's SUV. He threw his gear in the back and climbed aboard.

"How is everybody?" Mark asked. Sarah and Beth…are you guys okay?"

"Yes, we are," Beth said. "And it's all because of you. You saved our lives. We can't ever thank you enough."

"Ah, shucks, Ma'am. I'm only doing my job." He turned to Sarah, who was leaning against Megan, and patted her on the shoulder. "You all right, munchkin??"

Sarah lifted her head off Megan's shoulder, her eyes swollen and red with tears. She nodded her head and smiled.

"Good. I have to say…the two of you were incredibly brave out there. And you pulled off the plan perfectly."

Max turned in his seat and looked back at Mark. "Nice work. I assume you displayed your extreme skills in your dance with the chopper."

Mark grinned. "Let's just say I terminated its fuel tank with extreme prejudice. You should have seen the grouping of my shots. It was a thing of beauty."

"I'll bet. And it's sure to put a major dent in their travel plans."

"Major," Mark agreed. "I don't know where they're headed, but I'm thinking they may be able to make it to Denver on fumes. They'll crash land if they try to reach any place further."

"Right. Let's head to Denver ourselves. We can all fly to Cali and hire someone to drive the SUV back."

"Want me to call it in?" Mark asked, cell phone out and ready.

"Yeah. We better do that now. Full report. Thornton and his crew are sure to make a run for it. They should try to head them off. Sure hope that kid Eddie is all right."

Chapter 59

Three months after the rescue, life had pretty much returned to normal for Max and Megan. At least as close to normal as could be expected. There were changes in their lives, good changes that continued to unfold and surprise them as time went on.

And one of the best of these was Sarah.

She had come to live with Max and Megan the night of the rescue and had stayed with them ever since. In the time they'd been together, Sarah and Megan had grown inseparable, spending almost every waking moment together. Max filed papers with the court for temporary custody of Sarah and met the school officials at Megan's school.

He pushed to have Sarah tested and admitted to the gifted students' program and placed in a more challenging grade level than the first grade. Her test results were stratospherically off the charts, and the school officials conservatively placed her in the fourth grade. They agreed with Max that skipping three grades might not be enough to challenge her, but they would try it out and see how it went.

This providential decision thrilled Sarah and Megan. They ended up in the same class.

Soon after the rescue Max and Beth had petitioned for the police to obtain a wide-reaching corporate search warrant of Viralvector, Inc. They had been allowed to accompany and participate with a police detective team on a physical search of all three corporate office and properties. They found no evidence that Sarah's mother had been kept as a comatose patient at any of them.

A police investigative tech team undertook an extensive search of all the company's computers and complete electronic records, many of which were encrypted. The team discovered that Sarah's mother had been an anonymous twenty-one-year-old desperate for money who had agreed to become a surrogate mother.

She had been artificially impregnated with an embryo created in vitro using DNA samples from Megan and her mother Carol's cryogenically preserved eggs. They had used internationally outlawed human cloning techniques first developed and successfully performed in Asia before international outrage halted further legitimate research.

Immediately after the birth, she'd been paid twenty-five thousand dollars for her efforts and sent on her way with the one-way ticket to the east coast she'd requested. Never to be heard from again.

Sarah didn't know any of this, and Max and Beth decided that they would wait until she was older to tell her the entire story. For now, they simply said that the woman she had seen in the hospital bed was not her mother and that they couldn't find any information about her mother's names or whereabouts in Viralvector's records.

Three months after Sarah was placed in Max's house as a foster child, he applied for full legal custody. In his mind and heart, Sarah was already his daughter, and he wanted to officially adopt her.

Over the months that followed, the tantalizing and mutual feelings of attraction between Max and Beth had sparked into a full-fledged romance. Their feelings for each other quickly escalated into a dizzying, all-encompassing love.

Max couldn't get Beth out of his mind. He could see himself spending the rest of his life with her. She had walked into his life and changed it forever. They would explore the future together and see what joy and adventures awaited them.

Them. Life partners. Soul mates.

It was a wonderfully complicated concept that resonated in his head and mind and continually surprised and thrilled him. He was enamored with everything about her: her character, her kindness, her intellect and beliefs, her strength and beauty. Her love for Megan and Sarah.

Max took the unit motto of his former Marine 3rd Battalion to heart. *Fortune favors the bold.* He knew what he wanted. He just had to be bold and reach for it.

When he planned a special dinner for the two of them, he knew it would be one of the most important moments of his life.

Dinner was enchanting, filled with warm conversation, mesmerizing glances, and laughter. He ordered a bottle of Dom Perignon champagne to celebrate the moment.

They lifted their glasses to toast. Max reached out and placed his hand over Beth's before she could take a sip.

"Beth?" He cleared his throat.

"Hmm?"

"Beth, you are the most special and wonderful woman I've ever met. I think of all we've been through these past few months, and I just marvel at the magic of it all. I get lost in your eyes and the curve of your face. I love your heart, your mind, your strength and beauty. And I'll open up my heart right now and say it...I love you, Beth Collins. More than you'll ever know. You are the rarest of all jewels...and the perfect diamond of my life."

Beth's eyes grew glassy. She swallowed. "And you're the man of my dreams, Max Tyler. You're strong, thoughtful, heroic, a man of true character. You're an incredible father. And not to mention...*very* easy on the eyes." She tilted her head, a beatific smile on her face. "And I love you too. *Afire* love. Always."

They clinked glasses, and Max watched as Beth raised her glass to her lips and took a sip. Her eyes grew wide when she noticed something slide up from the bottom of the glass.

A diamond ring.

Max stood up from the table and dropped to one knee.

"Beth, I'll love you always and forever. Will you marry me?"

She stared at him and at the ring. Her mouth dropped open. Max felt his heart soar in the pinnacle moment of his life.

"Yes!" She shrieked in excitement as she leaped up and hugged him. 'You know I will!"

They set a wedding date for only two months from then. The time would pass in the blink of an eye.

As for Richard Thornton and Viralvector, Inc.—the threat had vanished into thin air.

The helicopter that had taken off with Newt, Eddie, Thornton, and his team crash landed halfway to Denver, courtesy of the multiple bullet holes Mark had shot through the gas tank.

A few people received minor injuries including Eddie. But Thornton was unscathed. He managed to call 911 on his cell phone, and his emergency call triggered a Medevac helicopter rescue and evacuation.

Two hours later, after they had all been successfully transported and admitted to a Denver Trauma Care hospital, Thornton, Newt, and Calvin Lynch slipped out of the hospital unseen. They disappeared into the city and hadn't been seen since, despite an intensive search.

Eventually, they were traced to a flight to Europe that had left the day after the crash. Their tickets had been purchased in cash. Their itinerary ended at London's Heathrow International Airport. Evidence was uncovered later that suggested they had split up and traveled on through Madrid and Rome. And possibly into France and Germany.

What was certain was that upon arriving in Europe, Thornton had liquidated all of his tangible assets, including large blocks of Viralvector stock, and had the funds wired through a maze of multiple banks that stretched from the Cayman Islands through all of Western Europe. The convoluted trail of banks split again and again, ultimately becoming untraceable. Investigators speculated that the bulk of the cash—nearly three hundred million dollars—ended up in Swiss accounts.

Thornton was gone. The terrifying nightmare was finally over, and a new dawn was breaking.

Max and Beth's wedding was coming up. Legal custody of Sarah was sure to come through soon. Megan and Sarah were safe and happy and thriving. Max, Beth, and the girls would make a wonderful family together. They were even going to see Eddie again soon.

Life was good. Better than good.

At least until the night when pure evil came visiting.

Chapter 60

"Could you believe the look on Amelia's face when she saw us today?" Sarah asked. She caught Megan's eyes, and they started to giggle.

"Who's Amelia?" Beth asked. She was standing by the coffee machine in the kitchen, and the girls were sitting at the kitchen table finishing an after-school snack.

Megan raised her eyebrows and bulged her eyes at Sarah, and they both burst out laughing.

"What?" Beth couldn't help herself from chuckling.

Megan stopped and took a breath. "Amelia's the new girl in class. Today was her first day."

"Yeah!" Sarah chimed in. "She looked back and forth at us and almost crossed her eyes. It was so funny!"

"Total bug eyes!"

"That's hilarious!" Beth said. "Is she nice? Did she ask why you look alike?"

"Yep," Megan said. "We just shrugged and said we're twins. We're the two Musketeers. 'All for one, and one for all!' We laughed about it. She seems super nice. She said it felt like she was in an episode of *Stranger Things*, and it was *so* cool."

Sarah nodded. "She asked if we wanted to come over to her house to play sometime. Maybe even this weekend."

"That's great, girls! We'll definitely plan that. I don't know about this weekend, but maybe the next." Beth put her coffee cup in the sink. "Okay, you guys. Finish up your snacks. Gymnastics class starts in half an hour."

It was almost midnight when Beth at long last got Megan and Sarah settled down in their beds for the night. They had just finished watching *Toy Story 4*, capping off a fun night of games, M&M's, Skittles, root beer floats, popcorn, and more M&M's.

"Okay, you two..." Beth said. She stood in the doorway of Megan and Sarah's bedroom and smiled. "I had a lot of fun tonight."

"You said it!" Megan chirped.

"Yeah!" Sarah added with a Cheshire grin.

They looked at each other and giggled.

Beth smiled at them and shook her head, tired but amused. "Look, I know you two are wired for sound, but it's time to close your eyes and go to sleep. Tomorrow's a big day."

"What are we doing?" Megan asked. She looked wide-eyed at Sarah, and they started giggling again.

"Well...we have a picnic and swim party at your friend Jordan's house. And then your dad gets back from his trip late in the afternoon. I'm sure we'll barbeque something. Maybe play some games. We might even go on a bike ride."

"Good...I hope so!" Sarah exclaimed. "I love the new bike you got me!"

"Yeah, it's sweeeeet!" Megan agreed.

Beth grinned. "I'm glad you like it. Now it's time for lights out...and no staying up talking."

"All right," they both said at the same time.

Sarah tugged her sheets up to her chin. "Can you leave the nightlight on?" she asked timidly.

"Sure I can, pumpkin." Beth reached down and switched on the plastic Cinderella nightlight that had been in Megan's room since she was five. She turned and flipped the wall switch, turning off the overhead light. "Sweet dreams. See you in the morning," she said, pulling the door closed behind her.

As Beth got ready for bed, she thought about Max. He was out of town leading a two-day training class for new SWAT team members. She was surprised at how much she missed him and was really looking forward to seeing him when he got back tomorrow. It was nice to have someone to miss, and it was going to be nice having him home again.

Their wedding was only two weeks away, and then she would move into his house permanently. A new life. Max and her and their incredible girls

She smiled in the dark. She climbed into bed, pulled the covers up, and let her body slowly unwind and relax until she drifted off to sleep.

Larry Drake carefully slid the window up and stepped into the utility room of Max's house. He stood motionless, counting to ten as he listened for any noise or movement from upstairs. The air conditioning was running, and the soft whoosh of air streaming through the vents into the room was barely audible. It ran for another full minute as Drake waited. Then it shut off.

Silence.

He tiptoed toward the door and stepped out of the utility room into the kitchen. He paused by the island counter. The mournful howl of a dog in the distance interrupted the perfect stillness. Drake listened to it as it faded off. Then silence resumed.

Drake waited a few moments longer and didn't hear a sound.

It was two o'clock in the morning, and everyone was asleep. Just as they should be. Just as he'd planned.

He'd been staking out the house over the past week, cataloging the comings and goings of everyone and paying particularly close attention to when Max left in the morning and returned at night.

But always, he watched Megan. He wanted her. Wanted her bad. And this was his best chance to take her.

Ever since the incident at the hospital, his fantasies of Megan had grown progressively more twisted and titillating until they were unbearable. He'd made up his mind he had to grab her at night, snatch her out of her bed and take her back to his place. And then the real fun would begin.

There was just one problem: Max the SWAT cop.

He'd almost succeeded in injecting and killing Megan right in front of Max...what an icy thrill that would have been. But then things went to hell in a splintery handbasket with that doctor Collins lady yelling at him to stop.

Then Max had exploded out of his chair and attacked, tackling and driving him out into the hall where they got into a major knife fight, ending when Max stabbed him through the shoulder and pinned him to the wall with that wicked, jagged knife.

It had hurt like a mother when he'd ripped it out of his shoulder, freeing himself to run off. Even after several months, when the wound should have been completely healed, excruciating shocks of pain still rocketed through his shoulder when he moved his arm certain ways. He didn't think it would ever get back to normal.

Max was going to pay. Big time.

Drake planned to ambush him and shoot him a couple of times, then make him beg for his life before he killed him.

But first, he was going to take Megan tonight and unleash his fantasies on her before he killed her.

Afterward, he'd leave easy clues for Max to find her body, and best of all he'd watch Max die with sorrow and despair, right before he died for real.

Revenge was going to be perfect.

Drake hadn't believed his luck when he'd watched Beth arrive the previous evening, and after a while saw Max throw a suitcase and duffel bag into his Suburban, kiss Beth goodbye, and leave.

He hadn't returned. So tonight was the night. Time for fun.

Drake stretched a black stocking mask down over his face and started up the carpeted stairs to the second floor. He held his breath as he crept to the landing at the top of the stairs.

He stopped and listened. Nothing but his heartbeat and the silence of the house.

During his surveillance, he'd figured out that the girls' bedroom was the second door on the left. Their window faced the front yard, and on consecutive nights, he'd watched their bedtime routine through his binoculars.

He reached into his backpack and retrieved a halogen flashlight the size and thickness of a dime and clicked it on and off, covering it with his cupped hand. It gave off just enough light for him to see.

Dropping it in his shirt pocket, Drake removed a narrow sheet of plastic that had strips of precut duct tape stuck to one side and plastic police wrist ties taped to the other. He'd need these right away.

He'd also need the razor sharp folding knife he took from his other pocket. It was time to play.

Drake inched forward until he stood in front of the girls' door. Turning the knob, he slowly pushed the door open and slid into the room, easing the door closed behind him.

Moonlight filtered into the room through the gauzy curtains. Drake's eyes swept the room, glancing at the glow of the nightlight as he took in the sleeping forms of the two girls illuminated in the shadowy light.

Perfect, he thought. There was no need for the flashlight. He took a few steps toward the bed on the left and stopped. That wasn't Megan. The figure under the blankets was too small. *Must be the little sister.*

He was tempted to try to take them both, but he'd already thought about this, and there was too much of a chance that something could go wrong if he grabbed them both.

Megan was the one he wanted, but first, he had to take care of the sister.

He walked over to Sarah's bed, quickening his pace when he realized his good luck: Sarah was lying on her back, eyes closed and head tilted slightly toward him. An angelic picture of blissful, carefree sleep.

He peeled a strip of duct tape off the plastic sheet and pushed it across Sarah's mouth. Her eyes blinked wide open as she jolted awake. She reached a hand up toward the tape. Drake stuck the razor sharp point of his knife against her throat and moved in close.

"Stop," Drake rasped. "Don't make a sound, or I'll kill you...and your sister. Understand?"

Sarah's eyes widened in terror. She nodded.

"Put your hands together," he ordered. His mouth was close to her ear, and she gagged at the sour, rancid smell of his breath.

She lifted her hands and pressed them together. Drake slipped two of the self-locking plastic ties around her wrists and pulled them tight.

With Sarah quietly immobilized, he pivoted and crept over to Megan's bed. She was thrashing in her sleep. *Your nightmare's only beginning,* Drake thought.

He peeled off another strip of duct tape and leaned down toward her. He was about to put it on her mouth when she sat up. Her eyes flew open, and she glared at him with unsurprised awareness as though she knew all along that he was there.

Drake pressed the duct tape on her mouth, driving her back down on the bed. He raised his knife and pushed the blade against her throat. "Keep silent and do exactly what I say, or I'll slit your throat. Got it?"

Megan nodded in terror. The pressure from the blade caused a thin cut that began to sting, and Megan felt a line of blood on her skin. Her heart leaped into her throat. It seemed to stop altogether. She'd never been so scared in her entire life.

"If you don't cooperate, I'll kill you here and now. And then I'll kill your sister. Put your hands together."

Megan did as she was told, and Drake put on the wrist ties and yanked them tight.

He jerked her forward and checked the ties to make sure they'd locked. Megan peeked over his shoulder at Sarah, who was staring back at her with a tear-filled look of terror that mirrored her own. Their eyes connected. Windows of each other's perspective opened and dilated in their eyes, doubling the intensity of their escalating fear in a parallax vision of horror. A third image began to open…

Beth tossed and turned in her sleep, her mind swirling in the netherworld throes of a terrifying dream. Twin images crystallized in her mind. Intense. Disturbing.

Sarah came into view, eyes wide in terror, pleading. A band of gray duct tape was pressed across her mouth. The view shifted, and she saw Megan sitting up in bed. A band of gray duct tape was sealing her mouth too.

And even more disturbing…the back of a man who she could tell was wearing a stocking mask. He was busy doing something to Megan's hands.

The images crystallized in ever-increasing clarity and resolution.

Beth bolted upright in her bed, instantly awake and alert. Her eyes flew to the closed door. She stared in the direction of Megan's room. She was watching the events take place in Megan's room. And somehow, beyond all possible doubt, she knew the images were real.

She scrambled off the bed and leaped to her feet. Adrenaline pulsed into her bloodstream, triggering a massive fight or flight response.

Weapon, she thought frantically, switching on the bedside lamp and scouring the room with her eyes.

There. Leaning against the dresser. A baseball bat.

It was Max's Louisville Slugger, the one he'd used on his varsity baseball team in high school.

Beth grabbed it as she sprinted to the bedroom door. She paused with her hand on the knob. Inching the door open, she peered down the hall at Megan's room. The door was closed. The house was silent. The images in her mind intensified.

There was no time to think. No time for caution. Inaction was not an option.

Beth raced down the hall and charged the door with a visceral rage that obliterated all fear. She would not let Megan or Sarah be hurt, or abducted, or worse. Not here. Not ever.

Grabbing the doorknob and crashing open the door at a full run, Beth flipped on the wall switch with her left hand, then gripped the bat with two hands, cocking it back for a full swing.

Drake whirled around in an awkward pivot to face her. He hesitated a fraction of a second before raising his knife and lunging at her.

He was a moment too late.

As he rushed towards Beth, Sarah dove off her bed and landed with a bouncing belly flop on the carpet in front of Drake's feet.

He was so focused on rushing to attack Beth that he never saw her coming, and he tripped over her body.

What happened next unfolded in surreal slow motion for Beth.

She saw the man facing her, his black stocking mask stretched over his face, his wild-looking eyes locking on her as he raised his knife.

All her senses heightened with preternatural sharpness, and she unconsciously decelerated the pace of her attack, timing her forward motion with Drake's approach. Three years as a star player on her high school softball team had honed her skill with a bat. As Drake approached, knife poised for a downward arcing slash, Beth began stepping into her swing.

Sarah's body tripped both of Drake's feet, rocketing him forward and downward. Beth adjusted her upward sloping swing, powering it with every ounce of adrenaline-enhanced strength in her body.

As he fell face forward, the bat caught Drake squarely on the front left side of his face. The high-speed impact crushed his skull into the left prefrontal cortex of his brain, and the arcing rotational path of the bat torqued his head around with such force that the cervical vertebrae in his neck cracked and shattered, severing his spinal cord.

He crumpled to the floor in a lifeless heap. Dead when his head hit the carpet.

The blood-stained bat slipped from Beth's hands to the floor. She jumped over the body and swept the girls into a hug.

"Thank God you're all right!"

She untied them and removed the duct tape from their mouths. They buried their faces in her neck and sobbed.

"It's okay," Beth said. "It's all over. We're safe now…"

They stood there, clinging to each other, for five long minutes, and then Beth took them by the hands and led them to Max's room. The girls curled up on either side of her and fell asleep in her arms.

Beth stayed awake for an hour watching their breathing and feeling an all-encompassing love for them fill her heart and her soul. Then she quietly slipped out of bed and took her cell phone downstairs to call 911.

Epilogue

Six months after Drake's attack, Max and Beth were informed that the police investigation was officially closed. Drake's death had been ruled a clear open-and-closed case of self-defense, and the detective team investigating the multiple hospital deaths had obtained direct DNA evidence linking Drake to three of the four deaths.

Max, Beth, and the girls did their best to put the attack behind them and move on with their lives. Max and Beth were married, and their wedding—graced with two bewilderingly identical flower girls—and honeymoon had been a wonderful storybook dream with no foreseeable end.

Their new life with Megan and Sarah unfolded in perpetual joy-filled adventures and wondrous heartfelt events.

The first and most overwhelming of these came about a month after the wedding when the paperwork came through, and they were notified that they would be able to legally adopt Sarah.

The four of them had hugged and cried at the news. Max took them all on a camping trip to Yosemite National Park, and for days they continued to celebrate that Sarah would become an official member of the family. Max and Beth's daughter. Megan's sister.

After months of cerebral PET scans and radioisotope uptake tests, neurology experts had determined that Megan, Sarah, and Beth's brains were no longer adding cells or neuronal axonal connections. Everything seemed to have stabilized.

The special ability that Beth and her daughters shared remained with them throughout the years. It faded over time, but never entirely, forging a special closeness between them that words could never describe because it lived in their hearts.

And in the shadows of their dreams.

CPSIA information can be obtained
at www.ICGtesting.com
Printed in the USA
BVHW031956011219
565305BV00001B/114/P